BOTH SIDES

BOTH SIDES

Stories from the Border

Edited by Gabino Iglesias

Copyright © 2020
Introduction — Gabino Iglesias
The Letters — Rios de la Luz
Los Otros Coyotes — Daniel A. Olivas
Fundido — Johnny Shaw
American Figurehead — Shannon Kirk
Colibrí — Nicolás Obregón
Buitre — Michelle Garza and Melissa Lason
The Lament of the Vejigante — Cynthia Pelayo
Fat Tuesday — Christopher David Rosales
The Other Foot — Rob Hart
Waw Kiwulik — J. Todd Scott
El Sombrerón — David Bowles
She Loved Trouble — Sandra Jackson-Opoku
Grotesque Cabaret — Isaac Kirkman
Empire — Nick Mamatas
90 Miles — Alex Segura
Cover and jacket design by 2Faced Design

Hardcover ISBN: 978-1-947993-87-7
eISBN: 978-1-951709-12-9
Library of Congress Catalog Number: 2020933989

First hardcover publication: April 2020 by Agora Books
An imprint of Polis Books, LLC
221 River Street, 9th Fl., #9070
Hoboken, NJ 07030

TABLE OF CONTENTS

THIS IS ABOUT PEOPLE

An Introduction
Gabino Iglesias

My first border was the ocean. It was always there, surrounding me on all sides, dictating the limits of my life. It was an endless blue thing that kept me away from a world I didn't know. Then I grew up and started realizing how borders are everywhere. I hated all of them.

I grew up and the ocean was still there, blue, eternal, and relentless. Planes helped me break its power over me. Planes shattered an invisible wall and showed me borders were meant to be crossed, to be ignored. I refused to remain landlocked.

Years later, I made peace with the ocean and sat before it regularly. I kissed girls, got drunk, bathed in it. I also sold stolen jewelry in front of that ocean because being poor is also a border, a boundary that keeps you within something you want to break free from.

As the years passed, my name became a border, an unpronounceable amalgamation of vowels that many monolinguals struggled with and butchered. My parents hadn't gone to college, and their history became a border. My country became a border. My lack of education, my age, and the fact that I didn't speak English all became borders. My hatred grew. It became a force, an unstoppable weapon.

BOTH SIDES

Borders. Limits. Boundaries. Lines. Confines. Fuck them all.

They are there to be demolished, jumped over, overcome.

In 2008, I moved to the United States. I was naïf and believed education was a surefire way to upward social mobility. It wasn't. Moving to the United States uncovered more borders. My second-class citizenship became a new border I had ignored before. My accent became a border that affected the way others saw me. My socioeconomic status was a border that kept me living in certain places and wearing certain clothes and stealing toilet paper from work to survive. And you know what? I was lucky. I was lucky because I had a blue passport with an eagle on it. Sure, it wasn't good enough to make me a full citizen or grant me the privilege others enjoyed, but it was good enough to keep me here and not make me fear deportation. Which is luckier than most with my borders.

I won't bore you with the details of my life in this country. What you need to know is this: my doctoral dissertation was done with DREAMers, I spent a year teaching ESL night classes to undocumented workers in Austin, I worked with an immigration lawyer doing translation, and I now teach a public school in East Austin where there are many undocumented kids and even more undocumented parents. I'm an authority on immigration, and everything you think you know about immigration is wrong.

The US-Mexico border has been militarized and politicized. It has been turned into a talking point. It's not; the border is a humanitarian crisis, an open wound, an interstitial space where idiots work really hard at stopping progress and spend a lot of money and time strangling the American Dream. Well, I believe the most important thing fiction can do is tell the truth, and that truth is crucial right now. The anthology you now hold is a tool that will help us do a little bit of the most significant thing contemporary American fiction can do: rehumanizing la frontera.

I've heard that being too political can hurt your book sales. I don't care. I care about humanity. I care about people. I care about the Haitians who move to the Dominican Republic and the Dominicans who build boats to go to Puerto Rico and Puerto Ricans who leave everything behind and move to Florida or New York because we all want to live better lives. I care about every family crossing our border, about every parent fearing for the safety of their child, about every separated family member sending money home, about the tears and the fear and the injustice. I care about the fact that migration is the history of the world, and stopping migration is stopping progress. I care about every writer in this anthology because they care about the same things and are willing to write about them from their perspectives: an angry lawyer, someone who used to work for the carteles and now does water drops in the desert, a Boricua struggling with her identity, a man who was in the middle of the action as a federal agent fighting Mexican cartels in their smuggling routes. They are all here. They make this a beautiful, incredibly diverse book that looks at the issue of borders and immigration from a plethora of spaces, and enriches the discussion as it illuminates what a lot of people ignore.

Al carajo todas las fronteras.

This anthology is about borders. However, this is a book about people. Why? Because too many forget that people are at the core of every immigration debate. Yeah, this isn't about borders, this is about the people on both sides—and across—those borders.

Bienvenidos a la frontera.

Gabino Iglesias
December 2019

THE LETTERS

Rios de la Luz

Emiterio and Alonso sprint across the 375 Border Highway. A violet semi-truck with spiked hubcaps wails at the two of them. Alonso's shoes are falling apart at this point in the journey. They used to light up when he first got them. They were a gift for his seventh birthday. He is almost eight, but he thinks of himself as an old soul. His Bart Simpson socks have holes in the heel and big toe. Rocks and stickers become the cushion in between his small toes. He wears his favorite T-shirt with a dragon and gargoyle battling. He follows his dad because Emiterio is the only person who understands his quirks. The way he chews on his tongue when he is nervous. The way he pops his knuckles before he interjects his opinion into an adult conversation. The way he never looks someone in the eye until he becomes comfortable with them. Emiterio is running because he wants to be like the coyote puppies who cross between Texas and Mexico. The ones who howl and scavenge and survive. He is running because he needs to feed his son and his other two children, who stayed behind with the love of his life. He needs a second chance.

The Sanchez family helps the priest lug in his suitcases filled with Bibles. The priest explains it is better if the family chooses the Bible they want to hear a prayer from. Grandma Lala is dying. Tumors in her stomach erupted and she coughed up blood. Within an hour, she started vomiting blood. Then it escalated to her begging for an exorcism. Her eldest son, Esteban, looks at the open suitcases on the floor and picks out the Bible with the gold-and-red-striped cover. The words inside are printed in red. An ink drawing of the crucifixion is scribbled on the last page. He hands the Bible to the priest and leads him to the back room, where Lala has slobbered down her chest and is reaching at the ceiling. *Moths on the moon. Dirt in my throat.* She keeps repeating the words, over and over until she falls back to sleep.

Screaming erupts from the cement front yard. Two Border Patrol agents have a man and a boy pinned to the hood of Esteban's car. The boy is tiny. Nine at the oldest. Esteban grabs his phone and films the two agents. The boy is crying and gagging as he sobs. The Border Patrol agent slams him into the cement, spits on him, and says, "Better luck next time."

Emiterio and Alonso are separated. Alonso gets placed in a tent city outside of El Paso. Emiterio gets deported without his son.

Esteban's video goes viral. The video cycles through the discussions of online scholars, online bigots, and news outlets. A month after the replays wind down, both of the Border Patrol agents in the video end up dead. One agent falls headfirst from the second story of the mall. The other suffers a brain aneurysm while eating breakfast.

11

Cops have started to show up at Lala's house. Every single day. Someone waits for Esteban in the front yard. He is mourning. Lala died the night before spring started. As she was going in and out of consciousness, she told Esteban the world was going to end underwater. *We will all drown and the earth will devour us.*

Esteban went on a cleaning spree and scrubbed every crevice of the house after Lala's body was taken to the morgue. A cop he doesn't recognize bangs on the door. Curious to feel out the aggression, Esteban opens the door and extends his yellow dish-gloved hands to greet him. He's not a cop. His name is Gustavo. Gustavo takes a count of the golden crosses on the living room wall. There are thirty-three total. He looks at the quaint bookshelf filled with self-help books. He asks Esteban if he can take a look around Lala's house.

"What are you looking for? She just died, man."

Gustavo bites his tongue and sighs. "I had a dream with Lala in it."

Esteban steps back and looks for possible physical traits that this man could be related to him. Esteban asks for more details. Gustavo claims something in the house belongs to him. Gustavo's throat seizes up and he ends the conversation in a coughing fit. Esteban feels the weight of discomfort slamming against his temples. He asks Gustavo to leave. Maybe another time. A small shadow appears behind Esteban and watches Gustavo get into his blue Mustang and drive away.

Three more Border Patrol agents die. Three days apart from each other. The first agent is crushed under a semi as he crosses the street. The second agent slips on a hiking trail in the Guadalupe Mountains and tumbles through the desert until she blacks out and dies minutes later. The third one has a food allergy. His throat closes as he rides up an elevator. Esteban keeps track of the deaths. He reads conspiracy theories online claiming the Border Patrol agents have been taken hostage in other timelines.

Alonso dreams about his family every single night. They travel together. They eat together. Sometimes he sees them in the distance, he screams for them, but his voice is inaudible. ICE agents whisper about him in English and he understands them, but he knows better than to give himself away. They claim he cursed the agents who took him away from his father.

Alonso spends his nights reading under a table with a flashlight. The boys have made it into a cardboard fort. Alonso has read travel pamphlets, a bible, a book on Greek mythology, and a choose your own adventure thriller inside the fort. The boys take turns sitting inside when they want to be alone.

Alonso convinces every boy in his tent to start a silent protest. They will start in the morning and vow only to say something if someone is in grave danger. Alonso holds little trust for the ICE agents. They always say the same thing: "If you don't behave, we'll send you back where you came from." He doesn't want to waste his words on them. In the morning, the boys look at each other and pinky promise in a silent shuffle as they go outside for their allotted hour. The sun stings their eyes as they become exposed to the desert. The dry air warps the sun into an oven. The boys step out and look at their feet. There are hundreds of holes in the makeshift soccer field. Alonso reaches inside one of them and pulls out a letter from beneath the earth. The dirt smells fresh. The envelope has gold trim around the edges and a name written in red ink on the front. He slips the envelope into his pants. Alonso looks around and gestures to another boy. He hands an envelope over to him and then motions for the other boys to dig. One by one, they find envelopes and hide them.

After their play hour is over, Alonso opens the envelope labeled "Elena Villalobos." The letter tells her birth story. She was born in the morning on a blustery day. The winds knocked over power lines throughout the city and mourning doves attacked people with blond hair with no explanation. The letter states she was to die the next morning. Alonso's heart races. As he reads each word, they disappear. He collects the envelopes and reads them carefully inside the makeshift cardboard fort they were allowed to build. Name after name, he vows to stay silent.

Then, he recognizes one of the names. Ricardo Quevedo, an ICE agent who punished the boys by hitting the backs of their legs with a wooden meter stick. His other favorite punishment was making them sleep in a dog kennel if they didn't listen to his instructions when they were lining up to eat dinner. He was fired because of a DUI. The kids called him Alacrán and tried their best to protect each other from receiving his punishments while he worked at the camp. Alonso could picture the satisfaction on the Alacrán's face when the boys looked up at him in fear. The name alone fills Alonso with dread. The letters go into no details of their deaths, only the day of their conception. Ricardo was born in Lawton, Oklahoma, on a muggy day during tornado season. Like Elena, he was sentenced to die the next morning. Alonso feels his guts tighten. He memorizes each name and recites them one by one, not knowing how he is to keep track of whether or not the letters are factual.

When the agents dig into the holes overtaking the soccer field, all they find are fire ants and burrowing owls.

Esteban dreams about Lala. She's in a red gown with a train so long, he can see it ribboning around the mountains. Lala is cutting into meat and bone with a machete. Over and over until a small creature emerges. It's a coyote pup who starts to howl as soon as it opens its eyes. With her claws, Lala starts to dig at the cement in the backyard. The cement turns to ash as she digs further down. She digs into a room filled with stacks of books. The puppy follows behind as she pulls out a book filled with names. The language is symbols and formulas. Esteban wakes up before Lala explains what the codex means.

Alonso waits to hear news of any deaths in the campsite. One ICE agent had a heart attack after posting a selfie of herself in her uniform. Another choked on his vomit after binge drinking with his friends. Alonso had listened for the whispers of their names. Both of them were named in the letters. Alonso's anxiety torments him. He questions if his memorization of each name started the cycle of deaths. He starts to loathe being in the tent, but isn't ready to fess up to being some kind of death magician. One morning, the holes in the soccer field fill up with flower petals. Roses, lilies, and orchids. The boys take turns sniffing the petals. Some of the fragrances smell like nostalgia. Alonso pictures his mother receiving roses from his dad and cries so hard it hurts his chest. One of his tent mates holds him and lets him melt into more tears.

BOTH SIDES

It has to do with Lala's ghost. Esteban has convinced himself Lala has something to do with the surge of deaths.

Lala shows up in Esteban's dreams again. This time, she's younger, her hair is long and black, and curls cover her shoulders. In a black pantsuit, she's standing at the gate of a pool. Lala's tongue is black. She scratches at her tongue and spits dribble into the stale water at her feet. The residue trickles into the pool. Swirls of black and purple oil infest the pool. She chugs liquid from a goblet and eyes the two kids who show up. A young girl in a pink polka-dot bathing suit and a boy in dinosaur swim trunks. They hang around the ledge and doggie paddle together in giggle fits. Clouds gray the sky and the pool water becomes darker. The bottom of the pool disappears. A midnight blue. The water erupts. Stingrays jump in and out of the water. The girl and boy continue to play. The girl steps out of the pool and sprints around the ledge. In a matter of seconds she trips over her feet and thrashes into the water. Waves take the girl under and Lala can't move. The gate begins to grow so tall; it can't be seen past the clouds. Lala watches as the young girl floats up lifeless after the water calms down. The young boy tries to save her, but he flounders around until the waves shove him against the gate.

Gustavo can see Lala in his dreams. She's in the background. She never says a word to him. Sometimes she leaves photographs behind. Photos of forests and ocean waves. Photos of coral reefs and starfish. Lala shows up when there's water. She watches him as he travels through the geography and architecture of his subconscious. In some dreams, Lala carries his baby sister in her arms.

Alonso continues his vow of silence. He has yet to utter what he's feeling or thinking to the ICE agents, who have grown aware of their own mortality. He has listened for names and erased them from his mental list. The list has dwindled down to only three. Ricardo was confirmed dead by one of the agents who used to flirt with him. The agents talk amongst themselves, how they're scared and feel helpless to this phenomenon. Alonso's sense of time has warped. He's apathetic to the concepts of life and death. Two months away from his family has made him lose weight. He can't eat and he's grown lethargic. He still dreams about his family. When they are together, there is always light. There are full meals. There is warmth. There is tenderness. It hurts Alonso to wake up in the tent day after day. He wishes the accumulation of his silence could convert into something other than small satisfaction that the agents are irritated with him for never speaking to them.

Lala kept a memento of that evening. She took a photograph of the pool where the girl died. As the girl was drowning, Lala was inside, cooking for a man who would leave her three months later to chase drug money going back and forth between the border. A high-pitched scream of terror came from the boy. He was shouting for help. Lala watched the way the man she loved followed her with his eyes, ensuring he was taken care of first. As soon as she served him his dinner, she washed her hands and went outside to investigate the commotion. Two tiny feet were sticking up from the hole of a floating yellow duck. The boy was curled in a ball, gasping for air and crying. Lala jumped into the pool and grabbed the girl. Her face was blue. No one else came to aid them. Lala called 911 and an ambulance took the girl and the boy without an adult because Lala was summoned back to the apartment to serve the man in her apartment another plate of food.

Esteban has dreamt of the backyard the entire week. This pushes his impulse to search through the shed in the back. He digs through piles of collected stamps and decks of cards. He digs until he finds old photographs stashed away in a neon pink duffel bag. He sifts through hundreds of photos belonging to unfamiliar faces. These photos are up close, sometimes blurred, and some of them have dozens of floating orbs around their brow. Then he finds a stack of photos with Lala crawling around tombstones, collecting pebbles and feathers. As he gets further into the pile, there are images of her digging up animal bones and photos of her wrapping fruit in yellow ribbon. There are photos of her burning gold paper. Another photo features people whose faces are painted gold with black cloaked robes. The photo underneath reveals them in a circle with a blood-splattered offering in the middle of a yellow field. Esteban gasps at a picture of Lala with vials of blood in her hand.

Lala could feel out when someone's luck was shifting. She caught people in the midst of crisis and sold them her money spells and protection spells out of her apartment after she was left to figure out financial stability on her own. She stopped being subservient to men who could not love at their full potential. She started a reciprocal business model. Every time her protection spells worked, she became bedridden. She needed something in return to balance out her bodily sacrifice. As she continued her craft, she understood how much power she could convert through magick. She made this deal: if her work changed someone's life, they needed to live in ways which never harmed another soul. This was a stipulation not only for them, but for their family members as well. If any family member conducted cruel acts, they were cursed to become sick or even die. It was all dependent on the severity of the cruelty.

Gustavo shows up at Lala's house again. This time, he has a sledgehammer. Esteban lets him in and gives in to his search. He thinks the guy is after secret money or a biological revelation. Gustavo takes the sledgehammer and starts to bash into the ground in the backyard. Esteban tries to stop him at first, but he sees Gustavo crying. He digs out the broken chunks and Esteban helps him start digging. No more than four feet in, Gustavo starts digging with his hands. He's weeping and frantic. Esteban cleans the mess they've made as Gustavo continues to throw dirt out of the miniature crater they've forged. Gustavo finds the remains of a small body and looks up at Esteban, who shakes his head and mouths oh-my-god.

"Lala told me guilt manifests in interesting ways."

Gustavo runs to grab a small coffin from his car and places the bones inside, one by one, kissing and whispering to each piece.

Alonso pretends he's in purgatory. The adults around him are cold. As they've gotten more accustomed to their jobs, they get sloppy. They get cruel. Mean. Sometimes the boys are stuck inside the tent all day. There are days where their trays of food are delivered to the front door. Someone knocks and the boys pass the trays around, making sure to ration any shortages so everyone can eat.

Alonso dreams about his father. On the beach, they run beside each other and chase waves. Sometimes Emiterio shows up as a coyote puppy. Alonso holds onto the puppy with all of his strength. The puppy responds with face licks and then pounces around the desert dirt as soon as Alonso lets him loose. They howl together.

Eleven of the deaths were consequences of Lala's binding contract. The other hundreds remain unexplained. Alonso can't remember the names in the letters anymore. He tries to go through his mental scroll and nothing happens. He keeps this secret until it all seems like a blurred memory. He dreams of his family often and waits for Emiterio every single day.

Eventually, Emiterio will find him, but not while Alonso's still a child.

LOS OTROS COYOTES

DANIEL A. OLIVAS

"Espero que la salida sea alegre,
y espero no volver nunca más." — Frida Kahlo

Nadie construye muros mejor que yo, créeme.

The guard gently led Rogelio out of the lookout room. The boy shook his head so hard that tears flew from his eyelashes, hitting the guard's green uniform and making dark, petaled blotches on the thick fabric. Rogelio tried to shake from his mind the image of his huddled, sobbing parents. But he couldn't. And though he was only in fifth grade, Rogelio was smart enough to know that he'd never be able to wipe away the memory of waving goodbye to his parents through the cloudy, bulletproof Plexiglas.

The President's executive order explicitly laid out the design of the detention centers connected to the Great Wall, and explicitly prohibited the expenditure of funds for more humane farewells. Children who belonged in the United States—because they were born in the country or were otherwise naturalized—could have no more than thirty seconds to gaze upon their soon-to-be deported parents through the Plexiglas. Because the President prohibited the installation of microphones and speakers, the goodbyes would consist of silent, tearful pantomimes and mouthed expressions of love and promises to behave and never forget.

Soon Rogelio and his older sister, Marisol, would be packing their meager belongings and sent to live with their tía Isabel in Los Angeles. And his parents would be with the other sobbing parents on a large, black bus that would take them through one of the reinforced gates in the Great Wall and back to Mexico regardless of which Latin American country they called home. The grieving parents would disembark in Tijuana and be left to fend for themselves. The President had designed this process, praising himself for coming up with such a clean, fast, and beautiful way of MAKING AMERICA GREAT AGAIN! He had tweeted: "Only a Very Stable Genius could come up with this very GREAT system! And Mexico will someday PAY for my Great Wall!"

The guard led Rogelio past the other children who waited in two snaking lines—one for boys, the other for girls, as the President had decreed—along the walkway toward the nurse's office for a quick visit before going back to the barracks to pack. Above the cries, shouts, and laughter of the other children, Rogelio could hear the recurring audio loop of the President's voice blaring over the intercoms that spotted the ceiling: "I will build a great wall—and nobody builds walls better than me, believe me—and I'll build them very inexpensively. I will build a great, great wall on our southern border, and I will make Mexico pay for that wall. Mark my words." Rogelio's teacher, Ms. Becerra, had noted in class one day that Mexico had yet to pay for the President's wall, which cost more than $21 billion to build.

As he walked with the guard, Rogelio blinked away the last of his tears and looked out the large floor-to-ceiling windows that allowed perfect views of the Great Wall. The enormous spotlights that were trained on it in intervals also lit up the cool San Diego evening. Rogelio thought the wall was a dreadful, hideous thing even though the President had paid "good money, the best money" to one of his most supportive Twitter followers—a contractor from Alabama—to design the outlandish, golden curlicues that were painted along the wall's top and bottom edges. Between the borders of gold paint, the President wanted to share with people on either side of the Great Wall his life's accomplishments as depicted in captioned bas-relief scenes beginning from his childhood (*I was the BEST son!*), his education (*Only the GREATEST schools and TOP grades!*), beginning careers in business and television (*I had the HIGHEST ratings!*), running for president (*Biggest victory EVER!*), the swearing in (*So Presidential!*), and the President signing executive orders (*Making America Great Again!*).

The President saw on Twitter that the bas-relief scenes on the Mexican side of the Great Wall had been defaced in obscene ways, but his staff convinced him that photographs of the defacement were nothing more than fake news designed to embarrass him. And this attack on his greatest accomplishment simply confirmed in the President's mind that he was justified in imposing martial law and suspending the 2020 election four years ago. The President had seen numerous pre-election polls that showed him losing the general election in a landslide he blamed—in an early morning tweet—on the "Lying Liberal Media, Fake Polls, and Chinese Interference!" He had no choice but to call off the election and order the military to keep "the peace." In a rambling, hour-long primetime address to the world on October 15, 2020, the President had promised that once a full, televised Senate investigation into traitorous activities could be completed, he would lift martial law and only then could free, fair elections resume. He was true to his word: Most evenings during the last four years, the Senate held hearings that were broadcast on Fox, the only television network with a federal license to disseminate news, where witness upon witness divulged in exquisite detail the plots against the President and America. The hearings would take another two or three years, said the President, but they would eventually come to an end, and a full, unredacted report would be released. This is what the President promised, and who but only the nastiest traitor could question his sincerity?

The guard brought Rogelio to another line, this one in front of the nurse's office. Unlike the lines to say goodbye to their parents, there was only one line here, where boys and girls could mix and talk. The guard gently touched Rogelio's shoulder and said: "Wait here until it's your turn." The boy nodded, and the guard turned on his heel and went back to the lookout room to fetch the next child.

Rogelio looked at the nurse's office. A sobbing girl came out, rubbing her right forearm. Another guard was waiting for her, and slowly guided her toward the girls' barracks. Rogelio sighed. He hated shots, and he figured the children were forced to receive some kind of booster inoculation. Rogelio liked that word: *inoculation*. He let it roll around in his mind. He learned from his teacher that all words had origins—roots—in other languages. French. German. Latin. Where did "inoculation" come from? And what about the very first words? How could those words have any roots if nothing existed before?

Rogelio's turn finally came. A guard opened the door for the boy and said, "Go in." Rogelio complied, stepping into the darkened room that was lit by a lone lamp over phlebotomy chair. The moment the guard closed the door with a loud click, the President's audio loop about the Great Wall disappeared, and the room was enveloped in the most beautiful song Rogelio had ever heard. The two women's voices sang in a language he did not understand, and seemed to come from every corner of the dark room.

The nurse stood to the left of the chair and swiped at an iPad. The nurse reminded Rogelio of his cousin Mateo who lived in Los Angeles, the only son of his tía Isabel, except the nurse had blond hair and a neatly trimmed beard. The nurse suddenly stopped swiping and looked up at the boy.

"Beautiful, isn't it?" said the nurse.

The boy nodded.

"It's called 'The Flower Duet.'"

The boy nodded again, feeling calm for the first time since Homeland Security had rounded up his family in their home in Chula Vista two weeks ago.

"It's from an opera called *Lakmé* written a long time ago."

The boy listened.

"Here, this part, it's so beautiful when the two voices play off each other."

The boy nodded.

The nurse sighed, then looked back at the iPad. "Rogelio Acosta?" He pronounced "Rogelio" as "roe-JELLO-o."

Rogelio had heard his name mangled too often to even notice. He nodded.

"Show me your dog tag."

Rogelio pulled the tag out from the top of his T-shirt and showed it to the nurse. The nurse bent forward, squinted, nodded, and then typed something onto the iPad.

"Please sit."

The boy went to the phlebotomy chair,. It was a green, padded contraption that had seen far too many children. The right arm of the chair that was set in the down position was cracked and revealed white stuffing, and the seat betrayed the many bottoms that had nestled uncomfortably waiting to be poked. The left arm of the chair was propped in the upright position, which allowed Rogelio to slide in.

"I'm getting a shot?" said the boy as he settled in. He tried to sound brave, but his voice cracked, something that was happening more often. He then tried to impress the nurse: "An inoculation?"

25

The nurse let out a muffled laugh that ended in a sloppy snort.

"I guess you can call it that," the nurse said as he grabbed what looked like a long fireplace lighter from a table that stood in the shadows behind him. "It'll feel like a shot." He used the other hand to grab a bit of cotton. The strong smell of alcohol suddenly hit Rogelio's nostrils.

"Put your arm down, keep still," said the nurse. Rogelio complied. The nurse quickly swabbed the boy's forearm. The boy's entire body tensed.

"Look up at the corner," said the nurse with a nod of his head to a spot above and to the left of Rogelio's head. "It's better not to look. It'll be over fast."

Rogelio turned his head and looked up to the dark corner of the room, just to the left of the door he had entered. The music seemed to grow louder, and the women spoke to him in a mysterious language he was on the verge of understanding. The corner's darkness filled his eyes, and the music removed all thought from the boy's mind. Rogelio felt the nurse grab his wrist. He heard a click, felt a small pinch on his forearm, and it was over.

"Good job," said the nurse. "We're done here. Just let me put a bit of cotton and tape on because it will bleed a little for the next couple of hours."

The nurse worked fast. A few seconds later, Rogelio looked down at his forearm where the nurse had expertly wrapped a wad of cotton with blue, stretchy tape.

"Easy-peasy," said the nurse. "You can go now."

Rogelio stood. The women's voices reached an apex of beauty. He couldn't move.

The nurse smiled. "Stunning, isn't it?"

The boy nodded.

"Almost as if God is singing."

Rogelio nodded. "What are they saying?" he whispered.

The nurse shrugged. "Beats me. But does it really matter?"

Before Rogelio could answer, the music ended, and a sharp rap on the door shook the two out of their mutual reverie. The door opened, the President's audio loop invaded the room ("...nobody builds walls better than me, believe me..."), and a different guard stuck her head into the room. A teenage girl stood silently near the guard waiting for permission to enter.

"Time to go," said the nurse.

The boy nodded and slowly walked to the door.

A mí la muerte me pela los dientes.

The large, black bus rocked back and forth on the I-5 freeway toward Los Angeles. An hour earlier, it had made its way from the six-level parking structure at the base of the Great Wall to the freeway entrance. Rogelio rested his head on Marisol's shoulder. His sister snored softly. He felt safe with her. The forty-two children on the bus made little noise, save for exhausted snores, muffled sobs, terrified whispers. The bus driver had turned off the interior lights just before backing out of the parking structure, explaining through the intercom system that it could take several hours to drive to Los Angeles and "deposit" the children at their designated new homes. She'd said that the children should enjoy the box of snacks that had been set on each seat containing bottled water, a bag of pretzels, an apple, and a wrapped mint. Not much, but their new families would feed them, she was sure of that. In the meantime, enjoy this free and very excellent nourishment courtesy of the President, and then try to get some shut-eye. Most of the children had quickly made their way through the snacks. With the lights turned off, few could fend off the brutal fatigue that encased them in the aftermath of the farewells with their parents.

27

BOTH SIDES

The rhythms of the freeway and the traveling shadows that shifted across the bus's interior soothed Rogelio. Before drifting into an unavoidable slumber, the boy remembered his father's favorite dicho when things got difficult: A mí la muerte me pela los dientes. When he first heard his father say this, the boy had wondered why would Death peel anyone's teeth? And could teeth even *be* peeled? But as he now capitulated to inevitable sleep, Rogelio believed he finally understood that old Mexican saying.

"Marisol and Rogelio Acosta!"

Rogelio's eyes popped open at the bus driver's announcement of their names on the intercom. His sister was already zipping up her backpack. Rogelio figured Marisol must have been awake, reading a book with her mini-reading light. His sister loved poetry and novels and short stories. That's why Marisol did so well in high school, their mother often said. Loving books will lead to success in life. Rogelio preferred to entertain himself with video games when he couldn't be outside playing basketball or soccer. But he hoped that someday he'd like to read books as much as his sister did, and maybe then he'd get better grades.

"We're here," Marisol whispered. "At Tía Isabel's house."

Rogelio looked out the window and saw his aunt standing in her driveway. She looked so much like his mother, even though Tía Isabel was eight years older than her sister, Alma. In fact, there was a time—when Alma was in her mid-twenties and Isabel in her early thirties—that many who met them thought the sisters were identical twins. Sometimes, at family gatherings, whether in Chula Vista with Alma and her family, or here in Los Angeles with Isabel and hers, the sisters would sometimes play along with the confused neighbors who had been invited over to celebrate.

28

And despite the 127-mile distance between Los Angeles and Chula Vista, the sisters' families remained close. In fact, Rogelio knew his tía Isabel well because he had interviewed her for an oral history project last year. He had learned that, with the cunning and expensive assistance of a coyote, Isabel and their now late mother, Abuelita Belén, had come to the United States seven years before the infant Alma and their father could. And for this simple accident of timing, Rogelio's aunt and grandmother had become United States citizens under President Reagan's 1986 Immigration Reform and Control Act. Tía Isabel did well in school, majoring in business administration at San Diego State University before landing her first job in Los Angeles working the registration desk at the DoubleTree in downtown. Now, Tía Isabel was the hotel revenue manager at the Courtyard Marriott near LAX. At age fifty, she looked years younger than her actual age—betrayed only by a streak of white hair that ran from the top of her forehead that she brushed back over an otherwise full head of black hair. The women on that side of the family kept their youth, Rogelio's father, Alejandro, often said. Good skin, great hair, nice teeth. Alma would always add: "And we're smart, too."

Yes, Tía Isabel was healthy, but her late husband, Tío Manny, had suffered from Type 2 diabetes for years, surviving three strokes before a heart attack took him on Christmas Day 2016. Rogelio's father said that it was really the election that killed Manny, but Rogelio couldn't figure how an election, even *that* one, could cause a heart to stop. A few years after Manny passed away, Tía Isabel's son, Mateo, came down from Sacramento, where he had earned a master's in English literature at UC Davis. He didn't want his mother to be alone, and he could easily find a teaching gig at a high school in Los Angeles. Mateo didn't need much to live, just enough to keep himself clothed and fed while he worked on a novel. He moved into the small house that stood in the large backyard Abuelita Belén had enjoyed as her haven. But it had been vacant since her death, so, in many ways, it was a perfect way to make use of it again. Mateo saved money on rent and helped his mother stave off sadness and loss. He quickly found a teaching job at Cathedral High School. "Not a big paycheck, but enough to keep body and soul together," Mateo liked to say, "while I write the Great American Novel." But his mother knew he had sacrificed the full life he had fashioned up in Sacramento to help her with the loneliness widowhood had brought. Though young when she had Mateo, Isabel could not conceive again. "Quality, not quantity," Mateo joked whenever his mother fell into a funk because she could not give him at least one sibling. And he'd add: "And that way, I have you all to myself."

Rogelio and Marisol stepped off the bus. The night had gotten very cold. The crickets chirped loudly. Tía Isabel opened her arms wide and said, "Come here, my babies."

Rogelio and Marisol had settled into a comfortable—if not wholly normal—routine in the month they had been living their new lives with Tía Isabel and Mateo. The house had been built in 1933 in a part of northeast Los Angeles that was just six miles from downtown, in an area known as Glassell Park, near Eagle Rock and Highland Park and Mount Washington. These communities had undergone some of the most aggressive gentrification over the last fifteen years, and her modest, 1,450-square-foot home was now worth well over a million dollars, at least according to Zillow and Redfin. But Isabel would never sell. She and her late husband had toiled for the down payment when they were newly married, and it held too many memories. And now that her niece and nephew were living with her, Isabel needed the house more than ever. She had converted the study of her wood-framed home back into the bedroom it had been when Mateo was young. Isabel furnished it with sturdy bunk beds, two dressers, and two small desks that she bought at IKEA. She knew she could never replace their parents, but at least she could make it as comfortable as possible.

Marisol enrolled as a high school senior at the Sotomayor Learning Academies on North San Fernando Road, a short drive away. Rogelio enrolled at the same campus, but in the middle school program. Because he had been identified on the enrollment form as one of the relocated children, the school granted a waiver so he could enter the sixth grade early to be on the same campus as his sister. "Small kindnesses," his aunt had said when the waiver was approved. Each morning, Mateo would drop off his cousins at school and then head to his teaching job at Cathedral High School. The children would then stay on campus doing schoolwork or attending club meetings until 6:30 p.m., when Isabel would drive onto campus and gather them up for dinner. Structure. Activities. Near normalcy.

And part of that normalcy was the once weekly, government-sanctioned—and monitored—video call with their parents. Each Sunday night, Isabel would set up her laptop at the kitchen table for Rogelio and Marisol, click on to the Homeland Security–approved link, type in her family password and code, and connect with her sister and brother-in-law, who sat 1,576 miles away in a small apartment in Ocotlán, Jalisco, their hometown about 150 miles south east of Guadalajara. They were allowed fifteen minutes each week to gaze upon each other and share as many bits of news about themselves as could be shared in that short time. Since all cell phone and internet connections to all Latin American countries had been blocked by Homeland Security under Executive Order 9066, they were forced to savor each of these minutes. At the end of the video calls, Rogelio's mother would always break down in tears, and his father would valiantly try to comfort her as tears fell freely from his own eyes. The one thing that kept their parents sane was knowing that the children were in safe hands and clearly thriving despite the pain of separation. And so this was the new normal: Parents on a computer screen, fifteen minutes a week.

Rogelio had his suspicions about Marisol.

At first, he thought he was dreaming what was happening. But one night, as the glowing alarm clock numbers read 11:02 p.m., Rogelio forced himself to stay awake while pretending to sleep—complete with fake snores—as he waited in his perch on the upper bunk. Marisol whispered: "Are you awake?" The boy did not answer. Then after a minute, Marisol slowly got out of bed. Even in the shadows, Rogelio could see that his sister was fully dressed in a sweatshirt and jeans. She slipped on a pair of sneakers, grabbed her backpack, and gingerly opened the window. Within a few seconds she was outside standing in the flowerbed. Marisol closed the window and was gone.

Rogelio blinked in disbelief. He heard a car start up—he thought it sounded like Mateo's battered Honda Civic that was always parked out front—then a car door opened and closed, followed by the sound of the engine revving and then slowly making its way down the street. As the last sounds of the car disappeared, fatigue overcame Rogelio, and his fake snores soon became real. His final thought was that he would confront Marisol and Mateo in the morning as they drove to school. Rogelio had no choice.

Los caminos de la vida.

"Put it louder," said Marisol, even though she could have reached over and done it herself.

But Mateo complied and pushed the volume control on his steering wheel. Marisol sat in the front passenger seat and bobbed her head to the song. Rogelio thought it was funny how his sister had gotten into a habit of exploring their aunt's vast CD collection. So old school. Fortunately, Mateo's ancient Honda had its original CD player, so Marisol could bring the music with her on the rides to school. Lila Downs had become Marisol's musical crush of the week. Rogelio's Spanish was not as good as his sister's, so he strained to understand the words to "Los Caminos de la Vida." He eventually gave up and remembered the task at hand.

"Where did you go last night?" asked Rogelio as he kept his eyes trained on the back of his sister's head. It stopped bobbing when she heard her brother's question. Marisol turned toward Mateo as if for guidance, but he kept his eyes on the road, wary of the children who were walking to school and crossing streets.

"Are you two dating?"

"Oh, gross!" said Marisol.

"No, dude," said Mateo. "I wouldn't date my cousin, and I certainly don't date seventeen-year-olds. Want me to go to prison or something?"

Then Marisol said: "Look, we were going to wait to tell you." She kept her eyes on Mateo, who nodded his approval to continue.

"Tell me what?"

Marisol twisted her body so she could look at her brother. "We go to meetings," she began.

"What kind of meetings?"

"Planning meetings," said Mateo.

"And we volunteer after the meetings," added Marisol.

"For what?" said Rogelio. He kept his body still, his voice under control. He wanted the truth.

"Meetings of Los Otros Coyotes," said Marisol, keeping her eyes on her brother. "They help reunite separated families."

"Where do you do this…meeting and volunteering?"

"They have an office downtown, at the Bradbury Building," said Mateo. "They pretend to be event planners. You know, special events like weddings, quinceañeras, and retirement parties."

Rogelio knew the Bradbury Building from that old movie *Blade Runner*. Marisol was a self-proclaimed sci-fi nerd who made her little brother watch that film with her three times, though she believed the Philip K. Dick novel on which it was based was far superior—she even thought the novel's actual title was more "evocative" than the movie's. The five-story office building was a Los Angeles landmark almost from the moment it opened in 1893, a year after millionaire Lewis L. Bradbury died. It is best known for its astonishing skylight atrium, marble stairs, tiled walkways, and wrought-iron elevators. With a shiver, Rogelio remembered the creepy scene where Harrison Ford, blaster drawn, makes his way through the darkened, dank, dilapidated atrium in search of a renegade android. The Bradbury Building of the film becomes the private lair of J.F. Sebastian, a genetic designer who is not allowed to emigrate off-world because he suffers from Methuselah Syndrome: He is a young man whose body has prematurely aged. He attempts to defeat his isolation by creating android companions. *This* was where Marisol and Mateo snuck to each night? Marisol could discern confusion on her brother's face.

"The Bradbury is filled with businesses and law offices," she said. "It's nothing like what you see in *Blade Runner*."

Rogelio appreciated his sister's explanation. Now he could move on with his next question: "Can we be reunited…with Mamá and Papá?"

Marisol again looked at Mateo for guidance, but her cousin kept his eyes on the road. She turned back to Rogelio.

"Do you want to?" she said.

Rogelio blinked. Before he knew it, tears filled his eyes. He nodded.

"Okay," said Marisol. "Okay."

Mateo pulled into the school's drop-off lane and said: "We're here. We'll talk tonight."

Rogelio nodded again. "Yes," he finally said. "Tonight."

El Señor es contigo.

After dinner that night, Tía Isabel opened her laptop at the kitchen table to work on bills. Marisol and Mateo saw this as the perfect time to get out of the house and take Rogelio to the Bradbury Building.

"Tía," began Marisol as Rogelio handed her the last dish to dry. "Mateo said that he'd take me and Rogelio out for ice cream at Grand Central Market."

Isabel kept her eyes on her screen, nodded, and said: "Well…"

"It's Friday, so no school tomorrow," added Marisol.

"Okay, I guess so," said Isabel.

Marisol continued: "Do you want us to bring anything? McConnell's has your favorite: double peanut butter chip."

"No thank you," said her aunt without looking up, but betraying a hint of temptation. "I'm gaining too much weight. Go have fun. I need to finish the bills."

Marisol nodded at her brother. Rogelio smiled. He appreciated how his sister plotted.

Mateo drove his Honda down Broadway through Chinatown. The evening was warm, so the streets teemed with people enjoying the weather. But dotting each side were dozens of tents and jury-rigged structures of multicolored tarps, where people who could not afford apartments made their homes. The happy pedestrians skirted around these makeshift abodes without stopping. Marisol rifled through her aunt's CD holder, found what she wanted, popped it in the player, and "La Cumbia Del Mole" came on. She was still on her Lila Downs kick. Rogelio liked this song—and truth be told he preferred the

English version that comes later on the CD—but he wanted his sister and cousin to explain the next step.

"Tell me," he said from the backseat. "How do we get to see Mamá and Papá?"

Marisol turned down the music's volume and twisted back toward her brother.

"We have to volunteer tonight anyway, so we can go early and introduce you to them."

"Them?"

"Vivaporú," said Mateo, catching Rogelio's eye in the rearview mirror

Rogelio blinked. "Vivaporú?"

Marisol nodded.

"That's how Mamá pronounces Vicks VapoRub," said Rogelio. "You know, because of her accent." He closed his eyes and tried to remember the feel of his mother's warm hand as she rubbed the ointment on his chest whenever he got a cold. She'd whisper an Ave María as she slowly applied the Vicks onto her son's narrow chest. He could almost hear his mother's voice: "Ave María, llena eres de gracia, El Señor es contigo...." Rogelio opened his eyes, which were now moist. He said again: "Vivaporú?"

"That's the name they go by," said Mateo.

"They?" said Rogelio again. "How many people am I meeting?"

"Just one," said Marisol. "And they go by the name Vivaporú, okay?"

"Okay," said Rogelio, still feeling confused, but he didn't press the issue.

"We'll park in the structure on Spring Street and then go through the courtyard to enter the Bradbury from the rear entrance," said Mateo. "It's safer that way."

"Okay," said Rogelio. "Okay. And tell me about Los Otros

36

Coyotes."

Mateo said, "We've told you all we should for now."

"Vivaporú will explain," added Marisol. "Be patient."

Rogelio nodded. The boy knew he had little choice but to wait.

The three took the elevator down from the seventh level of the Broadway Spring Center, a large parking structure on Spring Street.

"We cut across here," said Marisol as they exited.

Rogelio looked across the courtyard toward the red-bricked building where his sister pointed. Along the pathway stood a long, gray wall that looked like the kind of reverse timeline that he and his classmates made for their history class. As they walked, he looked up at that first section of the wall that had the year "1900" at the top over the words: "Los Angeles mourns and reveres Grandma Mason."

"Biddy Mason lived right here, after the Civil War," said Marisol. They stopped in front of a photograph of the former slave. "She ran the city's first childcare center out of her home and founded the city's First African Methodist Episcopal Church in her home."

"Wow," said Rogelio.

They started to walk again, but slowly, so that they could read the legends on the wall.

"She was born into slavery in Georgia," said Marisol. "A Mormon family owned her. But when the family moved to Southern California, she sued for her freedom because California entered the Union as a free state in 1850."

"You mean when Alta California was stolen from Mexico," added Mateo.

"What happened?" said Rogelio.

"She won," said Marisol and Mateo in unison. They laughed. "Jinx!"

BOTH SIDES

As they read the timeline, Rogelio learned that after winning her freedom, Biddy Mason worked as a nurse and midwife, delivering hundreds of babies during her career. She also was one of the first African American women to own land in Los Angeles. Biddy Mason became a successful businesswoman who shared her wealth with charities. She spoke fluent Spanish, was much loved, and even dined on occasion at the home of Pio Pico, the last governor of Alta California. They got to the end of the reverse timeline with the year 1810 and the words, "Biddy Mason born a slave." Rogelio shivered, but he didn't know why.

"Up these stairs," said Mateo. They marched up the ten concrete steps. Mateo opened one of the large wood and glass doors, and they were in the Bradbury Building. As they walked down the hallway, Rogelio was not impressed by what he saw. Yes, the floor was beautiful with its Italian marble and Mexican tile—which Marisol proudly pointed out as if she'd designed the building herself—though it was nothing like what he knew from *Blade Runner*. They turned, went down a few steps, and then entered the magnificent atrium area. *Ah! This was it!*

"Pretty fucking amazing, eh?" said Mateo. Marisol elbowed her cousin.

"What?" said Mateo. "I suspect he's used that word before."

Rogelio blushed, but he liked how Mateo treated him like a peer.

"Okay, fine," said Marisol. "Now up to Los Otros Coyotes. Let's take the stairs."

Rogelio could not hide his wonder. The Bradbury was a functioning office building, and even though it was after the dinner hour, tenants—and a few tourists oohing and aahing and taking photos—wandered about. On the second floor, they passed several large doors with beveled glass windows that had painted names of different businesses and law firms such as "Charoenpong, Eskandari & Lundgren LLP," and "Elisofon+Van Gelderen Architectural Concepts," and "Pletcher & Jones Designs." They finally arrived at a door with the name "Los Otros Coyotes: Party Planners." Under the lettering was a painting that resembled a woodcut of three coyotes howling beneath a full moon. Marisol pushed a small button, and they waited. After a few moments, a thin, young man opened the door. He smiled at Marisol. She smiled back. The young man said, "Come in."

They entered. A dozen young people were at standing desks typing away on laptops, their faces aglow from the screens, almost all with earbuds listening to their own personal soundtracks. At the back of the room, a large table groaned with soft drinks, bottled waters, plates of fruit, coffee pots, and paper cups and plates. To the left of the table was another door with VIVAPORÚ painted across it in bold, black letters.

They walked to the door, and Marisol knocked.

"Adelante," came a voice that was the most beautiful Rogelio had ever heard.

Marisol opened the door, kissed Rogelio on his forehead, and said: "Don't be afraid." He nodded and walked into the dark room as Marisol closed the door behind her brother. Rogelio turned and set his eyes on a figure who sat in an oversized green leather chair in front of a large, old, wooden desk. A brass lamp at the desk's edge offered the only illumination in the room. Seven or eight books in Spanish and English sat in a stack just beneath the lamp. Rogelio could discern titles on four of the spines: *Under the Feet of Jesus*, *La Metamorfosis*, *The Children of Willesden Lane*, and *La Hija de la Chuparrosa*. The figure looked up from a large ledger. Rogelio lifted his eyes from the book titles. He just then noticed that, unlike the main office, there was no computer or laptop in this room. And instead of earbuds, the person in front of the boy had a turntable on a credenza just behind the large chair, the words "love supreme" repeating out of two large speakers.

BOTH SIDES

The figure reached back and lowered the music to a whisper.

"Siéntate, por favor," said Vivaporú, pointing to one of two guest chairs that were stationed at angles in front of the desk.

Rogelio sat. Vivaporú stood and looked down on the boy. Rogelio had never seen such a perfect person in his life. Vivaporú wore a luminous white three-piece suit accented with a shocking green shirt, collar spread open wide across the suit's large lapels. Vivaporú's earlobes were stretched with large golden gauges, accented by a great golden Chai—Rogelio thought it was a dog or some other animal—that hung on a thick chain around their long, muscular neck. Vivaporú's lustrous black hair was parted neatly down the middle and hung to their shoulders. They must have been at least six feet tall, with the lean proportions of a ballet dancer. Vivaporú's hazel eyes almost never blinked, and their smooth brown skin gleamed. They pointed down at the ledger while keeping their eyes on the boy.

"Rogelio Acosta," said Vivaporú—not as a question, but a statement of fact. Rogelio remembered how the nurse at the detention center had said his name before checking the boy's dog tag. But where that nurse had spat out a mangled version of his name, Vivaporú said "Rogelio Acosta" in an almost musical manner, softly pronounced in Spanish, as if the boy were a melody to be shared with an invisible audience. Vivaporú's voice reminded Rogelio of a sound he once heard while hiking at the Mother Miguel Trailhead with his father a year before the separation at the Great Wall: a beautiful bird's song that filled the boy's mind with thoughts of his home back in Chula Vista.

"Yes," said Rogelio. "That's me."

"Your hermana tells me that you want to be with your parents again," said Vivaporú. "¿Es cierto?"

"Yes," said Rogelio. "It's true."

"They're in a safe city. Safe for children. We know this."

40

Rogelio listened silently.

"Show me your right forearm," said Vivaporú. The boy was confused at first, but then he realized Vivaporú wanted to look at the inoculation site. Rogelio pulled up his shirtsleeve and showed it to Vivaporú. The skin had healed, leaving a small, square, shiny scar.

"Do you know what that is?" said Vivaporú.

"My inoculation."

Vivaporú let out a gentle, melodious laugh.

"No," said Vivaporú. "A microchip."

Suddenly, a black-and-white cat jumped onto the boy's lap. It purred wildly and made itself comfortable. Rogelio smiled and petted the feline.

"Su nombre es Sophie," said Vivaporú.

"I like Sophie."

"Sophie likes you."

Rogelio extricated his right arm from beneath Sophie and showed Vivaporú the scar again. "Why did they put a microchip in me?" he said.

Vivaporú leaned forward. "So that Homeland Security can track you to know that you're still in los Estados Unidos."

"What for?"

"Pues, because they need us as much as they hate us," said Vivaporú with a loud sigh. "The country desires young people to grow up and then take the jobs that need taking. *¿Entiendes?* All kinds of jobs, from janitors to engineers. The white population is aging, not— *¿cómo se dice?*—reproducing as fast as we are. Too many jobs, not enough people."

"I want to be with my parents."

"Por supuesto," said Vivaporú. "But I don't know if that's possible."

The boy sat up straight. "You said it was safe."

41

Vivaporú shook their head. "No, niño, I said your parents are in a safe *city*. That is a different fact."

"What do you mean?

"It is a dangerous journey back," said Vivaporú. "Children have been caught by Homeland Security before they could get back to the other side."

"And what happens to them?"

"They get sent far away, to places like Kansas and Nebraska and even South Dakota. They become—¿*cómo se dice?*—foster children, put with families that are not blood."

"I don't care!"

"No, it's too risky."

"I need to be with my parents!"

Vivaporú sighed, turned, walked to the turntable, and increased the volume. Vivaporú closed their eyes and swayed slowly to the rhythm of the jazz. Rogelio sat in silence for several minutes. Tears fell from his face. The track ended. Vivaporú turned off the turntable and turned to face the boy.

"The answer should be no," said Vivaporú.

The boy held his breath.

"Pues, the first step will be to remove that microchip."

Rogelio wiped the tears from his face, smiled, and sat up.

"Yes?" the boy said.

"Sí."

Rogelio then grew serious and looked at his forearm. "But the government will know it's been removed," he said.

Vivaporú laughed. "¡Qué inteligente eres!" Vivaporú walked around the desk to the boy and pulled Sophie from Rogelio's lap. "My beautiful gato will become you."

"What?"

"We usually use rescue pets. I had been saving Sophie for a special person, and we have one here: you!"

Rogelio shifted in his seat. He was trying to follow what Vivaporú was saying. Vivaporú returned Sophie to the boy's lap, sat down in the other guest chair, crossed their long legs, and leaned toward Rogelio.

"Once we have identified a child who wants to be with their parents, we contact the parents by hacking around Homeland Security," began Vivaporú. "Your sister is already in contact with your parents because she works with us. That's what those beautiful young people are doing in the front office. ¿Entiendes? First, we remove the microchip from that child and put it into a dog or cat. That way, to the government, the chip is still on this side of the Great Wall even as the children are transported back to their parents on the other side. It is like a reverse—¿cómo se dice?—Underground Railroad."

Rogelio nodded. His class learned about the Underground Railroad last year when they studied the chapter on slavery. He thought of Biddy Mason, who didn't have to use a secret escape route because she successfully sued for her freedom when her owner brought the family to California.

"How will I get back to Mexico?"

Vivaporú took in a deep breath and smiled. "In the belly of the beast."

"What?"

"Those big black buses that take the parents through the Great Wall and into México, like the one they put your parents on. ¿Entiendes? We have identified several sympathetic drivers and guards who have gotten more sympathetic with a little mordida—¿cómo se dice?—bribe. And we do not charge you. We are supported by many churches, mosques, synagogues, and temples of all types."

Rogelio nodded. "And what about my sister?"

"She has decided to stay here, for now. Marisol is one of our best hackers, and she has become invaluable. Ella es brillante. And she has excellent ideas for the Reconquista."

"The what?"

"No es importante," said Vivaporú. "At this moment, the question is: Do you want to be reunited with your parents even though it is risky?"

"Yes," said Rogelio after a few moments of thought. "Put my microchip into Sophie, and get me into the belly of the beast."

Vivaporú clapped their hands and stood. "Your hermana will alert your parents and get you ready."

En el vientre de la bestia.

After Mateo and Marisol had finished their two-hour shift at Los Otros Coyotes, they walked Rogelio to a place called Tina's Café, two blocks from the Bradbury Building. They strode in silence, the evening's cool breeze beginning to make itself felt. In the back room of what was an otherwise normal coffee shop, a man removed the microchip from the boy's arm and placed it in a tube of disinfectant for eventual implantation into Sophie. The chip's slow descent through the blue liquid enthralled Rogelio. Removal of the microchip hurt the boy more than expected, but he was happy that it would soon be in that lovely cat.

As they drove back home through Chinatown, Marisol explained the plan. She would contact their parents in the morning so they could begin their journey from Ocotlán to Tijuana. In one week, before dawn, a small group of children, including Rogelio, would be picked up by a school bus a few blocks from their home. It would look like any other bus taking children to school, but in their backpacks, instead of books and folders, the children were instructed to have several changes of clothes, toiletries, water, snacks, and anything else needed for the trip to San Diego and through the Great Wall and reunion with their parents in Tijuana. About a mile from the large parking structure where the black buses were parked, the children would be moved into a van of the kind used by Homeland Security, and from there, they would be taken to a predetermined black bus where the luggage compartment— the belly of the beast—would be waiting for its young cargo. Bribes would be paid at each step. Once the bus crossed through the Great Wall into Tijuana, if all went well, the children's parents would be waiting to take them back to their homes. Many of the parents who had lived in places like Guatemala, El Salvador, or Honduras were given asylum by the Mexican government, and so their children would settle with them in their new homes in Mexico. Marisol would not tell their aunt until after Rogelio was safely with their parents. Tía Isabel would be upset, no doubt, but it was the only way.

The belly of the beast was hot. The black bus rocked back and forth as it made its way down three levels toward the exit gate at the base of the Great Wall. Even over the rumbling of the vehicle's engine, Rogelio could discern the audio loop of the President that was broadcast in the detention center and parking structure: "…I will build a great, great wall on our southern border, and I will make Mexico pay for that wall…."

The five other children who had ridden with Rogelio were huddled together in the dark. Two of them softly whimpered. The beaten-up luggage and duffel bags of the parents who rode above made the small space feel even more confining, like an ancient tomb. Rogelio sat in a corner and hugged his backpack. He willed himself not to cry. He had cried too much already. He was done with tears. He would soon be in Tijuana. He would soon embrace his mother and father. And after a few weeks of living in Mexico with his parents, Rogelio would contact his sister to find out more about this thing Vivaporú called the Reconquista. This was the boy's promise to himself. And he always kept his promises.

The bus suddenly jerked to a stop. Rogelio heard shouting in both Spanish and English. He held his breath, and the other children's whimpering grew louder. What was happening? Rogelio could hear cars honking and speeding by the bus. He then heard footsteps on the gravel of the freeway's shoulder. More shouting, men and women. Arguments, cussing, both languages mixing into one cacophonous commotion. Then silence, adults whispering, a clicking and sliding of the locking mechanism that kept the children in the belly of the beast. Suddenly light—three, maybe four flashlights aimed at the children. And then Rogelio—blinded by the flashlights—heard a woman scream, "Oh my God!"

FUNDIDO

JOHNNY SHAW

Gordo should have been in bed with his wife, but instead he was driving a van full of corpses to a demonio necrófago's lair. It wasn't a complaint. It could have been worse. He could've been in the back of the van with the dead.

The phone had rung, he had received his orders, and he had gone to pick up the kid. Whatever had happened at that nightclub was none of his business. Gordo may have been Raul's cousin, but he was still only told essential details. The cargo and the destination, that was all.

Gordo had been to Barranco Seco a few times. He would never get used to the place, but he had learned to tolerate its ghoulish creepiness. This was the kid's first time. When the compound came into view, the kid inhaled deeply and let out a whimper. The place didn't look like much, just a trailer and an old barn surrounded by a high fence. It was the stories of what happened in that barn that made the kid's face lose its blood. Like everyone else, he had heard the stories of El Fundidor.

At the gate, the kid got out of the van and unlocked the padlock. Gordo drove onto the compound and waited. He wanted to see the kid's face when he caught sight of the skulls.

From a distance, the barn looked stuccoed. As they approached, it became evident that it was covered with animal skulls of all shapes and sizes. Perforated, bleached, some skulls fused together. Dogs and pigs and goats and cattle. But it was the writing that made Gordo shudder. Strange sigils and markings written on each skull. Curses or spells, he didn't know, but they were definitely a warning.

This was an evil place. A place where death wasn't the worst thing that could happen. Where death was the beginning.

The man they called El Fundidor heard the gate open outside. He heard the gravel under the van as it entered the compound. He didn't rush to greet his guests. They would wait. El Fundidor went back to his work. It required concentration.

Too little acid and the process took days to complete. Too much and the froth overflowed from the edges of the barrel. Precision was everything. Dissolving a human body was both science and art.

The early years had required considerable trial and error. At first, he used roadkill and carcasses supplied by feedlots and farmers. A series of brews that showed mixed results: boiled water, acids, caustics, oxidizers, dozens of multisyllabic corrosives. Some ineffective or slow. Others dangerous alone, worse in combination. He wrote his recipes and notes on the animal skulls as a record of his progress.

The patchy scar tissue on El Fundidor's arms stood as a reminder to the primitive experimentation that had led to his mastery. His persistent cough the product of almost a decade of melting flesh. The two missing fingers on his left hand had been a hard-learned lesson in overconfidence. He had never tried to perform the process without measuring again.

After hundreds of melts, he had little doubt that he could perform the entire procedure by eye and feel. By the fizz of the liquid solution. By the creamy color of the tallow. By the acrid, yet meaty aroma. His grandmother had never needed a measuring cup to make pozole, but

El Fundidor was making a very different soup.

It took no added effort to carefully measure. To stay humble. To get it right. It was the least he could do for the dead, to show them respect before he erased their existence. Each corpse was once a human being, one of God's children. The Lord God had chosen El Fundidor's purpose. It was his obligation to perform his task with the same care and precision each and every time. Anything less would be a sin.

There had been many changes at the top since El Sanguinario had conscripted him into his service. He had been a butcher's assistant, not yet twenty. Old for a new recruit, he had thought he had evaded the cartel's reach, but El Sanguinario had got it in his head that someone who worked with meat would understand how to disintegrate a human body. He had not been wrong.

He had hated the name El Sanguinario had given him. El Fundidor. It sounded like a villain in *Batman*. It wasn't until the cartel leader died that he realized its value. While later leaders controlled him and gave him his orders, they also feared him. After all, he had been the one to dispose of El Sanguinario's body. He had dissolved a king. The stories spread from the barren ranch outside of Tecate to the cantinas and backrooms of Tijuana and Mexicali. His reputation was known throughout Mexico. El Fundidor was a brujo, a vampiro, the cucuy de la frontera de California.

His prowess made him useful. His gruesome legend kept him safe. As long as he performed his distinct function, he was left alone. And so was his family. That had been the arrangement.

He continued to send money home, even if he hadn't heard from his family in years. He was losing his sense of purpose. The work no longer challenged him. The routine, the burn in his lungs, the living conditions.

He hadn't left the property in months, living on a diet of beans, potatoes, and tortillas with the sparse orange trees supplying breakfast and dessert. There was a television in the small trailer, but the rabbit ears only got XHBC from Mexicali, and even then he had to watch fútbol through static and snow. He needed a vacation. He longed for a swim in the ocean. Something clean. But he was El Fundidor. The devil didn't get time off.

"Six of them," the fat man said, waiting for his young partner at the back of the van.

El Fundidor had interacted with the fat man before. He was one of the few men who made eye contact with him. The fat man didn't look like much, but he was more than a lackey. He was familiar with death, comfortable among the dead.

The fat man's young partner looked even younger in his fear. Probably tougher in the city, the young man kept his eyes to the ground, glancing at El Fundidor when he thought the monster wasn't looking. His hands shook enough for him to stuff them in his pockets.

El Fundidor considered shouting "Buu" to see if he could make the kid piss himself, but he knew he wouldn't. He wasn't a cruel man.

The fat man opened the back of the van. The bodies sat piled in a pyramid like rolled carpets. El Fundidor admired the fat man's efficiency of space. Too often, the bodies were packed haphazardly, which could create rigor in unworkably awkward poses. El Fundidor preferred to do as little dissection as necessary. It was time-consuming and the last time, he had injured his shoulder trying to snap a leg from the hip joint.

Usually the corpses were delivered concealed in canvas or plastic tarp. None of these dead were wrapped. It took a lot of cojones to drive around with six dead bodies uncovered in the back of a van. Even in Mexico. Something unnaturally bad had happened. Something unplanned or rushed. There had been no time for discretion.

"All women," El Fundidor said.

The fat man nodded and threw a body over his shoulder. The woman was small, light. She would melt easily. He indelicately dropped the woman on top of the two-day-old body in the corral near the barn door. Flies billowed from the ground in a gray cloud.

"Hijo de puta!" the fat man shouted.

"Over there," El Fundidor said, pointing to the other side of the corral. "I work in the order they arrive. And be more careful."

The fat man nodded, dragging the young girl's body off the older corpse, displacing more flies. His young partner waited with a dead girl in his arms. When the fat man moved to the side, his partner gently set her next to the other girl.

"Why women? What happened?" El Fundidor asked, unsure where his curiosity came from. He could not remember ever asking about the dead they brought to him.

"I don't know, carnal. I drive the van."

The men carried two more bodies, treating them more gently. One of the dead girls was nude. She was either very young or shaved. From the wounds and bruises, the death had been violent. From her suppleness, it had been recent.

"Where did they come from?" El Fundidor asked.

The fat man gave him a questioning look. He opened his mouth to answer, but before he did, a soft moan came from the back of the van.

The three men looked at each other, then in unison they turned. Another faint moan filled the silence.

El Fundidor and the fat man stepped to the van to get a better look. The young partner remained where he stood, visibly shaking.

Inside the van, one of the two remaining girls moved impossibly slow, folding herself into a fetal position. Like a dying fly, her arms and legs receded toward her body.

"She's alive," El Fundidor said.

51

"She shouldn't be," the fat man said. "Kill her and be done with it."

"I don't kill people."

"You are El Fundidor," the fat man said.

"I have never harmed a soul."

"Are you fucking kidding me?" The fat man laughed.

He should not have laughed while standing near a frightened and suffering girl. It was cruel and disgusting. It lacked empathy and compassion. It was almost as if the fat man could not see that this person was in pain.

"I will not kill her," El Fundidor said. "It is not the gravedigger's job to do the work of the executioner. She is alive. She has earned the right to live."

"A la mierda. I'll get my gun," the fat man said, walking to the front of the van.

"Vale," El Fundidor said and walked to the bone pile that had been overdue for disposal. The acid effectively disintegrated the meat, but only blanched and perforated the bones. Every two weeks, he had to grind the bones to be picked up and distributed throughout the desert. El Fundidor found half a femur in the pile, the shard at the end sharpened to a point. The tip drew blood across his palm. It would do. He met the fat man at the back of the van.

Suso Rivas pulled down the steel grate and locked up. He appreciated the quiet after a long night. The bass of the repetitive dance music still pounded in his head. It was what every club played, but Suso didn't know anyone who actually liked it. It wasn't like people came to his place for the music.

Early Sunday morning was the only peaceful time on Paseo de la Reforma. The cantinas and men's clubs appeared abandoned without their neon and flash. Suso looked at his own establishment, Adelita Bar

& Girls. In the day, the chipped plaster and pornographic graffiti were more pronounced. He considered calling Pepe to give the exterior a once-over, but it wasn't worth it. It wasn't like his customers cared about anything but tits and getting laid.

He clicked the key fob and walked toward his car at the far end of the small parking lot. Two big men stood between him and the car. They dropped their cigarettes on the ground, crushed them underfoot, and met him halfway. He instinctively gripped the knife in his jacket pocket.

"Jesus Rivas," the smaller of the two men said. Smaller, not small. He was six foot five and thick, which gave a hint to the size of the other man.

"I'm not carrying any money," Suso said.

"We're not here for money. We're looking for your brother."

"My brother?" Suso laughed. "I'm sorry. It isn't funny. It's that I forgot I had a brother. I haven't seen Cesar in ten—no, twelve years. I didn't know that he was alive."

The smaller man turned to the bigger man. "Do you believe him?"

The bigger man moved quicker than Suso would have thought possible. Two seconds later, he picked Suso off the ground and lifted him over his head like a barbell. Only for a moment, then he slammed Suso onto the asphalt.

All the air left Suso's body. His wrist bent backward underneath him, the crack both suffered and heard. It felt like his organs and brain had shifted inside his body. Suso's mind told him to get up, to fight, to try to survive. He was vulnerable on the ground, but his body did not respond. He could not breathe. His heart raced. He saw spots.

"Where is your brother?" the smaller man said.

The words came out in gasps. "I don't know. He left when I was fourteen. The last time I saw or heard from him."

The bigger man picked him up again, cradling Suso in his arms.

"No. Please," Suso said.

"I'm going to believe you," the smaller man said. "If you see your brother, call this number. Or we'll be back." He placed a slip of paper into Suso's jacket pocket.

Suso nodded.

"Thank you," the smaller man said and turned to his partner. "Let's go."

The bigger man nodded, lifted Suso overhead, and dropped him to the ground again.

Suso woke up in the back of a van. While the surroundings were strange and his vision unfocused, the smell was sharp and alarming. Familiar, but unreal. It smelled of a butcher shop, of the hair on a barber's floor, of a sewer drain after a storm. It reeked of rot and decay. Of death.

He rolled over and immediately recoiled at the sight of the young woman next to him. Her face was inches from his own. She looked half-dead, her breathing raspy and shallow. Dried blood matted her hair and covered her face. Her tattered clothes were stained with blood and other fluids.

"Not all of the blood is hers."

Suso turned toward the voice. A man sat on a crate at the front of the van. His hair was grayer, his eyes sunken, his face gaunt, but it was most definitely his older brother. Cesar had been twenty when he had joined the cartel. The twelve years had aged him forty.

."Two men beat me. They were looking for you. What's going on?" Suso pressed himself to a sitting position against the side of the van. His whole body hurt. His wrist was definitely broken.

"I killed a man a few hours ago. He was cartel."

"You what?"

"He shouldn't have laughed."

"What do I say to that?"

"I didn't know they would send men for you," Cesar said. "Family had always been forgiven."

"Who is she?" Suso pointed at the girl. Her shallow breath continued. One hand shook as if warding off an attacker.

"A girl."

Suso waited for Cesar to say more. He didn't.

"Where have you been all this time?"

"Close," Cesar said. "Our mother? Is she?"

"Yes. Buried with Papá."

"At least they are not in danger."

"Why are you here? Why come to me?"

Cesar nodded toward the girl.

"I don't understand," Suso said.

"You need to take care of her. I cannot."

Suso looked at the girl once again. "She looks bad. Like really bad. She needs a doctor."

"There were men at the hospital."

"I can't help her."

"She needs sanctuary." Cesar held up the piece of paper the man had placed in Suso's pocket. "Find her safety and I will call them. I will end this. You will be left untouched."

"Won't they kill you?"

"They'll try."

With the young girl in his arms, El Fundidor followed his younger brother down the underground corridor.

"They might be watching the front door," Suso said, leading the way with the flashlight. "You'd be surprised at how many tunnels and connecting basements there are in Mexicali, especially near La Chinesca."

BOTH SIDES

"Mexico is like an anthill. There are tunnels everywhere."

They walked through a tight doorway of broken bricks and reached a staircase. Spider webs stuck to their skin and clothes. Suso climbed to the top and unlocked a trapdoor. El Fundidor followed him into a large room. They stood on a stage with two poles on it.

"Welcome to Adelita," Suso said.

From the stage, El Fundidor got a full view of the entire place. The room was filled with tables and chairs. A long bar took up the entire back wall. Mirrors decorated the remaining walls. He stared for a moment at his own reflection, not recognizing the man who stared back at him.

"It is a strip club establishment," El Fundidor said.

"My strip club establishment. Partly yours, I suppose. I used the money you sent to open this place four years ago."

"You used the money I sent for this?"

"After Mamá died, I didn't know what to do. This was an investment. It didn't take long to turn a profit, but the real money comes from the rooms upstairs. Come on."

El Fundidor followed. The girl was so light in his arms, he hardly noticed her. She didn't weigh much more than a sack of lye. They went up a flight of stairs, down a long hallway, and into a bare room. A bed, one chair, and a toilet in the corner. No windows. He set the girl on the bed, pulling the thin blanket to her chin.

"You are a chulo," El Fundidor said. "This room is used for sex."

"It's business. I treat the girls well."

"That money could have been used—should have been used—for something else, anything else."

"There were no instructions. I was alone when Mamá died. You weren't here."

"I did things to earn that money. To protect you and Mamá."

"We did not ask you for that. I wanted my brother. She needed her son."

"I will pay for my sins."

"We all do," Suso said. "You are asking for my help. This is the help I can give."

Suso walked to the girl and felt for a pulse in her neck. He lifted one of her eyelids. The glassy pupil remained unchanged in the light.

"I need you to promise to take care of her," El Fundidor said. He reached into his pocket and pulled out a handful of money. Most of it fell to the ground. He took the dead fat man's gun out of his pocket and set it on the chair. "Please."

Suso nodded. "I will take care of her."

El Fundidor's parents, Maria and Jose Luis Rivas, were buried in the old cemetery, El Panteon de los Pioneros. His father had won four grave plots in a game of La Viuda back in 1988. After marriage and two children gave him a family of four, the drunken win felt like fate. His father had provided so little in their lives, the least he could do was cover their deaths.

El Fundidor had bought flowers from the woman who ran the stall at the entrance. He set them at his mother's grave. His relationship with his father had reached its natural end when he had attended the man's funeral. No more to say or do. The loss of his mother was new. He had thought he had felt the loss years back. A sense of change within his body, but it wasn't a feeling he trusted at the time. He was disappointed with how little time he would have to mourn her.

Kneeling on the hardpack—only the new cemetery had grass—he recited *Padre Nuestro* because it would have made his mother happy. On the "Amen," he kissed his hand and placed it on the stone. "Adios, Mamá."

El Fundidor walked back toward the dead fat man's van and took out the dead fat man's cell phone. He dialed the number on the slip of paper they had given to his brother.

"Bueno?" the man on the other end said.

"It is El Fundidor. The girl is gone. She is beyond your reach."

"What girl? I don't care about a girl. You murdered my cousin."

"The fat man."

"You will die for him."

"We all die."

"Yes, but as long as you are alive, your brother is not safe."

"Then I must die sooner," El Fundidor said. "Promise to leave my family alone and I will come to you."

"You don't tell me what to do."

"I am not demanding. I am asking. For years of service."

"Return to Barranco Seco. It will end there."

"That is where it should end," El Fundidor said. "One hour. There's one more thing I have to do."

Until that morning, El Fundidor had never killed a man. Until he drove another human being's femur into the fat man's neck, he couldn't think of any harm he had done to another living creature. He had let the fat man's young partner go, left to run the eight miles through the desert to the main road. Even the flies in the old barn were never killed on purpose, but by their density. It was hard to lean on a surface without squashing one underhand.

Looking down into the dry wash where his former compound was located, he counted at least a dozen men. An army to stop one harmless man, not a soldier, an amateur when it came to killing. They feared him because of superstition.

El Fundidor backed down the hill and found the dead tree that acted as a marker. He pushed the dirt away with his fingers, slowly revealing the edges of the metal plate. His brother had been right. There were tunnels all along the border. It had taken six years for El

Fundidor to dig this one. A man needed a pastime when he was left alone in the desert to dispose of the dead. A man's life couldn't only be focused on his career.

The tunnel had been dug as a precaution. To escape from the barn, if necessary. He had never thought he would need it to break inside. It wasn't fancy like the smuggling tunnels they had in Tijuana. This was a three-foot-diameter pipe buried in the ground. He would have to snake his way the one hundred meters.

He had no light, but there was no way to get lost. At the halfway point, the air thinned. He panicked for a moment when he ran into an area where dirt blocked his way. He got his fingers and hands into it and realized it wasn't a complete collapse. He managed to pile dirt to the side, squeezing through the narrower section and finding his way to the other end.

Most of the soldiers had taken positions outside. Only two young men were posted inside the barn. They had been given the least crucial assignment, which telegraphed their inexperience. One looked frightened. The other looked bored. The bored soldier curiously inspected El Fundidor's equipment. When he opened a three-day barrel, he fell backward and vomited all over himself. The other soldier laughed nervously.

The two of them never had a chance. El Fundidor emerged like a ghost from the shadows. They had time to respond, but instead froze in fear. The machete El Fundidor used to separate joints struck them down with two efficient blows. They hadn't thought to scream.

He dragged them onto the pile, now eight corpses ready for disposal. Whoever took over his job would start with a backlog that would take weeks to catch up on. And that was only if the regular influx of new bodies died down. He didn't envy his replacement.

El Fundidor managed to close one of the barn doors undetected, but as he pushed the second door closed, a man in the yard pointed and yelled. Another fired a shot that chipped the wood near his head.

The commotion on the compound rose as he got the doors closed and locked. El Fundidor poured gasoline in a line along the base of the door. He dropped a lit match, flames rising quickly. That would give him enough time.

El Fundidor had prepared the mix in advance. He stepped into the warm acid bath, at first a tingle and then a sting.

He heard the men at the door, but the fire kept them back. Two gunshots fired near the far wall. Men pounded on the wood, the ends of their axes splintering the boards.

Pinpricks stung his entire body. A heat enveloped him. He could feel the skin on his legs melting, liquefying, sliding down.

Part of the barn wall exploded. A half dozen armed men entered the barn and circled around El Fundidor. They froze when they saw him in the fuming barrel, unsure of what to do, no instinct for this scenario.

El Fundidor made eye contact with the men in front of him. He wanted there to be no doubt that it was him.

He couldn't decide if it was better to hold his breath or end it sooner by taking the acid into his body. His curiosity ended up being greater than his impatience. He grabbed the lid and took in a big inhale. El Fundidor submerged himself in the barrel and placed the lid above him.

The acid burned the sight from his eyes, the sound from his ears, and the smell from his nose. He entered into the comfort of his own pain. It was excruciating, but it was his. And then there was nothing.

Suso lifted the sheet over the dead girl's face. He didn't know her name or anything about her. He only knew that his brother had tried to help her. And even though he had failed, her final contact with another person was a man who made every effort to be her savior. That had to mean something.

The girl had had no pulse when he had checked, but Suso hadn't had the heart to tell Cesar when he had been in the room. He didn't see the point in turning his victory into a defeat.

Suso had promised to take care of the girl and he would. He would bury her in the cemetery next to his parents. He would use Cesar's plot. His brother wouldn't need it. When the cartel eventually caught up with Cesar—and they would—there would be no body. That was a dead certainty. Everyone knew about the horrors of the man they called El Fundidor.

AMERICAN FIGUREHEAD

SHANNON KIRK

We passed the point where jokes were okay. Even biting satire became improper. Regardless of our insistence on First Amendment rights, only vicious verbal rejections and fact recitations became appropriate to speak. We turned literal in our divisions, and uncompromising in voicing the extreme justice we sought to impose, in order to course correct. We were screaming about horrific injustices, at the injustice of everything. As history had taught us many times before, we came to a place where law was not followed, nor norms nor established decencies. Everything had been blown to fuck, crimes out in the open, flagrant. And so, I do not regret my actions nor the flaunting of my oath to be an officer of the court.

There was no court.

I joined the judge and jury of The Maples.

I'm in hiding now. A woman is screaming outside my French cave to be let in. A band of soldiers not far behind. I can hear their commands and whistles, the *pop, pop* of their guns in the distance, hot on her trail and closing in like a slick, cold, black and strong fisherwoman's net. I may not let her in. I don't foresee me letting her in. We are past the point of forgiveness and understandings.

There is no valid "other side." In short, she's too late for absolution.

Besides, the First Oath of The Maples is an uncompromising commitment to "merciless eradication of the complicit." We don't want any smoldering embers of what we just went through to flare again. I suppose it began two years ago, with my rage. Or two years before that when the then American Figurehead came to power.

Maybe my rage has been boiling since I met her in our Texas law school twenty years ago. Kristine Nelson—the same exact one from Torts class—is the same exact one screaming for help outside my French countryside cave.

Here now, I move to extinguish the last flames on the entrance's bolted-to-limestone torches.

"Please! Your lights, they'll see. Please snuff them out, let me in," Kristine pleads.

I extinguish the torches to allow myself to weigh the options in front of me, give her pause, allow her to stall in her screaming. These are my options: Let her in or leave her for the soldiers. There is a stone barrier around this cave opening, which some ancient ancestor of mine erected thousands of years ago. This is my family's land, and no person may trespass that granite moa—a full two feet thick and four feet high—unless I utter one specific word. She knows this is Undeniable Law, as this is the law everywhere now, on every property, the whole world wide. In fact, it is mandatory, and my requirement as landowner—and certainly as a decorated officer of The Maples—is to eradicate her even if she falls off the granite wall and onto my property before I say the one magical, legally-mandated word aloud: Enter.

I do not say enter. I am still weighing options.

If she jumps off the wall and onto my land, I *must* shoot her, decapitate her, butcher her, boil her, draw and quarter her, tie her to a tree and leave her for bees and bears, tar and feather her. Drown her. Dissolve her. In any which way I choose, I must—I'm required to—

eradicate the infection of *her* completely. I must take everything that has any meaning to her and sell it to the highest bidder.

We are a world of lawless rule. And I am in high command in this cave. A throned empress presiding over my walled-in world.

She stands on the flattened top. She is barefoot, her toes bleeding, parts of her wounds matted black, some seeping crimson, all of which is visible under a full moon. Kristine must have fled Texas after the *Big Event*, not long after I fled, which was the very day of the *Big Event*. She must have been struggling, scraping and begging, hiding on ships and walking, crawling, scurrying like a cockroach in the cover of night, slinking like a snake, finding her way here for two years. I assume this is the only place left for her to run, my French property, where I brought her once to study for our third-year law school finals. That was twenty years ago. Eighteen years before my rage flared to unrelenting heights and Kristine's and my entanglement truly began to backslide. She must have assumed I'd forgive her, as none of the revolutionaries who know of her and her kind would forgive her.

I, she must assume, am her last chance.

Or did I ensnare Kristine? Sometimes it is difficult for me to untangle all that has led up to this moment. Two full years of rage will do that. Four full years of rage will do that.

Kristine is careless, reckless, to be standing so bare, so high, on my rock wall, between the V opening of foliage canopy, full fat of deep, dark greens and bursting with leaves in this hot August. Any soldier worth her ration of baguette could sneak up and snap her neck, sniper her brains from the moonlit ridge above the nighttime lavender field, aglow in a ground cloud of purple haze. Mist and steam and humidity, green and purple and slate. Everything glows at night in France.

Kristine is the months-old-bottled-blonde kind of arrogant. So arrogant, always so arrogant of roots and light and laws—as if she could defy or deny them. She never learns, which is odd, since her downfall already came. Her screaming now is her begging for more punishment.

My rages started four years ago when the then American Figurehead came to power. It was wrong, and we all ached, millions and millions of us ached. My true red rages began two years after that—two years ago—after eighteen years of corporate defense practice at an Am-Law 100 firm. Read: high-stakes white collar crime. Meaning, I was a bigwig, fancy-pants female partner at a major international law firm. I was the ruler of my kingdom then, too, with a corner office in Austin, Texas, and access to all the corporate secrets. I was a watcher to the machinations of unchecked capitalism, convoluted schemes that would seem more fictional and concocted than *Mission Impossible* plots, but were all true. All true.

Kristine was in-house counsel, Head of Compliance, in fact, at Stranderham Equity, LLC, a private equity firm, also based in Austin. And she was my client. I mean, that's how it works. College and law school relationships are how the monied class manipulate the "trickle-down." *Manipulated.* Past tense—*manipulated* before the *Big Event.*

Two years ago, I walked into Stranderham's freezing-cold conference room. The wall-sized windows looked out over Austin's downtown cityscape. I sat near the head of the table, as I was the one presenting to my client, Kristine—then Head of Compliance—and to her internal clients, the General Counsel and the CEO, who took the head of the twenty-person, heavily lacquered conference table. It was made from a grove of mahogany ripped out of a Central American jungle, and displaced several tribes, making for widespread corruption between loggers and local governments, pushing populations into overcrowded cities, fueling drug running and gang violence, and thus feeding into a constant northern migration of innocents. The bloody river of consumption for consumption's sake. Four years ago, the *then* American Figurehead, before the *Big Event,* blamed the Central

Americans for unlawful migration. A laugh riot of a gaslight. But you know what? We don't speak in code or jokes or satire or metaphors or euphemisms now. We are literal, so I'll say this: The fucking asshole was a disgusting liar and you either knew that or you *chose* to not know that. And it's insulting to have to spell out all the reasons why, so I won't.

My hands were blue from the arctic air-conditioning in Stranderham's conference room. The lukewarm meeting coffee in a poorly-insulated, double-gallon pump thermos did nothing to warm me. Not even adrenaline or nerves helped, that's how cold I was. Kristine—in an unlined shift dress with no sleeves—seemed impervious to the male-set temperature—because she's a vapid, cold-blooded bitch. And true, perhaps back then I didn't realize, or admit, she was a vapid, cold-blooded bitch and this is my historical perception painting my characterization—which is a true characterization—but I would note she was also wearing the most complacent shoe choice: sling-back kitten heels with gouges in the heels from stomping in sidewalk cracks. I will afford myself such flippant, shallow, woman-corporate-lawyer thoughts now, as I stare down my archenemy, who currently begs for my forgiveness from atop my stone moat in France.

She put us in this situation.

But back then...back before I was a merciless, cave-dwelling officer of The Maples. *Back then.* Back when I suffered cold conference rooms and canister coffee, plumbing and electricity. Lined suits and wine in crystal goblets. Back before the *Big Event.* Two years ago.

I'd just finished my outside counsel role of conducting an internal investigation into some...odd...historical financial transactions Stranderham's new accountant flagged in a whistleblower letter. Given the circumstances, Stranderham was obligated to investigate the accountant's claims that funds were being sent to an offshore company with ties to a possible future justice of the Supreme Court, a senator, and the then incumbent American Figurehead, then routed back, in depleting sums, through other disconnected corporate strands, cleaned subtractions, to dozens of unnamable Stranderham acquisitions. If true, if the lines between the known dots could be drawn, and other speculative dots identified, Stranderham would have a potluck of federal and state offenses on its hands: money laundering; tax evasion; mail fraud; violation of campaign-finance laws; bribery; extortion; straight-up fraud. And those were just the immediately obvious legal violations. The whistleblower didn't have access to all the records. Unless you were a forensic accountant, holding the actual corporate records and books of all of these various entities in between, there's not a chance you would see the connection, or the implications—that was the whistleblower's point. And somehow, he saw enough to see those implications. When I first read the whistleblower letter, I did not think anything of such a salacious nature could possibly be true, or if true, proven.

Then I read the emails we'd collected from several Stranderham executives. Bold outright statements of complicity and fraud, the whole scheme, right there in emails. Not hiding a thing. And I became irate when I saw one of the ending points: a particular entity I'd been battling for a *pro bono* asylum client for almost two years at that point. And Kristine had known. *She fucking knew.* We were friends on Facebook, law school classmates, and I'd posted about my attempts to get this Central American *child* asylum in the United States.

I presented my investigative findings about the whistleblower's letter in Stranderham's cold conference room by way of a slick PowerPoint, loaded up with .jpegs of the most egregious emails, right there, presented straight up, unvarnished, naked, bold, to one of the offending parties himself: the fucking CEO sitting at the head of the conference table. I shivered as I spoke, rubbing goosebumps that felt like pulsing mountains on my arms. Perhaps, yes indeed, the freeze was from nerves and not air-conditioning. The CEO didn't blink.

I plowed ahead, straining and pushing myself to pull up my big girl litigator pants and suppress all emotions. Be robot. Be a Big Tough Sociopathic CEO-type Man. A no-conscience clinician. I said everything I'd found, how I'd substantiated the whistleblower's accusations. Simply put, the entire leadership team at Stranderham wanted a certain justice on the Supreme Court, come hell or high water and no bodies to care for in between, because certain cases were percolating in the lower courts regarding tax havens and shelters for corporate entities. Also, it was good political capital and good business for money to end up at a certain end-point acquisition of Stranderham's—the very one I'd been battling for my pro bono asylum client. A privately-owned jail on the Texas border.

The CEO slammed his palm, flat, on the corrupt mahogany table. Stood. Walked out.

The General Counsel stood. Walked out.

Kristine remained. Her face had inextricably sucked flat into some retractable point in space, aligned in a one-dimensional plane with her neck, like a dormant accordion. Her eyes were the size of poker chips.

Then the GC barged back in, crashing the heavy conference room door against the marble wall. The wall-sized windows opposite shook, and a pyramid of K-cups for an unplugged Keurig toppled, spilling onto the light-gray vacuum paths in the dark gray carpet.

"I thought you said this wasn't a problem, Kristine!" he shouted. "And how the damn hell, damn fuck, fuck, fuck, Kristine, did you get Arnold's emails! That was never authorized!" (Arnold being the CEO who'd flat palmed the table and stormed out.)

Kristine looked to me and shrugged in an aggressive manner, suggesting I was to blame for whatever breach was brewing to overshadow the *actual* breach of law presented in my PowerPoint.

"Arnold's emails were not collected from the company server," I said. "However, he emailed with Stan and Roger quite a bit, actually, and from a personal email account, so that is how we saw the ones I used here today."

The GC shook his head, his nostrils flared. "And you didn't think to warn me before accusing the fucking CEO of fucking fraud? Kristine, did you know this was the finding?"

Abandoning any connection we may have had as law school friends, study-mates, forgetting too how I let her cram for a week at my family home in France, she crossed her arms and snorted. "I absofuckinglutely did not, Jim. This is an ambush. Very unprofessional," she said, turning to me.

I stood.

"I had hoped," I said, "this would not be your response. I did hope. But the world has gone to shit, hasn't it, Jim? Hasn't it, Kristine? Unraveled. And you're just another set of architects. This scheme was so outright flagrant once you took a moment to look, I highly doubted you didn't already know. But I had hope. Son of a bitch, I had one last thread of hope. Did you think I wouldn't find all this because you sent my firm over ten million emails and gave me a week to do the investigation?"

They both looked to the gray carpeted floor.

"That's what I thought. Kristine, you're a fool. You never listen. I've told you a million times, our technology weeds through millions of emails in days. There are clear violations of law here. Ones the company is required to report."

"You will keep your fucking mouth shut, you hear me? I'll have your license if you break attorney-client privilege," Jim the GC screamed. "Kristine, clean this up. Close this out."

He turned and left the room, toe-kicking fallen K-cups and smashing some in his stomp-slide to leave. He pulled the door shut with the same venom as when he entered. I swear, the glass panels almost shattered.

Kristine, the still accordion-faced version of her, stared at me. "Holy shit. You couldn't give me a heads-up, Lacy?"

"A heads-up to *what*? You're in the thick of it."

She looked away, not denying anything.

"So brave of you to make me think things were clear and done, setting up this meeting so, with no alarms. No warnings. You've always been, you, just so fucking...pure." Her sarcasm was tangible, like a thorny blanket thrown down from the ceiling.

"Don't be saccharine, Kristine. How dare you try to whitewash this through my firm, as if I'd give a clean bill of health. You used me. And why? Why would you put your own license on the line for obvious violations of law? *Why?*"

"Please."

"No, why?"

"Look, I'm just doing my job."

I snorted. Disgusted. I saw where this was all going, and frankly, I knew why she was doing this. Money.

"Whatever. I know why. You're so predictable and revolting. I saved one document I found, just for you."

Still standing, I leaned over the table and shook the wireless mouse to enliven the screen once again. I clicked forward a few blank slides to the one I'd pinned for this moment. One I had hoped I wouldn't have to pull, hoping with the last, last, last thread I had of hope for humanity she would confess during my presentation and announce how she'd used my investigation as proof, as a way to call authorities to crash the sordid enterprise.

But no.

Money.

Blossoming first onto the stark white was a .jpeg of a sheet with columns of names in minuscule font. I enlarged the image. The page was headed CURRENT STAKEOWNERS OF BORDER CARE HOUSING, INC. Kristine was listed in the column with a forty percent return on investment, from two years prior to the then current "elected" tenure of the American Figurehead. The American Figurehead had been, for two years by then, notoriously criminal, objectively vile, shitting on the constitutional and humanitarian treaty rights of refugees and asylum seekers. In one year alone, *at least* seven children died in immigration custody. An untold number of adults had died. Children had been ripped from parents and shoved in freezing cages. And too many to count had been molested by government officials and private jail employees. Exactly like my fifteen-year-old Guatemalan pro bono client, an asylum seeker housed illegally, all my papers claimed, at Border Care Housing, Inc., in a town outside El Paso, Texas.

"*Border Care*, Kristine? Border Care is accused of sexual molestation of asylum seekers. You know this, you know I'm involved. I have one of the clients. She's pregnant, you know. And how'd that happen in an all-woman facility? She's fif-fucking-teen. You knew. You knew I had this conflict. I didn't know Stranderham had acquired Border Care. And here, fuck, here you're set to reap profits?"

She sucked her lips in. Didn't speak.

"Kristine?"

"They cross the border illegally, they take the risk," she said.

"Fuck you. Fix this. I won't be a part of a crime."

I walked out.

I sent her a text: "You report this or I will. You have one week."

And as storms were brewing mad in the air, and my personal convictions and professional obligations were colliding, my rage grew and then amplified when I received two certified packages the very next week.

One was a Motion for Temporary Injunction to stop me from speaking anything about Stranderham, which, the Motion said, would jeopardize their attorney-client privilege. Also included was a letter Stranderham, signed by Kristine, had sent to the Texas Bar complaining that I'd violated my ethical obligations.

The second was a notice that my Guatemalan client, eight months pregnant, had been transferred to an ICE facility, out of Border Care Housing, fine, but straight into solitary confinement. She would be confined in the same small town outside El Paso. She'd violated the terms of her holding, they said.

A text message came in from Kristine, who must have timed her message when she knew I'd have received these packages. It said, "I've always been better at timing. But you don't listen."

She'd sent her messages. She used my client in our war.

That was two years ago.

Twelve hundred phone calls led nowhere.

I had gotten in my car and driven west toward my client's ICE facility.

In my drive, the radio warned about surprise and fast-moving, colliding air fronts raging in and hovering around the entire state and beyond. The dramatic adjectives they used seemed to mirror the political fronts that had been colliding for two years by then, two years of furor and rage under the then American Figurehead and others like him in other parts of the world. The weather reports during my drive were, no other way to say it, apocalyptic: "Polar opposite temperatures of wild disparity"; "volatile winds, blowing at cock-eyed, broke-neck angles"; "vicious, speeding vortexes touching ground, helter-skelter." But I drove on, clocking the flatness of the road, the drop-dropping of the gray stew of sky, the bulbs and nodes of the ominous clouds blemished by the straight edges of rapture-preaching religious billboards. The insane weather adjectives likely amped my rage, but I tamped it down by staring straight ahead in a relentless trance. I had one mission: get my client out of solitary. Somewhere in the middle, halfway to the town outside El Paso, a minor hill broke up the monotony of the otherwise flat drive. After I crested and began to descend, driving on to more straightness, another blemish billboard came into focus. In navy font against a dingy white background, it read: "THE RIGHTEOUS HAND OF GOD WILL ERADICATE THE DARK UNWASHED," and in smaller font, "Donate to God through the GOP for a better world." A red cross adorned a corner.

That billboard. My nostrils flared at that billboard. I slammed on the brakes, moved over to the side of the desperate and desolate road. Brown dirt on both sides for miles. I got out of the car and stood and stared for a good long while, and I note now—as I stare down Kristine in France, who begs for entrance and forgiveness from atop my stone wall—that I focused on just one word: *eradicate*.

I got back in my car and drove on to my client. The weather reports unhinged further: "Wind tunnels of freight trains"; "Furious plates of air mass fighting in the sky"; "Freefalling columns of arctic air, spiking through broiling heat and angry humidity." In a word, the weather was in chaos. Indeed, my car shook from the whipping wind. Tumbleweeds, branches from trees not visible from the road, and a few pieces of torn-apart signs whipped around me. One gust pushed the car off the road, but I righted myself and jammed my foot on the gas until the pedal hit the floor. I sped on, fighting my shaking wheel. The muscles in my forearms burned.

The sound outside the car was of invisible monsters screaming at each other in variations of high whistles and growls and howls and wails. The newscasters frizzled as the reception fried. "Shelter… take…[static]…gusts of unprecedented [static]" and so on.

Scientists had never seen anything like it. They extrapolated what they knew, overlaid that knowledge on what they did not yet understand, and attributed the strange blowing winds and disjointed air streams to the undocumented shifts of climate change. The people who worshiped at rapture billboards said funnels were the literal fingers of God, *eradicating* the unwashed, picking them off, suggesting the weather was sentient and consciously choosing sinners by destroying their progressive-friendly organic farms and splatting their lust-filled bodies against barns. If a God-fearing worthy citizen was picked off, they said it was because God had raptured him up to paradise. For my part, I considered the unhinged weather an obstacle to me getting justice for my client, as it was slowing my drive.

By some miracle, I arrived at the ICE facility. I parked my car. Grabbed my briefcase, which held the immigration judge's affirmation of the USCIS's officer's finding that my client had, indeed, met the "low threshold of proof of potential entitlement to asylum," required by law in order to obtain an asylum hearing. In fact, she'd blasted the low threshold by leaps and bounds, having a "substantial and realistic possibility of success"—which standard is even lower than the "preponderance of the evidence" standard. I never once heard anything about these standards and legal process facts when talking heads screamed their binary immigration positions on the news. My client had shown border control physical burns and knife wounds from being tortured for being a woman in her home country, plain and simple. I also never heard any of the pundits read from any of the country conditions reports, the ones that document all the horrors from these impacted countries. Maybe I had missed a segment. But I doubt it.

Yeah, she met the legal standard. One particular group within ICE, however, taking advantage of the tangled nature of multiple agencies and confused reporting lines, would not release my client on parole until her very legal asylum hearing.

Am I bitter? Yeah, I'm fucking bitter. I'm living in a cave. I haven't had a moment's peace in two years, four if you count when the awful American Figurehead took office. I haven't taken a proper, peaceful hot bath in two years. Haven't read a romance novel. My hair is half gray. Dirt is permanent under my jagged fingernails. I ran out of contacts, because I didn't grab any before I fled, and the eyeglasses I plucked from an abandoned store three villages over are several degrees off my prescription. My eyes ache. I live on baguettes and wine. And I can't tell if my lack of menstruation is from early menopause or unrelenting stress from being in constant survival/war mode. I have no lover here, so I'm doubly unable to get pregnant, it seems, which is the only silver lining. There's no relief. But these inconveniences are merely that, inconveniences. Others have endured far worse, far longer.

Right now, shadows dance on the limestone walls, light casting off the fiery torches, held aloft in the hands of the approaching soldiers. They are closing in on Kristine, but she can't see, because she faces me. And she's ignoring the shadows on the cave wall behind me, because she was never smart enough to read Plato. On a flat rock at the cave's entrance, I pick up the chipped mug of red wine I'd set there. A light and fruity Brouilly, bottled at a vineyard not far from here. Mona, a soldier, one of the ones approaching, in fact, it's her vineyard. I barter baguettes for her wine. I take a sip, watch Kristine.

"Say the word. Say 'enter,' please," she pleads. Her knees are bent as if she's about to jump forward onto my land, closer to this cave. If she does, she knows the rules require me to *eradicate* her.

I say nothing. I sip my wine. I listen to the advancing soldiers' shouts and footsteps, crunching leaves in the forest. I think my favorite soldier, Kenterwil, hoots, and her companion soldier, Mona, hoots back.

A grove of crickets hum in the underbrush. The full moon in the clear sky pulses gray to white, white to gray. A purple haze hangs in humid mists atop the lavender field in the beyond. And there's the roof of my barn, light within aglow, movements inside choreographed.

Other soldiers are readying the vats. The blistering vats.

I contemplate my decision again, silent, head cocked, Kristine screaming and begging right in front of me.

I take another sip of wine.

There I was, two years ago, in the ICE parking lot in Texas. After all those rapture billboards and hysterical weather reports, after the mindless drive under a dropping gray sky and brown sand on all sides, my temper was a hurricane. I could not stop the cyclical rage in my brain over Kristine's intentional actions after my PowerPoint. How she went to work right away to silence me and then punish me, by punishing my client. She was the hand on the crank of the machine, grinding my client into solitary. She was the architect, and so she was the architect of the country's disintegration into chaos and humanitarian blight. She, as far as I was concerned, *was* the American Figurehead. In my mind, every single thing, every single rage, was due to Kristine's entitlement to more money, more return on investment, which, and I've done the math, amounts to, at most, at the tip-top most, $20,000 at her investment level and tax bracket. Twenty grand for her to upgrade her Toyota to a Lexus is what it all comes down to. Last week, the shortwave said the entirety of downtown Hong Kong had burnt to the literal ground. Millions perished.

Two years ago in Texas, I stepped toward the one-floor gray concrete ICE facility, which was a square with two side rectangle wings. No windows. Four white trailers spoked out like sun dials off the sides of the side wings, and those looked to be administrative offices.

The howl of a train blared to my left, making me drop my briefcase. But there were no train tracks anywhere in this part of the state. And to my right came the sudden whooshing engines of an aircraft. I froze, stuck in the center of these colliding noises, as officers with ICE in yellow letters on navy shirts exploded out of the white trailers and out of the cinderblock building. A few people in civilian suits and khaki pants spilled out as well.

I overheard all I needed to know to know what the jet sound was to my right: "Air Force One is making an emergency landing. The tornado. The tornados." I heard fractured variations of these frenzied reports from isolated pockets of shouting. "Manchester is on board." "Air Force…" "Category Five, off the charts." "Three funnels. Converging here." "Thirty more, all throughout the state and beyond." "Nowhere safe, nowhere safe." "Cover! Get cover!"

Manchester was the Secret Service code name for the then American Figurehead.

I looked to my left, toward the howling train in the sky, which sounded closer and louder, a barreling train off its tracks, mutating like some malevolent Transformer into a carnivorous wooden rollercoaster with rusty tracks and metal-wheeled carts with no ball bearings. Clinking and clanking in a loud surround, as if we were in a factory with a thousand unoiled conveyor belts dumping empty paint cans into a thousand steel drums. Long ago, I watched Helen Hunt's movie *Twister*, riveted by the funnel the graphics team had concocted. Cows tossed in the sky, street signs thrust like murderous spears. But this was nothing like that. This was so much bigger, so bad, so deadly, so otherworldly and alien, so fast and furious, and actually spinning in three separate phases like an upside-down, three-headed dragon, the gray merged clouds of the bulging sky the body. Off in the distance where the three funnels coupled and uncoupled and coupled again, I watched an entire prairie house leveled and disintegrate in the air. Human figures in and around the prairie house were visibly sucked up like ants in a vacuum, and I could not see where they landed, if they landed.

The tornado, tornados, I'd call a collective Category Fifteen, roared on toward us, coupling and uncoupling, and so on. Out of the disparate stampede of officers and civilians coming from the trailers and building, an ICE officer, like a charging football player, grabbed around my waist and thrust me up on his shoulders. He ran toward some far-off distance, and I didn't fight him, but I watched behind us as he ran, my stomach on his shoulder, my feet bare—I'd lost my shoes somehow—at his stomach.

A huge white barrel of a bird cut through the gray mass overhead and dropped fast toward the ground—its jet engine kicking up the loose dirt into brown clouds, the sound deafening, drowning out the howling dragon tornado. The parking lot, I noted then, served as a runway of sorts, given the cleared strip between parked cars and the ICE facility. Officers and civilians, likely lawyers like me, ran in the same direction my officer was taking me, albeit, nobody in straight lines. The Air Force One bird was about five feet from touching down on the makeshift runway, when a phase of the Category Fifteen dragon uncoupled from its mates, sped up, and chugged straight on forward, smashing head-on with the plane. The tornado didn't change course; instead it slowed, as if it found itself a righteous meal, and ate the plane like a glutton, chomping metal and gears and blades and those Air Force One letters, in a humiliating meal. Pieces and parts of the plane dropped and flew around the parking lot and overhead, some landing on some of the running people. But somehow, nothing hit me or my officer. The other two phases of the Category Fifteen spun and picked off all of the other running people, tossing them hundreds of feet in the air and either consuming them whole or spitting out their bones to fields of dirt. But my officer and I were spared.

He stopped running, thrust me down to stand beside him, bent, lifted a hatch, pushed me to stairs, and told me to climb down, "Now, now, now." Which I did, and he followed.

When we got into a steel-reinforced bunker, about twenty feet belowground, the clanking, screaming, conveyor belt sounds softened some, but I could still hear the roar of those judicious funnels.

The officer looked at me.

I looked at him.

"The Commander in Chief, and his entire staff and family, were on that plane."

"I saw. I heard."

"They're all dead. Everything is different," he said.

"We have to let the refugees out. Everyone's gone, no one to take care of them."

He sucked in his cheeks.

"I'm the one in charge now at this base. My commanding officer was in that prairie house, blown apart."

"Well then," I said. "As soon as it's safe, we release the refugees and we get out of here."

"I…"

I stared.

"We'll release them," he said.

And that's what we did.

I don't know whatever happened to the ICE officer. Don't even really know what happened to my client, once we released her and the others. I knew I had to leave the country and get to France before the borders closed up everywhere. This catastrophic event was the one the cards and the clouds and the broiling tensions of two full years of the just-obliterated American Figurehead were working up to. Nobody anticipated an Act of God would be the catalyst to all of the tensions boiling over. Everyone had anticipated a colossal act of man-made violence, something beyond even the horrors of daily mass shootings. But they were wrong. The catalyst was climate, a three-headed dragon tornado. One might say God's wrath was gorgeous that day. One might say weather is, despite all our studies and calculations, charts and Dopplers and sensors and graphs, unpredictable. Unhinged. And I say Mother Nature is a vengeful, merciless bitch, and thankfully, she left me unharmed that day.

They named the funnel that ripped Air Force One apart "Maple."

My car had been untouched. After the twisters passed, and after we freed everyone, I drove through a littered minefield to the closest airport. I always had my passport on me, something my father, a man of dual citizenship, had taught me. I bought a one-way to Charles de Gaulle, made my way to my family property, and waited. And the world burned for two months. Revolutionaries took the opportunity from the Big Event in Texas to fight all the growing dictators around the world. After two months, different sects of revolutionaries convened and agreed on a set of rules and a mission statement to *eradicate* the complicits. And it is this ground war, this mission, the world has been living under ever since.

One day shortly after the revolutionary sects convened, a woman in a brown jumpsuit and purple handkerchief tied around her forehead threw pebbles from the dirt road against the door of my French countryside home until I answered. A second woman stood behind her, on guard.

"We're The Maples," the woman in the handkerchief said, still standing in the road. "We seek to eradicate all forms of complicity with the prior regimes attempting to destroy democracy. We have rules and the new law of the land is this: each property owner must eradicate any persons who step on their property unless you voice the word 'enter.' Also, if a person known to you to have been complicit tries to enter, you must eradicate that person. Are you in?"

The day was sunny, and I looked off to the lavender fields, rolling and purple and green. In the farthest distance was a field of sunflowers. My red barn hid in a divot of a valley, surrounded by tall cypress.

"Did you say *eradicate*?"

"I did, ma'am."

"Your name?"

"Kenterwil." Pointing behind her, but not looking, she said, "And this is my companion soldier, Mona." Mona nodded.

Kenterwil had a smudge of soot on her nose, and her brown hair hung in a ponytail beneath the compression of her purple handkerchief. Her accent was French, and given that she was speaking English to me, I surmised, correctly, she knew more about me than I her.

"In exchange," she said, "we will protect you and your property. And, if I may, I know your land from grouse hunting with my father years ago. You have a cave surrounded by a stone wall. I'd suggest removing yourself to the cave for a bit. It's too vulnerable here in your wooden house, even with our protections."

"I've heard of The Maples, on the shortwave," I said. "I know of the sects' agreements and rules. The mission statement."

Kenterwil shrugged, as if to say, *of course.*

"Enter," I said. "Both of you."

Once on my doorstep, Kenterwil's eyes were strangely captivating and intelligent. A uniform ice-gray. I'd only ever seen such irises on cats.

"I'm in. Actually, I've been waiting for this. I have some personal objectives, but I'd like to be an officer."

Kenterwil looked to Mona, who threw her hands in the air in a gesture of *so be it.*

We shook hands, my initiation and admittance that fast, one sealed in soul and blood.

And now, now, two years after the Big Event, after Kenterwil, Mona, and I shook hands on my doorstep in France, here is Kenterwil gaining closer to my cave.

I set down my mug of wine and stare at Kristine, still perched on the rock wall.

"Please, please. I'm sorry. You were right. You were so right. I am sorry. Please let me enter," she cries.

I strike a match and hold it to my cave's entrance torches; the flames explode into two amber bubbles around the mouth. I allow Kristine to appreciate my wine-stained lips grinning at the women soldiers closing the snare around her. I begin to laugh, prompting the soldiers to laugh along, too. Kristine is not in on the joke.

These are my soldiers. My hill. My cave.

Two years ago when I landed in France, I made one phone call. Kristine picked up after two rings.

"You're watching the news?" I asked.

"Of course. Where are you?" she asked.

"In France. I fled. Good luck on that side of the ocean."

I meant it then as a taunt and a trap and a not-so-subtle seed of an option for her. I knew, I just knew, someday she'd follow the crumbs and come to my property. Seeking refuge.

So, I have been waiting all this time, and no, not once has my rage waned.

I flick all ten fingers into fans and dance them. This is my verdict to the soldiers, who await my sentence. This silent gesture says everything, and even nitwit Kristine can read this message. It means, "Dissolve her in the acid vats."

She is screaming again as Mona cantilevers herself to the top of my stone wall and arm bars around Kristine's neck. With her other arm, she grabs and holds around Kristine's chest and dangles her off the wall, so that Kenterwil, my favorite, yanks her down and pulls all her rings off her fingers, plucks everything from her pockets, and rips her backpack off her back. Mona and Kenterwil will get the spoils of this take, I had promised them last night over baguette rations, after they delivered word they'd heard through the French grapevine of a woman named "Kristine" asking for directions to my property.

Mona and Kenterwil drag Kristine down the forested hill and

toward the moon-glow barn that sits like an innocent haven between purple lavender fields. So charming, that ruse of a red barn, full of hungry poison, gluttonous acid, that will eradicate the complicity of Kristine. And though I think in only literal terms with respect to these current world politics, I will allow myself the metaphor that Kristine is indeed the American Figurehead, the one eaten by a tornado, the one who could be eaten ten times more, and ten times again.

Because she fed him, and he fed her, and you are what you eat, so he was her, and she was him.

COLIBRÍ

Nicolás Obregón

Milagros Posada put down the phone and went over the note she had just scribbled. *Lone male discovered on cattle ranch. Decedent described as "young" + Mexican-looking." Body found near a painted picture of a bird.*

"Who wuzzit, Milly?" Across the room, Sheriff Jim Fraley was combing his eggshell-white slickback in the mirror. "I know you ain't about to tell me we got another one."

She nodded and Fraley swore. He was early sixties, perennially sunburnt, a small man of good humor but ill temper—like somebody had dressed up a firecracker in a leather waistcoat. "Had to be today, huh." He hand-licked a final silver strand behind his ear. "Where is it?"

"Out by El Hundido. Irvin Hoglund found the body."

He fixed her in the mirror as though this was all her doing. "That's near on an hour's drive."

Outside, a truck choked gravel and the sound of men convivial on lunchtime beer scudded through the window. Fraley's scowl ossified into a grin as he put on his brand-new Stetson.

"What do I tell Hoglund, Sheriff?"

"Tell him it's the goddamn Fourth of Ju-ly. His stiff'll keep till Monday." At the door, Fraley paused and winked crinkles. "You're in

84

charge now, Milly. Don't go doin' nuthin' I wouldn't.'"

Milagros heard wolf-whistling as he left. An engine rumbled, gravel popped, and the department was silent except for the old pedestal fan, slowly shaking its head, *please no.*

She shook her own head in agreement. Where once there had been thick black curls, there was now gray, and there were pouches beneath her eyes, heavy with years of insomnolence. When her son was little, he said she looked like the lady from *Sesame Street.*

His memory made her close her eyes.

When she opened them, Milagros read her note again. She took a breath. Then she picked up the phone.

Irvin Hoglund walked with one hand on his gun. His land was way out in what his seasonal hands called "La Nada." Out here, he never greeted anyone without suspicion, and always with his palm resting on the grip of the gun.

The summer heat was stupefying, like snorkeling through simmering cooking oil. An old black dog led the way. He was panting, quivering, eyes blue with blindness. Even so, the rancher followed him. Milagros too. The paths here were too broken, too treacherous for conventional tires. And so they followed the dog through a fraying patchwork of grazing lands dotted with creosote bush, catclaw, and mesquite. Past bees defending Indian paintbrush and pineapple sage. And beneath vultures circling high above like some recess game.

In the distance, Milagros saw the country of her birth. Nickel-colored thunderheads warred silently over estranged mountains. The dog paused from time to time to catch his breath. His face was gray, his eyes watered when he considered the horizon.

"Does he know the way?" Milagros asked.

BOTH SIDES

Hoglund grunted, *yes*.

"He looks blind."

"Only his eyes."

There was nothing else to say, so they said nothing.

For what felt a long time, Milagros and the rancher trudged through the lorn ranchland, the thick air branding their skin. The nameless trails that seamed through Hoglund's land led out only to the desert, ten thousand square miles of nothing—a barren ocean of silence.

"How many of these paths feed out to the freeway, Mr. Hoglund?"

"Just one."

He didn't have to tell her where the others led. Finally, the dog froze. His nose twitched. Whimpering, he ran down the dusty ridge. Milagros hurried after him as fast as she could in the heat. She heard the flies and the roaring sound of the freeway. It was a sound she had come to know. At the bottom the dog was barking. It was hotter down in the arroyo, a dusty furnace. The air was viscous with coyote piss. The flies were in flux, death's own pinball.

The boy was lying in the shade beneath the tall governess bush, head propped up on his sneakers as though taking a nap. His dark hair was down past his ears, lips badly cracked, eyes covered by a baseball hat. His body was dark and lean, the knockoff soccer jersey he had been wearing thrown off to the side. The jeans were too baggy, a belt looped around the upper branches of the bush.

"Must have thought about ending it." Hoglund stood alongside her, shaking his head. "Looks about fourteen to me."

Milagros folded her sheriff's department ID into her shirt and crouched over the boy. Some of the denim at his ankle was shredded and brittle with blood, flies zipping in and out. Peeking through, she saw deep lacerations and smelled infection.

By the boy's head, there was a dried puddle of vomit. His feet were severely blistered, Rice Krispies of pus riddled his soles, the skin of his toes like old newspaper. One foot had swollen way beyond the size of the other. Inside the sneakers there was the stench of filth, fine sand glittered in the fetid gloom. Milagros ran her fingers through the burning sand around the body. If this had been a murder, then this would be the murder weapon.

"Mr. Hoglund, when did you last pass through here?"

"Three days ago. Body weren't here then."

"Did you see anything out of place since?"

"No, but the night before last I heard a chopper fly low and hard over my land. You think maybe he got scattered?"

"It's a possibility. His feet are in bad shape. If he was with a group they probably would have left him behind."

Milagros had seen death this way many times before. By the time the boy lay down here, he would have been wracked by cramps, slurring his speech, hallucinating. The cells in his body would have shrunk as his dehydration worsened, his kidneys, lacking water and salt, would have shut down. After that, it wouldn't have taken long until the desert claimed him, same as it claimed all things. Lying down there, under that bush, Milagros was certain the boy would have known: *This is where I'm going to die.*

There was a cell phone a few inches from his open hand but it was smashed and dead. An empty black gallon plastic jug lay nearby.

Picking it up, Milagros sniffed. "Spray-painted."

"They all do that. How come?"

"Harder to spot in the dark."

"Well, he didn't have near on enough."

"No human could carry that much water." Slipping on some latex gloves, she delicately searched his pockets but found no ID.

Patting the old dog, Hoglund pointed southward. "You go back a mile or two that way, the boy starts to shed stuff. Backpack, rest of his clothes. Heat musta started to really get to him. Still, he kept his pens."

"Pens?"

The old rancher nodded to the small rocky outcropping across the arroyo. "Boy musta done that. Weren't there before."

Milagros turned to see the exquisite hummingbird drawn on the rock, a saturnalia of colored crayon, pastel, and Day-Glo blots from broken highlighters. In electric greens and deep purples, the hummingbird was in flight—iridescent wings drawn back, beak reaching for sky-nectar. The colors had bled down the rock, the hot wind already gnawing at them. Looking at its glimmering black eye, Milagros felt for a moment as though she were seeing some mythical creature and not the birds of her childhood that zipped beneath her window in the mornings.

Below the otherworldly hummingbird there was a small word scratched in black:

RUDI

"Was that your name?" Milagros whispered.

She allowed herself a single sigh. Then, locking away her feelings, she took out the department camera and photographed the hummingbird. She photographed every inch of the arroyo, the body, everything belonging to the boy.

When she was done, Milagros checked her watch. It had been less than forty minutes since they had set off from Hoglund's place.

"Why didn't he try and paint a whatyoucallit—SOS?"

"After what he'd been through, maybe he accepted the end."

Milagros crouched down over the child once more and lifted the baseball hat to look into his eyes. They were beautiful and dead, like cherrywood. Even in death he looked toward his hummingbird.

The dog raised his head now. Crunching metal and the growl of thick tires could be heard—a vehicle approaching. The Ford Raptor came to a halt at the crest of the arroyo. A door slammed and heavy footfalls chawed over dusty stones. A man in green overalls stood above them. Gold letters on his body armor read: BORDER PATROL. Clambering down the slope, he stopped in front of Milagros, two heads taller.

"Christ, Milly—" He took off his tactical sunglasses and pinched the bridge of his nose. "How many times?"

She tipped the brim of an imaginary hat. "Tom."

"*Agent Maloney*," he corrected. "And you, Irvin. You always gotta call her out here on your little picnics, huh?"

The old man said nothing, just patted his dog.

Maloney turned back to Milagros. He was tall and muscular, but with his straggly red whiskers he looked like a boy doing a man's job. "Does Sheriff Fraley know you're out here?"

"No, I'm just hiking."

"Always funny, Milly. But I'm curious. You still gonna be laughing if I call Fraley and ask if you're on official department business?"

"You call him while he's out drinking with his buddies on the Fourth of July, he'll tell you to take a long walk off a short dock. Now—" She nodded at the dead boy. "He can't stay out here much longer. Where's the ME?"

"Busy. They sent me." Maloney approached the body and swatted the hat off. "Just a kid. Real shame."

Milagros started climbing back up the arroyo.

"Then again, maybe he'd still be breathing if he'd gotten in line like everyone else, huh?"

"For him there was no line. You know that, Tom."

Milagros drove her son's old truck the twenty miles to Boca del Virgen, a tumbleweed town clutching onto the interstate like it would fall into the abyss otherwise. It was little more than a handful of breezeblock buildings and long-failed auto repair shops. Wares not stocked for decades were lies in peeling paint—*sugar, tubing, cottonseed meal.* An elderly couple watched TV outside on their porch, basking in the decline. The only functioning business was the diner. It didn't have a name, the place had no use for one. Two flags drooped over the door, the American and the Salvadoran.

Milagros parked next to the other trucks, all of them new Ford Raptors gleaming government-white in the late afternoon blaze. Entering the diner, she was blasted with air-con and gameshow fanfare.

Oh, my! Oh, my! Thank you. Thank you so much! Welcome to **The Price Is Right.** *Thank you, wow, that is really special, folks. Real special. I gotta tell you, there are some wonderful prizes just waiting to be won today for smart shoppers. Only here on...* **THE PRICE IS RIGHT.**

"Púchica, Mili." Grinning, the old-timer behind the counter set down a polystyrene cup white as his hair, then sloshed in coffee, dark as his skin. "*¿Qué onda, chera?*"

"Félix." She smiled. "*¿Todo en orden?*"

"Aquí me ves."

"¿El negocio?"

"Pues está bien yuca—" As he ground cinnamon into the coffee he lowered his voice. "Fíjate, Mili. Hay pericos en la milpa."

Milagros glanced over her shoulder at the only occupied booth and saw four men in green uniforms. She nodded. "Para esos estoy."

"Vaya pues."

She took out her purse but Félix waved away the silliness. Instead, he placed a repurposed coffee tin on the counter. "Biscochitos." He winked. "Tienes que comer más, Mili."

The men in the booth laughed hard now, and Félix took that as his cue to get back to work.   Milagros approached the booth. The smallest of the men beamed at her, a rotund middle-aged man with a neat, graying moustache and spectacles. His patch read: SUPERVISORY AGENT JOSEPH SALGADO.

"Well, look what the wind blew in. *Deputy* Sheriff Posada."

They sniggered.

"Joe."

"Thought you was Fee-lix for a second—" He propped himself up and shouted. "Hey, Fee-lix. Don-day es-tah la co-mida?"

The old man held up three fingers for minutes.

"Goddamn, at this rate it's gonna arrive by reindeer."

"We need to talk, Joe."

"Sure. Take a pew."

"Alone."

Milagros sat a few booths away and nursed her cinnamon coffee. She waited and listened to a few more rounds of laughter which she knew would be at her expense.

Finally, Salgado dropped into the booth across from her, sipping his soda. He probed her with his eyes, trying to discern the taste of her, same as the Dr Pepper rattling in his straw. There would have been a time when the scrutiny of such a man would have intimidated her. But that Milagros had dissolved a long time ago. Instead, she just stared right back.

"What can I do for you, Milly?"

"I have an unidentified decedent out by El Hundido. Need your help."

"How exactly?"

"Access to all the nine-one-one calls bounced over to CBP in the last forty-eight hours. He had a phone with him, it's possible he dialed for help."

"You know Fraley would have to request that."

91

"Fraley's out of office."

"And so here you are." Salgado sucked the last of his soda and dropped his cup on the Formica—enough was enough. "You know what? You was right earlier. We *do* need to talk. I heard from Agent Maloney. He tells me this is the third time this year you've interceded in his duties. That was the word he used: *interceded*. You know what that means? It means *fucked with*, Milly. I get that you don't like him but he's a good agent—"

"—Tom Maloney is an asshole."

"Maybe so. But you gotta stop this, I'm not kidding. Your little sheriff department ID is good for answering the phone and buying toner for the printer. That's it. Now we all know what your son did for us, and I don't forget that…"

Her glare was a dead end.

Salgado softened with a sigh. "Milly, what you're doing here? It's dangerous."

"This state doesn't identify deceased border crossers individually. John Doe here is John Doe. What am I meant to do, nothing?"

"The next time Maloney reports you, I have to send it upstairs."

Félix arrived with the food. "Jou' wan' for another Coke, Yoe?"

Salgado shook his head. He kept his eyes down on his chile until he was gone.

Milagros leaned forward. "The ranch owner says he heard choppers flying low and hard two nights ago. Chase and scatter, right? Prevention through deterrence?"

"Come on, what do you want me to say? It's sad?"

"Two nights ago that body was a kid, Joe. A *kid*. He had a name. A family."

"You jump into a fire pit, a name don't make you any less burnt."

"I want to talk to recent detainees up at Aguayo County

Processing. If anyone crossed over with him, that's where they'll be."

Salgado laughed almost with admiration. "I can't give you the nine-one-one calls and I sure as hell can't let you in there, Milly. So, if we're done here…"

Milagros finished her coffee and sucked her teeth for the last of its flavor. "How's your son doing?"

He looked down. "Jack's… changed."

Milagros hadn't wanted to go there but he had given her no choice. "Is he getting help?"

Salgado nodded. "I find him sometimes… in the middle of the night. He's out digging in the yard for IEDs. Thinks he's back in Kirkuk half the time. He still wakes up in the middle of the night screaming your boy's name." He looked up at her now with red eyes.

"But he's alive. My Rafael? When things got bad, you know what he did? He *interceded*. You know what that means? It means you owe me. Not just for a fourth time. Or a fifth time. But the rest of your life, Joe."

Salgado contemplated his chile, steam curling up from the deep green and red sauces—Christmas-style.

Milagros looked away and out the window at the scorched hills above town. There was only dogbane, smoke tree, and the occasional desert flower.

"Milly I… I need this job. I can't help you without Fraley's agreement. I'm sorry."

"Then enjoy your food."

The medical examiner's office was in the state capital, a three-hour drive away. As usual, Milagros skipped the sign-in process and entered through the rear, into the loading area. The whiteboard on the wall was split into cells brimming with numbers, nationalities, coordinates—corresponding to an unidentified body in the morgue. Beneath almost every cell there was a code relating to the lockers opposite which contained the items recovered with the remains. It was death's own lost property office: toothbrushes, photographs, cell phone chargers, coins, rosaries, medications. A separate kid-sized whiteboard from Target had been affixed alongside it, exclusively for data relating to lone skulls.

When Milagros had started her work, it was the brutal reality of biology that had shocked her, the unspoken obvious: people had jawbones, people had hips, spinal columns, different-colored eyes. But after a few years, the physical impact had faded.

Yet the lockers never failed to break her heart. They were a silent memorandum to the fact that human beings made choices in life—which shoes to wear, which gods to follow, which loves to cherish at the end. Each locker was a sarcophagus decorated with the ornaments of cataclysm.

Milagros centered herself and looked at the stainless steel table in the center of the room. The body bag was already out. Rudi's items had been stacked neatly next to him. They, too, would be bound for the lockers.

A door opened and Carly Hanlon, the medical examiner, entered. She was a tall woman in scrubs, her only visible features indigo blue eyes and sinewy, freckled forearms. Giving Milagros a nod, she unzipped the body bag and got to work.

"Okay, death by dehydration but you already knew that much... Some pretty gnarly ankle injuries here, likely consistent with razor wire. Where was he found?"

"Out by El Hundido. The nearest border barrier deploys concertina wire."

"Yeah, that jives with these injuries. El Hundido, huh? Ranch land?"

Milagros nodded.

"Figures. These blisters are severe. Even with a hundred gallons of water he wouldn't have made it far." She inspected the grubby sneakers. "Full of fine sand. Would have been like walking through burning glass." She inspected the label. "Panam—that's a Mexican brand?"

"Uh-huh. And probably the kind you buy in a city."

"So could be a clue to work with, no?"

"But, Doc, once you factor out the swelling, they look about two sizes too big."

Hanlon peered at the boy's feet again. "You're right."

"He probably didn't start his journey with them. Who knows what happened to make him switch up."

"What about this?" She held up the soccer jersey, once white, now stained with blood and vomit, caked with mud. Turning it around, they saw the large blue H over the heart.

"Honduras," Milagros said. "But no name or number on the back."

Hanlon proceeded to inspect the body inch by inch, jotting down notes. Approximate age, height, weight, cavities, fillings, medical devices, birthmarks, scars, tattoos.

Rudi's body gave her very few clues.

But then Hanlon felt something beneath the side-seam of his jeans. She made an opening in the denim, then prized out the gleaming object with forceps. It was a gold wedding band. "Stitched it in to hide it from the coyotes?"

"Or whoever else."

"Is it just me or is he a little on the young side to be married?"

"Probably wasn't his ring, Doc. Maybe his mother's. He would've pawned it once he got to ABQ or Phoenix or wherever he was dreaming of."

Hanlon logged the wedding ring and put it with the rest of the belongings. As she worked, Milagros scanned through the photos she had taken that morning. She spent a long time looking at the boy's hummingbird.

"Colibrí," she whispered. "*¿A dónde ibas?*"

"What you got?"

"Just this. He painted this on a rock near where he died—" Milagros handed over the camera.

"Kid could paint."

"Zoom in right there. You see he signed it?"

"'Rudi.'"

"Uh-huh. Which probably made him a Rodolfo."

"Rodolfo from Honduras who could paint—not a lot to go on, Milly."

They both contemplated the boy in silence for a while.

"When I was little my grandmother used to tell me, 'If you see a hummingbird, someone on the other side is trying to send you a message.' Thing is, we got a lot of them in Aguascalientes. In the mornings, I would look out my window as a little kid and would see them flitting from flower to flower. I asked my grandmother about it once. If the hummingbird is a message from the dead, how come I see so many, Abuelita? She laughed and said 'Milagros, the dead have a lot to tell us.'"

Hanlon smiled sadly, then began to zip the body bag back up. Something made her stop. She ran her finger along the dead boy's head. It came back gray and bloody. Flipping on her lamp, Hanlon inspected the scalp.

"Fairly deep cut right here. Looks infected, also. Some kind of sawdust or concrete around the wound?"

Milagros peered at it. "Someone hit him with something?"

"Doesn't look like it. Maybe he fell." Hanlon picked up Rudi's hat and looked inside. "Yeah, same grayish markings. Some blood too."

"Strange. I walked through that ranchland, all different kinds of terrain—" Milagros looked down at the dusty scuff marks on her own pants. "Nothing that color on me."

Hanlon's cell phone buzzed in her pocket. "Milly, it's late. I gotta head home. Sorry I couldn't be of more help."

They embraced. "God bless you, Doc."

At the cold first blush of dawn, Milagros Posada entered Mexico. The city was in an arid basin surrounded by mountains. Up on the largest, a colossal message had been carved with lime, a knock-off Hollywood sign:

THE GRASS WIZENS
THE FLOWER WITHERS
BUT THE WORD OF GOD LASTS FOREVER

At its grand old heart, Ciudad Cabral was made up of elegant colonias of belle époque townhouses where governors and bankers had once lived. There were nice schools and good restaurants. Students from the art school painted poetry on the walls of communal gardens:

—*La melodía de tu mirada baila con los acordes de mi alma*—

Normal lives could be lived beyond the sound of gunfire and screams. Here, Ciudad Cabral was not defined by its horrifying homicide statistics or black ribbons tied to doors.

But Milagros had come for Colonia Frontera, a city within a

city, the square mile that leeched onto the border crossing. Here, meth was cheaper than five minutes on a donkey painted in zebra drag. Teeming slums pushed up against the border wall, built out of American refuse, old garage doors, rusted metal sheets, useless car parts. People lived on top of one another, in rickety club sandwich houses made of whatever they could repurpose.

The population was made up of the rejected, the deported, the denied. Many had once come to find work in the border factories. Trapped in a loop of low pay and hard work, far from home, they had turned to cristal. The drug raged through the city like a river, wrapped in tiny balloons of varying color, each one denoting its cartel producer. Here, the perfume of cooking oil and spices mixed in with the sweet window-cleaner smell of cristal. Colonia Frontera was a chaos of colorful breeze blocks, crooked satellites, playing children, comatose hopheads, blood puddles. Voices carried. Music blared. Laughter and screams could be heard from the storm drains, from the *ñongos*, little bunkers made in the hills of silt and trash.

Standing up on a hill, Milagros surveyed the sub-city. On the broken brick wall across the street, somebody had painted in black:

¡BIENVENIDOS A COLONIA FRONTERA!
POBLACION: DEMASIADO

The little houses were most densely built nearest the border gates itself. Leading away from the crossing, they became more sparse. The paradox was not lost on her: the closer they were to escaping this place, the more Colonia Frontera *became* a place.

Following the river east with her eyes, Milagros saw the place she was looking for. On the fringes of the shanty town, the old jade-colored warehouse with a new sign:

SOLUCIONES TELEFÓNICAS INTERNACIONALES

As she made her way down the hill and toward the river, a series of men in hats offered her safe passage to America.

"Cross now! With this president, if you don't act fast, you'll never make it in."

The sun rose morosely behind dove-gray cloud.

Eddie Nieves struggled with his tie in the reflection of a puddle outside the call center. A cigarette bobbled on his lips as he mumbled to himself.

"Eduardo," Milagros called.

The cigarette dropped into the puddle. He had lost weight, the teenage linebacker she remembered replaced by a tall, skinny man. But it was how old he looked that shocked her most. It hardly seemed impossible that he could have been in her son's grade.

"Milly?"

They embraced amid laughter and tears, without words but both aware how different things were since they had last seen each other. He let her straighten his tie, then led her to a café nearby. It was just a few plastic tables inside a repurposed wedding tent but the place was packed. A European soccer match on a pirated stream played on the TV while corridos blared through tinny speakers. Though the words were sad, the accordion and trumpets were jubilant. That was México, Milagros thought. Forever wringing what joy it could from life's pain.

She chose the table at the back. Pink cursive had been woven into the canvas behind it:

♥ KELSI & ANTHONY — CONGRATULATIONS ♥

BOTH SIDES

The waiter came and Eddie ordered them two coffees.

Milagros nodded. "Your Spanish has improved."

"Eh, just a couple phrases."

"You're sure you won't be too late for work?"

"Nah, they won't can me, my English is too good—" He cleared his throat and put on an exaggerated smile. *"Good morning, sir. I see that you have a 2010 Chevy Cruze in your name and I just wanted to check that you were aware your lease was coming up?"*

She smiled. He had always been a funny boy. She had liked having Eddie come to her house because she knew it would mean hearing Rafael laugh all night. When she went to wake them in the morning, she'd swear they were still smiling in their sleep. For Eddie, he was like a brother. He would have followed him to the ends of the earth.

And when the time came, he had. Milagros had to admit it had made her feel better, knowing that Eddie would be shipping out with her son. If anyone would keep him safe it was the linebacker with rage in his stomach and love in his heart. But looking through the plastic window now at the dead river, she recalled her grandmother's words, "If you want to make God laugh, tell him your plans."

"How are you doing, Milly?"

"You know."

The coffees arrived. Feeling the heat curl up in her face, Milagros realized how exhausted she was. "What about you, Eduardo?"

He smiled sadly down into his cup with a shrug. He hadn't lost the gesture since childhood. The type of kid who'd dive headlong into a bee swarm on a dare but couldn't look his best friend's mother in the eye.

"I'm here. Still waiting, I guess. Sometimes I get hopeless. But then I think about what you used to say: *to the bad times a good face.*

100

I'm glad for those memories, you know?"

"I'm sorry it took me so long to find you, hijo."

"Nah, you don't get to be sorry. Not you, Milly. You've only ever given the world your love."

They both sipped their coffee in a maze of memories.

"Been meaning to give your this." Eddie took out his wallet and opened a secret compartment. Milagros picked up the crumpled photograph of Rafael and Eddie. They were both shirtless against a wildly violet Iraqi sunset, a football balancing on Eddie's head, her son toasting the photographer with a can of Coors.

"That was Kirkuk. The night before… You know. I wanted to give this to you sooner but, well, I guess deportation kinda threw me against the wall."

Seeing her son's face was a rush of nauseating pain and love. She knew Rafael's face as well as she knew anything in this world, yet the shock of his beauty always reduced death to a fairytale. How could this boy, so strong, so vital, no longer be with her? Without having the words to ask for it, she put the photograph in her purse.

"You know, Milly, since they sent me here I done two things. One, learn Spanish. Two, I started praying." Eddie laughed. "You wouldn't have believed that one, huh? Back when you was vouching for me in the principal's office?"

"Well, if He's there, He hears you."

"I hope so, right? Every night, I ask Him to look out for Raf."

Milagros finished her coffee. She hadn't come for this. "Eddie, hijo. Listen to me, I need your help."

"Whatever you need."

"You know where El Hundido is?"

"I ain't passed through in years, but I know it, sure."

"I want to speak to the pollero that runs the route into that land."

"Oh, Milly… I don't do that no more. That was a few months

when they first sent me here. But it was bad. Real bad. Now I been at the call center two years. If I wanna get back home, I can't have no convictions."

"I'm not asking for you to take any risks. I just need a name."

"You don't understand—these people will kill you if you go there asking questions."

She fixed him with her eyes, same as she did when he had gone too far as a kid. "Two men came to my door, Eduardo. One was a medic, in case I fainted. The other one spoke. 'Milagros Posada? I have been asked to inform you that your son has been reported dead in Kirkuk, Iraq, May 27th, at eleven-hundred hours. He was killed by enemy fire while attempting to protect his fellow troops. On the behalf of the Secretary of Defense, I extend to you and your family my deepest sympathy in your great loss. Ma'am, Rafael is an American hero.'"

Tears stung Eddie's eyes. "I'm alive today because of Raf. Jack, too. A few other guys. But if I send you to the smugglers… Look, I can't have that on my shoulders, Mil."

She took out her phone now, brought up the picture of Rudi, dead under the bush. "On that day those men came, my life ended. Do you understand that? Now I want you to look at this—" She handed over her phone. "His name is Rudi. The medical examiner thinks he was between thirteen and sixteen years old. He died in a desert, too. But his mom didn't get any flag, didn't get any visit. She doesn't know where he is. That's what I do now, Eddie. That's the only reason why I'm still here. I've come to make that phone call."

He looked at her as his loyalties warred within him.

Sighing, Eddie Nieves made his choice. "Goddamn it, Milly." He stood. "I'll point you in the right direction."

On the fringes of the city, up in the barren foothills, Milagros walked past garbage dumps, along dirt roads. Panteón Municipal Número 2 was pushed up against the border wall, a dusty tract of gray earth and graves. Many were open, a stack of wooden crucifixes in the corner ready for the penniless or the unknown.

The cemetery was empty. Milagros found no one, no mourners, no would-be crossers, no coyotes. From up here, she saw Ciudad Cabral's American Siamese sister city. It was a quiet, orderly place, surrounded by nature reserves, yoga retreats, and Instagrammable swim holes.

Though the border wall cut through two cities, it was as if they were intent on becoming one another, like two blobs of mercury. The wall itself was old, rusting, of underwhelming height, recycled landing strips from the Vietnam War. Though it was no more than iron and razor wire to the eye and to the skin, to the heart it was something else—a political equator, a socioeconomic trench, the definition between the developing and developed.

Milagros wondered if Eddie Nieves had lied to her. There was nothing here but emptiness and mournful views. She was about to leave, when she checked her GPS device. Considering the horizon, she realized Irvin Hoglund's ranchland was some ten miles due north—almost exactly. With renewed energy, she searched the cemetery. Amid the tombs, she found strange things. Guatemalan quetzal coins, spots of blood, shell casings, baby wipes.

Milagros spent an hour among the dead, searching for traces of life.

Finally, she found the empty grave. Peering into the dank gloom she noticed footprints in the dirt. Puzzled, Milagros lowered herself into the grave, cursing her age. It took her a second to get used to the dark. Then she felt it—a breeze. Feeling her way, she found the tunnel. The smell of coyote shit was strong on the warm air.

BOTH SIDES

Crawling through the snaggy hole, she squinted into the void. And there, sticking out from the "ceiling" of the tunnel, was a jagged outcropping of limestone. It would have been impossible to see at night, especially scared and rushing. Reaching out, Milagros ran her finger along it. It came back caked in grayish dust. Blowing it off, she licked her finger and repeated the motion. Now her finger came back pinkish with dried blood mixed in with the dust.

"Rudi," she whispered.

Milagros felt a swell of excitement; she was almost certain the boy had come through this way. But even as hope filled her, the truth crushed her: it was a pointless detail that did nothing to uncover the truth.

Climbing out of the dummy grave, she dusted herself off and looked up at the sky. Milagros was running out of time. And she was clean out of ideas.

Her phone rang now. The number was withheld.

"¿Bueno?"

"Milly, it's me."

"Joe."

"Keeping your nose clean?"

"You know me." She looked down at herself and saw a human stick of chalk. Dusting herself off, she created a small gray squall.

"Listen, I've been thinking 'bout what we discussed. Now I'm gonna send you something, but I need to know that you get that it didn't come from me. We clear?"

Her heart quickened now. "Never been any misunderstandings between us, Joe."

There was a marshy silence. "Happy Independence Day, Milagros."

He hung up. A second later, her phone beeped. It was a voice note. Taking a breath, she pressed play and put it to her ear. She heard a metallic crackling, heavy breathing fuzzing in and out of clarity.

—*Nine-one-one, what is your emergency?*

—*Por favor ayúdame, por favor...*

—*Sir, I can't make you out real well. Do you speak English?*

—*Ayúdame, me muero...*

—*Uh, la línea es mala. La línea se está cortando.*

—*No tengo agua. Por favor, Dios. Ayúdame...*

—*¿Cuál es su nombre?*

—*Alejandro Flores Solorio.*

—*OK, Alejandro. Intenta mantener la calma. ¿Dónde estás?*

—*No lo sé, no lo sé... Estoy viendo cosas... Cosas que no pueden ser...*

—*Alejandro? Voy a enviar agentes para buscarte, okay? Quedase en la línea, okay?... Alejandro? Alejandro?*

The recording ended.

Milagros put the phone away and closed her eyes. "Okay," she said. "Alejandro."

The Diódoro Latapí Migrant Refuge was high up in the hills above Ciudad Cabral—a large breezeblock structure on a street of broken shacks and lemon trees. Clumps of people sat in the shade. Some had been recently deported, others hoping to make their first attempt soon. Many of them wore clothes bearing American concepts: colleges, football teams, star-spangled banners, NYPD—as though Border Patrol would be fooled by such displays.

The place had the feel of a ragged airport waiting lounge. Milagros heard the Spanish language in all of its multifariousness— from Paraguayan mingled with Guarani, to the beat poetry of

Dominican, to the "vos" of El Salvador—a cosmos of colloquialisms heard in jokes, scoldings, tearful phone calls.

Milagros waited in line for two hours, trying to ignore the heat as best she could. When she finally reached the front desk, she explained the situation to the woman, who wrote down the name *Alejandro Flores Solorio* and asked Milagros to wait in the courtyard.

Sitting on the tile lip of an old tile fountain, she gratefully accepted a cup of water and watched the mothers talk and their children play. The sky above had turned an argentite gray.

A short while later, the woman returned and solemnly asked her to follow. At the end of the courtyard, there was an entire wall of color. Ten thousand Post-it notes, drawings, messages, prayer cards, photographs, love notes—a wall of remembrance made by those about to cross—those recording their own details before stepping into the void. Those who wished to say: I was here.

Milagros spotted a small hummingbird sketched in pencil. Though it was no bigger than the palm of her hand, it seemed to carry every gray that there ever was. The woman touched Milagros on the shoulder before she left.

Alone, Milagros read the note beneath the hummingbird.

Mi nombre es Alejandro Flores Solorio. Soy de San Pedro Sula, Honduras. Tengo quince años. Esta noche intentaré cruzar hacia a los Estados Unidos para encontrar trabajo y poder ayudar a mi familia. Que Dios bendiga a todos los que pasan por aquí.

Making this little sketch, writing this message—it was planting a flag against the hurricane of oblivion. And yet it had held firm.

Milagros ran her finger lightly across the letters, the hummingbird. These fingers had searched in Alejandro's pockets, touched Alejandro's skin, his blood. Now they met his thoughts, his art. Feeling grief for a boy she had never met, she wrote down the phone number beneath his message—a 504 number. Then she left the shelter.

Outside, it was almost dark. Milagros walked the four miles back to the border crossing. There she joined a line eight times the size the one at the shelter, snaking into the large metal shed that led into America. It was like an exhausted world record attempt at human assembly.

Up and down the line, kids juggled for change. Unblinking junkies scoured for opportunities. Vendors tried to sell sombreros and toy donkeys painted like zebras. More men in hats and hoodies offered a last chance to cross into America without papers. A row of stores stayed open late hopeful for tourists hankering for last-minute mementos. One such pudgy couple sized up Ciudad Cabral fridge magnets. The old lady waiting to make the sale watched them, oblivious as to why anyone would want to commemorate this day.

Up on the hill in the distance, the bullring was illuminated. There was a show tonight. Little plats of orange sodium vapor from the border lamps encircled this little kingdom of steel and plastic and hope and despair.

Milagros could see America in the distance. She looked now at the darkness of the mountains behind her—the word of God lasting forever still barely visible in lime. A scurry of bats flitted through the darkness, far above the wall. They were from two places. They were from no places. *Same as me*, she thought.

Taking a deep breath, Milagros took out her phone. It was time.

Three thousand miles away, a woman answered her phone after just two rings. "¡Colibrí! Bájate de allí. Esa fue la última, voy en serio — ¿Aló?"

"…Colibrí?"

BOTH SIDES

"Si, mi hijo, Rudi. El pequeño. Asi le llamamos, Colibrí. Siempre para acá y para allá. ¿Pero con quién hablo?"

"Señora, mi nombre es Milagros Posada del Departamento del Sheriff de Aguayo County. ¿Tiene otro hijo? Alejandro Flores Solorio?"

"Si." she whispered.

"Señora Flores, lo siento. De verdad, lo siento de corazón." Milagros felt a tear slide down her cheek. Her voice shuddered as she gave the woman the truth.

There were a few seconds of silence. For a suspended moment there was only the wooing of the wind through a flimsy border wall. Then the scream of a mother. It came from the woman's nethermost, deep from where she had given life to her son.

Milagros hung up and began to sob. She cried for this woman she had never met. She cried for Alejandro. She cried for his little brother Rudi. And she cried for her own son, blown to pieces a world away, in another scorching desert that claimed all. Milagros cried for a long time.

She only stopped when she realized that, through the fog of agony and death, the hummingbird Alejandro painted in his final moments had been for his little brother. In the delirium of human finality, he had seen clearly what he should cling to—love.

Up ahead, the American couple decided on their fridge magnet. Holding up the Ciudad Cabral sombrero that doubled as a bottle opener, the woman in the ONLY GOOD VIBES tank top posed with the mystified old lady who owned the shop.

"What's Spanish for smile?" the husband said.

"I dunno, honey. Just hurry up and take it."

The next day, Jim Fraley strolled into the sheriff's department in a good mood despite his hangover. "Morning, Milly." He rested his feet up on his bureau. "Any messages?"

"No."

"Did Hanlon call?"

Milagros stopped typing. "No, why?"

"She managed to identify Hoglund's stiff already—how 'bout that?"

"How about that."

"I tell ya, we're doing a man's work in this county."

"You said it, Jim."

Yawning, Fraley leaned back and covered his face with his Stetson. "How 'bout a little coffee around here?"

"Already brewing. There's bizcochitos in the tin."

"Goddamn it, Milagros. What would I do without you?"

BUITRE

MICHELLE GARZA AND MELISSA LASON

Nogales, Arizona 1992

The cab of the truck smelled like a dumpster. The warm, humid air trapped inside only made it worse, an overbearing passenger who couldn't be seen. The smells of old beer, body odor, and the remains of tacos de lengua wrapped in a greasy bag all melded together into an inescapable entity, a suffocating hand wrapped around the throat of the nuevo vato, but he remained calm.

Tener la cabeza fría es muy importante en los negocios, mijo.

"Dígame," Alfonso said.

Luis contemplated his response. He couldn't let the older man know his intentions, not just yet. His eyes scanned the cab of the truck; he knew Alfonso would have some form of protection with him; after so many years Alfonso knew better than to trust anyone in the business, especially this nuevo vato. He couldn't let Alfonso know he was there to collect more than just the money; he was there for his initiation.

"Estoy aquí por la lana."

"¿Lana, cuál lana?" Alfonso asked, waving his hands about. His dumb act irritated Luis but he still remained cool.

Alfonso was a wiseass drunk, a trait that dug his grave one caguama at a time over the years.

"Tu lo sabes."

"No, no…"

"Sí, yo vine para recogerla."

Alfonso wasn't going to let this pinche escuincle force him to hand the money over, even though he knew he was crossing a line he couldn't come back from. He had been skimming from their patrón, Kiki, for years, and now his number was up, but he refused to look like a marica in front of the new guy. His hand was a blur in the darkened cab of the truck; it disappeared for a second to his side and reappeared holding a snub-nosed revolver, but as he began to lift it, the cocky smile on his lips fell. With age and drunkenness came a dulling of skills, a hesitation in his hand, and it cost him dearly. Luis already held his gun inches from Alfonso's head. His eyes studied the pistol, and the engravings of a scorpion spoke to him of a man he never had the balls to fuck with. The kid holding the gun bore the same green eyes as el Güero. Alfonso swallowed the lump in his throat. He knew if this kid was the son of the legendary el Güero, he wouldn't be shown an ounce of mercy. He pointed to the glove box as Luis took the gun from his shaking hand, tossed it to the floorboard, and carefully retrieved a wad of billete. It had to be at least a grand, all rolled up and wrapped in a rubber band. It smelled of greed, of traición, and of shallow graves dug by poor decisions.

"Yo recuerdo a tu papá…"

"¡Cállate!" Luis ordered Alfonso who was now beginning to snap, his tough guy façade thinner than an eggshell, cracking under the pressure of la calaca breathing down his neck.

Luis couldn't blame him for turning into a nena, he knew other men who did the same when they were staring down their own deaths.

"Por favor, no me mates."

Luis knew he'd promise him everything under the sun to be spared a bullet in the brain, and the borracho did, but he was already blocking Alfonso's pleas out, his words became becoming a garbled whisper, the incessant hum of a bobito in his ears, one Luis meant to squash.

No escuches, mijo. Los muertos son unos mentirosos.

"¡Yo vine por la lana…y tu vida, puto!"

Aprieta el gatillo, es fácil.

This time he would make his father proud, he wouldn't look away. He would pull the trigger.

The city of Nogales had yet to replace the many broken parking lot lights, and the truck was cloaked in darkness but for a single flickering yellow bulb. It was in the middle of the barrio on the edge of town, a place forgotten by everyone but those who struggled to live there and the ghosts trapped in limbo roaming its streets. The silhouettes inside were hardly distinguishable, but Pancho and Martín had watched Luis climb into Alfonso's truck; they sent him there to do their bidding, órdenes de arriba. They watched as the short conversation took place, and laughed as Alfonso began waving his arms around.

"Mira, el mentiroso de Alfonso," Pancho said quietly, and Martín smirked. They were aware of the old drunk's over-animated way of speaking.

"Como una pinche gallina," Martín said and flapped his arms like a chicken trying to fly.

They knew, at that moment, Alfonso, the thief and traitor, was more than likely wishing he could fly away from Luis. The air outside their car windows felt heavy—the swampy humidity of a monsoon was building outside and the faint growl of thunder came to greet them from the night like a hungry predator.

"Odio pinche Arizona, odio gringolandia," Pancho complained.

He hadn't been happy with his reassignment to Arizona, a tour of duty encompassing a four-year stint in the land of güeros. He wished he was still back in Culichi. He lucked out by receiving a call from Luis, his replacement. Kiki agreed when he learned of the nuevo vato's bloodline, so Pancho had to train the new kid before he could return to his beloved Sinaloa, which involved testing his bravery, to see if he could kill. If he could, then he would be putting a few traidores tres metros bajo tierra.

"Llorón, aquí no es malo. Aquí hay güeras, billete y poder. Yo soy feliz aquí."

"¡Pero la comida es una mierda!" Pancho said.

"Aprende a cocinar, marica."

Martín went quiet as Pancho held a finger to his lips. They looked to the truck, to Luis performing his first job and walking through a doorway that, to all newcomers, was big enough to drive a bus through, but when they turned to exit it would shrink to the size of a fly's asshole. The monsoon brought streaks of lightning across the sky, and Pancho could feel la calaca gliding along on its dusty winds. In a momentary flash from the gathering storm, the cab of the truck was lit and they could see Luis holding his gun to Alfonso's head. His arm didn't tremble, it was steady. Luis was thin and with the shadows cast on his young face, the deep hollow of his green eyes and high cheek bones, his face looked like a skull before everything went black again—el rostro de la muerte. Martín crossed himself and watched as the cab of the truck lit up, and though it was faster than the hot white crackling of spider-webbing lightning, time stood till and the vision of Alfonso's head bursting—the brutal force of the bullet blasting through the front side of his head and emerging in an explosion of brain matter and skull fragments, a red mist hitting the windshield—was imprinted in Martín's memory.

Luis stepped out of the truck and walked back to climb into

Pancho's Cadillac. Martín could smell the blood and gun smoke and death hanging on the nuevo vato—and, like the smell of a night at the prostíbulo, it wouldn't wash out his clothes or off his skin or out of his soul easily. El primer asesinato cambia un hombre. Luis would be marked forever.

"Buen trabajo, muchacho," Pancho said.

"Gracias," Luis answered with no mirth in his voice. He was still stone cold.

"¿Quieres unas chelas?" Martín asked.

Luis nodded and put his father's gun back in the back of his pants. The two in the front seat chattered like birds about the changing times and how Kiki demanded they start carrying beepers, how el patrón even owned a mobile phone now. Luis was lost in his own mind, in a conversation with a man he hadn't spoken with in almost five months, and not seen in person in eight years—not since his fifteenth birthday—a man he knew was dead and buried somewhere in a forgotten grave.

Estoy muy orgulloso de ti, mijo. Como tu papá, eres un asesino, un hombre de verdad.

Luis felt his throat tighten and his heart hurt hearing his father's voice. The adrenaline that had rushed through him before stepping into Alfonso's truck, which intensified when Luis sent him to el otro lado, was fading away. He could almost hear his mother crying, like she had many times at the foot of his bed as he grew into a reckless young man, begging him to stay away from his father's line of work. She screamed at Pancho, who came to deliver a severance package from Kiki in the form of billete packed into a duffel bag when Güero never returned. She didn't want their blood money, she would provide for her son all on her own, but it meant a life of struggle, one not fit for the son of Alacrán. Luis tried to appease her, pero con dinero baila perro y sin dinero bailas como perro. He hated feeling powerless and penniless and so he had called Pancho.

"¿Oiga, pendejo, estás dormido o qué?"

Luis shook his head and the voices left him, he looked to Martín, who was leaning into the window of the car. Pancho was already standing on the sidewalk beside him, and both looked confused and a little annoyed.

"¡Venga, muchacho!"

Luis hurried out of the car and was surprised to see they were already at Pancho's place. His *canton* was at the edge of the city, a large house in a decent neighborhood. Pancho liked to be inconspicuous, keeping the outward appearance of an average upper-middle-class gentleman. He claimed it was better to spend his money on booze and women than outward luxuries;, it kept the chota away. As they stepped through the front door, Martín began his usual line of chismes, mocking Pancho's sense of style.

"¡Qué naco!"

He pointed to the bold paint job in the living room of turquoise and gold and then the heavy wooden coffee table made of polished wagon wheels and oak with statues of roosters made of stained glass posed in mid-fight in its center. The crystal shelving lined with bottles of liquor and shot glasses, and a cowhide sofa. It was tacky but spoke to Luis of the life he longed to live for too many years.

"Cállate, chilango marica." Pancho responded and went directly into the kitchen.

Luis could hear him as he called el patrón, declaring Luis to be igual que el Papa. It made the young man smile proudly, his insides trembling just knowing how close he was to becoming someone, and no gringo would ever make him clean up after them again.

Pancho came back holding three ice-cold beers. They twisted off the caps and clanked them together, salud.

"El patrón estará muy contento."

BOTH SIDES

"¿Yo estoy adentro?"

"Kiki necesita un trabajo más de ti."

Luis sighed. He had already suspected this first job wouldn't be enough to get immediate approval from el mero-mero. He thought for a second of walking away, of his mother's disappointment, but he could envision himself mopping floors at the Mercado again, and walking home at night with his stomach empty, so he nodded and said, "Dígame."

Pancho grinned and sipped his beer before speaking a name: "Buitre."

He mopped the sweat from his balding head with a dingy pañuelo, then blew a wad of snot into it from his prominent nose, su narizota had drawn many teasing smirks as a child, but those looks of disgust were replaced with the wide-eyed stare of terror as he became a man, one with blood on his hands and an important person in the eyes of the cartel. Buitre's nickname came from more than just his bird-like nariz, it came from his profession, and how he flew along behind death like a vulture to pick to pieces the dead he came in contact with. He was christened with his new name by the only woman he ever cared for, his abuela, ella era igual que el esta, podrido por dentro. She had made him into the beast he was, assisted him in his duties before she died, and watched countless corpses disappear in barrels of putrid human soup, sopa de pendejos, she called it, and would laugh until she wheezed.

His gut hung over his belt, bloated and rock-hard from years of stuffing it full of gristle and warm mescal. The rest of his body was thin, his skin dry and pockmarked from his years of being around the barrels full of toxic chemicals as the man who made people disappear. Buitre was more than just a pozolero, though. He took pleasure in his work and employed a multitude of ways to dispose of corpses besides vats of acid. His father and grandfather were carniceros, he took the

116

skills they taught him of butchering pigs and cows and used them on human swine and soplones. He lived in the darkness, a monster among men, and no one, not even Kiki knew him personally. If they had, they would have either ran far away from him or called the Catholic church to do battle with the devil in the flesh.

Buitre encendio el fósforo. He dropped it out before his feet and watched fire spring up and race across a line of gasoline before it ran up the sides of the shack he worked out of for decades. Kiki hadn't gone as far as sick la tira on him yet—it was against narco códigos until he got concrete proof Buitre was a threat to his organization—but Buitre knew los perros del patrón were already hunting him, seeking proof by any means necessary. He had been told so and his source had no reason to lie; he was already dead. He left the house of death smoldering in the desert on the outskirts of Culiacan, Kiki's territory, and headed for la frontera, for the gringo side of Nogales. There, in the land of güeros, he thought he could disappear, then head farther north and open up shop as a true butcher, the kind who skinned pigs and not men. He only had one more stop to make, one to secure his financial future en el gabacho. He had a drive ahead of him, but he didn't plan to make it alone.

Beside him on the front seat of the van sat a weathered, dirty sack, una bolsa de oro. The treasure inside was worth more than a thousand black briefcases given to him by Kiki's perros. Buitre put his hand on the sack and felt it move, grinning as it writhed under his calloused fingers.

"Dime tus secretos."

Luis felt as if he could drink a river dry;, a cruda muy fuerte kept him from opening the curtains and looking out onto the sunny street where the barking of a dog woke him from a restless sleep. His dreams were tormented by memories of his father, of the night Luis felt like he failed Güero completely.

BOTH SIDES

Luis had been media pedo. His father had brought him a bottle of tequila for his birthday and they drank it on the sidewalk around the corner from his house because his mother wouldn't allow it in her home. Güero brought Pancho along with him para celebra su único hijo su cumpleaños, un dia especial, su hijo se estaba convirtiendo en un hombre. Güero planned to get his boy drunk and buy him a woman, a birthday fit for his mano derecha. The young man's memories were still blurred, muddled together and for many years he didn't understand what truly happened, only that he looked away and his finger couldn't pull the trigger, and the vision of it played over and over in his mind como una mala película. Un fresito gringo, who was clearly out of his element, stumbled down the sidewalk. Too much booze made the gringo feel ten feet tall and bulletproof when he came across the three Mexican men.

"Get outta my way, wetbacks."

Pancho shoved the gringo back. "Vete a la verga."

"Don't get tough, old man. You want me to call la migra?"

Su película aceleró y el gringo culero estaba de rodillas en la calle. Luis sostuvo un fierro. Le temblaba el brazo como un rama en la viento.

"Hazlo, hijo."

The gringo's eyes were running tears and bloody snot hung from his busted nose and lips. Pancho's fists were as hard and as heavy as steel and the American's soft and pampered flesh hadn't known the sort of violence they were tempered in.

"Please, I'm so sorry. I didn't mean to offend you. I'm a little drunk…"

"No escuches, mijo. Los muertos son unos mentirosos," his father spoke close to his ear.

Luis felt his arm shaking. He closed his eyes.

"Es fácil, aprieta el gatillo." Güero's voice was calm, but Luis felt the urgency in the instructions.

"¡Hazlo antes que la chota venga!" Pancho said.

The seconds were an eternity for Luis, who couldn't pull the trigger. He felt his father's calloused hand remove the pistol from his own, and in a heartbeat a shot rang out. His head had hurt the following morning, but the agony of letting his father down was more painful than anything he had ever experienced. Güero and Pancho took the corpse to the desert and left Luis with his mother. It was a secret Luis kept locked in the tomb of his heart. He just hoped killing Alfonso proved to Pancho he was no longer a frightened kid; he could look a man in the eye and take a life, just like his father.

Luis pulled his clothes on and then wandered to the guest bathroom to piss. He always dreamed he would see a new man in the mirror after his first kill, a stronger man, but all he saw was the hollow look of a man who had too much wiskicito, and not enough sleep. The night before was a blur of alcohol, coca y putas. The third, Pancho kicked out onto the street long before dawn, but the first two continued to dance with the three men until the sky turned gray with the approaching sun and they stumbled to their beds. Luis could hear Pancho calling to him from the hallway outside of his room. The old man sounded more than a little hungover, but Luis knew they would be heading out soon, no time for menudo or chilaquiles, just una cerveza to kill the deathly feeling churning his guts to an acid soup and to calm his thrumming nerves.

"Abre la puerta. Es hora,." Pancho said.

"Voy," Luis answered but hesitated to splash a couple of handfuls of cold water on his face from the bathroom sink.

He pulled the door open to see Pancho running his hands through his graying hair. The older man sounded worse than he looked. He was already dressed, and had a gun tucked into his pants, its handle embellished with a gaudy crucifix. He had become accustomed to a lifestyle of constant movement, of doling out punishment, of answering to the orders of men like Kiki. Luis hoped to live as long as Pancho, but knew in his new line of employment it wasn't likely. His father never got to see his fiftieth birthday—he'd simply disappeared—but Luis knew men just didn't vanish, they were erased. He promised his father's memory he would avenge him, and with the help of Kiki's cartel he would find the hijo de puta who had ended his father's life.

"¿Listo?" Pancho asked as Luis followed him downstairs to the kitchen.

"Simón."

Martín sat at the kitchen table, a tortilla in his hand. He shoved it in his mouth and washed it down with half a glass of whiskey, the last of the hard booze from the night before. He looked to Luis and nodded as the young man opened the fridge and grabbed a beer. He cracked it open and took a drink before holding the cold bottle against his forehead.

"Desayuno de los reyes. " Martín laughed.

He stood and went to the stove. The comal was already heated up, so he tossed two tortillas de maíz onto it and threw cheese on top of them. It didn't even have a chance to melt completely before he moved them onto a plate and handed it to Luis.

"Buen provecho."

Luis shoveled the food into his mouth and drank the rest of his beer as Pancho talked on the phone. The nuevo vato could tell by the tone of Pancho's voice he spoke to el mero-mero, el patrón. Kiki was relaying the latest information on the whereabouts of Buitre, and from what Luis could hear, he didn't know much, only that the pozolero was suspected to be headed for gringolandia. Kiki's orders were to capture Buitre, beat any useful information out of him, and then kill him.

The voice of Luis's father ran through his mind:, Los Perros muertos no muerden.

"El muchacho y yo venimos a buscar al Buitre, tu nos esperas aquí," Pancho said to Martín.

Luis felt a rush of adrenaline as he followed Pancho to the car. He was so close to being one of them, un hombre de negocios. Martín would gather more men and be ready for Pancho to call him. Luis and Pancho were informed their target was moving toward the border, right to their waiting pistols. They would put an end to the living legend named Buitre and seal his role as the nuevo vato in Kiki's cartel. He was still confused as to how they would locate Buitre, but Pancho walked with the confidence of a man who had hunted many soplones, he would be un gran maestro in the arts of making a man que suelta la sopa. Luis couldn't fail, couldn't turn back. He had to live up to the notoriety of the man whose gun he kept tucked in the back of his pants. He, too, had to become un alacrán.

Buitre had a lead on Kiki's banks in the desert, el patrón's secret stashes of money he had yet to launder. Buitre had already helped himself to a chunk of change from one in order to test Fransisco's knowledge, and with the help of Fransisco he meant to withdraw an even larger bonus for himself, a pension plan of sorts. He could outrun Kiki's perros if he worked fast and kept driving. He laughed to himself. They would never have a clue as to how he obtained the knowledge because they believed their secrets disappeared along with the corpses of the men who kept them. If only they knew the truth.

They already sought Buitre's blood for killing a local puerco, una rata who had it coming. Buitre didn't often hunt—he didn't need to with all the carne that passed through his house of death on a weekly basis—but el tirra pansón had gotten too cocky with the pozolero, even tried to get a cut of his pay from Kiki to keep his mouth shut. So

Buitre went hunting, and found him in un prostíbulo. Buitre had cut his throat open and watched him bleed out on the feet of two cheap teiboleras. Kiki was enraged when he linked Buitre to the murder; the pansón was Kiki's eyes and ears within the local police department, an important element to evading capture. El patrón figured Buitre was tipped off to the inside man's location by Fransisco, whom Kiki promptly beheaded, but his lips only wagged after his heart stopped and not a second before. Buitre knew Fransisco while he lived, and sought out his corpse after he was killed, as any vulture would, by following the scent of death. Fransisco had been left in a shallow grave, a thin blanket of dirt in his open eyes, his head severed from his neck and tossed in the grave on top of his battered corpse. Buitre took the head; he knew death wasn't the silencer Kiki believed, his abuela had taught him so. Fransisco told Buitre all the secrets he knew from working for Kiki for so many years, including how many secret stashes of lana he kept buried.

"¡Dime, pendejo!" Buitre commanded.

The dirty sack wiggled and a harsh whisper issued from beneath its filthy folds.

"Malverde."

Buitre lit a cigarette and exhaled a throatful of smoke out into the van and then reached into his shirt pocket and fished out a finger. Its flesh was a pale gray, the pallor of death. He held it up to his nariz and inhaled the aroma of decay, his mouth watering como pero de taquería, his gut churning with hunger. He stuck it in the side of his mouth and chewed on it, savoring it like a stick of beef jerky. He drove with his knees, alternating gnawing on the finger like a chicken wing with one hand while the other brought the cigarette to his lips. The sack beside him moaned softly, a single plea, one Buitre had heard countless times and ignored. Por favor. He wouldn't give in until he had what he wanted. Maybe after he filled his pockets he would release the pitiful thing from being bound to him.

They sat in the car; a quick dinner of tacos de canasta was more than a way to fill their empty stomachs. Pancho was awaiting word from Kiki's other perros, of any clue as to the whereabouts of Buitre. After a day of hitting the streets of Nogales on both sides of the border, they still had no word on the pozolero but Pancho was still confident they'd locate him. The vendedor pedaled away on his bicycle before Pancho spoke.

"Pinche Buitre. El no es un fantasma. Lo atraparemos."

"¿Por qué está marcado el Buitre?"

"El sabe demasiado, y el rompio las reglas."

"¿Qué reglas?"

"El mato un güey importante."

Luis nodded and ate in silence. The pozolero had killed an inside man, something he knew would be punishable by death. It made his mind stray to his father, and he wondered what he could have done to become invisible, what deed left him marked to die.

Tuve que quebrarlo, era el o yo.

Luis froze, he felt a sickness twist his gut, a cold sinking into his bones. He looked to Pancho who shoved half a taco in his mouth, its grease running down his chin. Did he hear it? After years of only hearing reverberations from past conversations, Güero seemed to be answering the questions running through his brain. Or was Luis losing his mind?

¿Y cómo me lo pagaron?

Pancho glanced at the nuevo vato, talking over a mouthful of food. Luis was wide-eyed, his skin pale and clammy, his mouth half-open.

"¿Te gusto o qué?"

Luis shook his head; he needed to keep it together. He was looking like un pendejo in front of Pancho, yet he couldn't shake the chill his father's voice filled him with.

"No, no, tengo que cagar."

Pancho laughed. "¡Como ya te hicistes, muchacho!"

Luis got out of Pancho's car, laughter chasing him across the street as he entered a small tienda. He made his way to the restrooms and checked the stalls; he was alone.

"¿Papá, estas ahí?"

He stared at himself in the mirror and watched his face, filled with a strange, sickening hope, droop into a look of emptiness. There was no reply, only silence, like the months of not receiving a single phone call from güero güero.

Luis washed his face and went back to work. Pancho was waiting for him, sitting on the hood of his car, smoking a cigarette.

"¿Limpiaste tus pantalones?"

"¡Cállate!" Luis smiled in embarrassment, feeling himself loosen up a bit as the tension faded. He tried to push his father's memory to the back of his mind and focus on the job ahead.

"Te pareces a tu papá. El era mi amigo por muchos años."

His mother had always told him the same, both when she was happy and feeling sentimental, and when she had too much to drink and hated his father for the heartbreak he left behind. Luis was his father's twin in appearance, a thin güero with pale eyes and skin. His actions were like a mirror to his father as well, hotheaded, stubborn, both men who refused to give up something once they set their mind to it, destined for either great triumph or incredible failure. Luis had wanted nothing more than to be his father's mano derecha his whole life, but he would never get the chance.

"Tu nuevo nombre deberia ser Guerrito o Alacrancito."

Luis sighed. It was a subject he had been meaning to approach. Maybe that explained his father speaking to him so much; it was his conscience reminding him to ask Güero's closest friend how he disappeared.

"¿Que pasó con mi papá?"

Pancho flicked his cigarette out into the street and motioned for Luis to join him in the car.

"Tu papá estaba…"

"¿Estaba? ¿Entonces, está muerto?"

"No se, pero el desapareció, y en el negocio eso es una mala senal."

Luis nodded, he knew Pancho was tiptoeing around the truth, like everyone did. His own mother wouldn't say the exact words tu padre está muerto, pero todos lo sabían, Güero was dead. The sack of money Kiki had offered them was proof enough, Pancho secretly giving Luis his father's prized pistol and whispering to him to hide it from his mother—it all added up.

"Te lo prometo, encontraremos la verdad," Pancho said.

"Gracias, Pancho," Luis said.

It didn't make him feel any better to have Pancho promise to find the truth. He was sure the old man already knew it but refused to speak it out loud.

"Concentrémonos en el Buitre, y después…"

"Si, después de este jale," Luis spoke, trying to hide his disappointment and frustration.

Pancho left Luis to sit in the car while he gathered more intel. He walked across the street to the same tienda where Luis had escaped. It was one of Kiki's spots, a place where he knew the phone had yet to be monitored by la chota. He wasn't gone long when he came sprinting back to the car, face twisted into the visage of a hungry animal.

"¡Pinche ladrón, hijo de su puta madre!"

"¿Qué?" Luis asked, drawing his gun as Pancho climbed behind the wheel.

"¡El Buitre se robó mucho dinero de Kiki!"

125

BOTH SIDES

Pancho drove like a maniac as he explained how Buitre's shack was found burned down, and how Kiki's secret stashes in the desert had been discovered. So far, one had been pilfered, but there was a second very close to their location, hidden beneath an altar to Malverde in Nogales, Mexico. Only a handful of people knew the locations of Kiki's stashes of billete, and one of them was Fransisco, who was already linked to Buitre. Kiki was no idiot; it was clear Buitre was trying to flee, and needed a fortune to escape the reach of el patrón. Kiki needed Pancho and the nuevo vato to provide protection to his stash and capture the pozolero if he came to pick it clean, like a carcass.

The altar was visited on occasion by those loyal to the legendary Malverde, the poor, the downtrodden, those hasta el cuello con las drogas y los carteles. Ellos traen cigarillos y wisquicito, le lavan la cara con agua bendita, rezan por su bendiciones y su protección. The narco-saint was celebrated by those in every barrio, en muchos paises, en todo el mundo. The guard was accustomed to strangers showing up at all hours but he knew the face of Buitre; he had unloaded a few corpses at the pozolero's shack in the past. He was ready to blow a hole through his cabeza, or shoot him right in his nariz, it wouldn't be hard to miss.

Buitre sat in the van, from a stinking cooler he pulled out his dinner, a fetid assortment of organs he had scavenged from the corpses strewn in his shack before setting it on fire. The cooler didn't have any ice in it, as he didn't require his meal to be fresh—actually, he preferred it wasn't. He lived up to his name; he fed off the dead, ate the meat from their bones, and burrowed in the maggot-ridden flesh of the deceased. He ate feverishly, knowing it would give him the strength to accomplish what he came to do. The sack beside him moved, and he grabbed it and threw it in the back of the van. It bounced and landed next to another sack; it fell open and Fransisco's head rolled out. His clouded eyes stared at Buitre, his cracked lips parted, and an unearthly whispering came out.

"Por favor, déjame morir…"

The voice was like the scratching of dry tree limbs on a windowpane, the words no longer produced by lungs and breath. They came from the spirit world—a barrier which was hard to communicate through, unless you were gifted like el Buitre.

"Déjame morir…por favor."

"Cállate," Buitre ordered the head.

He climbed over the seat and opened the other sack; his abuela's head was hidden in it along with a few others. Hers was basically fleshless, except for a few areas where the skin was as hard as leather. He stared into her eye sockets and waited for her to speak to him.

"Apúrate."

"Casi listo," Buitre answered and returned to feasting.

He could feel the flesh empowering him, granting his body the strength to carry out the heist. It was the way his gift worked. He was more than just a cannibal; his powers were charged when he fed on the carcasses of men, and the voices of the dead and their secrets were more easily revealed after feeding. For the first robbery, he ate only the arm of some headless corpse left behind by the Sinaloa cartel. He filled a bag with lana and hauled it away. It was a test to see if he made it out alive, but this time he meant to fill his van full of stacks of billete, and through the hidden tracks of the desert he'd drive into el gabacho to the new life awaiting him. He binged on the contents of the cooler until he could feel the rotten flesh and maggots almost tickling the back of his throat. He belched loudly before forcing Fransisco's head into the sack with his abuela's, then he grabbed his pistol and stepped out of the van, carrying the sack like Santa Claus. He was a vulture, a scavenger of the dead, and la calaca was his bride.

Buitre crept into the warehouse through a side door, his eyes keen in the darkness. The altar was lit by a multitude of candles, the statue of Malverde was adorned with the many tributes of his followers, a king of the suffering bejeweled and bathed in holy water. Beneath the statue rested what Buitre came to claim—a hollow recess in the altar filled with bags of dinero would be his ticket to a new life away from Sinaloa and Kiki's perros, the American dream. The guard looked anxious. Buitre stayed in the shadows and pulled a knife from his belt. He moved silently until he was within reach. His eyes strayed to the altar and silently he asked Malverde to guide his hand. The guard wasn't expecting a blade to his throat, or that the last thing he'd see in the living world would be his blood decorating the walls and the unblinking eyes of Malverde with a rain of crimson. He spun weakly and his dying hand squeezed the trigger a single time.

Pancho and Luis parked across the street. The young man felt a strange static moving up his arms.

Esta noche sabrás la verdad.

"Vámonos," Pancho ordered at the sound of un disparo.

Luis drew his father's gun and followed Pancho into the warehouse. The scent of death hung in the air, and many of the candles had been snuffed by the shower of blood. The guard lay in a gathering pool of red. His eyes blinked once but Luis was certain it was just the misfiring signals of a dying brain. Pancho was jumpy and ready to kill anything moving; Luis could feel a strange sensation radiating from the older man—fear.

"¿Dónde esta ese hijo de puta?" Pancho whispered.

"Mira." Luis pointed out a second, smaller pool of blood.

"El esta aquí."

A gunshot from the dark brought Pancho to his knees, un disparo en las tripas. He gripped his stomach and screamed while he fired in return, each blast ricocheting wildly inside the steel building. Luis fired his pistol as he ran for cover behind the altar, but caught a bullet in the hip as Buitre and Pancho emptied both of their weapons in an attempt to kill each other. Luis brought his hand to the wound, a wave of intense pain made him vomit a mouthful of tacos de canasta onto the dirty floor. He fell forward onto a filthy sack and held his breath in an attempt to keep silent. The smell of it overpowered him and a movement within it caused him to flinch. He couldn't scramble away from it; his pain held him still.

"¡Mata al traidor!" a thin whisper urged him from the sack.

Luis shook his head, and despite his agony he dragged himself away from the altar and the stinking sack.

"¡Pancho!" a gruff voice hailed the sicarrio.

"¡Chinga tu madre!"

"Que lástima, no te quiero matar, pero ahora tengo que."

"Ven acá, puto."

Luis gathered his strength and forced the pain aside enough to stand up. He lifted his pistol and fired it. Buitre tumbled backward over an empty steel drum. Luis hobbled to Pancho and helped him to his feet. Pancho was searching his pocket for bullets to reload with when Buitre reemerged and shot Luis through the shoulder and thigh. His father's gun fell out of his hand and slid across the floor. Pancho pushed Luis to the ground and took a second bullet to his abdomen; he dropped beside the nuevo vato. They were both badly injured, and as Buitre came to stand over them they could feel the cold breath of la calaca stealing their consciousness and suspending them in darkness.

When Luis awoke, Pancho was already conscious and spitting threats at the pozolero. Luis tried to move, but found his arms and legs were bound. Pancho was hog-tied in torturous position, but he writhed like a worm to break free while Buitre gathered black bags from the destroyed altar to Malverde. A sledgehammer leaned against the wall, and all Luis could envision was crushing Buitre's skull with it. The pozolero was bleeding from the side of his neck, a deep wound that should have been fatal.

"Sabía que te me hacias familiar, muchacho," Buitre spoke as he pulled Güero's gun from the back of his pants.

"¡Hijo de puta!" Luis screamed.

"¿Yo?" El Buitre pointed to Pancho, "*El* es un hijo de puta, y un traidor."

Buitre dropped the black bag he was carrying and stood over Luis.

"Sabes quién mató a tu padre?"

Luis went silent as Buitre pointed to Pancho.

"¿No me crees?"

"¡Mentiroso!" Pancho cried.

"Pregúntale a tu papá." Buitre smiled and hobbled over to the sack behind the altar.

He emptied it on the floor and five severed heads rolled out, their eyes wide and their mouths open. He picked one up by its light brown hair and set it before Luis, who choked back a scream as vomit rose in his throat. Güero's pale eyes were clouded in death, and skin clung to his high cheekbones, but it was clearly him. There was a jagged hole in his forehead, the mark of his execution.

"¡Mata al traidor! ¡Mata a Pancho!" the head of Güero spoke.

"¿Quién, Papá?"

"¿Puedes escucharlo?" Buitre marveled.

The look on his face confirmed that he could. Buitre knelt beside Luis and began untying him. He placed Güero's gun in the young man's hand.

"Somos iguales," Buitre whispered, "Los muertos conocen todos los secretos si escuchan."

"¿Cómo pudiste, Pancho?" Luis asked.

"¿Qué? ¡No es verdad!"

Luis realized Pancho couldn't hear the voice of Güero, but the pozolero could. It was no madness, it was real. Güero was speaking the truth of his death.

"¿Cómo, Pancho? ¡El es tu major amigo!"

"¡No fui yo!"

"¿Si no estabas involucrado, por qué tuviste su arma?" Luis asked.

Pancho fell silent. He couldn't explain why he would have Güero's gun if he wasn't there when he was killed.

"Estaba siguiendo órdenes, hijo. Lo siento mucho."

Luis didn't tremble, even in the intense pain his heart was overcome with. He lifted his father's gun and pulled the trigger. A bullet hole in the right eye marked Pancho's end.

"Vámonos." Buitre said.

"¿A dónde?"

"¿Quieres venganza?"

Luis looked to his father's head and nodded.

"Pancho es sólo un perro, tu quieres al jefe," Buitre answered and pulled a knife from his belt. He began cutting Pancho's head from his neck. "El nos diré como."

Luis sat in the back of the stinking van, lodged between bags of money, a bloody cooler, and a sack of severed heads. He had no idea what the morbid pozolero had in mind but if it meant avenging his father he would do it, even if it meant becoming a buitre himself.

THE LAMENT OF THE VEJIGANTE

CYNTHIA PELAYO

My father taught me to believe in monsters. Most monsters are malevolent, but there's one monster—a saint—whose presence has blessed me with the reminder that we are neither from here nor there. We are Puerto Rican. Our island home exists as one of the three points making up the Bermuda Triangle, a supernatural place where some things just cannot be explained or reasoned.

One of the earliest memories I have as a child about being Puerto Rican is my father taking me to downtown Chicago to the Puerto Rican Day Parade. I remember I could barely see the glittering, colorful floats, even sitting atop his shoulders, because there were so many people waving flags. Red and white stripes, a blue banner, and a single white star. Cheers and car horns roared through the air. Whistles and the sounds of motors revving. Those people screamed with such feverish joy as they waved that flag. Even though I was too young to even be in school at that time, I knew deep within me that I was a part of that thunderous joy, that I was a part of something more, something greater than myself.

When my father brought me down off of his shoulders I faced a demon, and my life forever changed. It was dressed in bright, bold colors. Like a clown or a harlequin, it stood there with a theatrical command. Its clothes bore flashes of glitter and dashes of gold. An elaborate, flowing costume of red and orange silk. Ruffles and bells lined its collar and sleeves. Its face was a fantastical horror of long horns that jutted out from its temples and adorned its head. A crown of horns. A sharp beak, and a wide-open mouth with pointed teeth mocked me. Then the demon bowed, and it struck me softly with a rattle.

I screamed.

I ran, dodging through the crowd, pushing past people. Screams and blaring car horns followed me. Then, it was as if all went still. I found myself on the street. When I turned around, I finally saw it. The parade floats that stretched down Columbus Drive. No one moved. Parade-goers stood still. The floats stopped. When I moved to turn around, to see where all eyes were directed, I saw a splash of red on the asphalt. My father placed his hands on my cheeks and turned my face away.

"What happened?" I asked. "Are you okay?"

He didn't answer.

As my father led me away from the parade route I asked him about the monster.

"What was that?"

"El Vejigante," he answered.

I didn't know what it was and I didn't care what it was. "It hit me!" I snapped.

My father got down on his knees and looked me in the eyes. "That's good. That's very good, because that means he blessed you with good luck and strength. He'll protect you. Always."

That early memory also mixes and melds with another memory, of our Independence Day celebrations. On the Fourth of July, my parents would host a large cookout for family and friends. We would wave sparklers and shoot Roman candles into sky. The boom of illegal fireworks kept us all giddy and awake throughout the night. This was another day of joy, another moment of celebration, another day of identifying, of belonging to something greater than myself, because this was America, and I was an American, and because of that, I felt pride.

Eventually, my mother stopped hosting Fourth of July cookouts. Instead, we would visit my cousin's house. I remember visiting them on one Fourth of July, and I found it so odd that they weren't just watching Spanish television, but that they were so engrossed in it. They knew the language and that world, and I did not. In the evenings at home, my brothers and I watched programs like *Knight Rider, V, Quantum Leap, Alf, MacGyver*, and *The A-Team*. I couldn't understand anything people were saying on the programs my cousins watched, and I felt so disconnected from them. My aunts and cousins would make fun of me for not understanding, and then ask my mother why I didn't know Spanish. My mother would brush it off with some empty, non-threatening excuse. I knew the real reason: because my mother had grown to resent Spanish. She grew to blame our identities for all of our struggles and pain. She grew to blame Puerto Rico for everything bad that had ever happened to us. So at home my mother would stress, "In this house you speak *English*."

And so it went, we were Puerto Ricans who did not speak Spanish. Eventually, we were Puerto Ricans who did not go to the Puerto Rican Day Parade. We were Puerto Ricans who did not visit Puerto Rico. We were Puerto Ricans who didn't even own a Puerto Rican flag.

When my cousins moved back to Puerto Rico, my mother spoke about it like they would surely regret their decision. My cousins spoke about moving back to Puerto Rico like there was no better way of life. Chicago was dirty. Chicago was unsafe. Chicago schools were overcrowded. In Puerto Rico they could speak their language. In Puerto Rico they could be outside without the fear of a rogue bullet tearing through the air searching for a target. In Puerto Rico they could be successful.

"Those poor kids," my mother would say. "The opportunities they are missing."

My parents didn't meet in Puerto Rico. Had my parents each stayed on the island, I doubt they ever would have gotten together. My mother is from San Sebastian, a somewhat middle-class municipality in the northwest region of the island. The patron saint of San Sebastian is San Sebastian Martir, or St. Sebastian the Martyr. The patron saint was brought to San Sebastian by the immigrants from the Canary Islands in Spain.

My father is from the town of Adjuntas, a small mountain town, with one of the highest peaks on the island. Adjuntas is nicknamed La Ciudad del Gigante Dormido, because of a mountain formation resembling a slumbering giant.

The patron saints of Adjuntas are Saint Joachim and Saint Anne, the parents of the Virgin Mary. In Puerto Rico, every town has a patron saint, and so you could say every Puerto Rican has one, too.

Adjuntas was once a booming mountain town where sugar cane and coffee were the main source of industry, but when the United States instituted Operation Bootstrap in 1947 and moved the island away from an agrarian society to an industrial one, life on the island changed. As industry increased, the need for labor decreased, and there is, in part, what drove the great Puerto Rican migration to the mainland starting in the 1950s.

My father came to the mainland in 1958. He was sixteen years old and had twenty dollars in his pocket when he landed in New Jersey. He lasted one day there working on a farm and then made his way to Brooklyn, New York. In Brooklyn, he washed dishes in a nightclub and slowly learned English with the help of his black co-workers who treated him as one of their own. My father eventually found himself in Chicago, and when I asked him what brought him here he said, "Aventura."

Adventure.

My parents met in the factories along Michigan Avenue. Imagine, there were once factories so close to the Magnificent Mile. My father lived in Lincoln Park back then, which was also once the Puerto Rican neighborhood. Today, Michigan Avenue is a tourist destination and Lincoln Park is dotted with mini-mansions owned by the wealthy. In the 1970s, my parents bought a multi-unit greystone in Logan Square before Logan Square gentrified. After my mother's mother died, my parents sold the building, and they and my two brothers moved back to Puerto Rico, in search of healing and strength, and there they had me.

Shortly after I was born my parents returned to Chicago. My mother missed the city skyline, the public transportation system, and the ability to walk anywhere. We settled in the northwest side of Chicago, in the Polish-German-Greek neighborhood of Belmont-Craigin, in 1980. We were the first Puerto Ricans, and overall the first Hispanics on the block. By 1990 the neighborhood was ninety-eight percent Hispanic. White flight happens fast.

In 1985, when I was in kindergarten, I developed the skill that is still my best to this day: procrastination. I told my dad that I had show-and-tell one morning and needed something to present to the class. He didn't know what show-and-tell was, so I explained to him that I had to take something to school and show the class and talk about it. He took me downstairs to our unfinished basement. It was dark and moldy with exposed beams. In one corner of the basement, there was a heavy wooden floor stereo that held a turntable and eight-track player. There were boxes that held yellowed, faded documents and photo albums and loose black-and-white pictures. We moved to the far end where the basement sink and boilers could be found. There, my father pointed to a box that was still taped shut. He asked me to tear away the tape, and I did. Inside, I found aged, balled-up sheets of newspaper; the box was stuffed with them. He told me to reach inside, and I did. When I pulled the contents, I gasped. I held the face of a demon, similar to the one I had seen before.

It was brilliant, and grotesque.

"This one is very old," my father said. "It's made of a coconut shell."

It was unrecognizable as a coconut. The shell was painted an electric blue, speckled with yellow. Yellow horns jutted out from its head, and wide eyes and a wicked open-mouth grin stared on at me.

"It's scary," I said.

"That's the point," my father said. "You want him to be scary, to scare away the bad things. He can't get rid of all of the bad things that happen, but he can fight them off."

"The kids are going to laugh at me." I could feel tears well up in my eyes and I dropped the mask on the concrete floor.

My father didn't move. "The vejigante is special because he's magic. He helps people. He helps people who are struggling."

I remember stomping my feet and whining and saying I didn't want to take that mask with me to school. When I turned to look for my dad, I found I was alone there in the basement. He was gone. It was just me and that mask. I dove into the box, pulling out the remaining newspapers, hoping that there was something else inside the box that would be fantastic and exciting that I could take to school instead— but there was nothing. I begrudgingly took the mask of the vejigante with me to my kindergarten show-and-tell class. Other kids proudly showed off their Teddy Ruxpins, Barbie dolls, and Transformers. When it was time for me to present, I remember pulling the mask out from a bag. There was silence.

"This is a vejigante. He protects people."

And that's all I said.

No one said anything. No one asked any questions, and so I returned to my seat with my mask, embarrassed and angry that my father didn't have anything else to give me. I kept the mask in that plastic bag in the basement for a long time.

Years later, when my brother Tito went looking for a suitcase in the basement he found the mask. He brought it up to my room and said it would mean a lot to Dad that I keep it safe. When Tito went to the Army there were tears, but we all knew he was doing a great thing. He was an American fighting for America. Before he left, my mother gave him a scapular of the Guardian Angel; a cloth necklace with the image of an angel hovering over two small children. Tito spent time in South Korea, patrolling the Korean Demilitarized Zone. I remember what it was like to talk to my brother on the phone back then, and how soft and muffled and crackling he would sound, like he was a ghost calling from another dimension. When the Gulf War broke out, I remember being in my room playing Super Mario Brothers on my Nintendo and my mother screaming into the phone very early one morning. Tito had received orders to deploy. In a panic, she left the house and told me to stay in my room. She said she was going to fix it, and that she was not going to lose any more family. I don't know why or how, but Tito's friend went to war in his place. The friend was shot, but survived.

My brother Coco would go on to serve, too, a few years later, with the 101st Airborne Infantry. My mother gave him a rosary of Saint Michael, the patron saint of soldiers. He went to war, and my mother was not going to stop him. He fought and served in Bosnia. Coco didn't come back right. He screamed at night, and one time he choked me so bad I passed out. I started locking my door because he had a growing gun collection—antique weapons and semi-automatics—and because, in my brother's mind, he was still riding that tank at night, pointing his machine gun at enemies. One day, my brother came into my room and threw a stack of photographs at me. Pictures he had taken. They were mostly of the countryside, but many of them were of mass graves. He told me that was part of his job, locating mass graves; Christians killing Muslims. Muslims killing Christians. Humans killing humans, and piling their bodies in open-air pits. In one of the pictures I could have sworn I saw the shadow of horns and the outline of that demon.

Still, my brother had come back home, broken and shaken, but he came back home. And as my mother dealt with his wreckage of a human, I enlisted in the Army Reserve, because that's what we did, we served. In boot camp, my platoon had a handful of women and the rest were men. Most of them had never met a Puerto Rican—I had never met white men from the south. They became my brothers, my family. We stood out in the rain together holding our rifles overhead. We marched up and down hills for hours, and when one of them would collapse from exhaustion our drill sergeant would shout at us in the rear to stop and make sure we had taken care of our buddy. I don't recall why or how, but the men were woken up earlier than the women one day and they were marched for hours in the freezing cold. When they returned back to base, I remember some of them had snot and tears frozen on their faces. I remember running out of the barracks with blankets in hand to cover their heads. Through chattering teeth, they thanked me. When I was medically discharged, I remember hugging those men so hard. They were from Louisiana and Kentucky, and Georgia and Texas. Missouri and beyond. They called me their Puerto Rican sister, and told me to be safe up in the big city.

When I got home, ashamed and deflated because of my discharge, I went into my room, sat down on my bed, and cried. When I looked up, my father was standing there with a smile on his face. "It will be okay," he told me. "You will go to college, and you will be okay."

The first time someone called me "spic," I was sitting in a college

139

class. It was my journalism professor and she asked me what I thought of the word "spic." Honestly, I had never heard it before. When I got home I asked my dad what it meant and he laughed. He told me it would get worse before it got better, and it did.

"Do you still have that vejigante mask?" he asked.

"Yes," I answered.

"It would be nice if you hang it on your wall."

For some reason, I listened to him, and I hung that mask on the wall above my bed.

That first year in college I tried to get a part-time job at The GAP. I applied in person, a paper application, and the manager called me into his office for a quick interview. When he looked at the application and saw that it said Puerto Rico under my place of birth he asked me if I had papers.

"Puerto Ricans are American citizens," I said.

He literally laughed in my face. I told him that Puerto Ricans were made US citizens by an act of Congress with the Jones-Shafroth Act of 1917 signed by President Woodrow Wilson. He didn't believe me, and I didn't get the job.

A few days later a white guy in my Introduction to Reporting Journalism class said, "Oh, wow. I know about you Puerto Rican girls."

I genuinely didn't know what that meant. I asked him to elaborate. His face flushed red and he said, "Forget it."

When I asked my dad, he said the guy was trying to insinuate that Puerto Rican women were fast—sluts, prostitutes. I started crying and said I was never going back there.

My dad got the angriest with me he had ever been. "They used to send dogs to bite us. People would spit in our food, drag us out of restaurants. Police would pepper spray us. Hit us with clubs, and you are mad because someone called you a name?"

140

I went back to school and never complained again when someone called me a name, sneered at me, laughed at my clothes, my lack of a base education, or the way I pronounced or said something.

Before completing my undergraduate degree, I took two semesters off and worked as a flight attendant for American Eagle Airlines. I am my father's daughter and sought adventure. It was an easy way to travel and see much of the US. I got to visit the south and hear those accents I had come to fall in love with when I was in the Army. One of the pilots, upon learning I was Puerto Rican, told me Puerto Ricans didn't bathe, and each morning when I boarded the plane he asked me if I had showered. The next time I learned I was going to fly with that same pilot I quit.

My father was right. Things got worse before they got better.

While I was training for the Chicago Marathon one summer, a car slowed alongside me and a white guy leaned out of the driver's side passenger window and shouted, "Nice tits, you fucking spic," and he spat at me.

I finished my undergraduate without any friends. As people stood around hugging their fellow classmates, trading flowers and cards at graduation, I stood off to the side, alone, listening as they noticed my gold tassel and loudly whispered, "*She's* graduating with honors?"

After the ceremony, my mother pulled me into a tight embrace. I was the first in our family to graduate from college, and we sobbed right there in a crowd of people, many of whom had terrorized me over the years. Through the tears, I thought I saw its reflection in a mylar balloon. That billowing costume, that wicked, wild grin. Those wide-open eyes—black, and its horns. The vejigante had come to celebrate with me.

In my room that night, I noticed a small, worn wooden statue on my dresser.

"It was your grandfather's," my father told me. "It's Saint James."

141

Finally, I had received my patron saint.

I asked why Saint James.

"It's said that Saint James aided once in defeating his enemies by dressing up his troops as vejigantes. He's a symbol of our culture and resilience. He is a symbol of the fight between good and evil in Puerto Rico. You have overcome a lot to get here. Things will never be easy, but you will overcome them. If our ancestors could endure what they did, you will do the same, endure."

Graduate school went a bit smoother, but still, even the person who you think is progressive is often the person to be the most shocked to see you sitting in the classroom. Most of my college career I have been the only Puerto Rican sitting in class. Most of my life, I have been the only Puerto Rican sitting in that room, that boardroom, boarding that plane to another city, state, country, seeking what my father sought all of his life—aventura.

Looking back on it now, all I can think is that I wasn't supposed to be there. I was not supposed to be in college. I was not supposed to be working as a flight attendant. I was not supposed to be in graduate school, with two degrees and a PhD. Like my father, decades before, to them I was supposed to be just a Puerto Rican washing dishes and working in a factory.

I thought we had progressed. I thought we had moved beyond all of the hate. We had Sonia Sotomayor serving as a United States Supreme Court Judge, after all. J.Lo, Marc Anthony, Ricky Martin, Lin Manuel Miranda, Benicio del Toro, Rita Moreno, Bruno Mars, Rosario Dawson—all famous Puerto Ricans. They had seen us. They knew us. So, I assumed things had changed.

When Hurricane Maria hit, all of those words struck again. They sliced.

I know about Puerto Rican girls.

Do you have papers?

Nice tits, you fucking spic.

Did you take a bath?

When you're hundreds or thousands of miles away and your family is being engulfed by a hurricane and there's nothing that you can do, you sit there in shock, a penetrating sting. Days after Maria hit, I remember sitting in my living room, speaking with strangers through a walkie-talkie app, begging for any information on Adjuntas or San Sebastian. Tired of the silence, Coco found a flight and made it to the island with cases of supplies, many of which were stolen after he landed. He managed to make it past toppled trees, flooded roads, and through the decimation to my grandmother's house in Adjuntas. We learned that my cousin Papo had taken on the grisly task of chauffeuring bodies from town into San Juan because Adjuntas did not have a working refrigeration system in its morgue. A trip that once took two hours became a day-long, overnight trek. People did what they could to survive.

I finally got in touch with my cousins, those cousins my mother had felt so sorry for after they left the US years before. They sent us pictures of themselves with their post-hurricane stash, Tostitos tortilla chips, canned cheese, and canned sausages. They sent us videos of them singing in the night, serenading the spirit of Borinquen. They were tired. They needed clean running water, but through all of that suffering they still smiled. They still laughed. They were successful.

They endured.

When things stabilized on the island, my father said it was time for him to return. It had been years since he visited. Perhaps before I had even started kindergarten. I worried about that trip, because I was worried about how the devastation on the island would affect him. Thousands had died. The infrastructure was still damaged in parts of the island, and while Puerto Ricans were getting their life back together, they were pained by the slow response and lack of attention to their suffering. They were Americans, after all, so why were their American brothers and sisters delaying aid? It was difficult enough to watch the tragedy unfold on television, but to be there, with the pain so raw? I did not know how we could process it, but my father insisted it was time for him to go home.

I purchased a plane ticket and rented a car. With the roads somewhat cleared, the drive from San Juan to Adjuntas took us a little over the estimated two hours. During the drive, my father told me all he knew about his family, that his grandfather had come from Spain, but he could not remember from where. He did remember that his grandfather's surname was Mendoza, as well. He said my mother's family was as difficult to trace back, but that her grandfather had come from the Canary Islands. Their surname was Nieves—the same group of immigrants who had given the town of San Sebastian its patron saint.

I would later learn that Nieves translates into "snows" and Mendoza means "cold mountain." Snows and cold mountain. It's brilliant that my parents found each other, two people from a warm island who settled in a cold city, whose names were both related to the cold.

On the drive, my father started talking to me about jíbaros, people from the mountains where he was from. He told me about their way of life, waking up early morning, putting on their güayabera shirt and pava hat, and reaching for their machete. They spent hours each morning clearing brush from around their mountain home and cultivating coffee beans and sugar cane.

As the car wound up the mountain I noticed a mist settling over the treetops. We climbed up the Ruta Panorámica, and my father told me about when he was a boy, and the first time he had ever seen an automobile. It was a Model T Ford and had to be cranked by hand. He said a white man came out of his car and offered my father and his friends money if they would help him start his car. My dad remembered clearly how the man looked that day, with his clean, pressed clothes, and how he thanked them all for their help. He then told me how once on the mainland he stopped in a diner for a cup of coffee. When the waitress noticed he didn't speak English, she told him to hurry up and finish his drink and get out, unless he wanted trouble.

"There's the good and there's the bad," he said.

My father told me about home altars. How many of the jíbaros did not have easy access to churches in the mountainous region. How getting down from that mountain would have taken too long and so many of them created small altars in their house. The altars would be decorated with rosaries, pictures of saints, family members, flowers, maybe even Milagros—metal religious folk charms used for healing. And of course there were the Santos, wooden hand-carved statues of saints. I thought of that small wooden statue my father had gifted me so many years ago. About patron saints and protection. I asked him, too, why Saint James, and he asked me what had taken me so long to ask.

We came to a crossroads and my father told me to go left, continuing upward, farther up into the mountain. He asked me if I remembered now why I had not been to any more Puerto Rican Day parades, or why we didn't own a Puerto Rican flag, and why I had never been to the island before now. I nodded my head slowly and silently

"Do you still have the vejigante mask?" he asked and I smiled.

"It's above my bed."

"Good. That's a safe place to keep it."

"The statue is on my dresser still, too," I said.

"And that is where they both should always be, watching over you."

We drove slowly, along a narrow mountain road, pockmarked with potholes, and my father suddenly asked me to stop the car. He got out of the car and stood facing the jungle. As I looked closely I could see a small wooden house deep within the brush that had long ago been consumed by the mountain.

"This is where I grew up," he said. "This is my home, and it's time."

I told him I was not ready, so we stood there for a long time, him telling me about my grandfather who would sit on the porch and wave at cars that went by. My father told me ghost stories about the mountain, how at night he heard the whispers of his ancestors, the Tainos—natives of the island of Borinquen, later renamed Puerto Rico by the Spanish conquistadors who came to our island home. He told me through tears how they came to kill and then to conquer. He told me how 300 years passed under Spanish rule and how our island was then handed to the United States and wrapped in an American flag. Our ancestors, he told me, had endured more than we could ever imagine, but still, they endured countless horrors, the theft of their homes, their land, their language, their religion, their identity—but that those who survived did so that I could stand here right now. Neither words nor hate could hurt me, my father reminded me.

When it was time, my father walked into the house that was no longer a house, but now a part of that great mountain. As the cool wind blew I heard the rustle of banana leaves, or was that the fluttering of flags?

I then drove to the small cemetery there in Adjuntas and sat at my father's grave.

My father had been struck and killed by a car on the parade route so many years before, when he chased after me. After my father was killed, my mother knew he would want to be buried here, his homeland.

I knew, in all of those moments of sorrow and pain, of feeling as though I did not belong—that I really did. That I belonged here *and* there. That I was both. That I straddled lands, identities, and beliefs, and that my father had sent me blessings of saints and devils to remind me that I would be okay, that I would be safe.

In my car, when I pulled on my seatbelt and adjusted the rearview mirror, I saw in it that satin, billowing fabric and that demon mask. El vejigante waved to me as I drove away, but I knew it was not goodbye. I knew that he would continue to serve as my guardian, reminding me that if my ancestors could persevere and if my father could, that I would, too.

FAT TUESDAY

CHRISTOPHER DAVID ROSALES

Ruben opened the front door to see his son hanging from the arms of two other boys on the porch. His son's friends, their hair messy-long on top and the sides as bald as their peeled eyes, suspended James between them so that James' calves, ending in Converse, collected below. His head sagged between his shoulders, hung so that Ruben could see the bruises on one side of his face. Ruben took his son in his arms and brought him inside. He kicked the stacks of graded papers off the couch and laid his son down. "Oh my god, what happened? Mijo, you'll be all right."

He called the policía first, then he called his wife, but she didn't answer. With one hand he smoothed James' black hair back and felt the *Tres Flores*, blood, and dirt stick to his palm, rubbed the shiny tips of his fingers together. His other hand floated above James' forehead as if he were about to take his temperature. Instead, for no reason he could imagine to himself, he smelled the scent of his son's hair on his fingers.

He went back to the porch, where the boys told Ruben how they had been to Toro's house, north, across the border. In L fucking A, near the San Gabriel river. James had wanted to see about some firme chick

148

who turned out to be Toro's niece. Toro didn't like James for that. Toro had said something about who Ruben had been before he became un profesor del culo. James got pissed and called Toro a puto, so Toro had pulled a nina and beat him with it, right there in the driveway in front of everybody, said he'd kill him if he ever came back. "And tell your pops. . . I know he ain't got no payback."

"Who's Toro? Does he go to your school?"

"He don't go to school," answered the one on the left. "He old. Like you."

Ruben clenched his other hand into a fist at his hip before hiding it in his slacks' pocket. "What's he, some dumbass gangbanger?"

"Yeah. But he's been banging a long time. Since you was young, even."

The sirens approached now in the faint radar way noise is heard in the poorer parts of the city, where whispers downpour from distant alleys, the police sirens shriek, and the *whoop whoop* of birds overhead is a species of helicopter. The boys flinched at the sounds, and it was a moment before the one on the right nodded to the other that it was time to go.

Ruben reached for their wrists. "You have to stay and talk to the police."

They backed off with their hands up, as if to say don't shoot the messenger. "I think you know him, Mr. Flores."

"Who? Toro?"

They walked faster now, heading toward the low-walled stucco apartments across the street. "Mike G. Didn't he used to bang with you when you was kids? Before you got into all that University T.J. shit?"

The two of them vaulted up and over the brick wall, their baggy shirts and jeans billowing. Ruben heard them crash into trashcans on the other side. Standing in the doorway between the darkening city outside and the cramped and sweaty safety of his home, he hated this man, Toro; but he also hated himself for not guarding James as he should have. He watched his son's chest rise and fall, and he listened to the ghettobird's whoops overhead, and the approaching sirens, until the police arrived. He rolled the sleeves of his shirt down to hide his tattoos, and he buttoned each cuff, before waving his arms. The police and EMTs tried to squeeze past his large frame before finally asking him to move. When he did move he stepped to the window facing the street and stood there with his arms crossed over his chest, staring down the street, pretending to see through every building and wall to his past's role in now.

After the reports, the questions and the hours spent in Hospital Ángeles, a gray-lidded doctor told Ruben that he'd need to admit James for the night. Maybe two. But the boy would sleep for now. Ruben went into the room—the beeping machines, the hiss of the oxygen mask deafening after the silence of the hall outside. He kissed his son on the cheek. It was too loud a smack and he regretted the sound instantly. He knew that while he'd been on campus his son had been moving through a different kind of world; Ruben had been distracted by work—a way to avoid thinking about his wife—but now saw the recent changes in his son as clear as the stitches that ran up and down the boy's face. He realized that the two worlds could not exist as one; that, like life and death, you could only pass from one to the other. Ruben didn't whisper apologies to James from the door, just told him he'd be back soon.

The old Mercury traveled Avenida de los Heroes surrounded by pickup trucks with filigreed paint above the wheel wells, motorcycles shiny and motorcycles old, and the occasional decrepit Ford with rotten wooden fencing along its bed—appliances, or alfalfa, or corn inside. *Dang, man, nothing feels right.* Rosary beads hung from the rearview mirror and Ruben thanked the Virgin that his son was safe. The car roared around the corner and he parked in front of his old neighbor's house, the kind of neighbor who was there when he was thirteen and would still be there at thirty-two, and Ruben walked across the dry grass to the black steel door.

He pushed the button, and Yasmín answered before the brass doorbell ceased to ring. She wore a tacky kimono of cherry blossoms and looked as if she'd practiced every facial expression she tried. She smiled. "I thought you might not come." She propped her right arm high in the doorway so that Ruben could see inside if he lowered his eyes.

"We had an emergency. I need you to stay with James at the hospital."

"I don't guess you called his mother?" She tugged the kimono down over her thighs, then up over her breasts, and crossed her arms.

"As soon as it happened." He turned his head away and pretended to track a stray dog up the street but its receding hips were blurry to him even though he stared. "He got mixed up with the wrong people, I guess."

She rolled her eyes. "Oh, really?"

"Call me if anything changes." He handed her the doctor's card on which he'd scribbled the boy's room number.

"And if she does actually show up?" She pointed nowhere relevant. "If she finds me there?"

"Don't sound so hopeful." He was already walking away. "You'll be disappointed."

BOTH SIDES

Along the highway, the Merc rode smooth, round and black like a bomb it was called in his old LA neighborhood. From inside, the view of his old city was like the view from a tank, more horizontal than vertical, and low along the ground. That close, riding over the textured asphalt was like crawling over a rug in the dark, searching for its end. Instead of the street stable beneath the moving car, it was pulled beneath by a hand unseen.

On either side of Alondra Boulevard were trees with white trunks, and these gave way to smaller and darker trees, and these gave way to none—just telephone poles and jaundiced streetlamps. When he got to the square shop on the corner, the one with the enormous donut on top, he turned left on Atlantic. A yellow-haired woman in low-cut scarecrow rags stood on the corner and called out her price. He watched her in the side-view mirror flipping him off.

Down a side street and still another, he stopped before a small house guarded by a low, chain-link fence. There was dirt where grass should have been, and a white pit bull roaming out front. Ruben opened the car door and stepped out, but the dog charged the fence and Ruben ducked back inside. The dog snarled, leapt, and its head snapped back for the chain attached to its collar. It flipped backward. It wasted no time whimpering but growled and barked while its head jerked back and forth so quickly it seemed to have many.

From behind the metal screen door of the house a voice called out, "Who's there?"

Ruben shut the car door softly, holding the latch but keeping the keys in his hand. "It's me."

"Who the fuck is *me*?"

Ruben moved forward and the man inside opened the screen and pushed his face into the porchlight. There was the same horseshoe mustache running up over his lip, the same squinting eyes that seemed closed while he looked Ruben over. The dog kept barking and the old friend called Chino turned the porchlight off. It was as dark as the night can be in the city; radiant with the artificial light that fills the sky and fills the eyes with the falseness of what one attempts to see in the dark below. Chino cursed at the dog to shut up, but it didn't.

Ruben stepped toward the fence and the pit bull dove. Again, the chain snapped the dog back, but not before Ruben was hit with spit and the dog's sour breath condensed fog in the air.

"Watch out, pendejo. You're gonna hurt my dog. Stay back so she don't fight the chain." Chino walked off of the porch and led the dog back and out of sight. He returned, waddling, holding either pant leg at the thigh to keep his baggy jeans up out of the dirt. "She's worth a grip of cash." His white T-shirt hung from his skeletal frame as it would from a hanger. "She fights for me, so I'm protective."

"She looks like *she* needs protection." Ruben raised a hand to offer a shake. "It's been a while."

Chino slapped Ruben's hand away. "Shit, Profesor." They hugged and slapped backs. "Get the fuck in the house, homie. It's been about a minute."

When they entered they stepped on ragged, vomit-toned carpet. The walls inside bore sparse patches of '70s wallpaper in orange and yellow crescents, and a big-screen television occupied most of one wall. It wasn't a small wall.

On either side of the TV were enormous speakers, like columns beneath the low ceiling. Children's toys littered the floor, and a pile of weed centered the glass coffee table. Ruben focused on a Tonka truck near an end-table leg. An oversized black leather couch filled the room and, when Chino sat, it huffed, the protective plastic crackling the death-rattle of a dying rhino. Chino cleaned the weed, squinting his eyes at the green tufts between his fingers. "I didn't think I'd ever

153

see you again, ese. I thought you'd moved on. You know, bigger and better things."

"You haven't." Ruben stood in the center of the room, in front of the TV. "Seen me, I mean."

"Sure, I get it. Beef with the police? What'd you do, Profesor?" He looked up with a crooked smile on his face. "Forget to return your library books?" He laughed and the dog barked in the backyard and Chino laughed louder still, and then barked too. Ruben did not laugh and Chino's face went blank. "Serio, homes, you? You didn't do anything, did you?"

"Where's Toro?"

Chino plucked seeds from the shake on the coffee table. "Chingón."

"Where?"

"Stay the fuck away." He pinched some seeds into his mouth and rolled them along his inner lip. "Whatever it is, ain't worth it. You shouldn't be messing around, Profesor. Ain't you got rich white kids in Mex-i-co to teach?"

"Fuck you."

"I'm just being real here. You ain't seen me in years and now—"

"Toro beat my son. My *son*."

Chino set his elbows on his knees and leaned forward as if to see Ruben's face better in the dim light. He sighed in the stillness. "What do you want from me, ese?"

Ruben said, "Go for a ride with me."

"I don't go for rides no more. 'Specially not with people like you. If you got too much to lose you bound to lose it, hermano. Every time."

"No one changes much."

"Yeah, well I ain't gonna stick around to see you prove it."

"I did enough—back when. Where were you to kill those doubts then?" Ruben dropped his arms to his sides. His fingers opened and closed. "You don't have to come now, but I've done worse for you. Just tell me where to find him."

"Fine." Chino lowered his head and shook it. "I'll get the guns. You ain't going alone."

"No guns."

"Fuck you, no guns. You think I'm going for moral support? You want that shit, you take your wife."

Ruben grunted.

Chino stepped off into a short dark hallway. Ruben watched him stand before a dresser. Chino took a gun from beneath his shirt and another from a drawer and set one on the dresser. He began to load them with a jeweler's finesse.

Ruben stepped outside, smelled smoke, and looked down the street past the yards that grew narrow as the road curved away from the concrete riverbed. The 710 crossed over the thin river far below, and in the dark space beneath the overpass a trashcan fire burned. The firelight painted the men surrounding the can. They shared outbursts of laughter. Above them were blurry yellow and red light-trails of movement on the freeway and, behind, palm trees glowed in the streetlights. Ruben thought about what he wanted for his son, for himself, and knew that searching for it day and night wouldn't matter if he used the wrong map.

The metal door behind him screeched open. Chino pushed past him and pressed a towel into his stomach. "Take it, homes."

Ruben unwrapped the towel and a gun rested within: not cold and dead, as he'd expected, but warm and full of potential. God, he was losing it with the sentimentality already. He placed the gun inside the waist of his slacks and let the towel drop to his loafers. The two of them walked down the steps of the porch and out of the yard. The car rumbled to a start and they drove away from the freeway, turned left onto Compton Boulevard. Once, they had tried to change the street's name to Somerset. And on the safe side of town, they'd succeeded.

Deeper and deeper into the city the buildings were smaller but more colorful. It was depressing for Ruben to see his old neighborhood so dark and empty of any ornamentation, like the "Welcome to..." signs missing proper city names or stolen and replaced by graffiti.

"Do you still have your tattoos?" Chino thrummed his fingers on the dash. Turned music up. Turned it down.

Ruben looked at his arms and imagined the tattoos that covered his skin beneath the blue fabric of his collared dress shirt. Even now, on his mission, he hid the tattoos he once wore to show that he had kept company with other men who sought the very same things that he did now. "I thought about having them removed. Do you have any new ones?"

"I got these three ladies on my neck."

Ruben could only make out smudges on the side and back of Chino's neck as Chino turned in the seat. He realized that Chino had not registered much with him, that he had been a presence and nothing more: a thought in the back of his mind. He took out his cell phone and dialed his wife. Chino was still talking, but stopped when he saw the phone pressed to Ruben's face. It rang again and again, and finally Ruben left a voicemail saying, "James was beat up pretty bad. You should see him."

"You know, you might want to hear this shit." Chino choked his own throat, a caress. "I like these ones the best. The one on this side, she's my gangsta bitch. She's that bitch that backs you up no matter what, fool. And the one back here, she's my little hoodrat. She's that lady that's down for whatever you want, whenever you want it. She gives you that love and she don't ask questions. And on this side, the side above my heart, that's my decent woman. She don't ever mess up on you, and you always come home to her. She's the one you love and that loves you. When I meet a lady, I know right away which one she's gonna be. I never met one that's all three."

"Yeah. Well." Ruben grinned across the shiny leather cab. "Things aren't that easy."

"Hell yeah they are." Chino turned to face him. He silenced the radio. "I know what I'm up against. Serio, homes, you fooling yourself more than any other."

"I just mean that bad and good aren't mutually exclusive."

"What the fuck you mean *mutually exclusive*? Talk real to me."

"Forget it."

"I see, homes." Chino waited for Ruben to look into his eyes. "You thought you had one kind, but you got another."

A flash of blue and red flew through the rear window and bathed everything inside the vehicle. A siren chirped and buzzed and Ruben saw a piece of a police car in the rearview mirror, his rosary dangling from it, twisting and untwisting itself, swaying into and out of the headlights' flooding.

Ruben pulled over and the vehicle stopped behind him. In the side-view mirror he saw the chrome buckle and blue legs of the approaching cop. He rolled down the window.

"License and registration, please."

Ruben handed the cop his papers from the glove box and pulled his wallet from his pocket. He made sure that his university ID showed along with his driver's license when he handed the wallet over.

"Do you know that your vehicle is in violation, sir? It's too low, and the brake lights don't work."

The cop brought his mustached face down to the level of the open window. He examined Chino at length. Chino shifted nervously in his seat and he looked side to side and behind the way he always had, the way a boxer does. Ruben thought of the gun at Chino's waist, the gun at his own. He thought of James, of his reaction when he finds out his father had been arrested. Ruben feared there would be no one left to take care of him. He began to sweat, and conscious of this, became conscious that he had never felt this nervousness before. Not because he had never been in a similar situation, he had been in much worse, but instead because he had never thought about consequences. "I'm sorry, Officer. See, we were at a university down south. There's a car club for the underprivileged. I'm the sponsoring professor, and his car broke down. I offered him a ride. I don't normally drive this one. I guess I was just excited to show it off."

The cop handed everything back through the window. "It's not too smart for you to be driving a car like this through this city." The cop looked at Ruben's dress shirt and undone tie, and across at Chino's white T-shirt and tattooed neck. "There's a lot of trash around here." He stood up straight and spit down onto the street, scraped the foamy spot over with his boot, and walked back to the car. When he drove past, Chino reached to the radio and tuned it to an oldies station. He turned the volume as high as it would go. Ruben snapped it off and they glared at each other until Ruben shook his head and drove on in silence, Chino still staring, fuzzy in the periphery like Ruben's memories.

"Turn left." Chino snapped his fingers along with his order, smirking. "It's the house on the right." He jutted his chin at a crooked house shoved between a liquor store and an apartment complex. The fence-poles stood but the chain-links sagged over the yard like a safety net. A child's Big Wheel lay overturned in the patchy grass, black belly turned to the stars. The driveway was not like Ruben had imagined it would be; it was clean. In his mind's eye he saw Toro taking a water hose to his son's blood, washing it down into the gutter with oil and dirt.

"Fuck him." Ruben parked the car and threw the door open.

"He's probably waiting for you." Chino grabbed Ruben's arm.

"To him no one else exists." Ruben reached down to his waist and Chino put his arm out to stop him.

"I bet he has a lot of vatos with him. They probably don't know you exist, neither."

"They'll know soon."

"They could kill you."

"I could kill them." Ruben stood out of the car and walked down the long driveway, past the front door covered in weathered plywood. A brand new door packaged in bubble-wrap leaned against the wall beside it. Around back a dim light shone down through a broken pane of glass in the back kitchen window. Ruben took the concrete steps in twos and Chino shuffled up sideways and jumped in front of him.

"Maybe you'd better check on your son first. Just call."

Ruben paused, but he knew that if he stopped his forward momentum now he would never get it back. He knocked on the door and Chino pushed him down off the stairs. "Stop, puto. Just get out of here."

"What the fuck are you doing?"

Movement in the house. A ghost-white face appeared in the window and disappeared. The same face appeared in the doorway as the door creaked open: a young woman. Her delicate brown hand rested on the door and her white made-up face disconnected her from her body. "Who's this?" She looked at Ruben gently and that frightened him, her calm resting beneath high and thin brows and beneath still higher feathered hair, stiff like a cheap wig. She moved with otherworldly calculation.

"Where's Toro?" Ruben heard heavy footsteps inside. He said it louder, "Where's Toro?"

She tilted her head sideways. "Why would he be *here*?"

"Go on, fool." Chino pushed Ruben's shoulder. "Get outta here."

"Are you that boy's father?" She stepped down one foot, pointing a long maroon fingernail at Ruben. She looked at Chino. "Is he that boy's father?"

Chino reached his hand out for Ruben's shoulder and Ruben snapped his head toward him and back at the woman. "Let him see." Chino lowered his arm. The woman stepped aside.

Ruben stepped up into the darkness of a living room lit only by the television. It glowed on the floor in front of the fireplace and a naked toddler sat in front. A woman filled the expanse of a couch on the nearest wall; she looked him up and down and gave a bright grin before returning her stare to the television.

"Where is he?" Ruben turned a circle in the living room.

The fat woman looked up again. "¿Cómo?"

Ruben stepped back, bumping into the woman he came to realize was Chino's girlfriend. He tripped out of the kitchen and down the concrete steps, grasping at the wooden rail. "What are you trying to pull, goddammit?"

"I didn't think you'd take this shit so far." Chino made pistols with his fingers and pressed each temple. "I thought you'd puss out when I brought out the guns."

"Where are we?"

"This is my hyna's pad." He pointed at the woman and child. "My baby's mama. I tried to stall you out."

"Why bother?"

"No sé, ese." Chino pulled the gun out from under his shirt, where it had been resting next to a glinting silver buckle the shape of a marijuana leaf. "I figure some of us just belong here, others don't. Did you expect me to sell Toro out, homes? That fool would kill me. For what? For some buster who can't keep eye on his kid? Not even your own wife, vato." He pointed the gun at Ruben. "You been gone too long."

Ruben pulled his gun too and the girl in the doorway screamed. He looked up at her but she was not looking at him. She had pulled her wandering child back into the house and was crouched between the child and the guns in the flickering TV light. "Put them away, guys. Please, the baby."

"Yours ain't loaded, cabrón." Chino knocked the end of the pistol against his head. "Just go home."

Ruben looked down his arm, down the blue dress shirt to the buttoned wrist, to the hand that didn't seem his own. He opened it and he felt the gun slip. It clattered on the cement. He swept his eyes over Chino and the barrel in the air before him, over the girl standing in the doorway with the child wrapped in her arms, and back out onto the street where his car leaned its shadow forward under the streetlamps. He listened to Chino go inside, with the girl and child, and close the door, but he didn't watch.

Ruben got in the car and put the keys in the ignition. He pulled out his cell phone and called his wife but there was no answer, so he called twice more. About to put his hand back on the key, he stopped and flipped down the visor instead. There was a picture there of his wife and his son with him when he'd graduated wearing that ridiculous wizard's costume of a "doctor." He took the picture down. Even then his wife's eyes flared, haunted, summoned somewhere she felt lost.

He remembered that night when, screaming, crying, she'd kicked everyone out of their home. She disappeared for a week and returned looking strung out. She didn't speak. She just ate all of the week-old chocolate cake he and James had been saving to eat together when she returned. Then she passed out on the couch.

He returned the picture to its place underneath the rubber band on the visor and put the visor up. The white-faced girl stood on the lawn

161

beside his car. "I know about your son. I was there." She looked back over her shoulder. "Toro lives ten blocks down. Behind the old church. You can't miss it. There are always tons of people out front. He's too stupid to think he'll get caught. He'll be there."

Ruben started the car. "Thanks."

"You've got a rosary." She bent down to look at it hanging from the mirror. "It's pretty." She had a tattoo of the Virgin Mary on her chest and blue tears fell from the Virgin's eyes down into the darkness inside her halter-top. "What do you believe?"

Ruben looked over her shoulder, scared he believed he'd be killed.

"Yeah." She kissed two fingers and touched the half rolled down window. "I don't know either. Be careful."

He passed the church with its tall crucifix facing out over the street. Fat Tuesday had come and nearly gone, and in the morning the church would be full; everyone, even those who didn't normally go to church, would line up to confess sins, have ashes rubbed onto their forehead to mark the beginning of the fast. He doubted if wrongs could be righted so easily. He parked and walked around the corner.

Down the street, at the back of the old church, was a squat gray house with police cars out front. A crowd had gathered on the sidewalk and yellow tape was draped between the hydrant and the fence, then the fence and the orange caution cone, and then the cone and the hydrant. Ruben stepped closer, trying to see over the backs of bald heads and past the young cop telling everyone to back up, go home.

Ruben's phone rang and he pulled it from his pocket.

"Is he okay?" It was Sandra, but there was too much noise to hear her clearly.

"Not sure. I had to leave the neighbor with him for now. Are you going to see him?"

"I can't. Tell him I said I love him. I love you."

"What are you doing? Why don't you come home?"

The music in the background grew louder. "I can't hear you." A man shouted her name.

"I've gotta go."

"Sandra—"

"I've gotta go now."

He hung up and pushed past one man and then another. Ruben moved forward until, standing before the cop, his belly pushed against the tape. The feeling was so light but so exhausting. A broke-down car up the driveway leaked oil and some of it collected in pools within the taped off section. There were old stains on the cement but there also seemed to be different stains: lighter, the color of rust. In the back of one of the police cars sat a man about Ruben's age but Ruben couldn't see his face; it was disjointed by the metal grate dividing the criminal from the cops. Scrambled voices polluted the air, coming in bursts from police radios, and the police drove off. The crowd lost interest and dispersed. Only one child looked back, lips smeared by the clown makeup of chilied dried prunes.

Ruben stared at the driveway framed by the border of yellow tape, and reached. Though he was too far to touch any dirty cement, he squinted past his outstretched hand. He needed to know: Which stains oil? Which stains dirt? And which stains…not?

THE OTHER FOOT

Rob Hart

Bullets shred the front of the house, raining splinters on Nic's shoulders. He presses himself against the scuffed floor, holds his hand on the back of Rita's neck, pushing down hard to keep her from getting up. Her face is scrunched like she's crying, but he can't hear it over the sound of the bullets. Even if she is crying, he doesn't know about what: the fusillade, or the way his hand is yanking her hair, or the way he's pressing so hard his arm aches.

He resets his grip as the splinters of wood pile on his shoulders and in the crook of his neck, and then there's a great silence, the air thick with smoke and debris. Truck headlights glare through the windows and shredded walls, lighting the front room of the house in a vicious white glow.

Nic expects them to say something, to make some kind of threat or warning, but nothing comes, just the hum of truck engines. He can't remember the last time he heard engines. Weeks probably. Normally it'd provide a kind of comfort, like maybe the world was getting back to normal. Now the low rumble sounds like the threat of a wild animal.

"Stay quiet, sweetheart," Nic says to Rita, keeping his voice low. "Just, please, stay quiet, okay?"

Rita sniffles. Tears cut clean streaks down her dirty face. He wonders how much she actually understands about all this. He hopes she doesn't understand it. That one day she forgets this feeling, of being chased down by men who call themselves patriots, of having to push their way into a house that may offer salvation or may have its own hidden dangers.

Maybe it's good she remembers, because that'll mean she survived the night.

"Good girl," Nic says, looking around the house for something— anything at all—and he notices a door in the hallway leading to the kitchen, and behind it, a set of eyes, glowing in the light of the trucks. He shifts to get a better look. A hand snakes out of the gap, beckons to him.

He doesn't know what it means. Friend or foe. He just knows it looks like the door leads into the basement, and the basement is not outside.

"Okay, sweetie, listen to me," Nic says, turning Rita toward the hand. "Over there, okay? Crawl over there. Stay close to the floor."

Rita starts, moving slowly. She raises herself off the floor and he presses down on her butt, on her unicorn stretch pants, to make sure she stays as low as possible, in case the bullets start again. They get most of the way to the basement door when there's a crash behind them, then the thud of something landing to their left.

Nic thinks: grenade. He holds his breath, prepares to crawl over Rita's body, and prays the person in the basement is even the slightest bit kind, that they'll accept protection of a fatherless four-year-old girl, but in the corner of his eye he sees that what the men threw in was a human foot.

It's old, the skin gray, a piece of dull bone sticking out the end. Now that he realizes what it is, he registers the stink. He shifts his body so Rita can't see it.

165

BOTH SIDES

A voice rises up from outside, full of laughter and glee.

"Can't get across no border with no feet, can ya?"

That's met with a string of whoops and laughter. A fissure opens in Nic's heart—how can people be like this?—as he pushes harder for the basement door, and as they get closer it opens wider and the hand reaches for Rita, pulling her into the dark.

Nic follows, sliding down the staircase, staying low even though the bullets shouldn't be able to get him here. At the bottom of the stairs the shadows are gently shoved away by flickering candlelight, and he sees the source of the eyes and the hand.

It's an older woman, dressed in boots and khakis and a T-shirt, her graying hair tied back in an efficient bun. Her face appears kind, a snap assessment Nic hopes is true.

Rita stands next to the woman, gripping her leg. Nic's breath catches in his chest, and maybe it's because for two days now he's been giving nearly all his food and water to Rita, and delirium is buzzing around his head like a swarm of flies, but instead of the woman, he sees Maritza.

It's the way Rita is holding the woman's leg, which is how, before she learned to walk, she would pull herself to standing on Maritza's leg, and Rita would stand there and laugh, like this knowledge of how to move vertically was her first step toward conquering the world. Over the smell of mold and gunpowder Nic detects a hint of the perfume Maritza would wear, and he wants to reach out to her, to fall into her so she can hold him up, like the way she always did.

But then the woman says, "Follow me."

And her voice is wrong. Deeper, without the trace of Maritza's accent, and Nic swallows and wishes he could go back to the moment before, even if it wasn't true.

It was enough, though. It makes him remember the promise he made to Maritza.

He sets his back, tenses his shoulders, and follows after.

On the other end of the sparse basement is a room. The woman brings them inside and closes the heavy door. She pulls a chain hanging from the ceiling and a small lightbulb warms to life. The room is stocked with supplies. There's a cot, just the one. The supplies are neat and orderly and mostly untouched so she must not be living down here. Nic reaches over and pats the wall as the woman closes the door and spins the wheel on the door and there's a heavy *thunk*.

"Three feet of concrete," she says. "They won't get in here."

Nic nods. "They might wait."

The woman shrugs. "They could."

"You know them?"

The woman nods like she's remembering the death of a loved one. "The Liberty Boys. I've seen them around. This is the first time they shot up my house, though. Not too thrilled about that."

Nic notices Rita standing in the corner, arms crossed, looking down at the floor, the way she gets around other adults. He picks her up, presses her face to his chest, and she cries. He holds her tight, but not too tight, afraid of hurting her now that he's done having to push her into the floor, and he puts his free hand on the woman's shoulder and says, "Thank you…"

The woman nods. "Susan."

"Nic. This is Rita."

"Just the two of you?"

Nic hesitates before nodding, and Susan sees it, that chasm inside him, and reaches out and squeezes his shoulder, says, "Can she have c-a-n-d-y?"

Rita perks up a little, raising her face away from Nic's shoulder, recognizing the series of letters, and Susan laughs.

"Smart kid," she says.

"She loves to read," Nic says. "She reads to me some nights, even though she's making up most of the words. And yes, she can have some. I hate to ask since you're already putting yourself out for us, but I left my pack upstairs. Do you have any water?"

She nods, points to the cot. "Sit."

Nic does, and feels that weight of the world he'd been carrying for the past few weeks suddenly come off his shoulders a bit, if just for a few moments, and he wants to lie down and sleep, to just lie there with Rita and hold her and maybe even allow himself the indulgence of crying, but he doesn't, because he can't. Not in front of Rita.

He watches as Susan roots around until she finds a bottle of water, which she hands him, and he offers Rita a bit. She wraps her lips around the mouth of the bottle and immediately backwashes into it, and he laughs, lets her have her fill, and takes his own drink.

When they're done, Susan is holding out a chocolate bar. It's a wrapper he doesn't recognize, some kind of off-brand, and Rita eyes it with suspicion until she remembers she's four and it's candy, so she takes it and mumbles a whispered, "Thank you."

"Still has good manners. You're doing a good job, Dad." Susan sits on the far end of the cot, giving them space. "So, you headed to the border?"

"Thanks," Nic says. Rita is struggling with the wrapper so he takes the candy bar out of her hands and opens it. Considers taking a bite because his stomach is twisted up on itself, but it's more important that Rita eat, so he hands it to her and she leans against the wall, taking small nibbles. "Border, yeah. Is it true? They still have power on the other side?"

Susan nods. "They do. Not too far from here, even."

"Does anyone know why?"

"Some fella came through here a few weeks back," Susan says, taking a bottle of water for herself and cracking the cap. "Some kind of scientist. According to him, the electrical grids in the US are a lot more sophisticated than down in Mexico, which actually made ours *more* vulnerable to that big solar flare that hit us." She pauses, thinks. "Corona something…"

"Coronal mass ejection," Nic says.

She snaps her finger. "That's what he called it." She raises her hands, like she's cradling something. "So there's also a whole lot more bedrock north of the equator, and when the burst hit, all that energy wanted to go somewhere, which in the US was right into the grids. Whereas down in Mexico a lot of that energy dissipated into the soil. So essentially, the entire US grid got fried to a crisp, but Mexico came through it pretty good. I heard there are still some dark spots, but they're a lot closer to being back online. Up here, he said it'll be ten years at least, and that's optimistic." She drops her hands into her lap. "But who knows? I'm not a scientist."

"Why are you still here?"

"Folks like you and your girl," she says, glancing down at Rita and smiling. "People need a waypoint. Place to stop, rest up, get water. Hell, had those idiots outside not shown up, I'd probably be having this conversation with you anyway, just under less tenuous circumstances. Anyway, I moved out here for a reason. It's quieter. Whether I have electricity or not doesn't much change things for me."

"I can't thank you enough," Nic says. "I just… I wish I knew why those assholes…" He stops, glances at Rita, who doesn't seem to be listening. "I don't know why they're after us. I thought people like that just wanted to stop folks from coming into the United States. Why would they care that I'm going the other way?"

Susan leans forward. Takes a long sip of water. Sighs hard, her body nearly deflating as she does.

"They like to say it's because they don't want our sweat and labor helping another country get back online," Susan says. "They think folks ought to be *here*. But you know, it was never about whatever talking point they were clinging to...”

She takes a long sip of water.

“The cruelty was always the point,” she says.

She lets that hang for a moment, that pats the cot and slides to the floor, picks up a battered paperback. “Get some sleep. You look like you need it. I’ll keep watch. With any luck they’ll get bored and move on.”

Nic starts to formulate a protest, but Rita is already chewing on the last of her chocolate and curling into a ball next to him, so he kicks his legs out and wraps around her, pulling her little body tight into his, and he puts his nose into her dark, tangled hair. Says, “You are the very best little girl.”

He breathes in the smell of her hair and sweat, and by the time he exhales, he’s asleep.

He dreams of running, but his legs are slow, like he’s moving through water, his feet barely touching the ground, and he leans forward, trying to use his hands too, to pull himself forward.

He dreams of faceless monsters in the desert and the low rumble of their threats. He never sees them, just knows they’re there, lurking on the edge of the shadows.

He dreams of Rita and Maritza.

He dreams of fire.

No, not a dream. Something acrid strikes his nose. He coughs. Looks up at the vent in the upper corner of the shelter, sees thin tendrils of smoke seeping through the slats. Susan, kneeling down with her back to him, is looking up at it, too. She goes back to rummaging through a footlocker and turns around with two gas masks. “Don’t have a third.”

Nic nods. “You take one, give Rita the other.”

Susan thrusts one of them at him. “It’s yours.”

Nic smiles. “Women and children first.”

"First off, that's a bit regressive," Susan says. "Anyway, rules have changed. I don't have a little girl to look after. Take the damn thing, will you?"

Nic takes one and puts it over Rita's face, fiddling with the straps until it fits her. She protests and tugs at it and he pats her, trying to keep her calm. "Please, honey, just breathe deep, and don't take it off, okay?" Then he stands and is about to hand the other mask back to Susan, but both her hands are full with the AR-15 she's holding across her chest.

"Me and them boys out there were going to have this out sooner or later," she says. "They suspected I was helping people like this and they been waiting for an excuse, and, well, the law don't mean much around here these days. And I ain't going to let them win. The reason those chickenshits are burning the place down is because they're afraid to come in. They want us to run out."

She opens the door of the shelter, to a basement hazy with smoke. The engines still roar outside, interrupted by the occasional hoot and holler, or the crack of a gunshot into the night sky. Susan leads them across the basement to an old shelving unit heavy with painting supplies and rusted tools. She grabs it, and with a grunt and a groan she pulls it aside. It opens onto a dark corridor. She hands him a lantern, a small thumb of flame flickering in the middle.

"What is this?" Nic asks, peering into the void at the smooth walls, the aged wood beams holding it up. "This looks like it's been here for a long time."

"It runs about a half mile under the border and into the desert," Susan says, checking over the gun. "If you get lucky you'll come across the federales. They patrol the border, help people cross over, fight back against these idiots. Bit of a gamble, but hey," she says, glancing over her shoulder at a volley of gunshots from outside. "Pretty nice of them, considering how we used to treat their people."

Nic raises an eyebrow at her. "Something tells me this isn't an escape tunnel."

Susan shakes her head. "I've been looking to take a chunk out of these boys for a long time now. But let's just say..." Susan's gaze trails off along with her voice before snapping back. "Let's say I have some things I'm working on making up for. And that's why you need to keep that little girl safe." Susan reaches down and ruffles Rita's dark hair. "Make this count."

"You're going to hold them off with that?" Nic asked.

"Told you, I been waiting for this day. I got a few more surprises in store for them." She slaps him hard on the back. "Now go on, Dad. Keep teaching her good manners."

She turns and disappears into the smoke engulfing the basement. Nic wraps his hand around Rita's, her little fingers disappearing into his palm, and he pulls her forward into the dark, holding the lantern ahead of him, the light barely making a dent. When he's far enough he can't see the basement anymore, there's a great *thump*, and the tunnel shakes, dust cascading onto his shoulders, and Nic says a little prayer that Susan took out that chunk she was looking for.

When Rita starts to fall behind Nic pulls off his mask and yanks her onto his hip, holding the lantern out with the other hand, jogging until they come to the end, to an old wooden ladder leaned up against the packed earth.

He puts the lantern down next to Rita and tells her to wait. She nods, and he climbs up, presses his hands above him and feels plywood. He pushes hard, ends up with a mouth full of sand, but gets the thing aside and sees the sky above him, starlight scatted like diamonds. He reaches down and pulls up Rita and takes a fleeting moment to point up, to show it to her, because he wants her to see something beautiful.

"Aren't we lucky to have met someone so nice tonight? And don't the stars look pretty?" Nic asks, looking at her, desperate almost, and when she smiles his heart fills up, and he's glad to know that this night may include the seed of something good that might one day grow to blot out these feelings of terror.

"Daddy?" she asks. Then she states it: "Daddy."

"Yes, sweetheart?"

She leans into Nic and says, "You are the bery best daddy."

Nic swallows hard. Almost shatters, but holds it together. He takes that swell of emotion and uses it as fuel. His body simply forgets how exhausted he is, how long it's been since he's eaten. He climbs out of the hole, hears those engines in the distance. Behind him he can just make out the smoke against the sky, and the twinkle of the flaming house, red and orange flapping in the air like a flag.

Far in front of him, twin beams of light bounce in unison as they travel over the rough terrain. And beyond that, more starlight. In the last several weeks of traveling south through a powerless America, he hasn't seen anything close to this much light.

Everything is muddy and dark, so he holds Rita close and runs hard in the opposite direction of the engines, focusing on the ground, looking for the smoothest path he can. He knows if he stumbles or falls, twists or breaks an ankle, that'll be the end of it.

And he wonders, briefly, if him having a child with him would make any difference to the men chasing him. The men whose faces he hasn't even seen, whose lives he has never touched, whom he has never wronged or even interacted with, but who want him dead nonetheless.

It wouldn't matter, though. It never did.

The cruelty was the point.

With the rumbled threat of the engines growing behind him, Nic runs harder, toward those bouncing beams of light, and the promise he made Maritza.

WAW KIWULIK

By J. Todd Scott

"They can't," Joaquin says, glancing back at the camouflaged knot of men behind him, circling the spider hole.

"No, they *won't*," Nico answers, his eyes—his anger and frustration—hidden by dark Oakleys.

But not well.

Joaquin, his gray eyes now fixed on the fiery ceiling of a late afternoon Sonoran sky, shrugs.

"They're Shadow Wolves," Nico pushes. "This is what they do, Quino. *When one wolf finds the prey, it calls in the pack.* All that shit."

"No," Joaquin says, "this is what they *choose* to do."

"But not that?"

Joaquin only shrugs again, shouldering his AR-15, staring at the sunset.

Nico knows he's fallen into some sort of mystical, circular O'odham logic…as round and deep and mysterious as the empty spider hole it took their team three days to find.

He'll never quite get it—and never fucking escape it.

"What about you?" Nico asks, although he's already resigned to the answer.

"I choose to stay out of it, amigo," Joaquin says with a smile, and a resigned look of his own he doesn't even try to hide.

They check coordinates and take a water break six hundred feet above the desert floor in the long, dusky shadows of nearby Baboquivari Peak.

The rugged mountain is the most sacred site on the Tohono O'odham Nation.

More than two million acres of O'odham land stretch in all directions below them; raw, unforgiving, southern Arizona desert. The Sonoran Desert. The color of pale bone and dried blood; crisscrossed haphazardly by torchwood copal and mesquite and scrub and calcified ridge lines. Blocky mesas rise like teeth in the distant horizon. From up here, Special Agent Nico Costa can see into Sonora, Mexico, itself. The O'odham have always lived on both sides of the border, even though their ancestral lands were carved up more than 150 years ago by the Gadsden Purchase.

A sale no one bothered to tell them about.

As compensation, tribal members have been historically allowed to move back and forth freely over the border for religious pilgrimages; to visit southern family members, to buy and trade and sell. O'odham culture is a unique mix of Native, American, and Mexican. Sells, Arizona, the capital of the Nation, has both a Basha's grocery store and the Gu Achi trading post.

Supposedly, in O'odham, Sells translates to "Tortoise got wedged."

But over time, immigration and drug issues started to take precedence over tribal freedoms, and the US government forced them to use a handful of loosely monitored gates, little more than steel and concrete posts and wire in the scrub.

Now, they're down to one—the San Miguel gate. Or as the

O'odham call it, the Wo'osan Gate.

With a tribal ID card, tribal members can still cross the border at Wo'osan, but it bothers the O'odham *they* have to prove anything at all; that they need to justify their ancestral right-of-way across land that has always been theirs.

Every crossing is like cutting your arm to show the blood beneath your skin.

Once called the Pima, or the Papago, they call themselves the O'odham.

The Desert People.

Yet, even as the O'odham continue to adhere to laws they didn't make and borders they didn't draw, the cartels—the narcos—indiscriminately use their ancient and sacred trails. The reservation and Mexico share about seventy-five miles of border, and the narcos claim much of it as their own, spinning a tangled spiderweb of smuggling routes on both sides of it. They employ human mule trains and blacked-out vehicles stolen from Phoenix and Tucson—even horses—to move coke, meth, marijuana, and fentanyl through the desert. They leave their dead behind in the unforgiving terrain, and some have taken to marrying tribal members to increase their access to the reservation. And although the O'odham have always pushed back at these incursions, even allowing a broader US border enforcement presence and endless sensors and cameras across their sacred lands, it's never enough.

We always want more, Nico thinks. *Just like the narcos.*

Like this specialized border task force, made up of federal agents like Nico himself, and tribal police like Joaquin, and the last few Shadow Wolves—the infamous Native American trackers. The narcos put spotters high up on the peaks and ridges, young men armed with two-way radios and binoculars and even NVGs, to help guide drug caravans over the border, routing them safely past Border Patrol units and helicopters. They hide in caves, these spider holes, for days on end, drinking bottled water and eating Spam and beans and tortillas and oranges and scanning both the endless sky and the desert.

They make more money for their families in a week than they'd make otherwise in a year.

Last month, Nico's task force found a granite rock outside a cave that had been marked like a monthly calendar, each day gone by scratched off with a blade into the quartz.

They've been on the hunt for this most recent redoubt for days, and Nico figures they're less than thirty minutes behind the scout who was hiding here. They've nicknamed him Rabbit, something that sounds like "tobi" in O'odham, because of the man's small footprint and light tread. The Wolves joke that he hops across the desert, hiding behind the saguaros and barrel cacti. They've been after Rabbit for weeks now, almost all summer, and he's fast, elusive, and very, very good.

The remains of his small fire are still ashy and warm; a cracked Motorola radio has been unceremoniously left behind in a tangle of blankets and burlap and old clothing.

Three black jugs of sweating water still sit in the cooler shadows of the deep hole itself.

But the Shadow Wolves who found this remote cave have chosen not to go any farther. The mysterious scout has retreated up the flanks of Baboquivari Peak, what they call Waw Kiwulik. It is their most sacred place and the home of I'itoi, the god and creator of the O'odham, who according to Josef, the lead Wolf, lives in a cave on the mountain.

Nico doesn't know how much Josef, wearing a Phoenix Suns T-shirt under his camo jacket and checking his iPhone, actually *believes* this stuff...

But if Josef won't go, no one will.

BOTH SIDES

Joaquin went to University of Arizona, majored in literature.

He once admitted to Nico he wanted to be a writer but returned to the reservation to become a cop instead. He's got a young wife, twin boys, and maybe still writes stories in his spare time. Nico has no idea.

The reservation is a rough place, so many struggling with addiction, poverty, despair. Drugs and the lure of easy drug money only make it worse, a constant gravitational pull. The Nation is a battleground for the US government and the Mexican cartels, as the O'odham try to stay out of the line of fire.

It's a war they didn't ask for, never wanted.

No one lives here untouched, unscathed, and every family has its own stories.

Nico thinks Joaquin's a good cop, but he's in a bad spot, caught between two cultures. Two worlds. The Shadow Wolves, mostly elder tribal members, are tolerant of government interference but hardly cowed by it. Surprisingly, it was this older vanguard who voted recently to allow the Border Patrol to put up IFTs on the Nation, a line of integrated fixed towers more than a hundred feet tall, festooned with night vision cameras and radars. The hope is that these electronic deterrents will force-multiply law enforcement efforts across the border, while simultaneously decreasing the need for boots-on-the-ground teams like Nico's, or even the Shadow Wolves themselves. But it was a cadre of younger O'odham who argued vigorously against the surveillance towers, believing they'll only undermine tribal sovereignty, when so much of it has been lost already.

One thing the whole Nation agrees upon is they'll never allow a *physical* wall to be built across their lands.

But all Nico knows is that all these trail sensors and IFTs, the tracking and chasing, have only pushed the narcos deeper and higher into the mountains.

As Josef says, they're in wolf and jaguar territory now.

The home of I'itoi.

The Man in the Maze.

Joaquin glasses the next ridge, freshly painted in deep shadows the color of bat wings, and thoughtfully chews on a CLIF bar.

"It's getting dark soon," he says. "Time to head down."

"We still have daylight. An hour, maybe more. More than enough. We can grab this guy, Quino."

But night comes fast in these mountains, so Joaquin only shrugs; his irritating, universal gesture for *yes*, *no*, and *maybe*.

"Josef's already said no."

Josef and the other Wolves are kneeling apart, talking quietly in a mixture of O'odham and Spanish. They all speak perfectly fine English—Nico's even heard Navarro singing along with Tom Petty—but out in the desert, in the presence of I'itoi, they hardly ever do.

Nico figures they mostly do it so he can't make out what they're saying about him.

"Convince him otherwise," Nico says, nodding in Josef's direction.

"I can't." Joaquin offers Nico a CLIF bar. "And you'll never find this guy without Josef. Let it go. Let *him* go. It's been a long day. And he's already long gone."

But Nico can't either. Not now. Not sweating through his camo, tired and aching, his blood hot and pulsing fast behind his eyes. He never wanted the transfer out of Charlotte to this godforsaken place, this far corner of the world filled with furious sunlight and dust and creosote, where he's constantly chasing shadows back and forth over the border. So, he's decided to take this one personally. It's shitty, thoroughly unprofessional, but the others resent his clumsy presence anyway, and he's beyond frustrated at hunting these goddamn ghosts— at least this one fucking rabbit—thorough the mountains, forever a few moments too late.

Always another goddamn peak or ridge behind.

"Well, I'm gonna talk to him," Nico finally says, leaving Joaquin to simply shrug again.

Yes, no, maybe.

Or better yet: *Good luck.*

Josef is a big man with dark eyes and salt and pepper hair he wears in traditional rolls.

He sports a deep half-moon scar under his left eye where a horse kicked him when he was a kid, and he has a black tribal tattoo on his chin.

He wears a gold chain around his neck and a big Timex watch.

He's a tribal elder who represents the Chukut Juk District on the legislative council, and he is entrusted with handing down the himdag, the O'odham's cultural values.

He claims his people have been living in this desert for 10,000 years.

He started tracking when he was nine or ten, learning it from his father. The DEA once had an open case on Josef's father, who was both a tracker and a goddamn good smuggler.

There are a lot of ex-smugglers and former DEA file titles in Josef's extended family on both sides of the border.

Nico and Josef are hardly close, despite the hours they've spent in the desert together. There's a certain wariness, not quite distrust but something damn close to it, between the two men.

Nico is the nominal task force leader but they both know Josef is really in charge—his word is law—which is why Joaquin won't argue with the older man.

Unlike Joaquin, Josef's never left the reservation, not for any real length of time. He acts as if there is no world beyond these canyons and mesas, this desert valley. But despite his indifference to Nico and his overall reticence, Nico has come to respect the man's ability. As an investigator he admires it, even if he can't begin to explain it. Josef's a goddamn Jedi—although he acts like he has no idea what that is— able to cut for sign through the densest thickets or scrub. Even with all the high-tech surveillance at Nico's disposal, Josef still sees things in the land, reads the dust itself, in a way no camera or sensor can. And although Nico rejects any sort of Indian mysticism bullshit, he readily admits, as a practical matter, that he would never want Josef Montana chasing him.

That's why it's particularly frustrating the Wolf has decided to pull his pack up short now.

"Josef, c'mon, work with me here. Please. We've got light and time on our side."

The Wolves used to be near forty strong, but there's barely a dozen of them now, often no more than a handful together at any time. They're not all O'odham, there's a mix of Navajo, Ogala Sioux, Kiowa, Apache. But they're all old men—although there have been female Wolves in the past. Joaquin tells Nico there are too few younger tribal members interested in these sort of traditions now. Some start to take it up, but it's hard to learn, nearly impossible to master, and much easier to put down for cellphones and e-cigarettes and TVs and iPads.

The remaining Wolves watch Nico and Josef get ready to square off, and on some unseen signal, move away.

As Navarro walks by he's smiling and whistling to himself. Nico swears it's "Hotel California."

They all know how this is going to end.

Josef motions to the hole and the flotsam and jetsam of trash

181

around it. "Too late now. We're an hour behind, maybe more."

His voice is rough, old. Like nails in a coffee can. Navarro told Nico he used to smoke a pack a day and then gave it up.

He looks up at the fading sun as if that decides it.

"We can make that up," Nico counters.

Josef nods, slow, deliberate. "*We* can."

Nico doesn't miss the subtle jab. "Jesus, Josef, don't act like I can't keep up."

Josef outweighs Nico by maybe fifty, sixty pounds. Whenever they drive somewhere together, he occupies a seat in Nico's Durango, like a foreign army. But out here, the big man is nimble, graceful. He's in his element and glides through the greasewood. Nico was a midfielder for his college lacrosse team, one of the fastest players at one of toughest of the positions, and still he struggles in this goddamn desert.

Both Joaquin and Josef have reminded him it's not about speed, it's about knowing where you're going.

Their Rabbit is fast, too, and has always known exactly where to go, how to run and hide. *Until today.* Nico feels like they've finally chased him down, cornered him. There's no more room to run and no way even Rabbit can hop *over* Waw Kiwulik—seven thousand feet of granite rising from the desert—and Nico can't imagine the scout easily scaling it, either.

Its stony face is impassive; ominous and forbidding.

"It's just a pile of rocks, Josef, a fucking line *you've* drawn in the sand—"

Josef laughs, sharp, unpleasant. He puts a heavy, calloused hand on Nico's shoulder, turning him away from the peak and back toward the sun-scorched desert below them.

"And some lines mean just as much to you and your people."

"C'mon, Josef, not this tired routine again…"

But Josef uses a free hand to point at some distant mesquite, a few rugged prickly pears and massive saguaro. The knotty red fruit that ripens on the saguaro is important to the O'odham, and it's harvested for three weeks in the summer, before the desert monsoon season really hits. Nico never thought about rain over the desert, but during a monsoon, the sunny skies suddenly blacken and race; they spark and shine with endless chrome lightning.

The washes, the arroyos, churn with clay and angry water the color of blood.

Nico and his team have been trapped on the flanks of some these peaks in lighter squalls and can only imagine what it's like for Rabbit to face the full fury of a storm alone.

It must be a hell of a show, though.

They roll in and roll out again, a crashing symphony, but the water dries so fast in their wake, it's like they never passed at all.

Josef's continuing, still pointing this way and that. "You buy them, sell them, guard them. All these invisible lines, like your new IFTs, like your laws. And yet we are bound by them, abide by them. On one side is one thing and on the other is another, and only you get to decide this for us. But from up here, from Waw Kiwulik, it all looks the same."

The same invisible lines Josef is describing also cut the great mountain in half as well. The eastern face is managed by the Bureau of Land Management as part of the Baboquivari Peak Wilderness area. Waw Kiwulik's western face is still controlled by the O'odham, who've been fighting to get back their whole mountain for years. But both sides are a mecca for rock climbers, and, actually, anyone can visit Waw Kiwulik. Even the O'odham only ask visitors to fill out a permit, which makes Nico only more furious that Josef is invoking this sacred bullshit—some obscure tribal myth or *law*—now.

Josef's beliefs seem to conveniently come and go just like the monsoons. For reasons all his own, *he* doesn't want to follow Rabbit any farther.

Josef finally lets Nico go. "He's in the hands of I'itoi now. It is out of ours."

Nico now steels himself for an I'itoi story. He's heard several, from Joaquin, even Navarro, but never Josef. Myths about how I'itoi made the butterflies in every color imaginable but also made them silent, because the birds were jealous of such a beautiful creature also sharing their song. Old, bastardized legends about how Spaniards once came digging for gold on Waw Kiwulik—possibly a take on the Seven Cities of Gold—and how I'itoi made the mountain swallow them whole.

I'itoi is the Elder Brother and Waw Kiwulik is the navel of the world. The O'odham appeared from the cave after a great flood, maybe even a desert monsoon, and I'itoi exists at the edge of a great labyrinth, the maze of life. It's an image Nico has seen on O'odham pottery, and was even made famous in a popular cable show.

Some might say stolen, appropriated.

But Josef claims he's never watched that, either.

The maze represents a man's life; all his experiences, his choices. And like Joaquin said, Josef is *choosing* not to follow Rabbit up Waw Kiwulik, for whatever his reason. But he's making that choice for Nico too, and when Josef simply falls silent—no new I'itoi tale today— Nico wants to know why.

"Josef, Rabbit's probably helped move fifty thousand pounds of weed over the Nation. Hundreds of kilos of meth and coke and fentanyl. Hands down, he's the best scout the cartels have, and he's been a royal fucking pain in our ass all summer. But now that we've finally got him, really got him, you're ready to just walk away?"

Josef blinks at him, and he usually doesn't even blink when staring straight at the sun.

But it's the only answer Josef seems willing to give.

"Wolves my ass." Nico points at Josef. "Fuck it then, you and your so-called pack hang out down here. I'm going up after him on my own. I'll file my sacred permit or whatever when I get back."

Nico knows he's being disrespectful, belligerent. He's making *this* goddamn choice, trying to goad the older man.

"You won't find him," Josef says.

"Watch me. He's just a man, Josef, a—"

"No," Josef says, shaking his head, hair rolls swaying. "No. You're wrong, Agent Costa. He's just a *boy*."

And this stops Nico.

Mouth open, anger still smoldering.

He glances at the spider hole again, taking another good, long look at all the trash around the tiny campsite. It looks exactly like all the others he's ever seen and wonders why—*how*—Josef can be so certain. Is it the turn of a leaf, some fresh moisture on the rocks? A faint Nike tread crossed later by a thin trail of ants only he can see?

It's bullshit.

But Nico asks anyway, "How old?"

"Fifteen, no more than sixteen."

Now Nico is the one who laughs, still disbelieving. "You're really going to tell me you know that by how he walks? How he *runs*? You're good, Josef, but not that good. No one is."

But when Josef only shrugs, when he doesn't bother to argue or even try to explain when the other Wolves stare pointedly at their boots, and even Joaquin looks away—Nico suddenly gets it.

It hits him like a storm. The only thing that makes any sense.

"Jesus, you think he's O'odham. A boy from the Nation. Maybe even someone you started teaching to track."

Josef nods, almost adds a smile. "Not a rabbit at all. A wolf *pup*."

"When did you figure this out?" Nico asks. "Or did you know all along?"

185

Josef looks toward the peak, then at fresh, thin clouds scudding low over the desert; the real threat of a late monsoon blowing in. "If he's O'odham, he's in the maze now. There's no need to follow him. *You* can't walk his path. It's impossible."

"And I'm just supposed to leave it all up to your god beneath the mountain?"

"Or to the Nation. We will handle him, in our own way, in our own time."

"I'm not sure that's good enough."

But Josef only nods again…as if he knew Nico would say that all along too.

"If you do this thing, Special Agent Costa, you're not really chasing Rabbit anymore. You're only chasing yourself."

Joaquin tries to stop him.

"Nico, don't be stupid. It's getting dark, the weather's turning."

Nico wheels on him. "Did you know too? Know Rabbit was O'odham? A fucking kid?"

Joaquin hesitates, embarrassed. Ashamed. "I heard the others talking. They suspected."

"They're fucking *proud*, Quino. One of their own, getting one over on me. And what was the end game? Let me drag my ass all over the Sonoran Desert until I got tired of it? Everyone have a good laugh? At least now I know why we were always a few steps behind, and it wasn't because *I* was slowing anyone down."

"It's not like that."

But Nico knows it is.

"I don't understand, Quino. I just don't."

"You understand more than you know, amigo. You always have. You've listened, you've watched, you've learned."

"Until now."

"Until now," Joaquin agrees. And although he doesn't say it, it's still there: *On one side is one thing and on the other is another.*

Nico will always be on the other side of that invisible line from Joaquin and Josef and the others.

"That's bullshit," Nico says. "Josef doesn't want me here. I get that. I don't want to be here either. But I didn't make this situation or create this border or fuck you out of your land or your history. I've got a job…a duty. And if you and *your* fucking people could handle it on your own, I wouldn't even be here."

Joaquin steps back. "Not fair, amigo. Not even close."

"No less fair than all of you playing me for a fool. Just another fucking white man." Nico straps his own AR-15 behind his back and repositions his pack, eyeing the mountain ahead.

But Joaquin's not quite ready to stand aside. "It's just a choice, Nico. A choice."

"No," Nico says. "That's what you don't get. Now that I'm here, I don't have a choice at all."

It's not about speed, it's about knowing where you're going.

But as darkness descends on Nico, it's slow going all the way around.

Painfully slow—hand over hand in some spots, as Waw Kiwulik's sharp-toothed granite slices his palms deep. He can't cut for shit, not like the Wolves, so he's just guessing at Rabbit's direction, and now the foolishness—the futility—of this chase is painfully obvious, too.

He lost too much daylight arguing with Josef and Joaquin, which may have been part of their plan all along. He hoped to call their bluff by striking out on his own, but they simply watched him climb higher.

He can't believe they've left him out here.

187

But it was *his* anger, his ego alone, that goaded him into this, and he's going to get seriously hurt if he doesn't turn back.

He clings to a small stone lip, using his Surefire to sweep for more handholds, any sort of safe path, up or down. Flecks of mica reflect silver and gold in the bright beam, and it's no wonder Coronado once imagined the Seven Cities of Cibola were here.

The mystical Quivira.

Nico hopes the mountain doesn't swallow him whole.

He doesn't know if the Wolves are still somewhere behind him, but he has an audience of a thousand stars now. They're rising in the east, a vast, breathtaking sweep of them, and it's beautiful in a way he can't describe. Between the storms and the stars and the vast desert below, it's easy to imagine you have the whole world to yourself. It's easy to imagine getting lost here. But Kitt Peak National Observatory isn't that far off, and he wonders if there's some astronomer staring at all these same stars right now through one of their giant telescopes.

Nico doesn't need a telescope. High up on Waw Kiwulik, the stars flicker close enough to touch, to grab and hold onto.

Maybe they'll keep him from falling.

But even as he looks on, they suddenly, eerily, start to disappear, flickering out for good, one after another.

It's like the sky, rather than the mountain, is swallowing them. And when a bright, actinic spark erupts on the horizon, illuminating the rolling clouds from earlier, he knows why.

The monsoon hits him with its full force only a few minutes later.

The wind nearly lifts him off Waw Kiwulik and cold water runs like tears down the mountain's face.

Battered, Nico more or less simply lets go and slides down through scrub and shale as lightning, closer now, shreds the night again and again.

The sky is a series of black-and-white snapshots, one incredible photograph after another that no one will ever see.

Nico scrambles to his feet but then stumbles and falls, slipping into a darkened crevasse, a spider hole, that closes over him and holds him tight like a fist.

He struggles to get loose, to pry himself free, but the AR-15 on his back and his heavy pack and other useless gear act like a wedge, jamming him tight in place.

His boots can't even touch the bottom and he's suspended above an infinite hole.

Tortoise got wedged.

He doesn't want to panic but can't stop himself. Rainwater runs into his mouth and he remembers, for no reason at all, that he never wanted to be in this place and didn't always want to be a cop, or an agent, either.

He thought about teaching history, once upon a time.

A lifetime ago.

Now more lightning, nearly blinding, until a massive figure looms over him, blocking out the torrential storm, standing high above Waw Kiwulik.

Impossible, mythical.

I'itoi.

But no...not I'itoi. Not Elder Brother.

Just Josef. And at his side...

A girl.

A young O'odham girl, soaked to the bone, with braids in her hair.

Rabbit.

She's led the Wolves here to him, probably saved his life, but by the time Joaquin and Navarro and Josef pull Nico out of the hole, she's gone.

BOTH SIDES

Maybe she was never there at all.

Two days later Nico and Joaquin sit in Nico's Durango, AC blasting.

It does little to beat back the stifling heat outside, the bright sun flare on the windshield.

It does nothing to make the clustered buildings here in Sells look any better; a stark contrast of both the beauty and barrenness of the reservation.

No one lives here untouched, unscathed, and every family has its own stories.

And Nico knows most of the story now.

Joaquin's told him all about the girl, Alena, Josef's fifteen-year-old niece; daughter of his sister, married to a Mexican narco sitting in a cell in Florence, Arizona.

Those old smuggling ties in Josef's family still run deep, as deep as his sister's addictions; she's struggled with meth and pills for years. Despite all of Josef's efforts and support, Alena took it upon herself to keep her family afloat with the money she could make out in the desert; the eyes and ears for the Mexican cartels.

She learned tracking early from Josef himself and she was damn good at it.

And if things had been different, different choices made, she might have been Wolf herself, and not a rabbit at all.

Nico hopes she still can be.

He's not sure she ever truly was.

Nico's going back to Charlotte for a while.

Maybe a long while, he doesn't know yet.

The team is Quino's now, even if doesn't want it.

Joaquin says, "I've got something for you. Actually, it's from Josef. Something he wanted you to have."

From a folded bandana, Joaquin pulls out a piece of shale and painted on it is the maze of life.

"The rock is from Waw Kiwulik, right where we found you."

Nico takes it and weighs it in his hand. It's heavy, solid.

"Tell him thank you. I appreciate it."

"I will." Joaquin watches a kid on a bike race through the dust. He rolls down the window, letting in the full force of the sun and heat. He shouts something after the kid in both Spanish and O'odham and the boy waves him off with a hand.

Nico thinks he even flipped Joaquin the finger, but Quino only laughs and rolls the window back up again.

"What'd you to say him?"

"I told him to slow down, to be careful."

"You too," Nico says. "Be careful."

Joaquin smiles. "I will."

But Nico knows Quino can only be so careful. It's dangerous being a tribal cop, breaking up drunken fights, getting caught up in domestic disturbances, dealing with the narcos.

Nico knows there's every chance in the world Quino will die young because of the badge he's wearing.

But Quino chose this.

Or maybe, like Nico up on Waw Kiwulik, he just didn't think he had a choice at all.

Joaquin, who left the reservation to study literature but ultimately couldn't leave his people, has understood the truth all along.

Life really is like a maze...and sometimes every choice, every turn, brings you right back to the start.

"Josef will want to know if you found what you were looking for up there."

"I don't know," Nico admits. "I don't know. Tell him I'm still looking."

"Yeah, I get it," Joaquin says, as he shrugs and slips on his own pair of new Oakleys, a gift of the US government.

"We all are, amigo."

EL SOMBRERÓN

DAVID BOWLES

The late afternoon sun silhouetted the teen as she walked into the shelter at Sacred Heart Catholic Church. Pulling her eyes from the distressing news about the 2016 presidential campaign that scrolled across her phone, Sister Ana Lozano smiled and stood. The other nuns, volunteers, and Jesuit priests joined her, applauding and welcoming the new arrival. But the young woman barely registered the cheerful reception, and when Sister Ana drew close, she held out her temporary papers from Customs and Border Protection without a word, staring into space with hollow eyes.

"Okay…Luisa," the nun said kindly, referring to the wrinkled sheets to glean the girl's name. "Let's get you a quick shower and some dinner. You can rest for a while, too. Then we'll talk about what comes next."

Most of the refugees emerged refreshed and renewed after a few minutes beneath the warm spray of water, dressed in gently-used clothes. However, Luisa Orellana still appeared numb to the world, glancing about with harrowed expectation as she sipped some broth and bit reflexively into a slice of bread.

After she had eaten, Sister Ana guided her to a cot, where she sat listlessly for a while, refusing to lie back, until startled, not by any of the loud bustling of others, but by the soft instrumental guitar music that drifted from some volunteer's phone.

"Could you," she whispered hoarsely, "turn that off?"

Accustomed to the unusual requests of people at their wits' end, Sister Ana complied with a smile, apologizing to the owner.

Picking up a brush, she returned to her charge. "Do you mind if I help you with your hair, Luisa? We can chat a bit, discuss your plans and options."

Luisa nodded, though she winced when the nun's fingers touched her long, beautiful hair.

"So," Ana began, slowly pulling the brush down that cascade of black, "you're from Guatemala, aren't you? Do you have relatives in the US?"

"Yes. My aunt. She lives in Chicago."

"Are you going to wait for other family members before heading that way?" This was often the case with the refugees. They arrived singly or in pairs, joining up in McAllen for the final leg of their trek.

"No. I'm alone. No one else is coming."

Sister Ana drew a sharp breath despite herself. She had heard so many horror stories about the military and the maras that she simply assumed the worst. But Luisa's head twisted slightly beneath her palms.

"They're not dead if that's what you're thinking. When I left, everyone was fine. We live in a highland village, close to Lake Atitlán. We're farmers, and life is pretty peaceful there. Sometimes the guerrillas—or a hurricane—comes smashing into the mountains, but mostly we are left alone with the jungle, the sky, and the xocomil winds that sweep off the lake to purify our sins."

She fell silent for a time. Ana knew better than to press. The teen would tell what she needed to tell when she was ready to tell it. No use asking too many questions.

After a few more strokes of the brush, Luisa continued her tale.

"It was about a year ago when we found the first burro with its mane carefully plaited in small, smooth braids. Everyone knew what this meant. Word spread throughout the entire village, and every unmarried girl or woman age ten or older was given a curfew by the council of elders."

Luisa turned her face a bit to look askance into the nun's eyes.

"It was el Sombrerón. He had come out of the jungle, looking for a bride."

Unbidden, a shiver uncoiled itself along Ana's spine. She had heard whispers of the ancient goblin from other Central Americans who had passed through Sacred Heart. Short, barefoot, face obscured by a wide-brimmed hat, the creature at times ventured from his shadowy home, a guitar slung across his back. Some evenings, legends said, he would lead a pack of mules through a town, hoping to encounter a girl to enchant with his song. If he succeeded, he would ask to braid her hair.

Once his fingers snarled their way through those tresses, the girl would be his forever.

Forcing her hands to stop trembling, Sister Ana continued the grooming, chiding herself for being foolish enough to let the folklore of a distant land affect her so. As the sun began to set, she kissed her crucifix and said a silent prayer of thanks for her own blessings.

"I was always too independent, my mother used to tell me," Luisa mused wistfully. "Reluctant to obey tradition or accept the guidance of adults. So one night I decided to slip out and sit beneath my favorite tree, staring at the stars and imagining some different destiny.

"Then I heard the music. The plucked and strummed strings of an old guitar, shimmering and bright like the moonlight. And a voice so pure and lovely that I at first thought some angel had descended from heaven to visit me. When he stepped out of the shadows, though, I saw how wrong I was. It was el Sombrerón, wearing his patchwork clothes and smiling wickedly beneath the brim of a hat that made him seem even smaller and more impish. I wanted to run, but I was frozen in place by the music. He crooned to me sweetly, promising so many things—long life and beauty and adventure. All I had to do was let him braid my hair. 'A single plait,' he sang, 'so delicate and smooth that your parents will never see it.'

"I heard my mother, then, screaming my name in desperation. The spell was broken. I stood and ran back to my house, weeping. I told my parents everything, and they swore to protect me."

Luisa's eyes welled with tears. "We knew what was at stake. That single braid marks a woman as his, and though he appears to leave, he, in truth, lingers to feed on her despair. He sprinkles her meals with dirt and pebbles till she refuses to eat, wasting away from lack of food and a longing for his lovely voice, his deft little hands. Some survive his torture, but they age much too fast and spend the remainder of their days old and alone, untouched by any love beyond the memory of his songs."

The girl's hair had now dried and hung in a dark, luxurious sheet down her bent back.

"I tried to hide. But he returned again and again, and his song was harder and harder to resist. Finally, I left without a word, crossing into Mexico and riding la Bestia, that horrible old train, across thousands of kilometers—beaten and mistreated by some, protected and helped by others—just to escape the goblin's grasp."

There was bleak silence for a moment as the implications of her flight curdled in the nun's ears, almost making her shudder.

She shrugs off physical abuse as if it's nothing compared to the darkness she fears. Is it trauma? Is this how she copes, creating a monster to explain away the nightmare she's faced?

Sister Ana finally spoke, keeping her doubts about the story to herself. "Well, now you're here, my dear. Now you're safe."

Notes quavered in the air. Luisa stiffened, but Ana patted the crown of her head.

"It's just that volunteer again. I'll ask him to choose some other sort of music."

She didn't get a chance to stand, however. The notes resolved into a melody, strange and ancient, beautiful beyond description. Then came the voice, soothing and seductive, intoning words in a language Ana could not hope to understand. As she listened, though, she understood, as if the music had sent waves of images and emotions into her very soul.

He sang of a long-forgotten time, before mankind had lifted lofty temples to the gods, unfurling cities around them. A time when the Little Folk had ruled the world, their magic untrammeled and unrivaled, faithful servants of the Feathered Serpent. Then he sang of their fall, the rise of Man, and the further descent of one rebellious band, damned and disfigured, goblins scheming in the darkness until they had forged an emissary, a seducer, an angel of death.

El Sombrerón stepped out from behind the dividing curtain, his hands caressing his guitar bewitchingly as he weaved his way through the gloaming toward them. Luisa yanked herself away from the nun, a cry choking in her throat as she stumbled away.

Sister Ana, however, was transfixed.

Let me braid your hair, the goblin whispered. *A single plait. No one need ever know. I see your yearning, your long and bitter wait for a magic that will strip this empty world away. It can be yours now, Ana. Just let me touch your hair.*

She neither moved nor spoke as he slid his guitar to his back and clambered onto the cot behind her. Part of her was drawn to his seduction. Part of her was struck dumb and immobile by existential fear. But more than anything, she wanted to give Luisa a fighting chance.

Run, she urged with all her soul. *Take that ticket, get on the bus to Chicago. Don't look back. I'll give myself to him instead. He'll have to stay to feed on me. You'll be safe.*

Humming his ancient melody, el Sombrerón unpinned her gray-streaked hair, which fell loosely to her shoulders.

Then he took up three strands and began to braid.

TROUBLE

SANDRA JACKSON-OPOKU

1

I ain't never been one for tequila. Back when I was still getting shit-faced, rojo was my thing. I been tussing since I was a shorty, and I'm still short. But thank God and the Department of Corrections, I'm not a syrup head no more. Until two days ago, I hadn't touched anything stronger than Pepsi in all these years.

So why is there a monkey mouth in the bunk below me singing "Drunk on a Plane" when it should have been "Locked Up"? And why am I having a blinding hangover with puke at the back of my throat? Y por qué, finalmente, am I locked up again not even a year on the outside?

It's because trouble always finds me, no matter where I hide. Trouble in this case, being that gringa La Cindy, smothered to death in her own filthy bed.

And the trouble that led me there were these red-hot twins whose name is Trouble, even though you don't spell it that way.

BOTH SIDES

2

Credit where credit is due, okay? You can't say the Robles girls aren't muy guapa. But don't even try it with that mulata shit, because ain't no mules in the family. Black mixed with brown isn't what people mean by "mulatto" anyway. The twins call themselves Afro-Latino. I call them superfine.

Now, I'm not trying to say biracial is better. If you think so, it's because you got some mixed-race babies at home, you're a self-hating homey that likes what looks the least like you, or you're biracial yourself. I ain't hating on you, tato. If that's how you roll, then you do you.

You just need to know it's "a fairly outmoded and frankly racist notion that has never held water." I read that in a magazine. Oh, you thought with all these prison tats and Spanglish, I couldn't spit a word like "outmoded." Don't judge a book by the outside, ese. I got my BA when I was in the joint, so I be knowing what I'm talking about.

They've even done studies on it. The theory that biracial people look better don't got an ant's dick worth of science. Plus, I seen this online gallery of seriously hideous mixed-race people. I'm talking Julia Patrana, horse-face zombie, la llorona type of ugly. No, I ain't naming no URLs. What do I look like, Google? If you want to find that shit, look it up for yourself.

All I know is Katrina and Terri ain't on that list, you feel me? I'm not saying it because we're cousins, and all. And not to come off like a Trumpelstiltskin perv, but if we weren't related and raised up together, I'd smash either one of those two.

The Robles twins are this spicy mixto of Louisiana hot sauce and Cholula Salsa Picante. The mother is a tall south side Chicago sister, looks like she could have played WNBA. The father's a fly-ass Mexico City chilongo, the one I was named for. This man saved my ass before I had an ass to save. He's been saving it ever since. To me and my siblings, he was Tío Papi. I know, "Uncle Daddy" doesn't make sense, but that's what we always called him.

Eduardo isn't my uncle or my father. He's my second cousin once removed. Dude's almost old as Mami so I can't be all, "yo, primo!" up in his face. You got to give an OG his respect.

Both of Tío Papi's daughters are supermodel tall with bangin' bodies like porn stars. Katrina was vain enough to be a model for sure, though she gained some weight with the baby. Terri had the brass balls to be a puta, if that was what she wanted. With la policía for a mother and un abogado for a father, that was never going to happen.

Both of them went into the family business, Terri into the Chicago police department and Katrina into law. Eventually they wound up as private detectives, which nobody expected from either of them. And that's a story to tell, compañero. I know because I was there. It seems like a long time ago, but it's only been a few days.

Let me tell you how it started.

3

So, here's where I come in, Lalo Enrique Rodriguez. If you're a Lalo and a Mexican, then you must have started out as Eduardo. That's the name I was born with.

I read Obama's bio when I was locked up. Homeboy came on out with it. *I used to smoke weed when I was a teen. Oh yes, and I snorted cocaine.* His enemies had nothing to dig up on him. They had to make shit up.

I'm taking a page from *Dreams of My Father* and dropping a dime on myself. There's a whole lot wrong with me, and it's worse than some 'dro and blow.

For one thing, I'm short as shit. People think I'm a teenager before they see these hard lines in my face. Take off a couple inches and I could have been one of those "Little People" on TV. I never liked being pint-sized, but a homey don't make himself. The things in life that I could get right, I didn't always do.

I'm a convicted felon and a recovering addict. I been banging and slinging from the age of seventeen, dropping out of school when I started swigging cough syrup. But there were a lot more cholos out there that were better at thugging than me.

I never raped no woman, mugged no old lady, or molested nobody's kids. I had my share of fist fights, for sure. I dodged my share of bullets. But I never shot nobody, at least not to hit the target. I don't care what that pinche prosecutor said, I never jacked no car. Yeah, I might have taken somebody's ride, but not when they were in it.

When Mami left Mérida, she was seven months pregnant with me. My older brothers' father had a wife and another set of kids. Mami was his side chick. When she left him for another man, Oswaldo Colón tried his best to beat that bastardito out of her belly.

One "little bastard" turned out to be two—me and my sister, Ashley. Twins run in the family. I never knew my real pops but he might have been Maya. "Chinky midgets" is what my half-brothers used to call me and Ash. We might be small and dark with slanted eyes, but at least we don't look like birds of prey. It's obvious where they got it from. The proof is in the pudín.

I never met their father but I seen the pictures. That man is so butt ugly, you'd have to call him *bugly*. If you're gonna be fat, go ahead and do that. If you're gonna be skinny, be skinny. But thin, thin with a triple chin and a Santa Claus belly? That shit don't even look right. Oswaldo's bald head, beaky nose, and long neck made him look just like a vulture.

That cabrón beat up my moms and tried to kill me and my sister before we were born. I think about going down to Mérida, looking for Oswaldo Colón, and kicking his buzzard ass.

My mother, Imelda, was first cousin to Terri and Katrina's pops. Tío Papi found out what was going down and got Mami and my brothers fixed up with visas and airplane tickets. He even moved them into the first-floor apartment of their two-flat building on the East Side.

Ash and I were born just a month after they got to Chicago, the family's first US citizens. Otherwise, I could have been deported just like my brothers when they started getting in trouble. I'd be raising hell down in Mérida with Carlos and Big Snake.

Ashley is the only one who made it out safe and sound. When the boys in my family took to the streets, the girl took to the books. I guess it's because my sister got that gringa name. If Mami had named her boys Christopher, Jordan, and Edgar instead of Carlos, Jesus, and Eduardo, maybe we'd have turned out better. And then again, ¿quién sabe?

4

If that hen hadn't been pecking my nuts, none of this would have happened. I wouldn't have left home that day and everything would still be bueno.

My old lady was riding my hairy ass like she was a jockey and I'm a Galiceño pony. All right, I'm overexaggerating. Isabella Esposito ain't did shit to me. I was the one in the wrong.

BOTH SIDES

When she got home from night shift at the nursing home, I was eating a bowl of cereal and watching Jerry Springer. Izzy stopped by the TV, her stomach blocking my view.

"Your daddy wasn't the Invisible Man," I complained. "You know I can't see through you."

She shifted to the side and put a hand on her belly. "This baby's coming soon, Lalo. You still looking for a job?"

"Hell, yes. Got an interview out South in a couple of hours. I better go get ready."

Yeah, I know that was wrong. I shouldn't have lied to my girl. She was handling the bills and all, putting the food on the table. Izzy didn't like my smoking so she wouldn't buy no squares. I had to scrounge for loosies, but I was trying to quit anyway.

I just wasn't holding down the household like a man's supposed to. I felt real bad about it. When you come out the joint with "felon" tatted across your forehead, nobody wants to know your real name. You knock on doors and they're slammed in your face. A homey gets depressed. Sometimes you just want to sit and chill, watch your TV and eat your Cheerios. Because if you go to the streets for your coins, there's bound to be trouble.

I found the job-hunting outfit Izzy got on sale at Burlington. Those stiff pleather shoes always pinched my toes. Instead, I put on my black Chuck Taylors, went out the door, got on the El at Logan Square, and set off for Chi-Raq. I wasn't scared of no South Side. Aunt Lori used to tell me this story when I was a kid: A fox caught a rabbit, but bunny tricked fox into throwing him into the bushes. Born and bred in that briar patch, zorro. Born and bred.

I represent the Wild Hundreds, Illiana side of the city. When people talk about the barrio they think Pilsen or Little Village, Humboldt Park or Hermosa. But Mexicans been on the East Side for 100 years. We're sitting right on Lake Michigan, sandwiched between White Indiana and Black South Chicago.

I wasn't headed to home grounds though. I got off the Green Line at Garfield to catch the eastbound #55, shocked as shit to see a crowd of college kids on the bus. The hood had changed a lot since I'd been away. You used to couldn't find a gringo west of Cottage Grove.

It wasn't until I got to Hyde Park that a thought came into my head. Maybe popping up at Terri's wasn't a great idea. She's the little cousin that once looked up to me. The last time I seen her she was looking down like I was a pile of caca she had just stepped in.

I took out the cell phone Izzy had bought me and dialed my cousin's number. Either Terri wasn't there or she wasn't taking my calls.

5

I walked up to the Hyde Park Bank and Office Building finishing my last loosie. I pinched out the butt and put it back in the empty pack. Cigarettes cost too much to be throwing away the dog ends. When I collected enough of them I could make me a rollie and save a couple bucks.

I was pushing through the revolving doors when I saw the two girls walking up 53rd Street. They came into the building and got into the elevator after me. The take-out bags they had were smelling good and spicy.

My cousins were lost in their own little world, talking all that chick-talk. Neither of them noticed me in the corner of the elevator.

"I can't wait to lose all this baby fat," Katrina complained. She looked into the mirrored elevator wall, sucking in her gut.

"It's just post-pregnancy bulge," Terri told her. "You don't call it baby fat unless the baby's fat. Which Señor Apetito definitely is."

"Don't make fun of Gustavo and don't be talking down to me. Like you would know about post-pregnancy *anything*."

Terri shrugged. "All I know is, sucking it in won't help. You need to hit the mat and do some crunches."

"If you'd ever had a C-section, you'd realize it takes forever to get back your abs." Katrina muttered "skinny bitch" beneath her breath, just loud enough to be heard.

"Oh, you don't want none of *this* skinny bitch," Terri snapped. "I guarantee you that."

Katrina let her stomach sag. They got off on the seventh floor with me following behind them. They still didn't notice me. That's what I like about Converse. They don't squeak when you walk.

I watched my cousins moving down the hallway. I had to scamper to keep up with them. Both of them had legs for days, but you could tell the difference between them. Katrina was styling and profiling in a tight pencil skirt, a red silk blouse, and a pair of "fuck me" heels. Terri was dressed down to the ground in a black T-shirt, holey jeans, and a pair of Doc Marten boots. But the difference wasn't just wardrobe.

Terri was even more buff than when she was CPD. Katrina, not so much. If Teresita Robles was fit as a fiddle, then Katrina Amrani was broad across the butt as an acoustic bass. Okay, that's a little shady. Let's go with "chubby as a cello."

"Terri, did you notice that elevator smelled like cigarettes?"

"Yeah. What about it?"

"Well, this is a nonsmoking building. And you know what? I can still smell it."

"All I smell is jerk chicken." Terri shrugged.

"When we get back to that broom closet you call an office, I'm calling management."

My eyes were watering from pepper fumes. I don't know how Katrina could smell cigarettes behind all that. I took my pack of dog ends and sadly tossed it in the trash.

The girls stopped in front of a wooden door. Terri shook her head at a printed sign taped there.

T. Robles & Associates
"Your ethnic detectives"
(The world's first Afro-Mexican team of private investigators)

There was a clip art image, sister-girl in a trench coat with a magnifying glass. It looked something like this:

I know, right? Tacky.

I knew these girls since they were born so I could guess what they were thinking. Terri was frowning at the sign. This wasn't her idea. Katrina was smiling, so she must have put it up.

Terri fished a key from her pocket and began fiddling with the lock. "Ooh, this thing always sticks. It gets on my last nerve."

"If a crook was following you, girl, you'd never get away."

And if *I* was the crook I'd have them both by now.

Terri finally turned the key, then looked at the sign and shook her head. "This is false advertising. 'Your ethnic detectives?' Sounds like we're rounding up colored folks."

Katrina rolled her eyes. "Colored? That is so politically incorrect, it's almost a slur. I don't think detectives like us should be saying shit like that."

"Trina, you're not any kind of detective. You're a bored, rich housewife hanging around and getting in my hair." Terri tore down the sign and crumpled it. "And I'm not a private eye, I'm a digital investigator."

"I hear you, Terri," I finally spoke. "And that gumshoe cartoon is whack."

"What the fuck?" they hollered in unison, wheeling around to face me. Terri dropped her take-out bag, assumed a fighting pose with her key as a weapon.

"¿Que paso, Double Trouble?" I picked up the bag and handed it to her, hoping the food had survived.

Katrina gave me a sideways hug. "Nada, primo. What's good with you?"

Terri looked down at my feet. "Nice Chucks."

"Thanks, cuz. You're rocking that pair of Docs."

I leaned forward to give Terri a hug. She ignored my open arms. "Lalo Rodriguez, America's Dumbest Criminal. To what do we owe the pleasure?"

So that's how we were playing it? Oh, I could match her bourgie for bourgie. "As a reformed detainee and a father-to-be, I desperately need a job."

6

Okay, yes. I was stupid. I wasn't good at the game, I was good at getting caught. I still don't think it was fair for my cousin to call me *America's Dumbest Criminal.*

So, this was back before I got myself locked up. I probably should have asked Tío Papi to borrow his garage, but I didn't want to bother him. I knew he was busy taking care of his wife—retired from the force when she got sick, Aunt Lori was still recovering from her mastectomy.

I didn't even have to jimmy the lock. I still had a garage door remote from when I used to live there. Nobody ever parked in the garage so I knew we'd have space to spread out. A raccoon had spooked Tío Papi back there so he started parking on the street. Eduardo was scared of anything with fangs and fur. He would scream like a girl if he saw a mouse in a trap.

Me and my partner weren't trying to bother nobody. We just needed someplace to work on that Chrysler 300 junker Freddy had got. He wanted to break it down to sell the parts. He promised me two bills in cash to help him out. I needed money for my rojo and didn't ask no questions.

We had just got all the doors off the frame when I heard cars easing into the alley. Even when they stopped, I wasn't worried. I figured neighbors had come to park in their garages.

Then somebody started shaking the door. Freddy opened his mouth to holler. I held a finger to my lips, warning him to chill. If we stayed real quiet, maybe they would leave.

Shit, that didn't work. I heard my cousin Terri's voice, the same twin who used to follow me around when she was little. Katrina was Ashley's mini-me. Teresita was mine.

"I'll give you to the count of three to open that door. One…two…"

The door started rolling up. I should have known Terri would have had her own remote. A cruiser with lights flashing was sitting outside. An animal control van was parked behind it.

Freddy saw Terri standing with her service revolver drawn. He dove to the ground like an Olympic springboard champ and crawled behind the Chrysler. I stood my ground. Family is family.

"Hey, little Terri Sunshine. What brings you out this way?"

"What do you mean, what brings me here? This is my family home."

"Well, I'm family, too."

"We'll see about that," she sneered. "Daddy called and said he heard something bumping around back here. He thought it might be raccoons knocking over paint cans."

"My bad, prima. We'll try to keep it quiet. Me and my partner are leaving as soon as we get this work done on his hoopty."

Terri looked at the Chrysler and narrowed her eyes. "Who do you think you're fooling? Stevie Wonder could see what's going on back here. Turning my parents' garage into a chop shop, Lalo? This is stupid even for you."

"Terri, you don't mean that."

"The hell, I don't! And who's that cretin back there? Hey! I see you trying to reach up and open the trunk. Come out here with your hands up. Don't make me have to shoot you."

"Freddy Flintstone, for your information." He came out with both hands raised. "You don't have to be calling nobody out by his name."

"Dude, you just said your name was Fred Flintstone. I think you're the one that's calling yourself out of your name."

Once he saw that Terri had things under control, a white dude got out of the animal control van with two big cages. His uniform had an IWS badge to match his vehicle—Illinois Wildlife Services. "What's up, home-brays? These the zombie raccoons your dad called in about, Officer Rubbles?"

"That's *Robles*." Terri holstered her weapon. "And shut your hole, McInerny."

I don't know why a fine female like Terri joined the force in the first place. Those Chicago Police Department clothes don't do shit for a chick with a shape like that.

"Breaking and entering." Terri unhooked the handcuff ties. "I'm going to have to take you in."

"Why you gonna do me like that? Familia es familia, verdad?"

"You have the right to remain silent. Anything you say can and will be used against you…"

I heard the sound of police sirens. Backup was on the way. Terri was saved the shame of hauling her cousin down to the precinct.

When CPD impounded the stolen Chrysler, they found a backpack in the trunk with two unlicensed guns. One of them had been used in a drive-by two weeks before.

Look, you got to believe me. I would never bring no murder weapon to my family's spot. I didn't know caca about those firearms. That was Freddy Flintstone's deal. That is what I told the judge, but I still wound up catching a case.

7

Terri and Katrina split their Jamaican takeout with me. Jerked chicken, plátanos fritos, red rice and beans, salad and ginger beer. I told them they didn't have to share but damn, I'm glad they did. I was hungry as a horse. I didn't get to finish my Cheerios that morning and it was already past noon.

My mouth was burning afterward and the ginger beer made it worse. And they say Mexicans like to spice up our food. We ain't got nothing on the Jamaicans.

We ate scrunched up in a little seating area with a loveseat, two armchairs, and a coffee table. On the other side was a computer on a stand and an L-shaped desk with office chairs on either side.

Terri wiped her fingers and turned toward me. "So, tell me, Lalo.

What's this about a job?"

"I heard you had your own detective agency and damn, cuz. I'm proud of you. Making bank and taking names! That's what I'm talking about."

Terri tilted her head and gave me la mirada that said: *flattery won't get you shit.*

"So," I hurried on, "I thought I might come see you about a job."

"Even if I ran a detective agency—which I don't—there's no way I could give you a job. A convicted felon can't become a private investigator. It's Illinois law."

"Aw, Terri," Katrina begged. "Can't we find something for Lalo to do? He's family, after all."

"There isn't any *we*. I don't have money to hire staff, which is why I'm not paying you. Like you even need it with that rich husband of yours."

Katrina turned to me. "I'm interning with Terri to become a private eye."

"Digital investigator!" Terri hollered. "I've said it twice already. Am I talking to myself?"

"I've heard about P.I.s," I admitted, "but I didn't know *D.I.s* were a thing."

I was shocked as shit to find out Terri had gotten shot. When she took a bullet on the job last year, her father begged her to quit. She had a Criminal Justice associate's degree and went back for a Digital Forensics certificate. T. Robles & Associates was just getting off the ground.

"I use technology to solve digital crimes."

"Digital crimes like what?"

"Identity theft, cyber scams, and harassment. I can get legal wire taps, analyze security footage, and recover deleted data from computers and mobile devices. Although, right now I'm working on a simple case, your typical insurance fraud."

Terri was investigating a fishy workman's compensation claim. She had to find out if the suspect was too disabled to work, like he claimed to be.

"It's not exactly my line of investigation," she admitted. "But beggars can't be choosers."

"And how's it coming?" I asked.

"Just following the digital trail. I need to plan a stake to get some physical evidence."

"So you need to find out whether old boy is illin' or chillin'?" I asked. "Maybe I can help."

Terri sighed. "You just can't come off the street and do a digital investigation. No way, Billy Ray."

I found myself grinning. "Who you calling Billy Ray?"

As kids we decided the expression "no way, José" was racist and kept coming up with changes. No way, *Andre, Sister Fay, Sallie Mae.*

"But what if I could help you out? Then would you give me a job?"

Katrina shot Terri la mirada. It said: *he's probably going to fuck it up, so just humor him until he flops.*

"What about 'no way' do you not understand, Lalo?" Terri took a file from her desk and shoved it into a drawer. "I've got a package to pick up at UPS. This is an 'A' matter so make like a 'B' and 'C' your way out. The door locks automatically. And there's nothing of much value in here, just so you know."

¡Ay, mi corazon! That hurt my heart like hell.

"I'll go with you." Katrina jumped up. "We need some air freshener. That jerk chicken really lit the place up."

"What's with you and all these odors?" Terri fussed as they left.

"I'm sensitive to smells. It's been like that since I got pregnant."

"Well, you ain't pregnant no more."

The tiny office was left in silence. I opened the drawer, found the folder Terri put away, and began to leaf through it.

It got me to thinking about this old white dude I'd met in the joint. Donny Finklestein was his name. As city manager for some downstate town he'd been cooking the books for years and embezzled a shitload of money.

Donny had covered his footsteps so nobody even suspected. It was his public behavior that gave him away. The man had a serious gambling habit and the racetrack was his drug of choice. He got so wrapped up in it that he decided to invest his ill-gotten gains.

Donny bought a racehorse he named Patrician after his mistress. Nobody paid much attention until the year she took top prize at Arlington Park. The horse, not his side chick. Donny's picture was on the news with a cigar in his mouth and the prize cup in his hand.

That's when people got to thinking. How can someone who barely makes a hundred grand a year afford to buy a quarter-million-dollar race horse? And what about that Porsche he drives and that mini-mansion he lives in?

Donny would have gone to one of those country club prisons for white collar offenders, except when they came to arrest him, he shot it out with the cops. Donny didn't hit anyone but he took a bullet himself. Still they managed to take him in alive. What do you bet a Tómas or Tyrone wouldn't have lived to tell the story?

Anyway, that's how Donny wound up in the pen with chulos like me.

I looked at pictures in the file. Terri's insurance fraud suspect was White, fat, middle-aged, and balding. The picture was posed to make him look as pitiful as possible. In a hospital gown and a neck brace, he was leaning on a cane.

I started fiddling around my little technical know-how. Before my last stint in the pen I used to work with computers, hardware and software issues. I found the suspect's social media but all his networks were private. Some online searching gave me details of his high school graduation.

I didn't have no credit card to sign up for a yearbook service. With some back and forth, I found a story on the Homecoming Queen from his senior year. Thirty years later she still was looking good.

I made up a Facebook profile with her name and photo then sent him a friend request, which he approved right away. I clicked into his online photo album. It showed him golfing last weekend at French Lick Springs, minus his cane and neck brace. He was even posed with his golf club pointing at a Donald Ross Golf Classics banner, the date and year printed on it as bold as day.

When the girls got back to the office, I showed them what I'd found. "Your man ain't looking that disabled to me."

Katrina grinned and patted my back, just like she hadn't given her sister The Look twenty minutes ago. "Good work, Lalo! I knew you had it in you."

Terri frowned suspiciously. "How did you find this?"

"I didn't exactly break the law. I skirted it, familia.*"*

Terri wasn't down with the snooping and the fake Facebook profile. That didn't stop her from downloading the photos pronto and dictating a report into the computer.

I couldn't resist gloating. "That saved you a little time, huh?"

"Are you kidding me?" Terri groaned. "You're congratulating yourself for breaking—excuse me—*skirting* the law, when I clearly told you to leave it alone?"

"Glad I could help."

"You know you shouldn't have done what you did. Those materials were confidential."

"Sorry about that, cuz."

"I would have gotten to the bottom of it eventually," Terri

continued, "but yeah, I guess you helped. I can pay you like, hm. Maybe, two fifty?"

"Two hundred fifty bucks? Are you kidding me?" Holy shit, I'd hit the Lotto. First thing I was buying was a new pack of squares. Second thing, some flowers for Izzy.

"Sorry, but it's the best I can do," Terri apologized. "I know I should offer you more but things are really tight."

Terri had so many of these contracts, she was thinking of changing her business name from T. Robles & Associates to Insurance Frauds "R" Us. The cases weren't much of a challenge and they didn't pay that well. But she was in startup mode and she couldn't afford to be picky.

"At least I'll be able to pay the rent on time this month."

Back in high school Terri would type kids' homework for money. I know she could have done it herself, but Katrina, the retired attorney and overqualified intern, needed something to do. She listened to the recording and slowly typed it up with her two-fingered keystrokes. Terri looked it over, made some edits, and emailed it to the client along with the photos I'd found.

Case closed.

8

I was still chilling at T. Robles when Izzy called. "Hola, mi amor. How'd the interview go?"

Isabella Esposito was Sicilian but she grew up in a Puerto Rican hood. Her peeps thought it was straight slumming when Izzy tried to pass. The girl couldn't really speak much Spanish but would try to talk English with a boricua accent. It was kinda cute.

"Hey, Izzy. Things went pretty good."

"Thank God. I was worried. You've been gone a long time."

"Yeah, something came up but I'm leaving now. I'll tell you all about it when I get home." I didn't want to be all cháchara with my cousins sitting there.

When I said my hasta luegos and opened the door to leave, I whispered "¿Qué carajo?" *What the fuck?* Why was a mannequin standing there? He was frozen in the open doorway with a fist raised to knock. Dude must have done his shopping at Alcala's Western Wear. He was decked out from neck to toe in high end cowboy gear.

El dandi was a toasty tan with a high top copete on his head. I rock a pompadour myself, trying to make myself look taller. His 'do swooped up way higher than mine, though he didn't need the extra inches. From the top of his head to the tip of his leather cowboy boots, the man had charro written all over him. He looked like a Mexican cowboy on dress-up day. Only thing missing was the sombrero.

But why was the brother so guapo pero severo, good-looking but grim? What problems could somebody have who had it going on like that?

"Is this the Troubles agency?" he asked.

"T. Robles," I corrected. "Tee. ROE-blaze."

"I got this, Lalo," Terri warned. "Step back and let him in."

I backed up to give him way, but he just stood there doing his mannequin act.

"Entra, por favor," Terri ordered.

"No hablo español," he answered in the worst gringo accent ever. He stepped to me and stuck out his hand. "The name is James Hill, no middle name. But you can call me Jimmy."

Katrina was on his culo before the words were out of his mouth. "Just because you see a man in a suit, don't go making assumptions. Lalo doesn't even work here yet. He's certainly not the boss."

"And neither are you," Terri reminded her. She got up from the loveseat and went to sit behind her oversized desk. "What can I do for you, Mr. Hill?"

"I told you, it's Jimmy."

"So, Jimmy. What brings you to T. Robles?"

Jimmy looked around the office with a frown on his face. His eyes skipped over me and Terri, lingering on Katrina. They jumped to the water cooler in the corner (empty), the artwork on the wall (posters), and Terri's forensics investigation certificate (real, I'm assuming).

"Troubles, right?" Jimmy asked again. "You're an all-girl production?"

Both twins answered at the same time. They've been doing that since they were little.

"Why, yes. We are," Katrina gushed.

"You make it sound like lesbian porn," Terri barked.

"Porn?" Jimmy Hill squealed. You'd have thought the chupacabra himself had strolled across his grave. Jimmy looked over his shoulder at the open doorway, like he wanted to scurry through it. Instead he came in, shut the door, and sat in the seat Terri had just vacated.

Jimmy turned attention to the wrong person again. With Katrina's polished perm and designer duds, she looked the female version of him. He clicked on his cell phone and thrust it toward her.

"See," he told her. "I got one of these."

Katrina took the phone and grinned. "I knew this would pay off."

"What is it?" I asked.

"Let me guess." Terri sighed. "It's that Groupon offer, right? A thirty-minute consultation for fifty bucks. A whopping dollar and sixty-six cents an hour for time I'll never get back. And after Groupon takes its share, I'll barely have enough left to buy myself a Happy Meal."

"Shall I redeem it?" Katrina smiled.

"Go ahead. And you," Terri pointed to Jimmy, then tapped her desk. "I'm yours for the next thirty minutes."

Jimmy rushed over, sat down, and started talking fast. He was going to get his half-hour's worth if it killed him. "So, here's the thing. I've been Me Too-ed real bad."

"I bet you have." Terri grimaced. "Just who did you harass?"

"It wasn't me," Jimmy insisted, like the refrain to a Shaggy song. "I'm the one it was done to."

"How'd it happen?"

Jimmy started sweating and his eyes got panicky. He looked back toward the door before answering. "Cindy McGhee, my agent? She books me for these modeling and acting gigs?"

"Are you asking me or telling me?" Terri deadpanned.

"Cindy won't give me my money and she owes me twenty-five grand."

Terri shook her head. "Sounds like a contractual dispute. Where's the Me Too angle?"

Jimmy looked down at his twisting hands. If he hadn't been brown he'd be blushing. "She said I'd have to put out."

"What!" I'd heard of all kinds of heinous shit but this was a new one on me. "And did you?"

"I did." Jimmy nodded sadly. "Or at least, I tried. According to her, it wasn't good enough. And if I told the cops or anyone, she'll see me go down for rape."

I got a sick, sinking feeling in my gut. "That's not all, is it, Jimmy?"

Katrina looked horrified. "What could be worse than that?"

Jimmy looked at her helplessly. "On Friday she's got me going up for a part in *The Long Ranger*."

"The old TV show?" Terri frowned. "Or a new movie remake?"

Jimmy shook his head and clamped his mouth shut, looking miserable and ashamed.

I answered for him. "He said The *Long* Ranger. I think it's probably porn."

9

The office door closed on Jimmy at the end of his thirty minutes. Katrina got up and checked to make sure it was locked.

"That guy was a real femme fatale, wasn't he?"

"Jesus Christ, Trina. You don't know nada, do you?" Terri shook her head. "A femme fatale is the sexy, sinister broad in a hardboiled detective flick. Jimmy would be an homme fatale, if that actually was a thing."

"More like an homme pitoyable. What?" I asked defensively. They were looking at me like I'd grown an extra head. "I took French in high school. It means 'a pitiful man.'"

"Pitiful *and* shifty," Katrina added.

"Definitely shifty," Terri agreed. "He was tweaking like a cat with his tail on fire."

Katrina continued. "He claims his name is Jimmy Hill? Who does he think he's fooling? My six-month-old could come up with a better alias. If that boy's not Latino then I ain't."

She was technically only fifty percent but I didn't point that out.

Terri wasn't buying it. "You think he's lying about his ethnicity? What would be the point?"

"I don't think it's a lie," I agreed. "He reminds me of this dude I met in prison. He hung out with La Raza, but he wasn't one of us."

Terri tapped the desk impatiently. "I'm well aware of your gang affiliation, Lalo. What's your point?"

"*Former* gang affiliation," I corrected. "Old girl wants to put him in a blue version of *The Lone Ranger*. What role do you think he's up for? Probably not the masked crusader."

"And not his horse, Silver," Terri added.

"Tonto?" Katrina suggested.

"'The faithful Indian companion.' I'd say that Jimmy Hill is indigenous."

Terri steepled her hands thoughtfully. "Native American, huh? You might be onto something."

"I'd bet dollars to donuts he is."

We sat there mulling it over until Katrina broke the silence. "Damn, he sure was pretty though. Too bad I'm off the market. When this is all over, Terri, you ought to check him out."

Terri shook her head. "I don't ever date clients, especially ones with pompadours. And anyway, I'm not trying to taste the rainbow."

"What makes you think he's gay?" I'd been in the joint for six years. My gaydar was usually on point and nothing beeped when Jimmy showed up at the door.

"Lalo Rodríguez, do you need glasses?" Terri hissed. "There was a damned rainbow flag on his lapel."

Katrina came to my defense. "No, that wasn't a rainbow. It didn't have all the colors, only black, gray, white, and a stripe of purple."

"And just because he couldn't get it up, doesn't mean he's gay," I added. "Maybe the chick is hideous. Maybe she has halitosis."

"Maybe this is all a nightmare I'll wake up from in the morning," Terri complained. "That damn Groupon."

Katrina looked hurt. "What do you mean? I thought it would help drum up business. You told me I could try it."

"Sorry, Trina, but this isn't my kind of case. He got his thirty minutes. I told him to go to the police and find himself a lawyer. Let's leave it at that. I doubt if Jimmy Hill could afford me anyway."

"Well, he does have twenty-five grand coming," Katrina reminded her. "If he's telling the truth."

"And he is a brother from another mother." I added my two cents.

Terri frowned at me. "What do you mean by that?"

"Natives are the original us, before Latinos existed. They're in our blood."

Terri mimed playing a violin solo.

"A person of color is literally getting screwed," I insisted, "by a white woman who's stealing his money and trying to pimp him out to porn. You can understand why he doesn't want to take this to the police."

"Jimmy never said the woman's white," Katrina pointed out.

"Well, I doubt if she's Native or Latina. And how many black Cindy McGhees do you know?"

Terri grabbed her bag and headed for the door.

"All right, you win. Let's go to Virtue's, get some drinks and snacks, and figure this thing out." She looked back at me. "Well, Lalo. You coming?"

10

"How you gonna take a man's money then try to make him freak for the cameras?" Katrina picked over a kale salad. "That's the textbook definition of a pimp."

Terri dug into a bowl of shrimp and cheddar grits. "Back in the day in the hood, we could have solved this real easy. Where's a soldier when you need one?"

"Sitting right here," I told her. "Just say the word and we'll order up La Cindy an old-fashioned South Side beat-down."

"And you'll be back in prison in an old-fashioned South Side minute. Dang, these grits is good."

"It's not fair." Katrina stared at her resentfully. "You can eat anything you want and not gain an ounce. I just look at food and it goes straight to my hips. We're twins! We're supposed to have the same metabolism."

"Enjoying my food here," Terri reminded her, "not trying to go on no guilt trip."

I drank my Pepsi, ate my crab cake sliders, and listened to their good-natured sniping. It was an old familiar song I'd been hearing since we were niños.

Izzy was blowing up my cell phone but I didn't answer. I knew she'd be salty when I got home late, but what was I supposed to do? Say "no" to hanging out with family I hadn't seen in seven years?

I was working an opportunity and it wasn't just about money. I needed to make it up to my cousins. I'd pled down an accessory to manslaughter rap that I wasn't even guilty of. But I did commit a criminal act on their parents' property, the childhood home we'd all grown up in. I owed the Robles girls more than an apology. I had to figure out how to make things right.

Even though they weren't identical, the girls looked just alike, or at least they used to when they were young. They had very different personalities, though. Katrina was the nosy one, always trying to get in somebody's business. She'd been a high-powered sports and entertainment attorney before she married one of her clients. Terri was loyal and steady, but had a short fuse. Katrina was a girlie-girl, Terri had always been a jock.

I listened to Katrina brainstorm ideas to get the business on its feet. I watched Terri laugh, disagree, and roll her eyes. The girls had their educations and all. I had my streets and prison. But when we got together we slipped into the language of our childhood. Spanglish sprinkled with Ebonics and words nobody else used. It was almost like a secret language.

The "associates" part of T. Robles was just for show, since it was a one-woman operation. Katrina expected it would soon be two. She was a T. Robles too, if you called her by her nickname Trina, and forgot she was married to a soccer pro whose last name was Amrani.

"T. Robles and Associates," she sighed. "We're gonna be partners in crime."

"*Against* crime," Terri corrected her. "If I go along with it, that is. The jury's still out on that one."

Katrina ignored her. "Double Trouble. It's déjà vu all over again."

"You're lucky to have each other," I told them. "I wish me and Ash were still close like that. Remember when we were young? Your moms used to call us Double Trouble squared."

When my mother worked first shift on cleanup crew at Trinity Hospital, Auntie Lori would give us breakfast and take us to school. My aunt was on graveyard shift at the precinct. Tío Papi sometimes worked late hours as an immigration attorney. If he hadn't made it home by the time she left for work, Mami would bring Katrina and Terri downstairs, feed us dinner, and get us all into bed. My brothers Jesus and Carlos were in high school by then. Seven and ten years older than the rest of us, they were already running the streets.

When it was time for Aunt Lori to come home from work in the morning, Katrina and Terri would be waiting in their pajamas.

"What's that I see?" When she came through the door in her police uniform, the twins would throw themselves at her. "Double Trouble coming at me. Oof, y'all kids are heavy."

As soon as she finished hugging them up, me and Ashley would come running out to tackle her again. "Here comes another one, just like the other one. Double Trouble Squared."

The tone of her voice and smile on her face let us know she loved that kind of trouble.

11

My mother died while I was in prison. I couldn't even go to her funeral. That's the kind of thing a man doesn't forget, and never forgives himself for.

Mami always kept her life insurance up to date. I knew it wasn't much. I didn't find out what happened with it until I got out of prison. Ashley had used part of the money for our mother's services, which was fine. The rest she took to pay for her IVF. Not so bueno. Fertility treatments weren't covered by her health insurance. She and her husband were desperate to have a baby.

What could a brother say to a sister? You want her to be happy. You want her to have a child. But she never talked it over with you, she just did what she wanted to do. And you're out here in these streets without a penny to your name.

My sister never thought she was stealing from her brothers. "Borrowing" was how she put it. She swore she was going to pay it back, but her husband lost his job, and they were barely scraping by.

When I was ready to be discharged from the halfway house, Ashley wouldn't even let me stay with them until I got on my feet. "It's not that I don't love you, Lalo. Joe doesn't want an ex-offender in the house."

"The *ex-offender* is your brother."

"Don't blame me." Ash looked like she wanted to cry, but she didn't change her mind. "I'm not the only one making decisions. There's two of us."

She gave me $100 and said she'd repay my share of the money as soon as she could. Didn't mention anything about our older brothers, Carlos and Jesus. It'd been seven months. I hadn't heard from her again and I never got a dime.

And Ashley Starks de Rodriguez hadn't turned up pregnant yet, as far as I knew.

12

"Okay, it's a plan," Terri finally agreed. "We'll see my attorney first thing in the morning."

"Why pay a lawyer," Katrina asked, "when you got one sitting here?"

The girl was so flighty at times, you almost forgot she had been an attorney before she became a suburban trophy wife. Katrina surprised us both when she said her law license was still up to date. We went back to the office and had her draw up the documents.

By the time we were done it was getting dark, time to call it a day. Terri only lived a few minutes away. We both walked her home. The sunset bled a band of golden light onto Nichols Park. Huge flocks of crows flapped across the sky and settled into the trees.

Katrina had left her car in Trina's parking garage. When I pulled it out to the curb for her, she insisted on taking me home. I would have said, no, gracias, but Katrina offered to let me drive. Who could say no to a sweet-ass ride like that—a silver BWM X3 that looked brand-new?

I was surprised Katrina was hanging out with us so late with a husband and baby at home. "Oh, Zak is out of town on a road trip and the nanny has Gustavo. Today was one of those times I just needed to get away. I get so bored up in Kenilworth with nothing but time on my hands."

Katrina was curious about where I was living. When I pulled up in front of the shabby two-flat, I could tell she wanted in. I told her that my girlfriend worked the night shift and probably would be sleeping.

But when I came in Izzy was wide awake, sitting at the computer.

"You're late," she said quietly. "What kept you all this time?"

"I actually got a little job. It started it right away."

When I came closer to kiss her forehead, Izzy quickly darkened the screen.

"What's that you're working on?" I asked.

Izzy blushed and ducked her head. She picked up a gizmo that looked like an old-fashioned radio. "One of the girls at work gave this to me."

"And that would be…?"

"A baby monitor. Sylvia lost the instructions. I was looking for them online."

I picked up the machine and looked it over. "Why don't I give it a go? I'm pretty good with electronics and shit."

"No, thanks." Izzy took it back. "I really need to figure it out for myself. So, tell me about this job."

I gave her a rough sketch without any details. Terri had been particular about keeping it all under wraps. I expected Izzy to be excited for me, but she only shrugged and looked out the window. "Who's the girl you were with?"

"What girl?" I asked in confusion, then realized that Izzy's desk looked out onto the street. "Oh, that was my cousin, Katrina."

"You just said her name was Terri."

"They're two of them," I explained. "They're sisters, actually twins."

"Come on, Lalo. Tell me the truth. That's a black girl you were with."

Uh-oh. I could see it coming. No matter what I said in my defense, Izzy went through these episodes where she thought I was with someone else. The pregnancy had made it worse.

"I'm fat and pregnant, I'm short and plain, my boobs are too small

227

and my thighs too big. No wonder you want somebody else. That girl you were with is gorgeous."

I kneeled down to put my face against her belly. "Isabella Esposito, I swear to you. I haven't been with anyone else. I don't even look at other girls no more. I wish you could believe me."

She lowered a tearstained face onto my head. "I want to, Lalo."

Just then the doorbell buzzed and I got up to answer it. Katrina Amrani de Robles was on her way up to our second-floor apartment. She came in shifting from one foot to another doing what we used to call as kids the pee-pee dance. "Lalo, my bladder is bursting. I'll never make it home. Mind if I use your john?"

When she came out of the bathroom I introduced her as my cousin. Izzy looked confused and Katrina gave her a wink. "I know we look like Mutt and Jeff. My father is Mexican, my mother's black."

"And very, very tall," I said. "I feel like I'm in the land of the giants whenever I'm with those two."

Izzy smiled with relief. She seemed relaxed after that. She even offered Katrina some of the food she'd made.

Katrina shook her head. "Thanks, but I've got to be going. Plus, we had dinner already. Didn't Lalo tell you?"

"You already ate?" Izzy turned to me. "But I made caponata, your favorite."

"You lucky dog." Katrina whistled. "You got a girl who can burn. I thought I smelled something good. What do you put in your caponata?"

"I'll get you the recipe later," I said, leading cousin curiosa to the door.

But that wasn't the end of it. Izzy was upset all over again about the dinner I missed. Or maybe it was just those pregnancy hormones. She huffed over to the kitchen and started putting food away. She was crying again. I could tell by how her shoulders trembled.

"I didn't have more than a snack earlier," I lied. "Let me get some of that."

Even after I ate, it didn't make Izzy happy. She wouldn't talk to me and went into the bedroom and napped for the next few hours. I woke her up when it was time for her to get ready for work. She wouldn't even let me walk her to the El like I usually did.

I got her an Uber instead.

13

"Are those for me?" the woman asked, yawning and stretching. She licked her swollen bottom lip and reached for the flowers with shaky hands.

I quickly tucked the bouquet behind my back. "No, but I do have something for you." I held out a three-page document.

I hadn't expected the felonious Cindy McGhee to be such a looker. A petite freckle-faced redhead with bee stung lips, somewhere in her early thirties, she seemed like a sexy, grownup version of Little Orphan Annie. It surprised me that Jimmy Hill hadn't wanted to get a hit of that. Maybe extortion had deflated his libido. Maybe the drunk girl thing turned him off.

Having had a longstanding habit myself, I knew an addict when I saw one. La Cindy, as my cousins called her, was clearly a heavy drinker. You could see broken vessels in the whites of her green eyes, and the puffiness around them. Her swollen lips and shaky hands were dead giveaways, along with that dazed grogginess that comes with a regular hangover.

It was ten on a late spring Tuesday morning in Humboldt Park. This had been a Puerto Rican barrio back in the day. Now it was almost yuppie-fied beyond recognition.

BOTH SIDES

I stood at the open door of a small two-story building that was set off the street behind a brick bungalow. These coach houses were once horse stables with living quarters for a carriage driver above. Now they'd been refurbished and fancied up for the new monied set.

The bouquet was an idea that I hadn't cleared with Terri. Skirting it, amigo. Not breaking it. I figured that if La Cindy looked through the peephole and saw a Latino with flowers, she'd probably think "delivery man" and open the door. Which in fact, she did.

Yet when I tried to put the summons in her hand, she demanded that I wait while she went to get her reading glasses. Maybe she was more like forty.

Cindy stood in the doorway wearing a silky robe that gaped open in the front. There were flashes of a pierced nipple and navel that I wasn't quite sure were accidental. A glimpse of her trimmed crotch revealed that the carpet didn't match the drapes.

She paged through the document then dropped it to the floor. Fine by me. She had accepted the summons, duty done.

"Well, that's all a crock of bullshit," she said with a seductive smile. "Hey, why don't you come inside and join me for a morning cocktail?"

I backed away with my hands upraised. "Thanks, but no thanks. Just doing my job."

I didn't want to mix it up in any La Cindy mess. Terri hadn't wanted to use me in the first place, but she needed a process server who would work fast and cheap. While the law didn't exactly rule out a convicted felon, the "good moral character" part was open for question. Skirting and skating like I was on roller blades, tato. Skirting and skating.

Cindy McGhee narrowed her eyes and pursed her lips, giving me the once-over. She looked exactly like a pimp sizing up a prospect. "You ever do any acting, José?"

If I'd been counting them up, that was another strike against her. I hated when gringos called you by a generic Mexican name. I sneered and turned away. "Yeah, right. Because I am *so* the pretty boy type."

I hightailed it down the stairs and crossed the tiny yard. As I entered the gangway leading to the street, I heard her calling after me. "You're not bad looking for a Mexican boy. I get lots of calls for the ethnic type."

I sprinted to the sidewalk and took a deep breath. Finished, over and done with. I walked past a place calling itself the Ukrainian Village Tavern even though that neighborhood was a mile to the east. A hand-lettered sign in the window read, "Tequila Shot Tuesdays, half-priced." I came upon the El station where I'd gotten off that morning and decided to pass it by.

We didn't have too many perfect spring days like this in Chicago. It usually went from the freezer to the inferno.

I lived with Izzy in Hermosa, the neighborhood where so many boricua had fled when they got priced out of the area. It sat right on Humboldt Park's northern border. I was only a few miles away from home. I was gainfully employed, or about to be, with a full pack of squares in my pocket and a present for my old lady.

I decided to walk through the park, then out onto Grand Avenue. The further north and west I went, the browner the complexion. Puerto Ricans mostly, but a lot of Mexicans, too. No more than a handful of blacks and gringos. This used to be Latin King territory, though it's nowhere near as bad as it used to be. Still I was careful to keep my La Raza tattoos covered. When I had the money I'd get them lasered off.

The flowers hadn't just been a trick for La Cindy, they were for a treat for my old lady. I'd meant to bring some home to her last night, but hung out with my cousins and forgot all about it. There'd been that little trouble afterward, but I was sure it had blown over. I was on my way home to her with a peace offering in hand.

It was already Tuesday afternoon but I was feeling easy like Sunday morning.

14

I'd left the apartment that morning before Izzy got in from work. When I got back home she was at the computer again, still in her CNA uniform.

"For you, babe." Her hands were busy closing out her browser, so I put the bouquet on the desk. "I'm ready to get into that caponata again. Italian food always tastes better the second time around."

Izzy swiveled in her chair and gave me la mirada. "Where were you *this* time?"

"Just taking care of some business."

"Don't lie to me, Lalo. You were gone when I got home. Did you sleep out last night?"

My "easy like Sunday morning" mood flew right out the window. "Isabella, we're not going through this again. You wanted me to get a job. Fine, I got one. Now you act like a chica loca when I try to do my work."

Izzy bent forward over her belly, covered her face with her hands, and started crying. ¡Ya wey! Enough already. My simpatía gauge was running on fumes. I was tired of being accused of something I wasn't even thinking about.

Just then I got a text from Terri.

La Cindy just called. She says she has something for you, she won't say what. I don't know what to think. It smells kinda fishy. Maybe you should go check it out. Come by the office after, if you can.

I turned and walked back out the door. I heard Izzy call out my name but I didn't answer. I went down the stairs two at a time and came out onto the street.

No matter how crazy Izzy had been acting, no matter what my cousin had asked of me, I should have stayed at home to comfort my girl.

It was something I'd live to regret, probably for the rest of my life.

15

I didn't feel like walking back down to Humboldt Park again. A #53 southbound bus was coming, so I hopped on. My mind was at war with itself: Irritation at the friction back at home, curiosity about what lay ahead.

I got off at West Augusta and started walking east. I saw the Ukrainian Village Tavern in the distance and knew I was getting close. Then I heard a familiar voice, talking fast and loud. La Cindy was pacing the alleyway between the bar and Blue Line Station. I heard the desperation in her voice before I could make out the words.

"Dammit Stuey, will you listen to me? I told you I'll have your money…Yes, all of it. I swear…Oh, for Christ's sake! I just need a little time. A client has a project this Friday…Yeah, the studio pays out the same day. Just work with me, Stuart. I won't stiff you this time, I promise."

So, in addition to her drinking, La Cindy had another habit. It sounded to me like she might be owing money to her dealer. A tight spot to be in, I knew.

She emerged red-faced from the alleyway, cursing under her breath. The sunlight was harsh on her face. Maybe she was closer to tail end of her forties. Cindy's frown turned into a phony smile when she saw me coming closer. "Well, if it isn't charming José again. We've got to stop meeting like this."

"I was just on my way to your place. I hear you got something for me."

"Absolutely." She patted the side of her leggings though I didn't see a pocket. "Let's not transact our business on the street. Come into my office."

I followed her into the bar, where she led me to a corner with a pool table.

"What's this about?" I asked her.

"Just a friendly game of billiards, amigo."

I didn't like the sound of Spanish in her mouth. "I didn't come here to play."

She ignored me and racked up a set. "Twenty dollars a game."

"I don't play against women and I never play for money."

"Then we'll have to play for drinks." She grinned.

"I don't really do liquor, chica. Nothing more than a Corona every now and then."

"Aw," she pouted. "Is the wittle bitty Mexican a-scared of the big, bad Patrón?"

That's when I knew that Cindy was hustling me. She probably conned everybody she came across. La Cindy was hard up for money by the sound of that phone call. More likely than not, gambling was her co-addiction. That had probably been her bookie on the phone, leaning on her hard.

La Cindy continued to tease me. "I'll go ahead slum it with you for drinks. I usually play the big money crowd."

Damn straight, I thought. *With other people's money.* I made the second mistake of the day. "Fine, Cindy. Whatever. Let's get this over with. I expect you to give me what I came or when this is over."

The bartender lined up ten shots at the far end of the table. La Cindy chalked up her cue stick. "Loser pays all."

Here's the killing thing about it. The drunker she got, the better

Cindy played. The tequila seemed to sharpen her focus and steady her shaky hands. When I was down by two to her six, she called for another round of shots. By the time she had beat me eleven to eight, we were both wasted as fuck. La Cindy drank way more than me and was practically falling over.

I ain't never been down with spirits, chulo. It makes me stupid sick. I get hot and start turning red all over, which ain't easy for a brown-skinned Mexican like me. Couldn't handle booze is how I started tussing as a teenager. I didn't notice the after-affects until it was too late to stop.

The day was warm enough that someone had a side door propped open. La Cindy staggered over, sat on the step, puked into the alley, then lights out. She slumped in the doorway like a rag doll.

I went over and shook her shoulder. "You said you had something for me, Cindy. Come on, I ain't got all day."

The bartender came over with the check in one hand and a cup of black coffee in the other. He frowned at La Cindy lolling in the doorway before turning to me. "Drink up, pay up, and get her the hell out of here."

"Hey," I protested. "I'm not the one responsible."

"You came in with her, didn't you? You can't leave her here like this. We've only been open an hour and Cindy's already three sheets to the wind. Looks like you could use a little sobering up yourself."

"La verdad," I agreed. "You're not lying. José Cuervo ain't never been no friend of mine."

I downed the hot coffee, grabbed La Cindy around the waist, half-walked and half-dragged her home. I got us both up the steps of the coach house and fumbled through her purse for the key.

Suddenly the door flew open from the inside. A tall blonde in what looked like a men's suit stood there scowling at me. She might have been pretty if she didn't look so damned mean. I wondered if she lived there. She wasn't old enough to be Cindy's mother and they didn't look like sisters.

"What the hell is this?" she hissed. "And who the hell are you?"

I tried to climb out of my drunk to answer her coherently. "Cindy got drunk at the Ukrai… Ukrai…at the bar back there. They told me to bring her home. She lives here, right?"

The blonde stared at me another second before holding open the door. As I helped her inside, Cindy opened her bloodshot eyes and squinted at the other woman.

"Hey, Monica," she slurred. "I want you to meet my good friend. My very, very good friend. His name is…Wha' you say your name was?"

"José," I answered. "Where do you want her to go?"

Monica pointed to the sofa. When I dumped there, La Cindy pulled me down on top of her. She slobbered all over my lips and neck, then turn her head and puked into a throw pillow.

I looked back and saw Monica was still standing at the open doorway, gripping the doorknob so hard I was afraid she'd break it off. I realized the suit she wore was an airline uniform.

"Hey, what are you?" I asked stupidly. "A flight attendant or something?"

"Not that it's any of your business, José, but I'm an airline pilot. Now get the hell out of my house before I call the police."

I headed toward the door, then stopped in my tracks. "Wait a minute, Monica. Cindy and I got business. She owes big money. She's been ripping off my client."

"Your client?" she hissed in disbelief. "What kind of client do you have?"

"She's jacking Jimmy Hill for all his money and trying to force him into porn." I pointed to the summons lying on the floor where it had fallen. "If you don't believe me, read it."

Monica picked up the document and looked it over. She seemed extremely pissed off with what she saw but not all that surprised. She let the summons flutter back to the floor.

Monica walked over to a roll top desk, took out a folder, opened it, wrote something down, tore it off, and slid it in an envelope.

When she handed it to me, I looked inside and saw a check, the numbers and letters swimming before my eyes. Even as drunk as I was, I could see it was made out in the sum of twenty-five thousand dollars from Monica Weissman to Jimmy Hill. The memo section read, "Services paid in full."

I left the coach house and started weaving my way toward the El station. When I got there, I realized I didn't have my cell phone on me. I searched the Ukrainian Village Tavern and didn't see it. I tiredly trudged back toward La Cindy's house.

A Lincoln Town Car was double parked out front. Monica came out carrying a suitcase, a jacket over her arm. She opened the car door, got inside, then climbed back out again. When she ran into the gangway I followed in my Chuck Taylors, silent as the wind.

I came out into the yard and ducked behind a blooming snowball bush. Monica Weissman was muy intimidante. I sure as hell didn't want to mix it up with her again.

The coach house door was sitting open. The same one who'd been legless and puking into a pillow a few minutes ago was back on her feet. La Cindy stood in the doorway holding up a leather satchel and wearing the same silky robe she had on earlier. Monica took the steps two at a time, grabbed the bag from her hand, leaned in, and planted a kiss on the lips.

She was turning away when Cindy yanked open her robe. Monica couldn't resist. She reached in and groped around, mashing lips with her again. When Monica finally left, Cindy leaned against the doorway with her robe hanging open, rubbing herself between the legs.

If there was any question about their relationship, it was now clear as glass.

16

Katrina had brought her baby with her to the office. I hadn't realized that the kid was an Afro-Latino-Arab terrorist. Gusto Amrani was hollering up a storm, crawling around and pulling things down. Terri kept moving things out of his way and rolling her eyes at her sister.

The cousins couldn't understand why I came rolling in drunk as a sailor. When I tried to explain why I had to play pickled pool with La Cindy, it didn't make sense even to my own ears.

"You smell like a damned distillery." Terri frowned. "I don't remember you as a lush."

Her harangue was interrupted by the arrival of Jimmy Hill. This time he was styling in a light summer suit, complete with a pocket watch and panama hat. Our boy was looking *GQ* clean. When Terri handed him the check, tears came to his eyes.

"Is this for real?" he exclaimed. "You're not a detective, you're a miracle worker."

Terri inclined her head toward me. "With a whole lotta help from my drunk cousin. Get that check to the bank right away. I'm sending you my bill and I don't want it to bounce."

"Hey." Katrina smirked in Jimmy's face. "Wouldn't you like to ask the miracle worker out?"

"Trina!" we both shouted.

"No, thank you." Jimmy shook his head. "I'm not really into that."

"You see!" Terri said triumphantly. "I knew the man was gay!"

"Oh, I'm not gay."

Katrina wouldn't leave it alone. "What, so you don't like Afro-Latino women?"

"Your sister is very pretty. But I'm not attracted to anyone, male or female. I'm what's known as asexual."

"La verdad?" I stirred out of my drunk to ask. "They got Viagra and shit for that."

Jimmy Hill shook his head, pointing to the pin on his suit lapel. "I'm fine the way I am."

"Asexuals got their own flag?" Terri asked.

"The purple is for our community. The white is for our sexuality…"

"Which you say you don't have any of," Katrina interrupted.

"Actually," Jimmy explained, "there's a spectrum between sexuality and asexuality. The gray stands for demisexuality. Some people have urges now and again that they may or may not act on. The black is for strict asexuality, which goes for people like me."

"Well, he's about as useful as a broke-dick dog." Katrina shook her head when he left. "I'm so confused right now. That's a criminal waste of pretty."

"Even if Jimmy wasn't asexual," Terri told her, "I could never be with anybody so much finer than me."

"That's lies," I sang. "Ain't nobody finer in the state of Carolina in the morning. You're fine as wine, dolomite."

I went into Michael Jackson's "Pretty Young Thing," got up, and drunk-danced Terri across the tiny office before she pushed me away. "Get off me, you drunk fool. I've never seen you like this."

They sent me home in an Uber and told me to sleep it off.

17

It was beginning to be like *Groundhog Day*. I came home and found Isabella in the same place, sitting at the computer desk in tears. Her head was buried in her hands.

"You made me do it, Lalo. This is all your fault."

A splotch of blood was seeping through her pants and spreading upward.

"Izzy, this is nobody's fault. I think your water broke. We're going to have a baby."

I called 911, and an ambulance took us to Illinois Masonic. In the maternity ward we found out that Izzy was in false labor. Her blood pressure was dangerously high, so the doctor decided to keep her overnight.

They must have given her something because she was drifting in and out sleep. I tucked the sheets around her and noticed scratches and bruises on her wrists. "How did you hurt yourself?"

Izzy burrowed into her pillow. "I tried and tried to call you, Lalo. You never answered the phone."

"Yeah, I lost it somewhere. The last time I remember seeing it was at the Ukrainian Village Tavern."

"That's not the Ukrainian Village," she mumbled. "It's Humboldt Park."

"Don't worry about it, babe. Just try to relax."

I called Izzy's parents, though I knew they didn't like me. When Matteus and Marina Esposito arrived, the nurses told us Izzy could only have two visitors at a time. Mrs. Esposito gave me a dirty look when she smelled the booze on my breath.

"You go home now," she ordered. "When you are in good condition, bring nice nightgown for my daughter to wear. This hospital one is crap."

Since Izzy had her people with her, I decided to follow orders. When I got home I started on the overnight bag we'd never got around to packing. Suddenly I heard the sound of a cell phone ringing. I followed it to its source, the computer desk drawer.

I didn't know if I was still drunk or dreaming. My cell phone shouldn't be there. I'd lost it at the bar or in La Cindy's place. Or, could I have had it on me all this time, brought it home, put it in the desk drawer, and forgot it? No, I was drunk but not *that* drunk.

The ringing stopped then started over again.

"Hey," I answered to my cousin Terri. "Izzy's in the hospital."

"Is she having the baby?"

"No, not yet. They're keeping her for observation."

"I pray she'll be okay. Look, you haven't seen the news yet, have you? Turn it on and call me back."

It was so surreal that I couldn't believe my eyes or my ears. One Cinderelle Brandy McGhee had been found dead that afternoon in the Humboldt Park residence she shared with a friend. Cause of death, undetermined. The police were investigating.

I called Terri right back. "Cindy McGhee is dead! How did this happen?"

"I checked in with some of my CPD contacts. It looks like foul play. They're just waiting for the medical examiner's report."

"Terri," I took a deep breath, trying to push my way out of intoxication, "I had nothing to do with this. You got to believe me. Cindy was alive when I left there. Terri, you there?"

There was a pause at the other end, before she finally responded. "Yeah, I believe you. But you were probably one of the last people to see her alive. Don't be surprised if the police call you in for questioning. Who do you think could have done this?"

"Who knows? The girlfriend may have had a motive to kill her. It seems Cindy slept around. A guy named Stu—I think he's her bookie—was threatening her on the phone. Hell, Jimmy Hill himself wouldn't be sorry to see her gone, especially now that he has his money."

"I'm sending Katrina over there. You're going to need counsel on this one."

"Well, have her meet me at Illinois Masonic," I said. "I'm going back there now."

I picked up the overnight bag and headed for the door. My mind was ticking like a time bomb, banging against my brain. Something clicked in place.

That's not the Ukrainian Village, it's Humboldt Park. How did Izzy know?

You made me do it, Lalo! This is all your fault. What did Izzy mean?

My lost cell phone ringing in the computer desk drawer. How did it get there?

I went back, logged onto the computer, and found out what my girlfriend had been hiding from me. Isabella Esposito had had me under surveillance for weeks. The "Find My Phone" application was open, my telephone number selected. I went back through the history.

Izzy had been tracking the cell phone she'd given me. The last report showed it traveling from Humboldt Park to Hermosa, arriving back here at 2:37 p.m. But wait, I hadn't come straight home. I'd stopped at Terri's office first.

The realization kicked me in the gut like a mule. Somebody had gone to Cindy's house, found my cell phone there, and brought it back home.

When the cops rang the bell, I waited for them at the front door with both hands raised. "Officers, I'm confessing to the crime. But before you take me in, I need to use the john. I'm not trying to escape but I think I need to puke."

18

It's all your fault…it's all your fault! Those words followed me through the reading of Miranda rights, the handcuffing, the walk to the cruiser. They taunted me on the ride to the precinct, the lockup, the arraignment, and on to Cook County Jail.

You made me do this, Lalo! echoed in my head, nearly drowning out the monkey mouth in the bunk below me singing "Drunk on a Plane" when it should have been "Locked Up." It broke through my blinding hangover, puke rising at the back of my throat.

Everything was my fault.

A CO came to get me later. He said I had a visitor.

Katrina waited for me in the interview room. "Damn, you look terrible, Lalo. Don't worry. We're going to get you out of here."

"No, leave me," I said dully. "This is all my fault. Just do me a favor and check on Izzy, will you?"

"What the hell are you talking about? You're not making any sense."

"I don't need counsel, Katrina." I turned to the corrections officer. "I'm ready to go now. Please take me back to my cell."

19

It felt like I was hungover for three whole days. I will never, ever, EVER drink tequila again.

Thankfully I was sober by the time of my status hearing. I hadn't even had a chance to meet with my public defender. So, when they brought me into the courtroom I was shocked as all shit to see Katrina sitting in the counsel's chair.

I lifted my eyebrow in la mirada. *What the hell is going on?*

She gave me the look back. *Don't worry, cousin. I got you.*

Katrina Amrani de Robles may be vain and sometimes shallow, but when she was on her game the girl had it going on. Not only did she have the look down pat, she had the lingo and know-how to go with it.

"My client pleads not guilty, Your Honor. We have incontrovertible evidence that Eduardo E. Rodriguez could not have committed this crime. At one forty-seven p.m., the time of the victim's death, he was with counsel and his employer at a South Side location forty-five minutes away. I enter into evidence Exhibit A, the security footage from the Hyde Park Bank and Office Building. The recording is time-stamped with the day and time in question."

The judge interrupted when the prosecutor raised his hand. "Do you have an objection?"

"We request that the case against the defendant be dismissed. Another suspect has confessed to the crime and has evidence to prove it." The prosecutor consulted his notes. "One Isabella Esposito."

"No!" I shouted at him. "I don't want Izzy in jail."

"Counsel," the judge warned Katrina, "kindly inform your client that these outbursts will not be tolerated. While he may be regaining his freedom, I have no problem charging him with contempt and locking him up again. Is that understood?"

Katrina shot me a look that said, *shut your damned mouth.*

"Has this new suspect been arrested and charged?" the judge asked.

"Early in the day she was admitted to Cermack Hospital here at the Cook County Department of Corrections. So far as we know at this time, she's in the process of giving birth."

20

"I'm not the one who dropped a dime on Izzy." Katrina tore through rush hour traffic like a bat out of hell. "I didn't even know she was involved. The evidence came from Monica Weissman, the decedent's roommate…"

"Her novia," I corrected.

"Her partner, then. She gave the police security footage of Isabella letting herself in through an unlocked door then twelve minutes later, running out and leaving the door wide open. It all matches up with Cindy's time of death. I just don't understand what her motive could be."

"Izzy was crazy jealous," I sighed. "The pregnancy got her all paranoid and she hasn't been the same since. She was tracking my cell phone and found out I'd been by Cindy's place twice that day."

With the woman brutally murdered it didn't seem right to keep calling her La Cindy. The fact that her real name was Cinderelle seemed even more bizarre.

Katrina shook her head. "So Izzy went over, confronted Cindy, and smothered her with a pillow because she thought the two of you had something going? Damn, Lalo. That's…."

The twins exchanged looks.

"That's tragic," Terri finished.

"The bruises and cuts I saw on Izzy's wrists must have been defensive," I told them. "Izzy was eight and a half months pregnant and Cindy was sloppy drunk. She still tried fighting back."

Terri quickly blessed herself. Katrina whispered, "Madre de Dios."

"I know you can get better speed out of this thing," Terri told her sister.

'Don't be calling my car a thing. Her name is Betty Mae Wilson,

AKA BMW."

"Well, can't Miss Betty move any faster? We've only got twenty minutes to get there."

"Where are we going?" I asked.

"To Juvenile Court," Katrina explained, "to defend your parental rights. Isabella Esposito's family are trying to get custody of your child as soon as she's discharged."

Marilda Rodriguez was born yesterday, the day of my status hearing. It had taken overnight to get me processed. When I was released, I found Terri and Katrina waiting outside for me.

"The baby was transferred to NICU at Rush," Katrina explained, "but she's holding her own. The Espositos claim you're an unfit parent based on your criminal record, your lack of viable employment, and your drinking problem. We all know that's bullshit."

"Well, not exactly," I admitted. "My priors ain't no secret and I don't really have a job. I've struggled with an addiction before, but it wasn't alcohol. Maybe I should just let Izzy's family have her. How can I care for a newborn when I can barely take care of myself?"

Terri reached back and shoved me. "Don't even talk like that. You grew up without a father, don't do that to your child. That little girl is your flesh and blood. She needs you and you need her."

"As far as a job goes," Katrina added, pulling into the parking lot, "you are a full-time contractor with T. Robles & Associates. We had to get creative coming up with a job title. Until we get that felony expunged, we can't call you an investigator. So, for now, you are…"

"…Research Coordinator," Terri finished. "Professional-sounding but vague enough to cover a lot of bases."

I couldn't have loved those girls any more than I did at that moment. "I can't let you do this. You shouldn't be taking up for your older cousin. I'm a man, I should be taking care of you. I've never held you down. That's how I wound up incarcerated. I'm sorry I hurt you, Terri."

Terri frowned in my face. "What do you mean by that? That was my parents' garage you broke into. I didn't live there anymore."

"I never really knew the whole story," Katrina interjected. "I was away at law school. What exactly happened?"

"It was greed and my addiction. This negrón named Freddy Flinster talked me into helping him cut up a car that turned out to be stolen. I should have known better."

Terri nodded. "Yeah, I remember. Fred Flintstone, he called himself. I didn't like busting you, but I had a job to do."

"When you saw him crawling around the back of the garage, Freddy was reaching into the trunk for a weapon. If that matón had shot you, I would have had to take him out."

"Well, good thing he didn't try it," Terri reassured me, "because if he had, I would have got him first, believe that. You've already paid your debt and you don't owe me nada."

"Yes, I do. You've had my back for years. Remember that time you ran off those dudes that were coming for me in high school?"

21

When I started messing up at Washington High, Tío Papi gave me a lecture about hanging with losers. Then he got me transferred to St. Francis de Sales, where Katrina and Terri were starting high school that year.

One day these two kids decided to jump me. I don't think they were on no gangbanging tip. These boys were straight up nerds. News around school was that some ladrón had robbed a Black kid at the bus stop. I knew why the homeys were mad but I wasn't the one that did it. Even with two nerds against one fun-sized chavo, the odds weren't in my favor.

"We're fixing to play Whack-a-Mexican," one of them said. "Dantrell, you hold him down."

"Man, y'all tripping. I'm a straight up nigga." I pointed to Dantrell, who was trying to grab my arms from behind. "I'm twice as black as him."

"Did you say *nigga*?" The boy dropped my arms. "Jelani, you hear what he said?"

Jelani paused in mid-bitch slap. "Well, he is a whole lot darker than your yella ass."

"My ass ain't yella and that nigga ain't no nigga. I never seen no brother with hair that straight."

While they were debating my ethnicity, Teresita Robles came charging down the hall like a cheetah. She was wearing a jersey and shorts, so she must have bailed on basketball practice.

"You better not be messing with my cousin," she hollered. "I'll kick both you lames in the nuts."

The light-skinned boy let me go. The other one stepped back to gawk at Terri's long legs.

"That was on Dantrell," he told her. "I knew from jump street he was a brother. Hey, girl, can I get your number?"

"Matter of fact," she grinned, "you both can have it."

They looked at each other in shock. Dime-pieces like Terri didn't talk to lames like that.

"So, what's up with those digits?" Jelani asked.

"Come find me on September thirty-first. I'll give it to you then."

Terri grabbed my arm and pulled me away. The two boys stared after her. They knew they'd been tricked but couldn't figure out how.

"You didn't have to do that," I whispered. "I had it under control."

"What, I was supposed to just stand there and let somebody kick your butt? Katrina came into basketball practice and said some guys were about to jump you."

I would rather get a beat-down than look like a punk with my girl cousin saving my ass. True, she was almost six feet, nearly a foot taller than me. But she was a freshman to my senior, and she was a *girl*!

My twin sister, Ash, had already graduated from Washington and was in her first year at Chicago State. If I hadn't messed up I'd be finished, too. There I was, a whole year behind being rescued by my fourteen-year-old cousin. I learned the words for me in French class: homme pitoyable.

I'd gone through life having my family protect me, instead of me taking care of them.

Terri reached over the back of the seat and hugged me. "I don't even remember that. You'll be taking care of us soon enough, working with T. Robles. We need somebody who won't actually break the law, but knows how to…"

"Skirt it?" I winked. We got out and walked toward the Juvenile Court building. "Primas, let's do this thing."

22

I sat staring at the angel in my arms. There was no face more beautiful en todo el mundo.

I'd given her a bottle and she quickly fell asleep. Mari lay there in dreamland, her tiny red lips still sucking air. My daughter stretched, made a little grunt, and grinned at me in her sleep. Katrina had already told me three-week-olds don't smile. She was probably having gas.

When the doorbell buzzed I hurried to answer it. I didn't want the noise waking up Mari. I opened the door to see my twin sister, Ashley, standing there. She was holding a big bag of disposable diapers and an oversized stuffed beagle.

"Lalo!" She leaned forward and kissed my cheek. "Look at you. You're a daddy now. Ooh, can I see the baby?"

"Sit down and I'll let you hold her. Be careful, I don't want to wake her up."

"Que preciosa." Ash gazed at her sleeping niece, the hunger plain on her face. "What's the little's one's name?"

"Marilda Lorashlee Rodriguez." I laughed. "Yeah, it's a mouthful. She's named for both her abuelas, Mami Imelda and Izzy's mother, Marina. Her middle name comes from…"

"Me and our Aunt Lori. I'm honored." My sister reached out to tenderly stroke Mari's cheek. "You're so lucky, Lalo."

I smiled back. "Yes, I know."

"It's going to be hard on a single man raising a child alone."

"Yeah, but I'll have help. There's Katrina, Terri, Aunt Lori, and Tío Papi. Izzy's parents will be in the baby's life, too. They were trying to get custody, but I'm putting that all behind me. I'm not trying to keep Mari away from anybody who loves her."

Ash settled back with the baby against her chest. "Joe and I will help, too, as much as we possibly can."

"I appreciate that, Ash. There's no such thing as too much family."

"I know things are still tight with you. Joe had a change of heart. You and Mari are more than welcome to stay with us in Bolingbrook. It's a great place to raise a kid."

I shook my head. "Thanks, but my new job is here in the city. I just don't have it in me to make that kind of commute."

Ashley took a deep breath and blurted out: "Joe and I would like to adopt the baby."

"Ashley, that's not going to happen."

She held onto Mari in pleading desperation, so tight the baby stretched and mewled in her sleep. "I know it's a big decision, Lalo. Please, just think it over. We'd give her a stable two-parent home and love her with all our hearts. And I saved up a few thousand for a new course of IVF treatment. I could let you have that toward the money I owe."

My sister had always been the respectable one in the family. My brothers were thugs, gangsters, and ¿quién sabe? I hadn't done much better. Yet I was certain that none of us had stolen from each other or tried to buy a child.

Ashley and I had never been as close as the Robles girls. We'd grown even further apart the older we got. Maybe because she was a girl, and me being born a boy. Or maybe it was Ash choosing the straight and narrow path, with me taking the crooked highway.

I got up and gathered my daughter back into my arms. Then I walked to the front door, opened it up, and showed my sister out.

GROTESQUE CABARET

ISAAC KIRKMAN

Winter, 2018

We've been in the city of the winter king for seven days, watching the widow's house. Snow whirls like geraniums past our car windows, as we sit silently smoking. My new partner smells like leather, kush, and roses. He is young and short of patience. He sighs, and repeats to me how to operate the surveillance program on the new tablet. He is tattooed and pretty, the way Hollywood stars who overdose are tattooed and pretty. And his gun is gold-plated and engraved with roses and skulls, and expresses clearly on which side of the gangsters' axiom he falls: glory over encryption.

But we've been selected, because we wouldn't be seen, or noticed, just two white men—perhaps father and son—in a station wagon parked in the snow, on a road outside a white neighborhood.

In the distance, beyond the ice-wilted forest, is Canada.

As I slide my glasses on to see how to switch the camera POV in the house, he looks up at me the way I once looked at old men like me. As if he's contemplating how much trouble he would be in if he pulled the trigger and dragged my body into the snow and took my cut.

My finger swipes left, and the widow reappears next to my

fingernail, and we watch her move, solemn and solitary, from room to room, before she settles by the fireplace and opens a book. Cameras small as the hope that this violence will end, concealed everywhere along her property and inside her house. Her phones and computers are tapped. Everyone she Skypes, everything she searches online, every key tapped, we witness. Every message back to her family in Hermosilla, we track. But she does nothing wrong. She has not betrayed our covenant. Her silence is as steady as the wipers clearing the snow. It takes a few minutes to get the hang of the replacement tablet, but when I do, my partner goes back to scrolling through his phone. The minutiae of surveillance bores him.

My new partner was an altar boy at a church my ex-wife and I once went to but he does not remember me, he still wears the cross. He says God is with him, all around, like the snow, concealing us.

We weren't supposed to kill her, but there is a new boss, and everything is being renegotiated. Wounds cauterized, loose ends burned. Which is why I'm here, in this Chrysler instead of my Ford. Why I've been on the road, seven months now, in this endless scream of sunrises. Why, after seventeen years, I started taking these pills again.

I sink into the seat when we get the message that she is to be erased. The widow's husband owned a series of car dealerships—cars we used to traffic guns—'til his thievery grew a shadow too long to not see, but she was one of those sullen things, kept segregated from his affairs. It's not that I'm opposed to violence, it's just this feels unnecessary. As if we were a construction crew told to tear down the entire house because of a single warped beam.

We've monitored her for months, and perched tightly this past week to every transmission, and there has been nothing but a woman rebuilding a life, from the rubble of an old life she seems grateful to be free of. Even the Feds have left to follow other dying things.

BOTH SIDES

But there is a new boss, and I am an old man. And the snow is falling faster, through this world of crumbling factories, and cars rusting beneath the winter sun. I look at my new partner; young enough, and emotionally distant enough, to be my son, and think about my old partner, the synergy we had, and how much I miss him, especially on cold surveillance trips like this, but that too has crumbled, like everything my shadow crosses.

We get word and return to our motel, shower, shave, and change into our cable uniforms. I smoke a pill solitary in the bathroom. Its lunar white surface burns eclipse black on the foil as I fall to my knees as if in prayer. Outside, the snow erases the horizon, save for a single blue chapel cross pulsing in the distance. Everything softens. I return to find my partner cleaning his gun, silhouettes from the blunt smoke weaving across the gold muzzle. If I didn't watch him grow up, I witnessed his beginning. Blizzard warnings loop on the television taper. My partner turns to me and says the widow's cable box has been disabled and the company has called her to say we would be there this afternoon to fix it. He returns to cleaning the gun. Cocaine residue glitters across the glass. I notice his facial tattoos are gone, they've been concealed with makeup. Everything feels like a dream.

We exit and silently drive to the warehouse. My partner makes the sign of the cross at every church we pass. There isn't much to say, I'm too high to form words, and he has nothing to say that doesn't make everything more uncomfortable. The landscape is emaciated and buried in emptiness. Icy cornfields crackle like lake waves. I smoke more pills, these ones to wake.

Abandoned buildings drift past. An hour passes. The frozen trees all look like grotesque angels, weeping from the weight of ice on warped branches. I point, telling my partner the trees were planted decades ago as part of a downtown revitalization that has slipped into disarray. I aim for something cordial to break the silence. He shrugs and says if it didn't find a way to survive, it isn't worth telling him about, and goes back to his phone.

The killings are recent, but partners like this aren't. Smoke dances across the exposed skin of my fingerless wool gloves. Snow crystals swirl through the tiny crack in the window the smoke escapes through. I turn sixty this year. When I was his age, I pulled the trigger, but now, at least this past decade, or the past twelve years—it's hard to keep track—time blurs—I supervise. I accompany others. Like a father or a brother taking a child hunting for the first time, and showing them how to stay downwind, sharing the ache of knees in cold morning mist, quietly hunched in blind, waiting for the animal. The partners were promising once, but now they're mostly fuck-ups, psychos, or someone demoted, or sent because their boss doesn't trust my boss, but the boss above both bosses demands at least some attempt at synastry between factions waiting for the other to slip.

I never had a problem killing, but then everything changed.

In the distance, trains whistle through the icy abstract. A solitary sex worker shivers in the falling snow. The amphetamines tighten the colors, crystallize the edges, but heighten the unreality. We move through the industrial sector of town, the smoldering factories paralyzed from a holiday strike, remnants from protest banners flap from boarded up windows. We arrive at the warehouse. Our gangland money is life support for a community near breathless. We're buzzed in. Boots crunch snow. Cigarette smoke weaves. Our beige cable uniforms in conjunction to illusion. Inside the warehouse, a cable van with plastic wrap and supplies for the disposal of the widow awaits us. The fixer, bearded but anonymous as me, hands me the keys. We inspect the supplies and go over the traffic log and back road maps one last time before heading back to the widow's house. Our hackers are monitoring, ready to switch the traffic lights. To understand us is to understand we are agents of order.

255

BOTH SIDES

They fear she may know names of kings, of senators, maps, and memories connected to shadows, and she may not know not to speak, even if it's only the shivering movements of lips mid-dream.

My partner drives as I watch the snow fall, the way I did as a child on the way to hunt with my father, then shift my attention to the tablet, where I watch the widow read her book, her black hair falling like my ex-wife's. I slip into the memory of another life. One of Christmas, and children, and porcelain snow falling. Of a wife, a forever, a farm, failure. Of a tree struck by lightning burning like a votive. As we pass a church, I catch myself doing the sign of the cross mid-motion, but my partner does not see. For seven months the widow has provided a focus, a peace that is impossible to express, other than the degree of sadness I feel, as the snow leads us to hello. It's strange to watch someone nearly every day for seven months unseen, and then to say goodbye this way. It's like she's become a friend. There is also the haunting curiosity of this book she continues to reread. No matter the zoom or the angle selected, I can't quite see the title. There is part of me that hopes to ask her about it, before the snow seals everything in silence. All around the blizzard builds, yet my partner, hands steady on the wheel, smiles calmly. With the makeup concealing his tattoos he appears almost cherubic.

THE ROAD

The road always reminds you of your wife. The phone rings, or vibrates with text, but it's not her, not anymore. You are now abstractions to each other. Human connection is never constant, it slips in and out of focus, like radio signals from falling planes.

You had a wife on the other end of the phone, when there was blood on your shoes, and a body, broken, on the floor. And she asks how the trip is, and your words are blank and smooth as stones washed in the river, and she feels how automated you've become, how blank and vast the chasm, between who you were, and who you are now, like a painting of a forest in reverse, stroke by stroke receding into blankness. One leaf, then another disappearing. The barn, the birds in the sky erasing, colored layer by colored layer stripped, as you recede from realism to abstraction, from flat beams of color into white blankness. In that blankness, she fills it with fear of infidelity or another family, but there is only her, and the work, and this body that you opened for the first time. You watch the blood pour on the floor, as the angels read every memory and fear and dream they ever had, and wonder what the angels will read when it's your turn.

And you begin to measure the distance with loved ones, with everything you can't say. You know the phones are tapped, and if they're not, you know better than to take the chance. So, you only share parts of yourself, the rest you cloak, or you fracture. And if there is a you in bed with your wife, there is another driving through the desert with kilos, and a black book of the dead, or soon to be dead. There is you at the race track, and you as a boy with your dog, racing through the gold field at dusk, and you sitting on the boat with friends, who no longer can be friends, because this canvas that is being unpainted, the blankness spreads into them, and you grow into emptiness, cast down a very long hallway you interact with the world from.

But blankness is the death of form, and like a plant unwatered, each of these yous, these worlds, fall like leaves, onto the surface of unswept floors.

And then you wake up and you're fifty or turning sixty, and you're alone, even inside yourself, because you stop processing what's happening, so it doesn't show in facial expression, or some biometric or lie detector. You become unreal to yourself. You say you're saving for a boat, to retire on some long stretch of water, but at the time you're saving for this, you're spending the parts of yourself that can experience this world as anything other than something monstrous.

VAVILOVIAN MIMICRY

Summer, 2019

We're parked in a garage, miles from the border. I sit on the bench crushing pills as my current partner circles the station wagon, whistling and pressing stickers onto our windows and bumpers. This is our third job together. She's gained weight since our last one. Her weight makes our illusion stronger. The pills have left my body a permanent strobing sweat. Outside the sun incinerates. Shadows burn from saguaros. Birds tumble from the sky. Their broken wings blistered against desert caliche. Slashed water jugs melt in the washes. Migrants stumble, their skin sunray sabered, across ravines, to an American hope more trickster than priest. Normally, we travel south in migration with the snowbirds. A blizzard of credit cards and pale skin. We wear the same shirts and shorts as them, our eyes the same empty blue as theirs. The same sixty-year-old bodies, softened from success and desert winters. But the killings this winter, and the regime changes, require proof of our loyalty. So we migrate, not to escape the snow, but to cross the border for medicine and better smiles and to deliver these gifts from our bosses. On the radio they speak of tariffs and migrants in detention camps, and everyone is screaming. I lower my head and snort neon-colored lines. The room softens. Mexico eats our sins the way the desert eats the rain. Anything that falls has to be treated as a miracle.

We've waited a week for our Border Patrol agents to give us words to cross over. The gifts are these guns, and this widow's hand. There is only one gun shop in Mexico. American women, grandmothers,

mothers, students will buy a gun, and a buyer will buy from them, and we will dismantle and ship them south. The white woman's hand holds the chains, linked to a million tear-wet brown eyes. The news anchor says a sixty-eight-year-old anarchist was killed attacking an ICE facility. I hear my partner yell to turn the channel, but I do not turn, or shift or respond. I examine my empty features in the mirror. These guns are promises that nothing ends, everything watches, and America must be fed. My partner turns the channel and starts singing. Partners like this are more annoying than dangerous. They talk, they slather. But they are necessary. Alone in Mexico I am DEA or cartel, but beside her I am husband. Perhaps a grandfather. She is a cataract to the machinery of watchers that await us, a fat smudge of grease against the endless eye. In another life she was a prison guard, and a wife to a man, slipping away as the tidal currents of hospital gurneys and heart monitors swept in. Cancer falling like ash through the snowbank of his body. But he passed, and the debts grew like nooses from the shattered limbs of her family tree and she suspended, made a choice.

Together we are another in a long line of citizens crossing over for a better deal.

Together we are white; blank and anonymous as a virus.

My eyes slip shut, and the widow drifts through the watery routes between each breath. I see the shadow her body burned into the warehouse floor, and the look in her eyes at the betrayal of this stranger that I have become. The shadow looks like a womb. It looks like my son. I catch myself instinctively sliding my finger against the glass car window, but the widow does not appear. For months that motion brought clarity. It brought peace.

My partner taps the bumper at the final sticker. The last few hundred miles we've driven as a couple through rural America with stickers supporting Jesus and Trump. Now she is stripping those and layering stickers supporting national parks and coexisting and various yoga mantras. She does not know of the guns hidden in the station wagon compartments, nor the cases of bullets, nor the hand of the widow in ice beside the bullets. She doesn't care to ask. What matters is the sip of good drinks, and the turn of a beach read in a forever rotating paradise our company pays for.

On our phones are photoshopped pictures of us, as a married couple in this fictitious life, with fictitious texts. She did not know of the guns we moved last year, when we moved in migration with all the snowbirds with pale bare legs, across the desert like the strangest of snow. She did not know of the guns or the millions in cash stashed before, all she cared was when this was done, she would have more, that her tomorrow would always be better. No one wakes up wanting less. Who wants to give their tomorrow to someone else?

We make a final inspection and then depart. The sun drags behind us like a scythe. The road ahead, she drives and sings, and checks her crooked yellow teeth in the mirror and daydreams of the great American smile the dentist across the border will give her. There is no killing, there is no genocide awaiting. Outside our window flash billboards proclaiming Jesus is alive and buy Mexican insurance with cartoonish images of sombreros and mustaches. Flat high desert gives way to a leviathan hillside splitting two cities with its great keloid scar of razor wire and cameras.

MANIFEST DESTINY

I am simply a mechanic sent to make sure the assembly line keeps moving. An insentient cog of fingernails and teeth, turning my piece of this machine. Of black and brown parts, grinding black and brown parts, as men white as me stand watch, safe and rich and clean, inside my private atrocities. It feels somewhere, something shattered, in the repetition of coke-cloaked caravans and corpses. I am postmortem. I am sunlight frozen. I am on the curb, crying at the dying bird. I hope to god there is nothing after this life, that I'm just meat for the fire, but there is a fear growing that this will never end.

SOUTHERN MIGRATIONS

The widow's corpse lies in my trunk, as I sit idle, car to car to a white cop, waiting for the traffic light to turn. Snowflakes spin like children in the strobing colored lights. The game hums on my radio, and he leans in to catch the score, then smiles and nods as if looking at a mirror, and I smile back. A mirror must be loyal to perception.

There was a time, in youth, I felt cocky, that my ability to move unseen was because I was luckier and smarter than everyone else. Now that I'm older, and the jobs I am selected for are strictly because I'm old and white, thus invisible, or not a threat, it's clear that my strength was always that I was seen by those in charge as one of them. White, blank, anonymous. A dove in a snowstorm. A plate of glass against a blank page. I look in the rearview at the cars in the snowy distance.

They send us in caravans. Like today, they will send someone ahead of me, sometimes two, who are not white, but driving clean, to draw focus from the local law when what I'm transporting is particularly explosive. Kilos or cellophane-wrapped cash, or this body, wrapped in plastic like a raincloud, body arched in a bolt, ready to boom. We own the sheriffs in small rural towns where the respiratory system of the community, its breath, is threaded with the wrist of the quarterback and the rise and fall of rain on wilted crops. Or at least a county deputy or two. We pass through, and their mildewed school libraries have new computers and carpets, and the vultures circle the sky of other towns, and for a moment, when the children step on rival fields with new uniforms, they are not the decaying shame of an obsolete America. The drugs in my wheel wells power the stockbroker, and the college kid on sweat-haloed dance floors, where they'll rise and pop pills and pen papers that will critique this red state with the moral purity of a bloodless coco leaf. Somewhere in the caravan, another car heading south with guns or cash, or north with kilos, will be driven by an old white couple, or a white mother with white children. And eyes—we have cameras in roadside businesses and gas stations, drones, and hackers surveillance on points throughout the journey. Whoever has eyes, we see through them.

THE WEEPING IS ENDLESS

The widow is running, screaming through a black glass maze, in the same expanding universe as I float, naked in my mother's womb, tiny feet kicking. And stars are bending to the shape of a boom, of God's hello, welcoming humanity atom by atom into his loneliness. And all those atoms contain my mother's love, and the bullet and the hand that held the gun, and the hand that held the widow, as she was raised from her mother's womb, and it's all one singular Pangea, until the first wave breaks. I wake sweaty, in a motel in Sonora, the television a crackling black frost, and I am still living.

THE BEFORE: ENTER THE WIDOW

Winter, 2019

It's the first time in months I've seen the widow smile. Her bags are packed. I watch her on the tablet a final time, as my partner leans in and presses the intercom button on the box by the lonely iron gate. We're buzzed in, and we weave slowly up the driveway. The unkempt gardens sprawling like a fading scream. Deer race through the snowy kaleidoscopic. The sun is gone. Everything is white.

The mansion is massive, but collapsing into the lake. In its frozen state it looks like it's being stabbed by a long blade of ice. There is a tarp covered in snow over the hole, suspended, like a wedding veil. The rest of the grounds are disappearing into the overgrowth. Winter-decayed vines grip the sides of the mansion like talons, dragging what the husband stole into the frozen abyss. In my peripheral, shadowy things move. I turn. But all there is, is falling snow outside my window.

Somewhere there is a bullet, lodged in a skull of a body lost in a forgotten forest, and from that hole grew the Porsche collecting dust in the garage—another bullet, another body, somewhere in an algae labyrinth of water-buried cars and submerged trees paved the pool frozen with insects and sleeping frogs. Someone's child, someone's forever. That all of this is an exchange. We used her husband's cars to move guns into Mexico. Those guns silenced reporters, and mayors, slashed a line between us and them. The sun rises, the sun falls, and each morning, Americans awaking, bored and pharmaceutically intoxicated to a brown world, forever beneath. The cartel is everywhere. It is here, it is on every shore, in every foreign city—a perfect ballet of miracle and violence.

I don't understand this world, this country, this future we're moving through. I understand neither side. I am the gray inside the fear, the illusion of walls when everything is crumbling. We park the van and I see her shivering in the doorway, clutching her arms beneath her mink coat.

After seven months watching her, this feels unreal. As if she were a beam of light from some unseen film projector, disguised as a dying star, or something the mansion dreamt as it sunk into the lake, or something I dreamt drifting opiate-eyed across barren highways, of nights more weeping than miracle. But she is real, as is everything that follows this.

RIVER

You remember the last time you crossed over that time by the river. You studied the storm pouring into the crack that splits these worlds. The river, the sky and the rain forming one, single pulse. That's what you think of sitting here, as his body trembles on the silent earth. That the government, the cartels...the people they serve, they say it's separate, but like the storm, the government thrashes wildly from above, but it feeds the river, and the river rises back up and floods the banks, flowers the washes. Then returns to the sky. That there is no separation between the cartels and the government, they are one as the rain and the river. And all the cities, books, and shows and all our happy little lives are flowering from its fertility.

WIDOW

It's a strange feeling to surveil someone for months, then speak to them, like this, and pretend to be a stranger. I know the widow's sorrows, her wishes, her dreams. The songs she skips, and the songs she lets loop like an endless rainfall. You know which parts of the porn she replays before she cums, then falls asleep. Which picture of lost loved ones that are too much when she turns off the laptop or gets up and pours a drink. The emotions and memories that are the hardest to express when she continues to retype a sentence. I've fallen asleep watching her, and dreamed of her, of us, those dreams where you live entire lifetimes with someone. I watch her move toward the drawer, like I've watched dozens of times. But this time the gun is not loaded. While she was gone our workers removed the bullets and dosed the smoothie in her fridge so this will end as softly as possible. Her Australian sheepdog watches us as he gnaws a bone.

When you surveil, you know things about them their closest friends and lovers do not. In this line of work, it's not hard to see how something like god could exist. Not in any benevolent sense, but that there is something out there watching us. You know that if something isn't watching you, something is trying to find you.

It's strange to think if we'd arrived seven months ago, or even two, she'd have run or grabbed her husband's gun, but seven months solitary, she's open to trust whatever reality we've led her into. She stares solemnly at the snow falling through the forest outside the window. The book held softly in her hand.

For the first time I see the cover. It reads *Ishmael*. She moves dreamlike to the cabinet and removes the pitcher. She slices fruit and adds protein powder with the drugs in it. The ritual of blender and powders and citrus.

"You got a favorite show you're missing, ma'am?"

I point at the dusty movie theater screen as I unpack the cable tool bag. Her eyes shift to the book by the sliced fruit. Knife in hand. Without looking up she points the knife at the book.

"Not a fan of television. I prefer…"

My partner stretches plastic wrap down the hall and the pup rises and trots toward him.

"Is all that necessary?" she says, turning toward the shadow my partner is casting.

Her eyes shift to him then to me, then to the panel where her husband's gun was stashed beyond the fed's obsession.

My partner looks up with the charm of an angel, that leads the winged to great falls.

"Bad wires. We had a storm short things further up the grid. And some of the insulation they put in couldn't handle the jolt."

I point at the book. "What's that about?"

She turns back to me and studies my face.

"It's about a gorilla telepathically telling a man how the world began. It's about leavers and takers." She pauses.

"You seem familiar. Do I know you?"

I smile. "Nah, ma'am, just got one of them faces."

I watch her finger the smoothie, knife beside her. What is in there will make her sleep. Make her not experience this. What she will know is a nice chat on a lonely snowy day, then, just as the storm outside peaks and the world is blank, she will close her eyes and forget this life ever was cruel.

My partner removes the silencer.

We stand here talking, and for a moment, I can see the child she was, in monsoon-glimmering barrios, streets shimmering with wet datura petals, and me in a field of snow, hand still innocent, holding a rifle, holding my brothers' hands, holding this moment in the lines in my palm. She sips her smoothie then heads over to the bags.

"Getting out of the snow for a bit?"

She looks at me like I'm a ghost, and perhaps I am, that this unreality is the valium she takes, or the exhaustion of sleepless nights, but she moves as if dead or unreal and asks.

"Do you think someone can start over? Do you think there are second chances?"

"I don't know, ma'am. I guess. I'm a little old for tomorrows."

I smile softly, waiting for the smoothie to make things simple.

Then my partner fucks everything up.

As we're talking we hear her dog howling frantically, followed by my partner screaming, then the sound of something crashing, and the widow rushes over, and I follow. My partner is strangling her dog. His gold gun is out, and the arm holding it is bleeding. The widow screams and runs. My partner raises his trembling arm and fires. The first bullet hits the wall, the second explodes her kneecap. The book claps bloody against the wall. She whirlwinds against the china cabinet, shattered glass slashes her face and arms but she keeps moving. As she thrashes toward the hidden board where her husband's empty gun is stashed, I raise my gun and fire. Her body pops and stops, then collapses. She's on the ground convulsing, her eyes locked on mine crying, roll back. I step across the book, aim the gun, and fire again. Everything she ever was, stops. My hand is shaking. I look down at the blood sprayed against the words on the open book—this is the story of leavers and takers. I feel like I am dying. I feel like weeping.

The sky is still, and everything is perfectly, blank. The snowy landscape unspoiled by a single footprint, or fallen branch, and we are returning, with her body inside the trunk, alongside her dog, and I can't find it in me to look at my partner without pulling the trigger. He is staring silently into the icy entropy, whiskey flask pressed against lips.

WAKING JUST TO DIE

The widow is dead. You wake in the night, naked with rifle, and peer through the drapes at the movement outside. Outside the window, you see a hunched Christ holding a cross, stumbling wearily across what looks like red waves—but when you look, it's bodies, brown bodies. They are adorned in bright indigenous fabrics. The hemoglobin waves crackle then clot, and swarms of insects hatch from eggs beneath its surface. In the Christ's hand is a chain, wrapped around wrist, dragging children behind him, black children, garbed in strange clothes, and you recognize them, they are of the Orisha. These are the children of Ogun, and Oya and Oshun. Sweat burns down your face. As the blood parts, you see your female cop partner arrive in the taxi.

LA FRONTERA

Our car is parked on the American side of the split cities, with a hole in the trunk positioned over a hole in the parking lot that leads to the wish. Our guns and bullets are moving piece by piece through the ventricle. Beside sodden tunnels are sallow-cheeked hunched children navigating to hope. And here I sit, on cantina bench dripping with chemicals, watching the Mexican block of buildings shift like technicolored Rubik's cubes. One bright-colored bar opens, with fresh tunnels beneath, another bar closes as old tunnels are discovered and sealed. Construction workers swirl in dusty nebulas. Everything is a mask wearing a mask. Everything weeps with sweat. My body is a widow shaped hole. The Americans pour through the gates, in endless lines for medicine and new smiles. Holding tax-free liquor and smokes, eyes on whores and drugs and dreams. Everything watches. Everything scans. These guns we shipped will go to the local police, others to the local cartel. This is not about violence. Or evil. This is about balance. We are agents of order. I search the other blank white faces. Somewhere in there is a caravan of smugglers like us. The Mexican locals watch us all. Wondering what they can take from us, what we have come to take from them. I take a seat on the bench and the pills disintegrate me. My partner is in the dentist with the other wives. Our workers are moving the guns and the hand of the widow from the compartments in our station wagon, through holes in the parking garage, to the tunnels, that spider-web beneath the divided cities. In the streets, all around me, pharmacists announce their wares in mangled English. Everyone is scanned for what they have come to take. Dick pills for this one, opiates for that one. Every wound scanned, every hunger measured.

A white-haired American citizen, invisible as us, sits next to me. He is holding a carton of cigarettes bought in the tax-free border zone. Shadows drip across our plastic faces. The sun slowly suicides. I am empty, the killings fall through me like rainfall, and I am left clear. I wonder if he has come to kill me, but he chatters about whores and cheap booze. He is as meaningless as a dream. He is another American citizen in a swarm of white hair and blue eyes that collect like locusts. The border is where Americans feed their shadows. The hills swoop and descend, with crumbling technicolor houses, vibrating with eyes. In the sky are drones and Israeli satellites, and wonders of such paranoid splendors. In the passageways surrounding the cities, migrants tumble, bloody and dehydrated, through sun-blackened ravines. But none of this matters. I have no insights to the people who live and die, and dream and dance so beautifully here. They are alien. I am simply a silent ghost, a parasite. I say lo siento when I bump shoulders, and move with quiet grace. I see others like me. Moving in and out of shops. There is a quiet density to them. A control. The real sicarios pull silence and shadow around them like a funeral veil. On every corner someone is watching, a child or an old man, or woman, with a camera phone clicking and sending images of any stranger who is to strange. The city whirls with chemicals and curses and miracles. My partner is inside, with her teeth growing whiter and straighter. Everyone in the waiting room is one image closer to their online illusion.

There will be young brown children, strewn out like wilted crops, from these bullets. Fathers will hang from bridges, and mothers will kneel, crumbling like flowers from the sunlight of each bang. There will be innocents collapsing in marketplaces from bullets sprayed from mopeds from the ammunition moving silently from our cars.

BOTH SIDES

And I am here, as my son's face grows blurrier and blurrier, and my wife and the widow all drift down a long black river to the beginning of when I said yes. I see the widow in every child, in every cloud, in every rippling puddle. In the distance is a rusty fence, dividing these two worlds, the American side grotesque with razor wires and on the Mexican, beautiful paintings of angels, and migrants and la migra, and the psychic vision of the first Spanish boat that landed, with a cross and a promise and plague. The border is a scar, a weeping wound, a black hole. This is defiance. We are art when you give us violence. I wish I could be of this. I think of swallowing the bottle and vanishing into the lips of Santa Muerte; a soft blackened breath, inhaled into whatever cosmic emptiness I've sent so many, but instead I sit and wait for the cartel to signal that it's time to move south or cross over.

There are tariff threats and tomatoes moving ton by ton in unison to every drug, inhaled through American lung or vein. Bodies burn like palo santo. There are warehouse rafters clogged with prayers. The desert eats children like communion wafers.

It is in Mexico that the American gangsters go to vanish each other. I have vanished many here. Some collapsed on concrete, spat at my face, others plead for their daughters, for mercy, but they all ended up in a pit that doesn't exist, a silent scream burned into the universe. Bloody rosaries. Pendants of children. Madres, memories, miracles—but none of it was enough to stop this machine of need. There are young brown girls going to colleges, beautiful in blue gowns, with rows empty of fathers who have disappeared, like one day I will disappear. The breeze dances, and I feel almost human in its movement. A vendor sells ice cream to dancing children. Grilled chorizo rises to a line of tired, but smiling workers. The citizen gets up and joins his wife with bags of medicine and crosses back over, in a line that leads for hours, to a camera and inspection for all that is brown or wounded, and dual-framed photos, one of a smirking

Trump with blue tie and Russian eyes. And another of the other, just as sinister but silent. There is musty ruin in the air, of sewage lines shattered from drilled tunnels. It clings like death to everything, but those who truly are flowers here. Everyone here is tired of stories of drugs and killings emanating in white beams. They want their beauty seen, their songs heard, true and cherished, yet we citizens across the razored wall return from work, tired, and turn the channel to whatever cinematic show of drug lords and killings help us drift to sleep. For the dream of America is always the dream of the gangster. A young boy sets a newspaper next to me. It is a signal that the job is done.

The transfer is finished. The guns are moved. The cars vanished. The widow's hand moves onward to someone's shelf. I sit and watch my partner leave the dentist, wave, then vanish into the line of hundreds, ready to pass back over the border. Perhaps another winter we will have another run. Of guns and dead children and the murders that make her beaches so bright. And all the halos that will quiver from my hands in between our next hello. Our maybe our bosses will tinker her engine, and she will drive off a Peruvian ravine, or she will take a drink and collapse in a bar in a blood-bought paradise, or a bullet will split her face, and she will be buried in a hole hidden as god, or maybe she will grow old perfect and clean as everything American. But the cartels close every story, and silence everything that it touches. And I walk and take a seat at another cantina and drink as the bodies pour, and screams build a wall and a country and an empty American dream. The old man on the corner whistles and extends three fingers. I have been requested to go deeper but alone. I finish my drink. I miss the widow. I miss seeing her each morning. I picture death falling over me like black sand.

BOTH SIDES

PAPER TIGERS BURN BRIGHTEST

I run bloody through the dark forest of saguaro. It feels like for hours, rifle in hand. Naked birds above are screaming. It's like I'm a child again playing tag, reaching to the safe tree that is base, and I race, bare feet blistering open, broken nose clotting, and arrive at the ranch. And here in the safe house, I burst through the door, my body weeping with blood, and I crumble against the wall, surrounded by shooters who know my name is clean. I see the widow in every shadow, in every endless memory. I tremble on the ground as they pour me tequila. I swallow the pills and erase myself.

TWO WINTERS LATER

I am steadier now. The new pills are helping. The colors feel cleaner. The orange juice doesn't taste like rainwater or rust. My skin is clearing up. The bruises have healed. My arm is no longer in sling. If volunteering at the soup kitchen doesn't stop the nightmares, it steadies my hands when the sun is relentless. They are flying me to another job. There is no killing this time, and I am not sure if it's because they sense I'm unsteady or that I've paid my dues, or that someone else— younger—must earn their stripes. But this is a negotiation trip only, or maybe it appears to be that, to lure me to my execution. It is a relief I hope finds me. Whatever mechanism delivered me this far is broken. I turn sixty-two this year. My eyelids flicker, opiate-glimmered, and I step into the airport magazine shop for something to segregate this sensation, but there are just books on killings and a cover that mirrors a memory. Of the widow we erased that winter.

And I flip it over, there's a writer white as me, writing the story of the widow we buried in the snow, white as the power behind his fame. This world is not his, but he writes like he has the right to our crimes, to her tragedy. I see the book stacked with the other white writers' books, at the airport stand, of missing girls and crimes, like mine, like ours, but their hands never twitch. They are family men and wives, who have never lived this life, but somehow need it more than I do.

I want to drive to his suburban house and show him the source of his words, but know another writer, white as he, will wake to the news of his killing, and write, on pages white as the cum on their fingers, dreaming of the awards all this violence will bring, and know their cycle of sorrow theft will never end, and put the book down, and purchase a book on the history of the rose, and a book on the universe, to remind myself that maybe all the atoms of me, and them, will one day be part of something more beautiful than what we've done with them.

EMPIRE

Nick Mamatas

El Warhol was a güero, so he was driving. His mask was mostly open-faced, basically a headband to hold his silver fright wig to his head, so the Border Patrol could see his face without him unmasking. Plus, he was a pluma, a featherweight, so wouldn't spark the machismo of la migra. He was no tough guy. El Warhol's partners in the back of the van had made less convenient sartorial and dietary choices. They were brutes. Donald Duck Jr., with his thick arms crossing his chest and fingers stuffed into his armpits, tried to look menacing but simply came off as insecure to El Warhol. A year ago, at a show in Reno, Jr. had found himself surrounded by people he took to police—blue uniforms, hands on their sidearms, tense and standing on the balls of their feet, thinking they're ready for anything—and by men he knew to be Mafioso. Nice suits, no guns visible, relaxed with weight settled into the saddle of their pelvises, actually ready for anything. Sunglasses at eight PM on a February evening.

Take off your mask, sir, the police said. *Take off your mask. You can't wear a mask on the gaming floor of the Eldorado, sir.* Like little white robots, Donald Jr. explained to his teammates after.

"Neta!" one of the Mafioso said to him, like a question. Good accent. Donald Duck Jr. shrugged at him. The Mafioso told him in

Spanish that the police were not police, just minimum-wage guards, and then told the minimum-wage guards, in English, that if he, the Mafioso, and his "friends" could wear their sunglasses on the gaming floor, so too could the illustrious luchador Donald Duck Jr., of the Estados Unidos trio team wear his mask.

You could run into fans anywhere, though only rarely did anyone at San Ysidro LPOE. El Warhol didn't need to take off his mask. Donald Jr. would take off his mask, if enough men with guns appealed to him to do so.

Then there was La Gran Depresión.

He was the newest teammate, after Super Coney was unmasked in the middle of the ring and forced to retire in humiliation. Completo, but really they needed a new weight class for Depresión. La Gran Depresión, had he been white and working for one of the US wrestling promotions, probably would have just been dressed in a comically oversized pair of hillbilly coveralls and told to stand in the middle of the ring while everyone else bounced off him. He was that big. El Warhol had trouble driving the van with La Gran Depresión riding in the back. It burned gas like a mother, and the handling was all screwed up.

But Depresión was a better fit for the United States theme of the team. Super Coney's cartwheel-focused move set and amusement park gimmick wasn't quite "Americana" enough, not like Andy Warhol, or the son of both a president and a cartoon duck, or the inevitability of the collapse of capitalism.

La Gran Depresión would not take off his mask. Not for la migra, not for the television cameras, not for a fifteen-pound gold belt, not for the Holy Virgin. El Warhol had to do something about that.

"When I was a kid," El Warhol said in his normal voice, not the fey affectation he used for cutting promos, "I went with my parents and my sister to visit Mexico. We lived in LA at the time." Donald Jr.

didn't say anything, but a grunt came from the very back of the van, so Warhol continued. "My dad is Puerto Rican, my mother Cuban—"

"That why you look Swedish?" Donald Jr. asked. "You could star in a novela. You could be a kid in a wheelchair."

"He doesn't look Swedish," La Gran Depresión said. His voice was deep, and he didn't speak much so it was a surprise to hear from him at all.

"So, like I was saying, we crossed into Mexico, no problem. Crossed back, problem. La migra decided my dad had fake papers and that I was some sort of reverse-adoption kidnap baby. We kept telling the cops that there wasn't a drop of Mexican blood anywhere between all of us. Boriqua and Cubana we told them, and don't I have my mother's delicate features? We asked," El Warhol said. "More than my sister, who looks like my father. She they figured was legit, but not me. Maybe they were watching the novelas, too. Anyway, they take me away from my parents, I was just five years old, and they separate me."

"They separate kids for real now," Donald Jr. said.

"Shut up," El Warhol said. "They take me too a little room and show me an orange. They ask me what they call it. I say 'orange,' in English. I'm from the States, right?

"They say, 'No, in Spanish, little boy. What do you call this in Spanish?' You see, they wanted to know if I would say chee-na or naranja. They cut me a slice and tell me to lick it, so I can see if it's sweet or sour. La migra knows a lot. Anyway, I said the right word, 'china', and proved my dad was Puerto Rican and they brought him back to the car and waved us through and the second I was back on US soil I shat myself and my sister started crying and hit me."

"That's a great story, Andy," Donald Jr. said. "Really helps with passing the time. Are you warning us that you're going to shit yourself again on this trip?"

"No, I'm telling you not to shit *yourself.* Just be cool," said El Warhol. "Everything is in order. La migra keeps tabs on things. There will be a way through. We just need to cooperate, though."

"Yes, they do keep tabs on things," said La Gran Depresión.

"I'm just thinking about your masks."

"You don't understand," said Donald Duck Jr. "The mask is sacred. It is not a mask at all, it is like a mirror deep in our heart, reflecting the real self."

"Do you have your checks made out to 'Donald Duck Junior' then, or to Francisco Valencia, Francisco?" El Warhol asked. Donald Duck Jr. didn't answer.

"How about you, La Depresión?" There was a shift in the shadows at the back of the van. El Warhol was surprised by himself for daring to ask, but his mouth kept moving anyway: "Is your mask your sacred self? You've never been north."

"Don't worry about it," La Gran Depresión said, casually yet definitively, like a gun in someone's hand.

El Warhol worried about it for the rest of the slow crawl up the highway to the port of entry. He recalled some photo he'd seen of a long line of climbers on a ridge near the summit of Mount Everest, all waiting for their moment of making it to the very top. A few more hours in subfreezing weather, a few more hours sucking precious oxygen out of a tank, shuffling ahead slowly for…what? A few people died on that line, and their bodies had to be left behind, to freeze and then over the years slowly thaw as the planet began to boil.

It just seemed like a lot to spend three days driving around southern California in the fifty-five-mile border zone, to wrestle in high school gymnasiums and at some taco truck street fair for a few hundred American dollars, plus all the free sleeps in the van their backs could handle. Warhol wondered if all the exhaust from the hundreds upon hundreds of vehicles wasn't getting to him. He glanced into the rearview mirror.

Donald Duck Jr. was asleep, his head resting against his shoulder, a line of drool glistening against the garish orange of his mask's "bill." He was snoozing like a child in a car seat. In the far rear, La Gran Depresión's black mask was lit by the light of the smartphone in his hands. He was holding it horizontally, thumbing away at something. El Warhol hadn't pegged the heavyweight as a phone game type.

"Whatcha playin'?" he asked.

"Shut up," La Gran Depresión said.

"Are you nervous, about the US?"

"Shut up."

"Just four car lengths left."

La Gran Depresión stomped his foot, sending the front of the van bucking like a low-rider. El Warhol nearly bit his tongue.

Now he was upset too. He'd always admired Andy Warhol's ever-placid expression, like a wax dummy or an android. And those long rows and columns of the same famous face—Marilyn Monroe, Chairman Mao—unchanging despite the assaults of color in the individual frames. It was even part of his gimmick; El Warhol never "sold" the dropkicks and forearm smashes and submission holds of his opponents, he just gazed out at the audience or into the camera lens, and took his beating until one of his teammates saved him. El Warhol was upset, worried, but he wouldn't show it. Not when he pulled up to the gates; not when the Border Patrol officer, himself a Latino darker than El Warhol, snorted and whispered something into his lapel radio; not when a half dozen men armed with rifles surrounded the van; not when he was told to wake up "that guy in the faggy mask."

He frowned, though, when they were taken into an office much like the one he visited as a child, sat at a well-worn table, and asked to present their visas. El Warhol just had his US passport. The armed Border Patrol members took up positions in the corners and by the one door.

"Oyola."

"Yes," said El Warhol.

"You're an artist," asked the Border Patrol officer. "Like that guy." His nametag read PAREDES, which El Warhol figured was appropriate, if a little on-the-nose.

"A performer, yes," El Warhol answered.

"You all walk around in your little costumes all the time?"

"Our masks are sacred," Donald Duck Jr. told the man. "They are symbols of our ancient culture and physical prowess."

One of the border cops left his position and showed Paredes something on a smartphone. Paredes smirked at it, then turned back to the trio. "And you're a duck. That's your gimmick?"

"He's also the former president's son," said La Gran Depresión. It was the first thing he'd said. He didn't even look up from the game on his phone. None of la migra were about to tell him to put it away.

"That's funny," Paredes said to La Gran Depresión. Then to Donald Duck Jr., "Your papers." After a glance. "Ah, a P-3 visa. Also an artist, is it? Sacred ancient culture performance art, right?"

"Right," said Donald Duck Jr.

"Walt Disney should sue your fucking ass. The Trump Organization too," Paredes said. Donald Duck Jr.

Nobody said anything for two minutes. El Warhol knew it was two minutes because he'd started keeping a mental count—"One, pumpernickel. Two, pumpernickel...ninety-seven pumpernickel." Parades worked up the courage to ask for La Gran Depresión's papers, but not to speak. He just held out his hand.

"Here," La Gran Depresión said as he reached into his fanny pack and withdrew them. He was big enough that his smartphone rested comfortably in his left palm.

"Turn that shit off," one of the other border guards said. He even gestured with his rifle, shifting it from pointing at the floor to gesturing broadly toward La Gran Depresión. He turned off his phone, or silenced it, or did something to it anyway.

"This is a P-1 visa," Paredes said.

"That's right," La Gran Depresión said.

"That's for athletes."

"I'm an athlete."

"For a real sport," Paredes said.

"I'm for real," La Gran Depresión said. The Border Patrol man said nothing. "I *am* for real," La Gran Depresión said, a second time.

"What about this guy?" Paredes asked, gesturing toward Donald.

"He's a duck."

"I'm for real, too," said Donald Duck Jr., but his voice quavered a bit.

"I am absolutely not for real," said El Warhol.

"You're the one who can go right now, if you want," said Paredes.

"We're a trio."

"Not with two different visas purporting to cover to the same event you're not," said the standing officer who had gestured with his rifle. Paredes glared at him, then turned to La Gran Depresión.

"Take off your mask," Paredes said. "I'll run your face, your prints. See how real you are."

"Maybe there's another way to find out how real I am," said La Gran Depresión, "and that's to try and take my mask."

El Warhol inhaled sharply.

"You used to wrestle, William Paredes," La Gran Depresión said. "In school. All-state. College scholarship. I looked it up. All you guys were doxxed years ago. I got fans, real nerds, they, what do you call it, 'cross-referenced' the names. Wrestlers, football players, lacrosse. Whatever wannabe tough guy signs up to cage kids and arrest gringos leaving water in the desert. It's just lucky that you used to know how to wrestle. So what do you say? We wrestle. You win, you get our masks. I win, we cross the border without having to take them off."

Paredes turned to El Warhol. "Is this guy for real?"

"Do I look like I am familiar with reality?" El Warhol answered.

"Look, I don't care about your bullshit," Paredes said to the trio. "You don't take off your masks, you're not crossing the border. You're not going to talk your way out of here, or do a springboard whatever over the fence, or dropkick me before Charlie takes you out. So just take off your masks, or get back in your van and go to Tijuana and get drunk and get crabs or whatever you want to do."

"We got a lot of cars out there to check," said the patrolman at the door. Charlie, El Warhol surmised.

"We take off our masks and we're allowed in?" asked Donald Duck Jr.

"He didn't say that," El Warhol said. "He said that if you didn't take off your masks, you wouldn't be allowed into the States, not that if you did take off your masks you would."

"Last chance, gentlemen," said Paredes.

"'Gentlemen'—listen to this maricón," said Donald Duck Jr. El Warhol twitched.

Paredes looked at Charlie. Charlie clicked a button on the walkie-talkie clipped to his lapel. The room filled with officers like a clown car in reverse. La Gran Depresión stood up and that was enough to put the officers on their heels. Donald Duck Jr. took a swing at one of them, and then was dog-piled. El Warhol kept his hands up, explained he was American, born in America, with an American passport, but nobody paid him any attention. When one of the officers reared back to kick at Donald Duck Jr's blue and orange mask, La Gran Depresión said "Don't," in a tone that used every molecule of air in the room. The officer stopped short, wobbling on one leg.

"Let him up," La Gran Depresión said. And they did let Donald Duck Jr. up, all of them peering querulously at Paredes as they stood—

Paredes who had his hand on the butt of his sidearm, and his lower jaw hanging open.

"Let's go," said La Gran Depresión.

In the van, El Warhol again took the wheel. "Fucking piece of shit," Donald Duck Jr., riding shotgun now to better glare at Ysidro LPOE. El Warhol understood that Donald was speaking universally— America was a piece of shit, as was la migra, as was the situation including La Gran Depresión's challenge, the visa situation, the ridiculous commitment to mask-wearing, all of it. A piece of shit you could stick your dick into. El Warhol too was a fucking piece of shit, for being an American, for being small, for having a maricón gimmick.

"I never cancelled an appearance in my life," Donald Duck Jr. said. "Not even Reno."

"You spent how much on that charter plane to the private airfield that happened to have a fan as the sole TSA agent thanks to the promoter pulling strings? And all to make sure nobody knows you have acne, eh?"

"I had a lot of money then. Pay-per-view. Action figures. Japan tours. Those were the days," said Donald Duck Jr. "It cost me more than your mother paid me to suck my dick, El Warhol."

"Warhol's seventy-year-old mother sucking your dick was 'the days'?" La Gran La Gran Depresión sounded almost jovial for once.

"Fuck you, man," Donald Duck Jr. said. "What were you trying to pull, with the challenge, and the P-1 visa?"

"I set up a little MMA match for a small audience of discerning fight fans. I guess I gotta cancel that too." He sounded sad again.

"No," said El Warhol. "We're going through."

"Tough talk, El Maricón...El *Americón*. Now you're a tough guy, like Andy Warhol?" Donald Duck Jr's sneer was audible in his voice.

"Let me tell you a story about Andy Warhol," El Warhol said.

"Fuck you."

"Shut up," La Gran Depresión told Donald Duck Jr.

"Andy was tough. He was shot once, you know? Point-blank range, by some crazy lady called Valarie Solanas. Two shots. Got him in the lungs, the spleen, stomach, liver. The bullets bounced around the ribs like two guys in a cage match. He had to wear a girdle for the rest of his life to keep his guts from spilling out." El Warhol made a lazy turn as he spoke, eliciting a few honking horns and shouts in three languages as he cut across the traffic lanes, nice and slow.

"Wow. Another amazing story," said Donald Duck Jr. "Hey, watch where you're going."

"That's not the end of the story," said El Warhol. "This is the end of the story.

"Twenty years he lives like this; a sneeze away from dying. The girl's crazy—she gets out of prison three years later. They share a city; they both live in Manhattan. Andy gets more and more famous. A writer, Fran Leibowitz—" More honking, the van rolls over something big and important seeming.

"Who? Hey! Watch out!" That was Donald Duck Jr. again. La Gran Depresión said nothing.

"Famous writer…she goes to Warhol's studio, the Factory. There's a big metal door, an intercom. The guy got shot years before; he built a fortress. You have to press the button and identify yourself to get in." El Warhol revved the engine.

"She presses the button. She hears Andy's voice asking, 'Who is it?'"

"Warhol…" La Gran Depresión said.

"She says, 'It's Valarie Solanas.'"

El Warhol takes his gaze from the road ahead—which is just a short span that ends with a barrier, a booth, and some of the armed men who had just escorted the trio back to the van—and looks at Donald Duck Jr.

BOTH SIDES

"And Andy, he opens the door."
And El Warhol, he stepped on the gas.

90 MILES

ALEX SEGURA

November 12, 1992

Joaquin Carmona tried to close his eyes. He knew it was a bad idea. Everything he'd been told said to do otherwise. Keep your eyes open. Don't lose sight of the horizon. Marta had said these things before they set off, knowing her husband, unlike her and their son, Angel, was not a water person.

Had the circumstances been better, he would have laughed at the memory—of beaches, uncomfortable dips in Cuba's crisp, blue waters; of his son's bubbly laughter as Joaquin picked him up and tossed him into the air, the sun casting half his small, olive-skinned face in shadow. But laughter was for another time.

Now they were in hell.

Rigoberto, the older man, was at the front of the small, rickety boat. He was the captain of their doomed vessel. A raft, really. A tiny flotation device of his creation that was supposed to carry the four of them to freedom. Actually, freedom didn't matter anymore. It was about safety. It was about land and feeling their toes in the sand or concrete. Anything, really. Joaquin didn't care anymore. He wanted off this maldito boat and to be anywhere else.

285

BOTH SIDES

Joaquin felt the raft lurch left, and his stomach turned right. His empty stomach. There'd been some tostadas before boarding but he couldn't bring himself to eat. Couldn't bring himself to do anything even mildly celebratory before they reached the other side.

Freedom. Miami. Or so they were told.

Manolo was nestled next to Marta, his tiny toddler face buried in her armpit like a tiny bird waiting for food. His mood was a blend of fear, anger, and sadness. They'd woken him up suddenly, rushed him outside of their tiny house, rushed him down the empty streets—sliding into alleys and dark corners if they caught wind of anyone. He was a smart boy. He caught on quick. He knew something was wrong. They weren't leaving de vacación. There were no bags. Plus, he knew—had known for years— that vacations and trips and adventures like that were for other families. Families with more.

Joaquin felt a sharp jolt of regret as he met his son's eyes—for a moment, before Manolito's dark brown pupils turned back to his mother. This was on *him*. He'd made this decision. He, in a fit of anger at their lot in life, had reached out to Rigoberto.

The bar—La Bodeguita del Medio, on Empedrado—had been dark and empty when Joaquin stepped in and met Rigoberto in the back. A cold beer was waiting for him. It was a tourist spot, that bar. The checkered floor, the writing on the wall, photos of American celebrities hanging everywhere. Joaquin didn't belong here. Would get kicked out if he stuck around too long. But this beer. This frigid dream materialized in front of him. He felt the dirt on his palms mix with the condensation on the bottle and he could almost taste the Presidente before he brought the bottle to his chapped, peeling lips. Desperate for the cold liquid to help fend off the tropical heat that had coated his body for what felt like a century. The bar's sputtering air conditioner felt like an arctic parka.

He slurped it down with gusto. Barely savoring the refreshment.

Barely feeling the alcohol pulse through his brain. Joaquin hadn't had a drink in at least a year. Not since Marta told him it was her—and Manolo—or the bottle. Bottles, rather. As life got worse, as their lives became more about scrounging and scavenging just to survive, Joaquin found himself turning more and more to release. Sipping his friend Osvaldito's gualfarina—the homemade, illegal liquor—with a frequency that bordered on obsession. It had gotten bad. Well, worse. He barely remembered those days. Stumbling into his tiny house, reeking of sex, sweat, drink, blood. He didn't know what he had done. Who he had met. How he had survived. Marta was having none of it. She knew they were in hell. She felt it, too. But she hadn't forgotten their son. She would not allow Joaquin to forget him, either. So the line was drawn: drink again, and we leave. No middle ground. So, Joaquin listened. And for a year, up until that moment in the bar, with the cold beer coming alive in his hands, he'd listened. He'd done what he was told. He went to work as a janitor, cleaning office buildings and government spaces when there was work to be done, sitting at home feeling his world fade into red when there wasn't. He bid adios to Osvaldito. He taught his son about baseball. He had sex with his wife once a month. He tried to remember the sound of his mother's voice, and a time when Cuba was a place where he wanted to be.

"Osvaldito told me you wanted...help," Rigoberto had said, his sun-crackled skin giving his appearance a wraith-like quality. He was a skinny, old man, his body frail and rigid. But his face had an unexpected expressiveness that alarmed Joaquin. A serpentine smile and tiny, obsidian eyes that seemed to pulse to their own rhythm. His hands were mangled, claw-like, from decades of working the fields and little medical attention. His teeth—what few Joaquin could see—were a dull yellow, the incisors sharp and vampiric.

"Yes, yes," Joaquin said, swallowing down the last bit of the beer. He tried not to look around the bar, not out of worry, but out of a need for another drink. He was not the type to have just one. To sip a rum and take a nap. No, Joaquin drank hard and long, like his father and his abuelo before him. He didn't know any other way. He didn't want to.

"Bueno, then tell me, hermano," Rigoberto said. "We are only briefly outside the eyes of the people who frown upon these kind of conversation."

"I understand."

"Do you, Joaquin Carmona, hijo de Salvador? I knew your father. He was a hard worker. Loved to sing and dance and drink. I have fond memories of him," Rigoberto said, his eyes glazing over slightly, the deep blackness now a cloudy, murky gray. "So when your friend called me, I came. I want to help the son of my friend, you see? I am a helper. I can get you where you need. But it's not free."

Joaquin felt the boat—the raft—lurch again. He felt Rigoberto's stare before he dared meet it. The dark, sludgy eyes on his, then trailing over to Marta, and settling on Manolo.

"It's just you and your wife?" he'd asked Joaquin as they walked back toward el Centro, where Joaquin lived. The first beer had blended into six more, and Joaquin felt wobbly. There'd been a time, not long ago, when six beers was an appetizer. A primer for the night. A necessity. But that was long ago. His tolerance was gone. He felt the rough edges of a brownout creeping into his vision.

"Just me and Marta, yeah, just two," he'd said, nodding fast. Why was he lying? Was it the cost? Was it habit—to lie, to deflect, to dance around the truth? The alcoholic habits came back fast, like sliding into comfortable slippers found in the back of the closet. It should've scared him, the ease with which the lies spread. But something inside him wanted these words, wanted this to be the truth—and that shook him to his core. Or, it would. Later.

"Está bien," Rigoberto said, slapping Joaquin's face softly as they parted. "Anything more and we'd barely make it off the island, mijo.

My boats are strong, but not that strong. They have to be fast, too, you know? To get past them."

"Them?"

Rigoberto laughed, a dry, crusty laugh that sounded like sandpaper on asphalt.

"Los tiburones, Joaquin," Rigoberto said. "The sharks."

Joaquin had heard the stories—of what men and women traversing the waters between Cuba and Florida had seen. The deep blue waters masking a deadly darkness. Sharks were fearless, and Joaquin had heard many a story of the giant, predatory fish snatching balseros from their rafts. He'd heard stories of bloodstained waters, arms and legs floating past. But that was just the sharks, Joaquin knew.

He'd stopped outside the rickety front door to his home and felt a jolt of clarity electrify his body. If the sharks didn't get them, there were many other paths that lead to a painful, brutal death. If they were captured—if they didn't make it past the twelve-mile area surrounding Cuba that preceded international waters—they'd be arrested. At best. Joaquin had also heard stories of balseros not making it back home, shot point-blank on the boats ferrying them back to the island. If they did manage to get past Cuban waters, and if they did manage to avoid a deadly encounter with a shark, they'd still have to navigate the waters—the massive Caribbean waves, some clocking in higher than fifteen feet—that could easily flip and destroy the kind of boat he envisioned Rigoberto captaining.

"What have I done?" Joaquin asked himself as his hand wrapped around the chipped and rusty doorknob, careful to not make any noises that could wake Marta. He cursed softly, remembering the drinks. Sure she'd sniff the alcohol on his breath as he slid into bed.

"What have I done?"

He made a beeline for their mildew-infested and cramped bathroom, sloshing water from the sink into his hungry mouth, rinsing and gargling in a vain attempt to clean up the stains of his behavior.

Rigoberto had laid out the plan as Joaquin worked on his fourth beer. He, unlike many on the island, owned a fishing boat, he said. And while he worked in the fields to this day, he earned a healthy income as a smuggler—ferrying people like Joaquin from Cuba to Miami. But the journey wasn't over once they hit international waters, explained Rigoberto. No. They needed to dodge nature's traps and man himself—notably, the Coast Guard. The US had enacted a "wet foot, dry foot" policy specifically designed to prevent another mass exodus along the lines of the Mariel swarm that hit Miami in the early '80s. Now, if balseros were caught on their way to Miami, they could be sent back. And a trip back to Cuba was certain death. No, they had to reach land. Their feet had to touch the ground. That made the Coast Guard the enemy, and it made international waters just as dangerous as the twelve miles surrounding Cuba.

Joaquim blinked, and he was back on the raft. Lying down now, his eyes staring up into the bright Caribbean sky—the sun bearing down on them, roasting his tan skin. His mouth was dry. His body limp. He heard Manolo whimpering behind him somewhere. He wanted to get up, but he couldn't.

"Halfway there," Rigoberto said, his voice a ragged croak.

How long had he been out? Joaquin had no idea. It couldn't have been that long. His mind drifted back to the morning—boarding Rigoberto's boat, just a few bottles of water, a bag of food, and nothing else. They were going fishing. At least that's what they wanted anyone who saw them to believe. There was nothing wrong here. Just a family paying an experienced fisherman to show them the waters.

Rigoberto's entire expression morphed once he set eyes on Manolo. The kid was pudgy, big for his age. But enough to create a problem on the old man's boat? Joaquin had tried not to worry, had tried to ignore the lie he'd drunkenly spat out at Rigoberto the night before—but now it all came back, and he saw the older man's eyes flicker with a flame that could only be pure hatred.

But they were out, in the open, and the old man couldn't deviate now. The plan had been set. People were watching. They'd boarded, and he felt Rigoberto's hot, angry breath on his face as he helped Joaquin onto the raft, the last crew member aboard.

"Pendejo mentiroso," he hissed. "Now we all die together."

Joaquin tried to ignore Rigoberto. Now, his back flat on the boat, the entire vessel bobbing up and down with a ferocity that he'd never imagined, he couldn't care less about the old man's petty concerns. He was worried, too, but it had little to do with a fat toddler. It had to do with *survival*.

Then they sprung the first leak. A small tear near the front of the raft— near where Rigoberto was seated, his makeshift captain's seat really just a cooler at the front of cheap, man-made raft. *Owned a boat*, Joaquin had thought when he and Marta caught a glimpse of Rigoberto's vessel. Who was the real mentiroso?

The water came into the boat slowly, but Rigoberto danced to his feet like a child stung by a bee, stepping back from the leak as if singed by flame.

"No, no, no!" he said, his voice an octave higher than Joaquin thought possible. "Now we die! Now it's over!"

Joaquin felt blood pump through his body. Felt life come back to his limbs. He saw—felt—himself sit up, yank his shirt off and stuff the tattered white cloth into the tear, trying to stop the flow. It seemed to work for a second, and his heart slowed, and he almost sighed in relief, but then he felt his shirt soaking in his hands and he knew it was over.

"Papi, no!"

Manolo's scream, shrill and desperate, didn't come soon enough to prevent what happened next. Joaquin felt the blade slide into his back, long and fat, the hilt touching his sunburnt skin. Then another scream—Marta—followed by a scuffle. Marta was strong. Forceful. She would not die quietly. And she would not die at the hands of some pendejo viejo, as she'd described Rigoberto that last night, as she angrily poured Joaquin a glass of water to sober him up.

"What have you done, Joaquin? To us? To our family?"

The raft bobbed up again, a larger, more powerful wave tossing the tiny boat up and off the water for a few seconds—and Joaquin felt like they were gliding on air. He fell backward, his face now watching the struggle: Rigoberto standing over Marta, his hands wrapped around her throat, Manolo cowering behind the old man.

"Puta maldita," Rigoberto spat, his body shaking from the effort of trying to keep Marta down. Joaquin felt the knife dig deeper into him, and he knew if he was going to act, it had to be now.

He was dying.

He stood, the lurch and lunge of the waves underneath them balancing out his own dizziness, giving his blood-drained body a brief moment of control as he grabbed Rigoberto's shoulders and pulled the skinny, jagged old man back and toward the edge of the raft—the raft that was now filling with water, the crystal blue ocean no longer something that surrounded them—now something that would consume them.

Joaquin felt his hands wrap around Rigoberto's scaly, tan throat, felt his fingers tighten around it, his thumbs pressuring the bones and muscle and life that took up space in there. He saw Rigoberto's eyes bulge open, a look of surprise and hate steaming off his eyes, like the exhaust from an old Ford.

"Estas muerto, cabrón," Rigoberto said, the words a sizzling whisper, a last gasp.

Joaquin felt the burning now. His back. The blood coating him. His hands hurt. His body was buckling. He couldn't hold on. He just felt so…so alone. So empty. So tired.

He'd tried, Martica, he really had. Even after everything—after prison, after that first failed attempt, she'd stayed with him. She'd cared for him even when the work disappeared. He'd tried this to save her, to save them, their life...their son. And now what?

He felt the crack in Rigoberto's neck before he heard it, a soft, wet *krrk* sound that he might have just imagined. But then the old man stopped fighting, though his eyes—red, the vessels burst and spreading—remained awake, as if looking for a final corner to cut, a last deal to make to ensure their survival.

Joaquin stumbled back. That's when the shark popped up, its sleek, gray-blue form sidling up to the raft, its mouth hooking onto Rigoberto's head and dragging him into the water, almost silent in its execution—a predator accustomed to scavenging for meals between an island and a peninsula.

Joaquin wanted to gasp, but found it hard to breathe. He felt a hand on his shoulder as he dropped down onto the floor, the water sloshing as he fell back, Marta next to him. She was crying. Manolo was crying. He could still hear them, but he found it hard to make words, to respond.

"Perdóname, Dios," he muttered. God, forgive me. Forgive me for what I've done.

He didn't mean Rigoberto.

"Think we got something, Lieutenant," the ensign said as he approached the edge of the small Coast Guard cutter and peered into the calm, teal waters of the Florida Straits. He felt his commanding officer, Lieutenant Osman, approach from behind.

"Already? Shit, we just left dock," she said, under her breath. She stood to the ensign's left and followed his gaze.

"You sure?" she asked. "Just looks like a bunch of wood...and

293

some clothes?"

They'd anchored the cutter at the first sign of something. They'd expected a small craft or boat in need of assistance. But this? This looked more like someone's overturned laundry bin.

Then they saw the red.

The kind of red that could only mean one thing. The kind of dark maroon that wasn't meant to be seen on the outside. At least not in these quantities.

"Shit, shit, shit," Osman said, more out of annoyance than genuine fear or concern. This wasn't her first trip off land. But as the image she was recording in her brain lingered over the next few months, it would, for all intents and purposes, be her last. "What the hell happened here?"

"Usual shit," the ensign—a good ol' boy from Pensacola named Gilbert—spat. "'Nother bunch of dead spic rafters, trying to swim 'cross these shark waters to get a taste of American freedom, y'know? Maybe next time, kids. Stupid."

Osman blinked, trying to reject the words slithering into her ears. She turned to face Gilbert, her expression immediately telling the junior officer he'd fucked up. Big time.

"Call it in," she said, straining to keep her tone calm and aligned with her job as a commanding officer, not shrill and enraged, which was how she actually felt. "People died here, Ensign. Do you understand? *People*."

Gilbert nodded nervously, and seemed relieved to be heading back to the comm station.

Osman looked down at the wreckage, at the bobbing debris that had once been something else—a ship, a construct. But not just that. It had been something more important. Something primal. Something good.

It had been hope.

ABOUT THE EDITOR

Bram Stoker Award–nominee Gabino Iglesias is a writer, editor, journalist, and book reviewer living in Austin, Texas. He is the author of *Coyote Songs*, *Zero Saints* (both from Broken River Books), and *Gutmouth* (Eraserhead Press). He is the book reviews editor at *PANK* Magazine, the TV/film editor at *Entropy Magazine*, and a columnist for LitReactor and CLASH Media. His nonfiction has appeared in places like *The New York Times*, *Los Angeles Review of Books*, *Los Angeles Times*, *El Nuevo Día*, and other venues. The stuff that's made up has been published in places like *Red Fez*, *Flash Fiction Offensive*, *Drunk Monkeys*, *Bizarro Central*, *Paragraph Line*, *Divergent Magazine*, *Cease*, *Cows*, and many horror, crime, surrealist, and bizarro anthologies. When not writing or reading, he has worked as a dog whisperer, witty communications professor, and ballerina assassin. His reviews are published in places like *NPR*, *Vol. 1 Brooklyn*, *Criminal Element*, *The Rumpus*, *Heavy Feather Review*, *Atticus Review*, *Entropy*, *HorrorTalk*, *Necessary Fiction*, *Crimespree*, and other print and online venues. He teaches at SNHU's MFA program. You can find him on Twitter at @Gabino_Iglesias.

CONTRIBUTORS

Mexican American author David Bowles has written multiple titles, including the Pura Belpré Honor Book *The Smoking Mirror* and *Feathered Serpent, Dark Heart of Sky: Myths of Mexico* (one of *Kirkus Reviews'* Best YA Books of 2018). 2018 also saw the publication of *They Call Me Güero* (2019 Walter Dean Myers Honor Book for Outstanding Children's Literature, 2019 Pura Belpré Honor Book). David's work has also appeared in venues such as *Apex*, *Nightmare*, *The Dark*, *Eye to the Telescope*, *Strange Horizons*, *Journal of Children's Literature*, *Translation Review*, and *Rattle*. In 2017, David was inducted into the Texas Institute of Letters in recognition of his literary accomplishments. Find him on Twitter @DavidOBowles.

Michelle Garza and Melissa Lason are Bram Stoker Award–nominated writers from Arizona. They're known as the Sisters of Slaughter for their horror writing but they also write science fiction and dark fantasy. They have been published by Sinister Grin Press, Thunderstorm Books, Bloodshot Books, Pint Bottle Press, and Wetworks. Find them on Twitter @fiendbooks.

Rob Hart is the author of the short story collection *Take-Out* and the Ash McKenna series, which wrapped up with *Potter's Field* in July 2018. He is also the co-author of *Scott Free* with James Patterson. His next book, *The Warehouse*, has sold in more than 20 countries and been optioned for film by Ron Howard. He lives in New York City. Find him online at @robwhart and www.robwhart.com.

Sandra Jackson-Opoku is a poet, novelist, screenwriter, and journalist. Her novels include *The River Where Blood Is Born* (1997), which won an American Library Association Black Caucus Literary Award, and *Hot Johnny (and the Women Who Loved Him)* (2001). With Quraysh Ali Lansana, she edited *Revise the Psalm: Work Celebrating the Writing of Gwendolyn Brooks* (2017). Jackson-Opoku's own writing on the cultures of the African diaspora has been published widely. Jackson-Opoku is the recipient of honors and awards from the National Endowment for the Arts, the Illinois Arts Council, and the American Antiquarian Society. She won the CCLM/General Electric Fiction Award for Younger Writers. On faculty at Chicago State University, she lives in Chicago.

Shannon Kirk is the awarding-winning, international bestselling author of *Method 15/33*, *The Extraordinary Journey of Vivienne Marshall*, *In the Vines*, and *Gretchen*. Shannon has also contributed to *Night of the Flood* and *Swamp Killers*. She has received multiple accolades: 2015 Foreword Review Book of the Year (Suspense); IBPA GOLD Winner; Winner of 2015 National Indie Excellence Award, Best Suspense; 2015 USA Best Book Finalist; School Library Journal's Best Adult Books for Teens (2015); Finalist in 2013 William Faulkner William Wisdom Creative Writing Competition; and the Literary Classics Seal of Approval. Shannon resides on Massachusetts' Cape Ann; find her on Twitter @ShannonCKirk.

Isaac Kirkman goes by 79797. 79797 is a mystic and poet based in the occupied Tohono O'odham land of Tucson, Arizona. He writes for *The Tucson Weekly* and assists Eva Sierra on the astrology-themed open mic event The Reading Series. "Grotesque Cabaret" is his last crime fiction story and his exit from traditional literary publishing. 79797 has done humanitarian aid work on the border for No More

Deaths and occult work with cartels. He is a devoted servant of the spirit world and the communities of the border and barrios and adversary to anyone who exploits these communities, be it Border Patrol, ICE, cartel, or literary organization. 79797's been published in many journals and taught in college, but is best known in the book world as Isaac the Visionero in Gabino Iglesias's barrio noir classic *Zero Saints*. You can follow his occult journey on Instagram @79797z.

Rios de la Luz is a queer xicana/chapina sci-fi loving writer living in El Paso. Her first book, *The Pulse between Dimensions and the Desert*, is out now via Ladybox Books. Her debut novella, *ITZÁ*, is out now via Broken River Books. Find her on Twitter @Riosdelaluz.

Nick Mamatas is the author of seven novels, including *Love is the Law*, *I Am Providence*, and the forthcoming *Hexen Sabbath*. His short fiction has appeared in *Best American Mystery Stories*, *Year's Best Science Fiction & Fantasy*, and many other venues. Nick is also an anthologist; his books include the Bram Stoker Award winner *Haunted Legends* (co-edited with Ellen Datlow), the Locus Award nominees *The Future Is Japanese* and *Hanzai Japan* (both co-edited with Masumi Washington), and *Mixed Up* (co-edited with Molly Tanzer). His fiction and editorial work has been nominated for the Hugo, Locus, World Fantasy, Bram Stoker, Shirley Jackson, and International Horror Guild Awards. Mamatas lives in Oakland, California. Find on Twitter @ Nmamatas.

Nicolás Obregón was born in London to a French mother and a Spanish father. *Blue Light Yokohama* is his first novel and he is currently working on its follow-up. Find him on Twitter @NicObregon.

Daniel A. Olivas (www.danielolivas.com) is the author of nine books and editor of two anthologies. His books include *The King of Lighting Fixtures: Stories*, *Crossing the Border: Collected Poems*, and *Things We Do Not Talk About: Exploring Latino/a Literature Through Essays and Interviews*. Olivas is also the editor of the landmark *Latinos in Lotusland: An Anthology of Contemporary Southern California Literature*. Olivas has written for many publications including *The New York Times*, *Huffington Post*, *Los Angeles Times*, *Los Angeles Review of Books*, *El Paso Times*, *California Lawyer*, and *Jewish Journal*. His writing is featured in many anthologies including *Sudden Fiction Latino*, *Hint Fiction*, and *Love to Mama: A Tribute to Mothers*. He makes his home in Los Angeles. Twitter: @olivasdan.

Cynthia Pelayo is the author of horror, mystery, thrillers, and poetry. Her first novel, *Santa Muerte*, was published by Post Mortem Press, followed by *The Missing*. Her poetry collection, *Poems of My Night*, was published by Raw Dog Screaming Press in 2016. *Santa Muerte*, *The Missing*, and *Poems of My Night* have all been nominated for International Latino Book Awards. *Poems of My Night* was also nominated for an Elgin Award. She lives in inner city Chicago. Find her online at: www.cinapelayo.com and on Twitter @CinaPelayo.

Christopher David Rosales is a winner of the International Latino Book Award. His fiction has appeared in anthologies, journals, and magazines in the US and abroad. His novel, *Silence the Bird, Silence the Keeper*, won the McNamara Creative Arts Grant. He is also the author of *Gods on the Lam* and *Word Is Bone*. Rosales was the Writing Fellow at The National Archives at Philadelphia. Previously he won the Center of the American West's award for fiction three years in a row. He has a PhD from the University of Denver. Follow him on Twitter @CDRosales. Website and Contact: www.christopherrosales.com.

BOTH SIDES

J. Todd Scott was born in rural Kentucky and is now a federal agent. His assignments have taken him all over the US and the world; he now resides in the southwest. His debut novel, *The Far Empty*, was published June 2016 by G.P. Putnam's Sons. His next book, *High White Sun*, was released March 20, 2018. The third, *This Side of Night*, was released July 2019. Find him at JToddScott.com.

Alex Segura is a novelist and comic book writer. He is the author of the acclaimed Pete Fernandez Miami Mysteries, which include *Silent City*, *Down The Darkest Street*, *Dangerous Ends*, *Blackout*, and *Miami Midnight*. He has also written a number of comic books, including the best-selling and critically acclaimed *Archie Meets Kiss* storyline, the "Occupy Riverdale" story, *Archie Meets Ramones*, and *The Archies*. He is the co-creator, co-writer, and executive producer of the Lethal Lit podcast from iHeart Media, named one of the best podcasts of 2018 by *The New York Times*. He lives in New York with his wife and children. He is a Miami native. Follow him at @Alex_Segura.

Johnny Shaw was born and raised on the Calexico/Mexicali border, the setting for his award-winning Jimmy Veeder Fiasco series, which includes the novels *Dove Season* and *Plaster City*. He is also the author of the Anthony Award–winning adventure novel *Big Maria*. His shorter work has appeared in *Thuglit*, *Crime Factory*, *Shotgun Honey*, *Plots with Guns*, and numerous anthologies. He is the creator and editor of the fiction magazine *Blood & Tacos*, which recently added a phone app, a Podcast, and a book imprint to its empire. Johnny lives in Portland, Oregon, with his wife, artist Roxanne Patruznick, when they are not traveling the world. Find him on Twitter @BloodandTacos.